When Christmas Comes

Center Point
Large Print

Also by Katherine Spencer and available from Center Point Large Print:

All Is Bright
Together for Christmas
Because It's Christmas
Christmas Blessings
A Christmas Secret

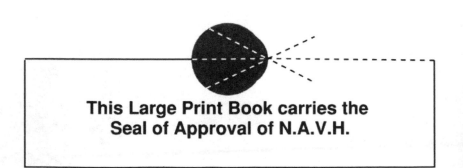

**This Large Print Book carries the
Seal of Approval of N.A.V.H.**

Thomas Kinkade's Cape Light

When Christmas Comes

KATHERINE SPENCER

CENTER POINT LARGE PRINT
THORNDIKE, MAINE

This Center Point Large Print edition
is published in the year 2019 by arrangement with
Berkley, an imprint of Penguin Publishing Group,
a division of Penguin Random House LLC.

The text of this Large Print edition is unabridged.
In other aspects, this book may vary
from the original edition.
Printed in the United States of America
on permanent paper.
Set in 16-point Times New Roman type.

ISBN: 978-1-64358-433-1

The Library of Congress has cataloged this record under
Library of Congress Control Number: 2019948904

For the faithful readers of the
Cape Light and Angel Island stories,
but especially those who asked for more
about the Inn at Angel Island.
Thank you for inspiring me to bring
Liza and Daniel home for Christmas.

Dear Reader

"Round up the usual suspects!" That's what I say when it's time to make a guest list for a holiday party at our house. By which I mean, close family and a few select friends. We're very lucky that practically everyone on that list lives close by.

But there are times when guests come from a distance. Their presence makes the party sparkle in a special way, because Christmas is the perfect time for reunions. It's the perfect time to renew our friendships and family ties. To recall shared memories and create new memories, too. It's the perfect time to put aside old grievances. To make a fresh start and go forward with love and peace in our hearts.

What better time than Christmas to bring Liza and Daniel Merritt back to Angel Island for a long-awaited reunion with Claire North and Nolan Porter? It's joyful moment that not only heralds the holidays, but a new season in their relationships, and the future of the inn.

But while writing this story, I found that reunions can be silent and secret; even invisible. At least, that's what Kerry Redmond hopes.

She's come to Cape Light to find the one person she loves most in the whole world, but lost years ago. Kerry vows she will not make her presence known. But her plans are no match for the magic of Christmas and the power of love.

Wishing everyone a joyful holiday season.

Katherine Spencer

CHAPTER ONE

~~~

I t wasn't her real home, not the way most people meant that word. It wasn't the remote, dusty village of Deep Wells, Arizona, where she lived with her husband and children, or even the Boston suburb where she had been raised. Liza had only lived on Angel Island a little over four years before she and Daniel were married and moved away. But as they drew closer, she felt a key slowly turn in a lock somewhere deep within and a door swinging open. She felt excited and peaceful at the same time. Angel Island was not her official zip code, but it was the place her heart called home.

His hands on the wheel, Daniel turned from watching the road to glance at her. "Detour through the village or straight to the bridge?"

She was curious to see Cape Light's Main Street again, but eagerness to reach the island won out easily.

"Let's just get there. Claire is probably standing at the door by now. I sent her a text when we got off the highway."

Daniel smiled. "I bet she is. I can't wait to see her."

"Me neither." Liza was so tired, she had dozed off during the drive from Boston's Logan Airport. Wide awake now, she watched familiar land-marks roll by, the vague shapes she could discern in the darkness—the winter woods and stretches of tall marsh grass, the sign for Potter Orchard and one directing them to the island, straight ahead.

Deep inside, she knew it all by heart. She had missed this place, though she didn't admit it much.

She glanced into the back seat. Max and Charlotte had been squirming like excited puppies all day; airplane seat belts could barely contain them. Now they were fast asleep, their small faces sweet and—deceptively—angelic looking.

"Should I wake the kids?"

Daniel shook his head. "Let them sleep. They're exhausted. It's too dark to see much anyway."

"Yes, it is. It will be like a first visit for them. I'm not sure if Max remembers anything from last time. Charlotte was a baby."

"How long has it been?"

"About two years. Max was three and Charlotte was just two months."

"That long, really?"

Liza heard a twinge of guilt in his tone. She felt the same. They had stayed away so long, though it hadn't been intentional. Their initial plan was to live in Arizona six months out of the year and return to the island in the summers to run the inn. That schedule had only lasted a year. Daniel's job share with another doctor at the clinic had unraveled and he had made a full-time commitment.

About the same time, the clinic was taken over by a large nonprofit health care organization, a change that had pluses and minuses. There was no longer a need for Dr. Mitchell, Daniel's boss and mentor, to search constantly for funding, but there was less flexibility in the job, too. Time off was rare, making visits east almost impossible.

One visit they had planned had been foiled when Max got the flu, and the last time they'd traveled east, they couldn't get past Chicago. A blizzard in the Midwest had grounded flights for days, and they were forced to turn back. Of course, Claire and Nolan had understood, but they had all been sad about not seeing each other.

The children would not remember Angel Island or Cape Light, but they certainly knew their Aunt Claire and Uncle Nolan. The older couple doted on Liza's son and daughter, visiting with phone calls and Skype. Nolan, an inventor by profession, was very capable with computer technology for his age. For any age, for that matter.

Liza's parents had passed away over twenty years ago, and Daniel's mother had retired to

11

North Carolina. Claire and Nolan were like grandparents to Max and Charlotte. Maybe even more loving and indulgent. Liza expected her children to be thoroughly spoiled by the time they headed back home next week. There was no way to stop it. It wasn't even worth trying.

"It will be fun to show the kids around. We have the whole weekend," Daniel said.

Liza looked forward to doing that, too. "Except for tomorrow. We'll be cooking and eating Thanksgiving dinner most of the day, and too stuffed to move off the couch after."

"My plan exactly. With some football watching tossed in. I'm sure I smelled Claire's apple pies baking somewhere over New Jersey."

Liza laughed. "That's funny, I smelled her sweet potato soufflé."

Claire North's cooking was legendary and well worth a six-hour trip from Phoenix to Boston, stretched even farther by a delay in Atlanta and a last-minute gate change. Liza's little family had been a sight, weighed down with duffel bags, backpacks, a stroller, and car seats. Daniel had tugged their son, Max, by the hand, then scooped him up under one arm, like a football player charging toward the end zone. Liza had jogged alongside, speed-rolling Charlotte's stroller as swiftly as she dared while the passenger inside shouted, "More, Mommy! More!" At least the adult craziness had not alarmed them.

12

"The gate is up. Good sign." Daniel pointed out the window.

They had reached the land bridge, and a slim yellow arm signaled it was safe to cross. The two-lane bridge was edged by large gray boulders piled on each side. A few tall lamps lit the way as they slowly drove along the black ribbon of highway that stretched across the harbor from the mainland to the island.

Midnight-blue water surrounded them; the same color of the dark night sky, where gauzy clouds drifted across a crescent moon, the rest of the sky scattered with a million stars. There were plenty of stars in the desert night sky, but even the moon and stars seemed different here.

Halfway across the water, Liza glanced back and saw the coastline curving around the harbor, a cluster of lights in the village. A gust of wind battered the SUV, and spray flew up from the waves that splashed against the road's rocky shoulder.

Daniel held the wheel steady. "Windy out here. I didn't realize."

"The island has its own weather. That's part of its charm. Part of what makes it a world apart. Didn't you tell me that?"

"So I did. Among other colorful bits of island folklore I employed to win your hand."

He caught her glance and Liza felt the familiar spark, still there after all their years together.

13

"It wasn't your folksy wisdom *exactly,* Dr. Merritt. But it did help." She grew quiet a moment, then said, "This reminds me of the night I drove out from Boston after Aunt Elizabeth died. After Peter and I inherited the inn. It was dark and windy on the bridge, and the moon and stars looked the same, too. A half-moon but very bright. That was the first time I ever met Claire, though my aunt had told me a lot about her."

"And met yours truly, not too long after," Daniel added.

"Don't worry, I'm not leaving you out. Two days after I arrived, to be exact. I'm still not sure why you didn't scream and run back to your truck when I answered the door. I looked like a bag of rags wearing sneakers."

Daniel laughed. "The prettiest bag of rags I'd ever seen. You had me at 'Who are you and what do you want?' "

Liza knew she'd been tart with him. At first. After her divorce, she was naturally defensive with all men. Especially the handsome ones. Thank goodness, Daniel had been patient with her. Their attraction had been mutual and immediate, but their long courtship had faced challenges. Their marriage had been well worth the wait.

When Liza's Aunt Elizabeth had passed away, she had left the inn to Liza and her brother, Peter. Aunt Elizabeth and Uncle Clive had no children of their own, and while growing up, Liza and her brother had spent every summer on the island, visiting with them.

Once the property passed into their hands, their plan had been to clean up the place and turn it over for a quick sale. But, as Claire often said, "Man plans. God laughs." He must have been amused that spring, watching His plan take her totally by surprise. She had been very invested in her career at the time. She never expected to quit her job at one of Boston's leading advertising firms and stay on to repair and run the inn.

But a short time after her arrival, that's exactly what she decided to do. Despite zero experience running a business of any kind. Somehow, with Claire North's experience and stalwart support, not to mention her amazing skills in the kitchen, Liza knew she had a fighting chance of making it work.

In the final years of her aunt's life, the Inn at Angel Island had been limping along, but with Liza and Claire at the helm, it quickly revived and thrived. Daniel had not been practicing medicine at the time but working as a carpenter and all-around handyman. Because her aunt had trusted him, Liza hired him for most of the repairs. And so they'd come to know each other very well, as if their romance was meant to be. Sometimes Liza wondered if her aunt, smiling down from some distant heavenly cloud, had been playing matchmaker.

As the years passed, Liza bought out Peter's share in the inn. She was now the sole, if absentee, owner. Claire and her husband, Nolan Porter, had been managing the place for almost six years, with as much care and attention as if they owned it. Liza knew she was extremely lucky to have such an arrangement. When Daniel took a job in a medical clinic on the Navajo reservation, their plan had been to stay out West for two years. Though they sometimes talked about one day returning to the East, they still had no idea when that might be.

Claire never pressed her, and Liza was thankful for her patience and understanding. She did hope that during this visit, there would be time for a talk about the situation.

The ride over the land bridge was brief, the winds just wild enough to hint at the island to come, rustic and untamed. Liza was sure that would never change. The year-round residents—a small but hardy bunch—would not abide it.

There were no lights on the curving road to guide them, save the headlights of their rented SUV, turned up bright. Daniel knew the way by heart; Liza didn't doubt it.

It all looked just as Liza remembered. Tufts of beach grass along the roadside, the rolling landscape, the dark shadows of houses popping up here and there, even the bent old trees that stood like sentinels and directed the way. Straight on Old Dock Road, veering right at the fork onto Mariner's Way, just past the huge willows at the crossroads.

The road to the inn ran along a high bluff. On the left side of the road, Liza saw the ocean shimmer in the moonlight. The sky had cleared, and stars sparkled like pinpoints of light on dark blue velvet. She heard the waves rolling to the shoreline, the sound muffled and distant, just the way it had sounded every night as she fell asleep in her summer bedroom.

Suddenly on the right, the inn came into view, and Daniel turned up the circular drive. She had always loved this house and, sometimes, still couldn't believe she owned it. Three stories high with matching bay windows on the first and second floors, the windows on the second floor fronted by a balcony. There was even a turret on the right side of the building, not far from the front door.

When Liza was a little girl, she had heard the extravagant Victorian called a "Queen Anne" and believed a queen had once lived there. *Why not?* she thought now. It was definitely worthy of royalty, a house right out of a fairy tale.

The large property sloped toward the road, and the house faced the bluffs and an expanse of ocean that stretched out below. In the summertime, the wraparound porch was filled with Adirondack chairs, straight-backed rockers, and wicker love seats. There was also a wonderful porch swing, enjoyed by visitors of all ages.

The big porch stood empty now, except for a few dark lumps covered with green tarps, but during the inn's busiest weeks, it was filled with guests from morning to night, sipping lemonade or iced tea, reading or knitting in the shade. Or simply gazing at the sea.

A light shone on the walkway, illuminating a sign that swung in the breeze. THE INN AT ANGEL ISLAND. ALL ARE WELCOME HERE!

Liza's aunt had painted the message so many years ago, trimmed with flowers all around. Somehow, with care and patience, and fresh paint each spring, Liza and Claire had managed to preserve her handiwork. The sign was precious to Liza, and it did her heart good to see it there, though the lettering didn't look quite as clear now, nor the colors as bright. Had Claire forgotten to touch it up this year? Maybe even longer than that?

I can work on that while I'm here. I wouldn't mind at all.

Even before Daniel stopped the car, the front door swung open. Just like the night Liza had arrived ten years ago, Claire stood in the golden light a moment, then rushed forward to welcome them. Nolan followed close behind, along with Edison. The aging chocolate Lab was a little slower down the steps than Liza recalled, but more than made up for his speed with happy barks and enthusiastic tail wagging.

"Here we are, finally," Liza announced.

Claire smiled, her eyes shining, and folded Liza into a huge hug. "And what a long day you've all had. You must be exhausted. And hungry. I have a nice supper all ready. Nothing special, just flounder and shrimp with lemon and butter sauce. I wanted to keep it simple the night before Thanksgiving."

"That sounds simply delicious." Daniel had scooped up Charlotte from her car seat and held her in the crook of one arm as he took his turn greeting Claire and Nolan. The little girl stared out sleepily, melting them instantly with her charm.

"Hello, sleepy one." Claire leaned close to Charlotte and gently kissed her cheek. Charlotte smiled shyly.

"Do you think she knows me? From the computer chatting?" Claire asked.

Before either of her parents could reply, Charlotte said, "Anticlear!" Her tone was very definite and full of pride.

Everyone laughed, Claire seeming amused and confounded by the nickname.

"And who am I?" Nolan asked curiously.

Charlotte looked surprised at the question, as if the answer was totally obvious. "Uncle No-man."

"You're exactly right. That's me, Uncle No-man."

"I think she's very bright to remember us at all." Claire picked up a duffel bag in one hand and a tote in the other.

"Where's the little man?" Nolan asked. "Where's my little Max?"

Liza had just pulled open the door to the back seat, where her son was still fast asleep. She leaned over and unsnapped Max's seat belt. He woke with a start. "Are we there yet? Are we at Aunty Claire's house?"

"We are. Everyone's waiting to say hello."

Max scrambled down from his seat and pushed past her. He ran straight to Claire and Nolan, then stared up at them shyly.

Claire leaned toward him. Liza could see she was aching to give a hug but was holding back, careful not to overwhelm him.

"We're so happy you're here, Max. You've grown so much since we last saw you."

"I'm the tallest in my class," Max said proudly.

"He takes after his dad. I can see that." Nolan crouched down to be eye level with Max. Edison, who sat at Nolan's feet, offered Max a doggy smile.

"Do you remember Edison? He hates to be left out, silly old fellow."

Max reached out and patted Edison's head. Liza wasn't sure if he did remember the big dog, but Max loved all things furred and four-footed and was eager to get acquainted.

"He's not silly. He looks very smart. Hello, Edison. I'm Max, remember?"

Edison stared back, boy and dog nose to nose. Then the dog lifted a large paw. Max took the paw and gently shook it.

"Nice job, Edison. He still remembers his manners." Nolan met Daniel at the open back of the SUV and grabbed a knapsack. Daniel already had a duffel bag in each hand.

"Let's leave the rest. We'll get it later," Daniel said. "That flounder is calling my name."

"My name, too." Nolan took Max by the hand and led him up the porch steps. "I wonder what a fish would sound like if it *could* talk? *No-man! Time for dinner. Come and get it!*" His silly voice made Max giggle.

Liza was the last to enter the grand old house. As her family followed Claire and Nolan into the kitchen, she stepped over the threshold and stared around the large foyer, happy for a moment's solitude to take it all in.

A fire was set in the front parlor. The logs snapped and popped.

The tangy wood smoke mingled with the scent of lemon verbena, from the bundles of scented herbs Claire tucked into every corner. Liza smelled the appetizing dinner that was cooking mixed with the sweet cinnamon aroma of the

Thanksgiving baking, which had likely gone on all day.

The long pine bench that stood against one wall was already piled high with her family's belongings. Nearby, on the oak check-in desk, a small china lamp cast the space in a warm, welcoming glow. Not the Tiffany-style lamp with the stained glass shade that had always stood there. It was a new lamp, one she had never seen before. It did the job adequately, in its nondescript way, but did seem mismatched in the midst of the elegant decor. Maybe the other lamp was being repaired?

Doesn't matter, Liza thought. She still felt the inn opening its arms to embrace her. She couldn't quite describe it, her heart rising with happiness and, at the same time, relaxing with relief. A feeling of safety, of returning to the place she was meant to be. Four full days was a luxury to squeeze from Daniel's schedule but now seemed like far too brief a time for a visit here.

Emily and Dan rarely hosted Thanksgiving for the family. Or any holiday, for that matter. Emily's sister, Jessica, was a much better cook and had a natural flair for entertaining. And her sister-in-law, Molly, was a professional chef who ran two successful bakery cafés, one in Cape Light and one in Newburyport, as well as a catering business. Molly was visiting her daughter for Thanksgiving this year, but her annual Christmas Eve party was the highlight of the family's holiday parties.

Even their mother, Lillian, had more space for a family dinner in her big, old house, and considerably more fine china and silver flatware to display. Which seemed the main point of family parties there, when you got right down to it. Emily was happy to help her relatives in other ways and to bring pies or cakes from the bakery to any holiday get-together.

But this year, she had decided to do a thing she thought she could not do, as Eleanor Roosevelt had advised. At three o'clock on Thanksgiving day, Emily stood at the top of the long dining room table, opened to full length. She smoothed the last wrinkle in the tablecloth and prodded a rebellious chrysanthemum in the flower arrangement, listening for the oven buzzer with one ear and the doorbell chimes with the other.

The oven sounded first. Emily set off for the kitchen, calling out to her daughter Jane. "Wait for me to take the turkey out, honey. It's heavy."

"Okay, but hurry. We don't want it to get all dried out and chewy." *The way it usually tastes when you make it,* Jane might have added. But she was too sweet to voice such a harsh critique, no matter how true.

It had been Jane's idea to have Thanksgiving at their house. She thought it would be fun. Emily hadn't known what to say. Hosting a family holiday was just the opposite of fun for her. But she didn't want her daughter to feel deprived of the experience; it seemed important to her. Jane was not her only child, but Emily had missed the chance to raise her older daughter, Sara, who was married and lived in Boston. Sara and her husband, Luke, were visiting Luke's family for Thanksgiving, but they would come to Cape Light for Christmas and stay a few days, Sara had promised.

Perhaps because she had missed out on raising Sara, or maybe just because of her natural, nurturing personality, Emily was a devoted and sensitive mother who never wanted to fail Jane in any way. If Jane thought they should have the whole family over for Thanksgiving, that's what they would do. It was comforting to see that Jane, who was adopted, felt such strong family bonds. Besides, as Jane had pointed out, it was only fair that they took their turn.

As part of the negotiations, Jane had promised to help with all the grunt work—shopping, cleaning, moving furniture, and setting the table just right. There was no need to ask if she would help with the cooking. Jane had practically made the meal all by herself. She had certainly been the head chef and Emily the kitchen helper. Emily was perfectly happy in that less-demanding role. While no one would deny Emily's many and impressive talents, cooking was not one of them.

Jane had taken an interest in the kitchen at a very young age, around the time she had noticed that there was more to eating than the healthy but plain meals Emily served. She loved watching cooking shows and baking contests, and she often reproduced the recipes she saw on TV or found on the Internet, with impressive results.

Even before her parents had agreed to host the holiday feast, Jane had collected piles of recipes and studied them every night, as diligently as she studied her chemistry and trig textbooks. Emily had to admit, the fun of preparing with her little girl had totally offset her usual entertaining anxiety.

Not so little anymore, she reminded herself. Jane was almost fifteen. Now, she stood in front of the oven and pulled on huge mitts, like a surgeon ready for the OR.

Emily opened the oven door and Jane peered inside. "The button popped out," she reported.

The not-so-infallible turkey button, Jane meant. Emily had learned through hard experience not to trust it. "Let's check the temperature, just to be sure."

She let Jane remove the pan and set it on the stovetop. Then she watched as her daughter stuck the thermometer into the turkey breast first and then the thigh. "The cookbook says to check the dark meat and the white. The dark takes longer."

"I think you're right." Emily always forgot that tip. No wonder her turkey was dry in one part and undercooked in the other. Or was that the time she had forgotten to defrost it completely?

"I think it's just right," Jane said. "Now it has to rest awhile before we carve it." Jane moved the pan to a rack on the countertop.

"Great. I'll shut off the oven."

"Just lower the temperature, Mom. We still need to warm the vegetables and stuffing. Everything will be ready by the time we sit down for dinner."

Jane stared down at a long list she had made of all the side dishes, which included timing for each. She wore a satisfied smile as she checked off *Turkey,* then checked the instructions for making gravy.

Dan poked his head into the kitchen and spotted the turkey resting under its foil tent. "Smells great. Has the bird landed safe and sound?"

"Thanks to your daughter. She's been giving me cooking lessons. I hardly did a thing."

Jane laughed. "You set the table and made the cranberry sauce, Mom. That was a big job."

It had been, for Emily, under Jane's watchful eye. Emily had not been permitted to use orange juice from a carton, only fresh squeezed; far less sugar; and loads of spices she would never dream of sprinkling anywhere near a cranberry. But the sauce had turned out very tasty, possibly the best dish she had ever prepared.

Still, she poked Jane with her elbow. "Wise apple." Then she leaned over and kissed her cheek. "I'm very proud of you. Maybe you'll be a chef . . . if you don't become an eco-lawyer, I mean."

Ecology law was Jane's latest career dream, an admirable one, Emily thought. Was Jane's attraction to public service possibly influenced by watching her mother hold the seat of Cape Light's mayor for so many years while she was growing up? Emily liked to think so.

But Jane's goals and dreams seemed to change every week, which Emily chalked up to her being fifteen. Emily only wanted her daughter to follow her heart and find work she loved so much that it didn't feel like work at all. She was eager to see where Jane's path would lead, to cheer from the sideline and help her whenever and however she could. But while Jane was still a teenager, living at home, Emily savored their time together.

Her younger daughter had come into their life in a strange and wonderful way. Emily and Dan had recently married, and she had almost given up on the hope of having another child, though it had been her dearest prayer. One that heaven had heard and answered in a way Emily had always felt was more than a blessing. To her, it had been a miracle.

The doorbell rang, pulling her out of her memories. "I'll get it," Dan called.

Emily looked at Jane. "Well, honey, it's show-time."

"No worries, Mom. Dinner is going to be fine."

"It's going to be delicious. My only fear is now we'll be stuck having Thanksgiving here every year."

They had the big dining room all to themselves. Claire had decided not to offer Thanksgiving dinner at the inn. Liza was glad of that. She didn't want Claire to be working all weekend. Their time together was too precious. And she didn't want to be working either. She always felt obliged to jump in and help when she was here.

They were twelve around the table, counting Audrey and Rob Gilroy, who owned the goat farm next door; Kerry Redmond, whom Claire had hired back in October to help with housekeeping and cooking; and all the children. The Gilroys had three, close in age to Max and Charlotte.

"We're ahead of you, Liza. You need to catch up," Audrey would tease her.

"True, but you had twins. Isn't that cheating?" Liza would reply.

Liza and Audrey Gilroy had been best friends for years when Liza had lived on the island. They remained just as close after she moved away, staying in touch with emails, texts, and phone calls. But technology was no substitute for the real thing, especially when it came to Audrey's

28

bubbly personality and irreverent sense of humor.

"More turkey, anyone? More of anything?" Claire came in from the kitchen, carrying a refilled platter of turkey and another bowl of stuffing.

Daniel was the first to lay down his fork and surrender.

"It's hard to resist. But if I eat another bite, I might explode."

Liza felt the same. She had tried not to gobble down the dinner as if in a race, but that had been a challenge.

Claire took her seat and covered her lap with a napkin. "Does that mean you're not interested in dessert?"

Daniel laughed. "You got me there."

"I'd like dessert." Max looked at Claire with a hopeful expression. The other children followed his lead. "Me, too," Audrey's boys, Ryan and Jack, called out.

"Manners, please?" Audrey reminded them.

"Me, too, please?" Jack said.

Claire was the only sympathetic ear. "Coming right up, my friends. I just need to clear these dishes, if everyone is finished."

"I'll help." Daniel stood up and grabbed a few plates, and Rob did, too.

"Don't forget to save some scraps for Edison," Nolan reminded them. He headed to the kitchen to supervise that mission.

Kerry did not say a word. Already holding a stack of dishes, she quickly followed him.

Liza had only met Kerry last night, but so far, had a good impression of her. She was like Claire in a way, quiet but hardworking. Friendly if you spoke to her, though she seemed a bit shy.

Not that Liza blamed her. Everyone at the table shared a deep history, and Kerry must have felt like an outsider and maybe a bit overwhelmed by their "catching up" conversation and inside jokes. Liza had tried to include her, but most of the time, Kerry sat back and listened. Either shy or simply private—Liza couldn't decide yet.

According to Claire, Kerry had been working at an inn in Bar Harbor, Maine, as a cook and housekeeper, and had come to Cape Light in October looking for work. Claire had posted a help-wanted notice on the bulletin board in Willoughby's Fine Foods and Catering, and Kerry had been the first to answer.

Claire had told Liza that Kerry was single, with no close family living in New England. Liza couldn't help wondering where her family might be and whether she missed them now that the holidays were here.

A short time later, with the dishes and food cleared off the table, everyone marched back into the dining room for the "grand finale." There was a pie per person, Liza thought. Not quite, but almost. Pumpkin, pecan, and apple, of

30

course. And a surprise addition, lemon meringue. Liza wanted to try a bite of each, but settled for a sliver of pumpkin and a dollop of the lemon meringue, which was quickly declared the hit of the dessert course.

"Kerry made it," Claire said. "I could never get meringue to peak that high, and her crust is even flakier than mine."

"I wouldn't go that far. You're a much better baker than I am." Kerry quickly countered Claire's compliment, but Liza also noticed a small smile.

She was a pretty young woman, though she didn't seem concerned much with her looks— her wavy, blond hair pulled back with a simple clip, her fair skin bare of makeup. A baggy blue sweater and jeans, plain and practical, completely camouflaged her slim figure. She had been working all day, helping Claire prepare for the sumptuous meal, and also taking care of a hand- ful of guests who were staying over this weekend. Liza guessed her age to be early thirties.

"I'll judge the pies and say which pastry is best," Daniel offered. Claire cut him a wedge and set it on a patterned plate.

"You're a brave man." Nolan glanced up at his wife. "I must recuse myself, since I'm happily married to one of the bakers. And plan to stay that way."

Kerry helped Charlotte with her spoon,

watching as the toddler maneuvered some apple pie into her mouth. "She's so sweet," Kerry said. "How old is she?"

"She was just two, in September," Liza replied.

"She's adorable." Kerry's gaze remained fixed on Charlotte. Then she suddenly looked away. "Both of your children are."

"They run us ragged sometimes. But we'll keep them for a while, see how it works out." She was joking, of course. She thought that was obvious. But Kerry's hazel eyes grew wide, as if she believed Liza meant it.

Before Liza could say more, Kerry smiled and nodded. "Kids that age are hard to keep up with."

"Do you have any children, Kerry?" Liza asked, then wondered if the question was too personal.

Kerry looked down and shook her head. Liza felt instantly sorry. She'd obviously hit on a sensitive topic. "I used to do a lot of baby-sitting," Kerry explained. "When I was in high school."

"I see. Well, you'll be well prepared when you have your own." Kerry quickly nodded and forced a smile.

Liza had a feeling that Kerry had a story, though she couldn't begin to guess what it was. The phrase "still waters run deep" popped into her head, seeming an apt way to describe Claire's new helper.

. . .

Liza stacked the last of the pie plates beside the sink. The kitchen looked like a tornado had hit, especially after the dirty dishes, glasses, and silverware from the dining room landed.

Kerry moved about the kitchen as if it were her own, directing how and where leftovers should be stored and whether dirty pots or dishes should be attacked first.

Liza had approved bringing in more help, but it was altogether different to see Kerry in action. Liza had never pictured anyone but Claire in charge of this kitchen. But her old friend seemed fine sharing her territory and her authority. Not fine, exactly, but resigned to doing things in a new way.

Everyone helped at first. The men were the first to drift off, taking the children with them, thankfully.

Finally, Liza and Audrey persuaded Claire and Kerry to let them finish. Liza was glad to have private time with Audrey.

Once they were alone, Liza whispered, "It's hard to get Claire out of the kitchen. Even for her own good."

"She's not exactly stubborn. More like . . . steadfast? Like the captain of a ship?" Audrey whispered back. "I'm surprised she let Kerry do so much of the cooking. Don't get me wrong," she quickly added. "I think it's great. Claire's not getting any younger, and she must get tired now and again, running this big place. Even though she never complains."

"She never does. But the work must be harder for her." Liza hadn't thought too much about that while living at a great distance. Partly because Claire never mentioned feeling tired or strained in any way by her duties at the inn. But now that Liza was here again, she was beginning to see that perhaps running the inn was a stretch for Claire at this stage in her life. And she was beginning to feel guilty about that, too. Guilty and self-centered not to have realized it sooner.

Liza scrubbed a small but very sticky pot, the first in a large, soapy pile. "Please don't mention I said this, but since we got here last night, I've been noticing little things that need attention. It seems as if Claire and Nolan aren't keeping up with the place lately."

Audrey snapped the lid onto a container of mashed potatoes. "Little things? Like what?"

"Oh, I don't know. Cracked tiles in the floor of the bathroom near my room. A water stain on the ceiling in Charlotte's bedroom. The handle on one of the dresser drawers is so loose, it fell off in my hand. And a shade in the side sitting room is torn, too. I don't know what happened to the Tiffany lamp in the foyer, and when I was coming down the stairs this morning, the finial on the post came right off in my hand. There's probably more if I really start looking." Liza sighed and looked at her friend. "I sound terribly petty, right?"

Audrey closed the refrigerator door and turned to her. "Now that you mention it, I've noticed a few things lately, too."

"You have?"

Audrey shrugged. "I'm sorry. I don't mean to upset you. It's nothing awful. It's just that . . . well, until recently, this place was pristine. I used to ask Rob, 'Do you think elves come out at night and freshen the paint and weed the garden . . . and arrange the flowers in the window boxes to look like a magazine cover? And do you think we could get them to stop at our place?' "

Despite Audrey's attempt at humor, Liza felt her heart sink. "And now? Have the elves abandoned us?"

"That's not what I mean, Liza." Audrey reached out and touched her arm. "I'm sorry I said anything. The inn is as charming and pretty as ever."

"I know it's still charming and pretty. But not as much as ever . . . right?"

Audrey meant well, but she had that tone friends get when they're trying to convince you a new haircut isn't *that* bad, even though you know it's dreadful.

"Don't apologize. I value your honesty. That's why I told you," Liza said. Her voice dropped as she heard footsteps in the hallway. The kitchen door was closed, but she didn't want to risk anyone overhearing their conversation.

When the steps had passed, Audrey said, "Maybe Claire and Nolan are still catching up with off-season repairs."

"I thought of that, too. Though the repairs are usually done by now. They might have fallen behind. Or there could have been more than usual."

Spring and summer were such hectic seasons, and with a steady stream of visitors shuttling in and out, it was impossible to keep up with repairs, except for the most crucial kind. All the summer traffic always left wear and tear on the building. Certain repairs, like painting, or even replacing tile if a leak was not a danger, were put on the back burner for the off-season. But by late November enough time had passed—usually—for the inn to look fresh and spotless again, and ready for more visitors.

"What will you do?" Audrey asked.

Liza plunged her hands back into the soapy water and pulled up a cast-iron frying pan. "I guess I need to speak to Claire. It's hard. I feel guilty for leaving her with all the work while I live two thousand miles away. I'm lucky she's willing to watch over the place for me at all. All things considered, maybe I don't even have a right to complain. I should be grateful to her and Nolan for staying here. I should be counting my blessings. Especially today. Not scrutinizing the property like a travel writer about to post an online review."

Audrey gazed at her with understanding. "You're in a difficult spot, no question. But I do think you have the right to say something. I know keeping the inn at a certain standard is important to Claire, too. She's always prided herself on this place, from the way the beds are made to her famous fish chowder. What does she always say?"

" 'God is in the details.' " Liza could hear her. As if she were right there in the kitchen.

"That's it. 'God is in the details.' I think she'll understand that you're not finding fault with her. Not really. You just want the inn to be as good as it can be. As good as it used to be? I think you both want that."

"I hope she doesn't take it personally. But if I were in her shoes, it would be hard not to feel criticized. That's the last thing I want to do. I love Claire. She's a dear friend. Even more than that."

Audrey met her gaze and nodded. She picked up a pan from the drainboard and began to wipe it dry.

Liza started on another pot. Audrey had made a good point. Claire had always taken pride in the inn's high standards and the awards and out-standing reviews garnered over the years. Maybe she hadn't noticed the place had slipped a bit? Or maybe her standards were no longer as rigorous?

"At least she hired help," Audrey added. "That suggests to me that she knows things aren't exactly right."

"Maybe. I never thought Claire would share her kitchen with anyone. I was always afraid to boil an egg in here."

Audrey laughed. "Mainly because you barely know how. But I know what you mean. It's almost shocking to see Claire share her turf."

Liza turned and looked at Audrey. "That was shocking, wasn't it? I nearly dropped my fork."

"Me, too." Audrey laughed and grabbed another wet pot off the rack. "The crust on the lemon meringue was very light. But I still like Claire's better. I think she wanted to make Kerry feel comfortable and give her some attention for all her efforts."

"I thought so, too." That was something Claire would do. She was modest to a fault and always quick to praise others. Even other cooks.

"Have you gotten to know Kerry at all?" Liza asked.

"Not too much. We chat a little when I deliver the cheese and produce. Unless she's busy. She's a very hard worker."

"Claire's told me that." And Liza had seen Kerry at work that day, cleaning the guest rooms and helping Claire put finishing touches on the dinner. "She seems reserved. The sort of person who doesn't tell you their whole life story five minutes after they meet you."

"Like me, you mean?" Audrey grinned. "I got that impression, too. But Claire thinks very well of her, and that's good enough for me. Claire is such a good judge of character."

Liza knew that was true. "Kerry has a nice rapport with the children. Especially Charlotte. She's very patient with them."

"Maybe she'd like to be a mother. I can't imagine why." Audrey made a silly face.

Liza had to smile. It wasn't easy to keep up with Max and Charlotte; she couldn't imagine handling three children all around the same age, and helping to run a thriving business, too. Audrey juggled it all well, she thought.

"You think you know what to expect . . . but you don't have a clue," Liza agreed quietly.

"Speaking of offspring, it's suspiciously quiet out there." Audrey set a pot on the table and opened the door a crack to listen. "Why aren't they running in here every five minutes asking for more sweets, or what game to play?"

"I was wondering the same thing, now that you mention it. Maybe aliens have whisked everyone away?" Liza dried her hands and untied her apron. "Let's go see."

Out in the front parlor, a football game with the volume low murmured on the TV. Daniel and Rob sat side by side on the couch, both fast asleep. On the rug in front of the TV set, Nolan supervised a circle of children—Flora, Max, Jack, and Ryan—working together on a vast Lego project. Liza couldn't tell what it was going to be. A giant robot or a skyscraper? Whatever the plan, Nolan had the group well in hand, their high spirits channeled into the effort.

"I love to see them playing quietly like that," Audrey said.

Liza agreed. "But where's Charlotte?" She wasn't among the older children.

Liza glanced around the room and spotted her daughter sitting in a small nook near the bay window, on a love seat with Claire and Kerry. Kerry sat on one end, reading from a picture book to the little girl, who sat on Claire's lap, though Claire had dozed off, her head slanted to one side, smiling in her sleep, one strong arm looped around her prize.

Liza exchanged a smile with Audrey. It was so good to be back here. She had so much to be grateful for. She had to remember that.

Chapter Two

As Emily had expected, every dish of their Thanksgiving feast was a hit with the family. And not because at her house, guests arrived with low expectations. Jane was showered with compliments and seemed overwhelmed by the attention.

"You'd better get used to it, young lady, if you keep cooking like this," said her grandfather Ezra.

"Maybe I can visit one night and make dinner for you and Grandma," Jane offered.

Ezra looked pleased and touched by the idea. "Wouldn't that be a treat. That's very thoughtful, Janie. You come anytime. Did you hear that, Lillian?" He turned to Emily's mother, seated on his right. "Jane is going to come over and cook for us."

Lillian looked as if she wasn't sure how to respond. She patted her mouth with her napkin and set it beside her plate. "As long as it's nothing spicy, and you bring all the groceries."

"Speak for yourself, Lily." Ezra turned to Jane. "Turn up the heat, honey. I can take it."

"Along with some antacid," Lillian muttered.

Emily's sister, Jessica, walked into the dining room with a pie in each hand, her husband, Sam, following close behind with a bowl of rice pudding and another of whipped cream. "Time for dessert. Jessica made a truckload of pies, and the whipped cream came from a real cow at our house. Her name is Zelda. Can you believe it?"

"Believe that the cow is at your house or that her name is Zelda?" Dan asked.

"Is the cow right *in* your house? I'm just curious," Emily added quickly. She didn't want her sister to take it as a criticism. It was entirely possible, these days, that the cow was living indoors, maybe near the kitchen? Emily did picture it there, from what Sam had said.

"The cow lives outside," Jessica clarified.

"She only comes in for meals," Sam added, raising eyebrows around the table all over again.

"Sam, please." Jessica gave him a look. "He's joking."

"Thank goodness for small miracles." Emily's mother grunted. "Cows in the kitchen. Bats in the belfry. I'm sure you've finally turned that lovely property into a barnyard. Not that it's any of my business."

About two years ago, Emily's sister had shocked the family—well, their mother, mostly—by leaving her job as a loan officer at the local bank to start an animal rescue, located on their spacious property. Jessica was managing it very well but sometimes had emergencies that required taking some of the animals indoors. Including livestock. Even if that were not the case, their mother had never gotten over Jessica's career switch, and was still appalled by any mention of the animals. Emily was surprised that Lillian had forgotten to use her favorite, hackneyed phrase about going to the dogs.

Jessica ignored her mother, but their youngest child, named Lily after her grandmother, did not. "Zelda doesn't come inside, Grandma. But we get milk from her every day and we even made butter this morning for the party. We just shook and shook and shook the cream. Like they did in the old days," Lily explained.

"Did you really?" Lillian sat back in her chair and stared at the butter dish. Emily could tell she was trying to remember if she had eaten any.

Lily nodded. "She's a very nice cow. You should come and meet her."

Sam laughed, and Jessica gave him a look. Sam and her mother did not have the best relationship, partly because he could rarely hold back his amusement at his mother-in-law's foibles.

"I can bring Zelda around sometime. It's no trouble, Lillian," Sam offered. "She's very tame. She'll walk right up the ramp into the truck bed."

Everyone at the table laughed. Her mother looked annoyed for a moment, then sighed with resignation, suggesting she was accustomed to being surrounded by inferior intellects and expected to be an amusement for them.

The pies had been sliced in the kitchen, and servings were quickly handed around. From the far side of the table, Emily searched for her husband's gaze with a look that said, *Time to change the conversation, please?*

Dan cleared his throat and stuck his fork into his slice of apple pie. "Who's going to church Sunday? We're lighting the first Advent candle."

Not the most stimulating conversation starter, Emily thought, but hardly a controversial topic, and one that did not include cows or some other sort of wildlife.

"We will attend. If someone picks us up and brings us home again." Her mother took a final bite of her pie and pushed the dish back, most of the slice still intact.

Emily didn't doubt that her mother had enjoyed the pie, which was her favorite flavor. But she had rarely, if ever, seen her mother clean her plate, no matter how delectable the food. Emily sometimes wondered if it was simply a trick her mother employed to keep her figure so slim all these years. Or if her mother believed that eating everything on one's dish was ill-mannered—or what she would call "bad form." Probably the latter, Emily thought now.

"Lighting the candle is fun. Reverend Ben asked us a few years ago," Jessica recalled. "Do you all know your lines?"

Dan glanced at his wife and daughter. "We could use a little more practice."

"We'll be fine," Emily countered. "It's only a verse or two. It's not a three-act play."

"I'm a deacon on Sunday. I'll take a video," Sam said.

Jane rolled her eyes. "Do we really have to make such a big deal out of this? It's only a candle."

Emily met her glance but didn't reply. When Reverend Ben had called to invite them, she had wondered if Jane would agree to do it. She was at an age when she didn't like doing anything in public with her parents. Emily had half expected Jane to make some excuse, like having basketball practice or too much homework, her favorite cards to pull in these situations. But she had gone along with the idea, and Emily hoped she wouldn't back out now.

"It's only a candle, but a very important one," Ezra said. "The ceremony marks the start of the Christmas season. In a spiritual sense. As opposed to all the sales kicking off at the shopping malls."

"Excellent point, Ezra," Dan said. "It's an honor to be asked, and we would definitely like a video, if it isn't too much trouble, Sam." He glanced at Jane. "Just for the family. No posts on social media. We won't embarrass you too much, honey," he promised.

"Just the usual amount?" Emily added. She finally saw Jane smile again and felt relieved. She wasn't going to jump ship. But Emily understood Jane's discomfort. It was another sign that her daughter was growing up. And much too quickly.

After the meal, everyone helped to clear the table—Jane and her cousins—Darrell, who was in graduate school, studying to be an architect; Tyler, who was in high school; and Lily, who was in fifth grade. Sam and Dan helped, too. For the first phase, at least.

Then the men headed out for a walk, including Ezra and Darrell. Jane played a board game with Lily and Tyler in the living room while Emily's mother started a crossword puzzle, then quickly dozed off.

Emily was not surprised when she and her sister were left to sort out the meal's aftermath. Jessica pulled an apron from the hook near the stove and tied it around her slim waist. "I can take care of this, Em. Why don't you sit inside with Mother? You've probably been in the kitchen all week."

"Jane would hardly let me do a thing. She had a grand plan."

"And pulled it off very nicely."

"She obviously got the cooking gene you inherited. I pulled Mom's DNA on that one."

46

Her sister laughed. "I do remember cooking when I was Jane's age. Mainly because there wasn't anything interesting in our house to eat. It's hard to believe Janie is already a teenager. She'll be learning to drive and applying to college soon."

Emily was packing leftovers for her sister and mother. "Don't remind me. I was thinking of that all day. We still have a little time left with her at home. I'm just trying to enjoy it." She glanced at her sister and smiled. "It's easier for you. Darrell is grown, but when Tyler goes off to school, you'll still have Lily."

Jessica stacked dishes in the sink. "I know, but it's still hard when they go off on their own. When Lily leaves, at least I'll have the animals."

Emily laughed. "Ah, so that's your secret plan. Very clever."

"Wasn't it? Please don't tell Sam," Jessica whispered with a grin. Her expression softened. "Jane is growing into such a wonderful young woman. You must be very proud. But I'm not surprised. She's had a great mom and dad."

Emily was grateful for the compliment. "I think she's pretty wonderful. I do know she's the best thing that ever happened to us. The day I found Janie was the happiest, luckiest, most blessed day of my life. And always will be. Not that I don't love Sara just as much. She's another miracle. But in a different way."

Emily knew Jessica understood. When Jessica and Sam were first married and faced great disappointment trying to start a family, Darrell had come into their lives. Nine years old and from a troubled home, the boy had won their hearts. Jessica sometimes said she wasn't sure who adopted whom—only that they couldn't imagine their lives without him. And as such stories often go, Jessica became pregnant soon after they adopted Darrell and their family began to grow.

"Darrell was our miracle, as you well know. I can hardly believe he's almost finished grad school. When he was about Jane's age, he began to get curious about his birth father. Has Jane talked to you about her birth parents yet?"

"Not really. She did ask that one time, a year or two ago. I think I mentioned it to you?"

"You did. That's why I asked. She's getting to the age when kids get curious about that information."

Emily knew that was true. But Darrell's situation was different than Jane's. Sam and Jessica knew when they adopted Darrell that his mother had died. When Darrell got curious about his family as a teenager, his father could not be found and there were no siblings, at least none that were ever discovered. He did have a grandmother, who had taken care of him for a while before he was adopted, and Sam had made sure Darrell visited her often until she passed away a few years ago.

Jessica and Sam had handled Darrell's search for his birth family with equanimity, Emily recalled.

But it was hard for Emily to even talk about the subject. Though she knew her sister only asked out of concern.

"Jane hasn't asked again since that one time, though I don't know if she thinks about it. Or talks about it with her friends. She knows how I found her in the crèche at the church that morning, and how I kept visiting her in the hospital until Dan and I got permission to take care of her here until her birth mother was found. And she knows that her birth mother was never found, and that we then made plans to adopt her. We've been very open about all that."

"I know you have, and it sounds like she accepts those facts. But at some point, she might decide she wants to search for her parents. Especially her birth mother," Jessica added. "At least, that's what I hear from other people who've adopted children. It seems to be an important phase they all go through, sooner or later."

"I've heard that, too. And read a lot about it, of course," Emily added. "But reading about it is one thing. Jane actually telling me she wants to look for her birth parents, that would be another. And if she does, it won't be easy, since there's no birth certificate. Not any that's been found."

Jane was a few months old when Emily discovered her in the crèche outside the church. It

49

was impossible to guess the baby's date of birth, so Emily and Dan decided to celebrate each year on the day their daughter had been found.

"If and when she decides to do it, I know I'll be supportive. But I also know, in my heart, I dread the day," Emily admitted. "So many things can go wrong in that situation. And I know I'll feel displaced and threatened," she confided. "It's hard to admit, but I will. I practically do already, just talking about it."

Jessica turned and touched her shoulder, her gaze sympathetic. "I know when the time comes that you and Dan will do and say just the right thing. Because you're a great mom and Dan is a great dad. No matter what Jane discovers, or who she encounters, she already knows that."

Emily covered her sister's hand with her own. "Thanks, Jess. You're so sweet."

Jessica shrugged. "It's just true." She rinsed off a heavy casserole dish and set it on the drainboard. "Let's talk about something happier. Did you realize Ezra's birthday is coming up? January fifth. He'll be ninety-five."

"That is a milestone." Emily had not realized that. "I feel as if he always gets deprived of a big party because his birthday is so close to Christmas. Everyone's tired of celebrating. We have to do something really special for him this year. If not for Ezra . . . well, I don't know what would have happened to Mother all these years."

Jessica laughed. "*She* would have gotten along just fine. *You and I* would be in the crazy house."

Emily couldn't help laughing. "He's definitely saved us. He has taken wonderful care of her, and with the patience of a saint. And he keeps her in line. Most of the time. Everyone in town loves him, too. People still ask for him at Dr. Harding's office, even though he gave Matt the practice at least ten years ago."

"There are people in this town who Ezra has brought into the world, and he's treated their children and grandchildren. He's an amazing person. I just don't know what sort of party we should have. A big bash? Just the family? A surprise? Is that dangerous at his age? He does have heart issues."

Emily knew Jessica was half joking, but it was true and something to consider. "Good questions. I'm not sure yet what we should do, but I think we better keep it just between us until we've decided. You know how Mother gets. Once she's involved, she'll insist on running the show." That was a diplomatic way of saying that their mother was so fussy and difficult, party planning would be complete misery once she became part of it.

"Agreed. We need to present it as a done deal. Maybe even sign contracts and make deposits with a caterer or venue. Otherwise, she'll sweep in and upend all our plans."

"My point exactly." Emily wrapped up the

last care package of leftovers and wiped off the kitchen table. "She's always imagining conspiracies, sure we're keeping her out of the loop about things. But this time, Mother will be right."

Before Jessica could reply, their mother walked into the room. Emily could tell from her curious expression she had overheard their conversation. But not too much, she hoped.

"I'll be right about what?" she asked, staring at Emily.

Caught off guard, Emily didn't know what to say.

Luckily, Jessica was faster on her feet. "About Zelda. A cow really is too much for our property. We're going to find a nice farm that will take her in. She'll be happier there. Though we'll miss the fresh milk and cream."

Lillian regarded Jessica with her head tilted to one side, her blue eyes narrowed. "You agree with me about the cow? I can hardly believe it. Surprisingly sensible . . . Or should I say *suspiciously* sensible?"

"Mother, what does that mean?" Emily hoped she sounded slightly indignant and not guilty.

"Never mind what it means. I'd like a cup of tea, please. Chamomile, if you've got it. I think that homemade butter disagreed with me." She rubbed her stomach with one jewel-covered hand. "Who ever heard of serving such a crude dish—on a holiday, no less?"

"The Pilgrims?" Emily offered. Her mother answered with a look.

"One chamomile tea, coming right up." Jessica grabbed the kettle and slid Emily a secret glance.

Emily fetched the tea and the sort of fancy china cup her mother preferred, all the while hiding a smile.

Not much got past Lillian. Unlike many seniors her age, she was still sharp and remarkably observant. The years had not dulled her radar for picking up subterfuge and manipulation. Emily knew that she and Jessica would have to be careful. If they could pull this off, it would be fun to surprise both her mother and Ezra. Though her mother would complain later of being kept out of the loop.

But it was all for a good cause, Emily reminded herself. A very good one.

By Sunday morning, Liza had discovered even more lapses in repairs—mostly small problems, but the mounting evidence weighed on her. She couldn't ignore it. She had to speak to Claire, but couldn't seem to find the time or the courage.

As she rose from bed she heard the children in the hallway and Claire's voice, too, leading them downstairs for breakfast.

"Let's see if Mommy is up. She loves pan-cakes," Max said, standing right outside Liza and Daniel's bedroom door.

"Oh, those sleepyheads. Let them have a few more dreams. There's plenty of pancakes. We'll save a few for Mom and Dad," Claire promised.

She was teasing, of course. Liza knew Claire would make a fresh stack as soon as she and Daniel appeared. Claire was so thoughtful to take care of the children so she and Daniel could sleep in.

She glanced over at her husband, his thick, dark hair standing on end, his bearded cheek squashed into the pillowcase as he clung to a rare opportunity to sleep past six thirty. Even with his mouth agape, he still looked impossibly handsome. Liza was tempted to wake him up and ask his advice, but he should have a few more dreams this morning, even if she couldn't. With a sigh, Liza headed to the shower.

When she returned, Daniel was sitting on the side of the bed, stretching and yawning. He picked up the clock and quickly looked up at her.

"Why did you let me sleep so late?" It was only a quarter to nine, but could have been noon from his expression.

"You must be tired if you didn't wake up. This is a vacation, remember?"

"I wasn't that tired. Must be jet lag."

He was already scrolling around on his phone, checking messages. Liza knew his work was important, but it seemed a shame he couldn't detach completely for even a day or two. Daniel loved being a doctor, though he had given it up for years before deciding to return to medicine. His specialty now was pediatrics, but the clinic was so shorthanded, he treated patients of all ages. He was well liked and very much in demand. And a very good doctor. Though the more he proved himself indispensable to the clinic and his patients there, the more Liza worried they would never leave Arizona.

She didn't think about it that much. Time just passed, one day melting into the next. But being back on the island reminded her of where they'd started and what they had given up. She still believed their stay in the Southwest was temporary. And yet, there was no end in sight.

"Looks like a beautiful day. Is it cold out?" Daniel pushed back one of the shutters. It squeaked ominously and dangled to one side. A screw on the molding was loose, threatening to fall out completely, like a bad tooth.

He quickly pushed the screw back into place and carefully folded the shutter. "I'll fix this later. It needs a little wood putty."

Liza pulled a sweater over her head. "I think this whole place is starting to need a little wood putty. Maybe something even stronger."

"What do you mean?"

"Haven't you noticed? All the little repairs that have been overlooked, here and there. Nothing really major, but when you add them all up, well . . . the inn is looking a lot more run-down than it was when we left."

Daniel frowned. "I didn't want to say anything and spoil the weekend. I thought we could talk about it alone, when we got back. But maybe it's better if we figure it out here."

"I'm glad you agree with me. For a while, I thought I was imagining things or just being picky. I know the place can't stay exactly the same as we left it. It can't be frozen in time. But it was kept to a certain standard. I hate to say it, but it just doesn't meet that mark anymore."

Daniel started making the bed. "I noticed a gutter was loose yesterday when Nolan and I were playing in the back with the kids. He said he's found a good handyman who's helped with the outside work. I think the fellow's name is Gabriel O'Hara. He's going to stop by this afternoon and give an estimate on the porch roof. I'll be interested to meet him."

Liza smoothed her side of the bed and set the decorative pillows in place. "The porch roof? What's wrong with that?"

"There's a leak. Nothing major, but Nolan certainly shouldn't be up on a ladder. Even if he wants to be."

Liza agreed with that. "And Claire found Kerry. She seems competent. That's some comfort. But I still need to talk to Claire. I just don't know how. I hate to seem as if I'm criticizing. I wouldn't hurt her feelings for the world. You know how grateful I am for the way she and Nolan have stayed on here, taking care of everything for us."

Daniel walked over to her and rested his hands on her shoulders. "I do know. And Claire knows that you would never intentionally hurt her feelings. But this has to be addressed, honey. It's better to work it out here, face-to-face, than to try to deal with it over the phone."

"That's true. We still have today and most of tomorrow."

Their time on the island was slipping away so quickly. Liza couldn't believe it was already Sunday. Mucking up the end of their wonderful visit with such a difficult conversation was the last thing she wanted to do.

Daniel searched her gaze with his own. "Do you want me to talk to her? I can do it. Or we can talk to Claire and Nolan together?"

Liza stared back at him, tempted to agree. "You're sweet to offer. I know you would say all the right things. But I can't push it off on you. It's my property, for one thing. And I don't want Claire to think I'm hiding behind my husband. I need to speak to her privately and work this out. I'll find the time before we leave . . . somehow."

"Stubborn as nails. But that's why I love you. One reason, anyway." Daniel nodded and kissed her forehead. Liza allowed herself a moment to relax in his embrace, to draw strength from his strength.

"I'm just worried about what might come after we talk. It might lead to some big changes, some big decisions. I'm not ready for that." She hadn't even realized that anticipating a next step, after the conversation, was the most disturbing to her. Now that she'd said it aloud, she knew it was true.

"One step at a time, Liza. You're stressing out about something that hasn't happened yet."

Liza lifted her head and smiled at him. "Now you sound like Claire. That's something she always tells me."

"That's why Claire is Claire . . . and why it might not be as difficult to sort this out as you expect."

Liza nodded but didn't reply. She also knew that Claire would advise that she pray about this challenge and ask Heaven to send just the right words she needed to say.

Liza didn't pray nearly as much as she used to when she lived here. Or attend church as much. Or at all, back in Deep Wells, partly because of the children being so young, and partly because their church was far, and Daniel usually worked on the weekends. So many excuses, she realized. Perhaps someday that would change.

Daniel ducked into the bathroom. "I'll grab a fast shower and meet you downstairs."

"Don't be too long. Claire made pancakes. Max might eat them all."

Daniel poked his head around the door. "Now you tell me? I wouldn't have stood there gabbing all morning if I'd known that."

He disappeared and Liza laughed. His tone was so serious. She wondered if he was really worried.

Down in the kitchen, it looked as if Max had eaten his fill. He was now busy steering a small plastic car in circles around the table while Nolan set obstacles on the course—a spoon, a coffee mug, paper napkins.

Charlotte sat next to Claire on her booster seat, her face a sticky mess, her expression content. Claire had cut a pancake into small squares and let Charlotte feed herself with her hands. It looked like many of the bites had actually made it to her mouth. Though Edison sat below the little girl's chair like a brown furry crocodile, and wearing a crocodile smile, too.

Liza poured herself coffee and sat next to Max. "How was breakfast?"

Max stopped pushing his car. "Aunt Claire's pancakes are good. Not chewy like yours are."

"Oh, Max, that's not nice to say. You'll hurt Mommy's feelings." Claire was already back at the stove, beating up the batter and pouring sizzling circles on the skillet for her new customers.

"It's true. I'm not the best pancake maker." Liza helped herself to one fresh from the griddle. "Besides, nobody makes them like you, Claire. Everyone knows that."

"Claire's should be called feather cakes." Daniel strode into the room, ready for the day in a navy blue pullover and white T-shirt underneath, his dark hair wet from the shower. He dropped a kiss on Max's head and then on Charlotte's. Then he tried to wipe his daughter's sticky face with a napkin, which only left tufts of tissue on her cheeks.

"Are there really feathers in them? I didn't taste any." Max didn't seem put off by the idea, just curious.

"I'm not sure. Why don't you ask her?"

Max looked at Claire. "Do you really?"

Claire laughed. "Your father is giving away all my secrets."

Liza could see she was pleased by the compliment. Daniel carried a plate to the stove, and she slipped a few pancakes on it. "Here are your feather cakes. Syrup and butter are on the table."

Kerry came through the swinging door that led to the dining room, carrying a tray of dishes.

"They've all finished breakfast, Claire. I just need to bring more coffee."

"I'll do it, dear." Nolan rose and walked over to the coffeemaker. Kerry was already at the sink, rinsing dishes and loading the dishwasher.

"Good morning, Kerry," Liza said.

Kerry turned and smiled. "Good morning. Did you sleep well?"

"Very well. Must be the sea air. Right, Claire?" Liza wasn't sure about that, but that's what Claire had always told her and told all the guests, and what her aunt had always said long before that.

"It is indeed. Scientists are just catching on. Nolan read me an article the other day, about ions or some such in the salt air. It's just common sense. The sea air is rejuvenating. Revives the body and soul and gets you right with the world. A long walk on the beach is almost as good as going to church on Sunday."

"Almost." Nolan had returned from the coffee run and grinned at his wife. Claire didn't seem to notice his amusement. Or chose to ignore it.

She was a longtime member at the old stone church on the village green in Cape Light. She'd been going there since her childhood, long before Reverend Ben's tenure, which was going on over forty years. Nolan had not been a churchgoer when they met. In fact, as a scientist, he had been skeptical of spiritual beliefs. But once he began living on the island and had married Claire, he'd joined the congregation. Perhaps for Claire's sake, Liza thought. He did seem devoted to her. Or perhaps because he'd begun seeing the world through Claire's wise and sensitive perspective and had experienced a change of heart.

"Which reminds me, would anyone like to come to church with us this morning?" Claire glanced around the table.

Daniel concentrated on his pancakes. Liza sipped her coffee, though there was little shelter to be found behind the mug.

"It's the first Sunday of Advent," Claire said. "Reverend Ben's sermons are especially thoughtful this time of year. I wonder what theme he'll focus on during the Christmas season. Last year, it was all about giving from the heart."

Liza tried to avoid Claire's hopeful glance, but it was hard. Having Liza and her family at church today would mean a lot to Claire. She was proud of Liza and Daniel and their family. She wanted to show off Max and Charlotte, her "almost grandchildren," to her friends. Liza could hardly deny her that.

"Of course we'll go. That's a nice idea. Thanks for asking us."

Daniel met Liza's gaze and nodded. "I love that church. We haven't been inside for years. Good idea."

Claire's blue eyes lit up and Liza knew they had said the right thing. The hassle of wrangling the children for an hour or two would be worth it.

"We'd better leave soon to get good seats," Claire said, removing her apron. "I think the Forbes family will light the first Advent candle—

Emily Warwick, Dan Forbes, and their daughter, Jane."

Claire's words were interrupted by the crash of breaking glass. Liza turned to the sink. Kerry stared down at a shattered dish, then quickly bent to gather the pieces.

"That was so clumsy. I don't know what happened. It just slipped out through my fingers—"

"It's all right. It's just a plate. It could have happened to anyone." Liza knelt down and helped her clean up the broken pottery. "Looks like it shattered. We probably need the electric broom."

"Don't bother, Liza. You should all get ready for church. I'll clean up in here. I don't want you to be late."

Claire shook her head. "Don't be silly, Kerry. We won't leave you all alone to work. Why don't you come? We'd love to have you join us."

"What about the guests? What if they want something?"

A good point, Liza thought. She and Claire had rarely left the inn unattended. Especially on a Sunday morning, when visitors needed help checking out.

Before she could suggest a solution, Nolan said, "You go along. I'll stand watch and clean up the kitchen, too."

"Thank you, dear. That's a perfect solution," Claire said, looking pleased at her husband's offer.

Kerry took a moment to reply. Finally, she nodded. "All right. I'll come . . . I'd like that. Thank you."

"Excellent. Let's meet downstairs in half an hour," Claire said. "That should give us enough time."

Half an hour hardly seemed long enough to clean and dress her children, but Liza would try her best.

Max tugged on the edge of her sweater. "Are there any more pancakes?" he whispered.

Liza smiled. "I think we've had enough of those for now." She took his small, sticky hand in hers. "Let's go upstairs and get ready for church."

Daniel walked back to the table and scooped up Charlotte from her booster seat. "I'll take the pancake princess upstairs and help you get them cleaned up."

"I think they both need a bath," Liza said.

Daniel followed Liza on the staircase with Charlotte tucked to his shoulder. "They seem to have already bathed this morning. In syrup."

Liza laughed, grateful for her sweet, if sticky, family. In church this morning, she would offer up thanks.

CHAPTER THREE

Emily hoped Jane would wear a dress to church, or even a skirt and a pretty blouse, or a good sweater. But she didn't say a word. Not even when Jane came to the breakfast table in a faded black turtleneck and worn-out jeans. Emily also managed not to comment when Jane ran back up to her room after breakfast and switched outfits several times, pulling clothes from her closet and dresser drawers in a frenzy and tossing them on her bed.

Dan hadn't said anything about the first combination either. Maybe he had intended to but had been warned off by Jane's mood.

He fixed breakfast for everyone—bacon, eggs, and toast—and Emily eagerly dug in. She loved it when someone cooked for her and would have eaten toasted cardboard. Jane had sneered at the offering. She was a vegetarian. Sometimes. It was hard to tell; her food ethics changed from meal to meal. She fixed herself yogurt and berries, then nearly snapped her father's head off when he asked if she was ready for the candle ceremony.

"Come on, Dad. It's just church. We're not going to be presented to the queen."

"Can't argue with that. Her Royal Majesty will definitely not be there this Sunday." He turned the page of his newspaper.

Dan had been dressed and ready by seven thirty. Two hours later, he waited at the front door in his parka and hat, car keys in hand.

"I'll go start the car. Get her down here, Emily. You know we can't be late."

Emily knew that was true. She was habitually tardy, and Dan, overly punctual. They were opposites that way, and Jane had unfortunately taken after her. She walked to the bottom of the stairs. "Jane? Are you ready? Reverend Ben wants us there a little early . . ."

Before she could say more, her daughter flew down the stairs, her honey-blond hair straightened with a flat iron. Jane's hair had a wonderful, natural wave. Emily would have given anything for that thick mane. But Jane was in a phase when she was often unhappy with her looks. This week, she didn't like her hair.

Jane wore a long, turquoise-blue sweater Jessica had given her for Christmas last year. It turned her hazel eyes a blue-green color. She was also wearing her "nice" black pants, saved for family parties and performing at school concerts. Emily felt relieved. "You look very pretty, honey."

"Thanks." Emily could tell from Jane's mumbled reply that the outfit was not Jane's first choice but what she thought she *should* wear, all things considered. She pulled on a jacket Emily thought was too flimsy for late November and headed for the door. "Let's just get this over with."

Emily zipped her down coat and locked the door. She was starting to feel the same but caught herself and reached for a little trick she used to avoid being bogged down in other people's bad moods.

She had relied on it all those years in village hall, dealing with so many opinions and difficult personalities. She thought of it as lifting her sights to the Big Picture. Looking beyond the difficult moment to her whole life from the long view, as if on a hilltop. Life would invariably look a lot better, the petty annoyances shrinking out of view. She began to smile as she walked to the car, feeling grateful for the bracing air and brilliant sunshine, grateful that her family had been asked to help usher in the Christmas season at church today, and very grateful for Jane.

Emily slipped into the car and fastened her seat belt. "Sorry to keep you waiting. I think we'll make it there in plenty of time."

Dan nodded and backed the car out of the driveway. Jane stared out her window, looking as if she might bolt at the first stop sign.

She won't be a cranky teenager forever, Emily reminded herself with a secret smile. *Even though it feels that way this morning.*

Kerry didn't expect that they would all fit into one car, but Daniel and Liza had rented a very large SUV with two rows of rear seats. She and Claire sat in the back row, and the children, in their car seats, sat in the middle. Kerry was happy to be in the back of the vehicle, alone with her thoughts, while Claire pointed out the sights to the children and chatted with Liza and Daniel.

Could anyone tell how nervous she felt? If they did, what would they think? There seemed no reason to be anxious about visiting Claire's church. Claire's friends from church would often visit the inn—Vera Plante, who rented out rooms in her big Victorian to visitors; and Sophie Potter, who used to run the orchard on the Beach Road, but now just lived in the old house there. Even Reverend Ben had stopped by one time when Nolan had a bad cold.

Kerry knew she was inclined to judge church-goers harshly; her childhood exposure to religion had not been a good one. Still, she had to admit Claire's friends had all been very kind to her, warm and welcoming. Not like some people she had known who had professed to be spiritual but felt themselves far above others who did not share their beliefs. Their hearts were cold and closed.

Though Claire often invited her to the Sunday service, Kerry had never agreed before. But when Claire mentioned who was lighting the Advent candle, Kerry knew she couldn't possibly pass up the chance to be there, to watch from a safe distance. To see with her own eyes, for the first time in almost fifteen years, the daughter she had abandoned as a baby and left in the crèche in front of the very same church, tucked in the cradle and wrapped in her blanket. Just about the same time of year, too.

It seemed more than coincidence, though Kerry's presence in Cape Light was not by chance. Kerry had come here purposely to find Jane—just to see her, to make sure that she had been raised in a good home, with loving parents. Of course, from the outside, it was sometimes hard to tell how a mother or father really treated a child. She knew that hard truth from her own experience.

Everyone who knew her father thought he was a saint, and even more so after her mother passed away and he was left to raise a little girl on his own. He certainly encouraged the impression. While in the privacy of their home, there was little joy or warmth, only judgment and criticism, and Bible verses, distorted and misused, undermining her confidence and squelching any vague dream she harbored of escaping to a different, brighter life.

Kerry already knew something about Emily Warwick and her husband, Dan Forbes. She hoped they were the decent, responsible, and kind people they seemed to be. She hoped she could somehow find out for sure. But being with her daughter under the same roof, breathing the very same air . . . that seemed enough to handle today. Kerry's hands were actually shaking, and she folded them together on her lap, watching out her window with unseeing eyes.

Claire touched her shoulder, and Kerry turned. "Are you cold, Kerry? I can ask Daniel to turn up the heater."

Kerry forced a smile and shook her head. "I'm fine, honest. But thank you."

They had almost reached the church. She hadn't even noticed. They were coming to the end of Main Street. The harbor and village green came into view, and then the old stone church, surrounded by tall trees that were mostly bare this time of year. Kerry's mouth felt dry. The very sight of the church triggered memories that were hard to face.

Since she'd come to town, she'd seen the church from a distance but had never gone inside. And had been inside only once before that. One fateful morning, one impulsive moment that she would regret for the rest of her days.

Daniel pulled up to the church's rear entrance. "I'll let everyone out and park the car. It will be easier with the children."

Claire handled Max, and Liza took Charlotte. Kerry jumped in to help, unfolding the stroller and grabbing the bag with toys, snacks, and other necessities Liza had hastily packed.

Liza was a good mother. She never seemed stressed and made handling two little ones look easy. Daniel shared the childcare, though from what Kerry had heard, his work as a doctor was very demanding. Most of the childcare was probably left to Liza, who also taught art part-time at an elementary school. Kerry wondered how she managed it. She had tried the single-mother route but had failed miserably, after a very short time.

But you were young and had no one to help. Very young, she reminded herself.

Kerry shook off her sad thoughts and followed Claire and Liza into the church. As they entered the sanctuary, she heard soft music from an organ. Many of the pews were filled, but the service hadn't started yet. One of the deacons showed them to a long, empty pew.

"Thank you, Sam," Claire said. Kerry wasn't surprised that she knew the man by name. Claire knew everyone in town, and many people sitting nearby greeted her. Claire was so wise and kind that people looked up to her. But Kerry had noticed that Claire never seemed to look down on anyone. She was the true model of what her father called a good Christian. Kerry had never met anyone quite like her . . . certainly not her father, who only acted the part.

Kerry had entered the pew first, followed by Claire. Then Max and Liza with Charlotte on her lap and an empty seat left for Daniel on the end. Kerry was pleased to be in the center of the row, with a clear view of the altar. They were not seated very far back; just a few rows. She could smell the flowers on the altar table, an arrangement of long-stemmed white lilies and greenery in a clear vase, circled by holly and pine branches.

She had no recollection of the sanctuary; the old wooden pews, smooth and polished; the high-beamed ceiling; the stained glass windows, arched on top. She had been here so briefly that day, mainly seeking shelter from the frigid morning. She only remembered it shadowy and chilly inside. She had slipped into a row at the very back and knelt to pray, as best as she was able.

She had been in such a state. Irrational, unhinged, totally desperate and at the end of her rope. Certainly not in her right mind. Otherwise, how could she have done what she did?

She opened her program, her gaze floating over the words. The candle lighting would come early, right after the entrance hymn, even before the announcements. That was a relief. She wouldn't have to wait. If it had come at the end of the service, she didn't think she would have been able to stand it.

The church was filling up now. She saw the choir line up just outside the double doors at the back of the sanctuary, dressed in long red robes with white collars, black folders of sheet music clasped in their hands.

She glanced around, hoping to spot Jane and her parents. *Her adoptive parents,* she silently corrected herself. She couldn't figure out who they might be.

I don't even know what my own daughter looks like. What kind of person am I? What kind of mother? No kind at all . . . I just want to see her one time.

She closed her eyes a moment and squeezed her hands together, trying to settle her nerves. When she opened them, she realized that Claire must have thought she was praying. The irony was almost amusing.

Though she'd never shared her father's religious zeal, Kerry had often prayed when she was young. But the last prayer she'd ever offered up had been right here, asking God to give her a sign. To either send help so she could go on one more day, or let her know that giving up her daughter was the right thing to do.

The organist struck a loud, clear chord. The soft murmur of voices grew silent, and everyone sat up with attention. Claire leaned over and gently stilled Max's toy car. "The choir is going to sing to us now," Kerry heard her whisper. "Get ready."

Kerry got ready, too. The choir marched down the center aisle singing a hymn that was vaguely familiar to her. Her father had taken her to church every Sunday, no excuses, short of a contagious illness.

The first soaring notes of "O Come, O Come, Emmanuel" filled the sanctuary. She saw the minister, Reverend Ben Lewis, at the back of the group. He sang in a hearty baritone, walking at a stately pace. He wore a long white robe with a bright blue scapular that draped around his neck and hung down over his chest.

He was not a tall man and looked to be in his late sixties or even a bit older. Reddish-brown hair was mixed with silver in a fringe around his mostly bald head. His thick beard was even more silvery. He had a friendly face. Even while he sang, she could see a slight smile, his eyes twinkling behind small gold-rimmed glasses. He looked happy and gazed fondly at his congregation as he marched by.

The hymn ended and a tall man with silver hair and a tall, slim woman with short, reddish-brown hair got up from their seats in the very first pew.

Dan Forbes and Emily Warwick, it had to be. Kerry had not even noticed them.

But where was Jane? Was she home sick? Had she decided not to come? Emily turned back toward her seat, and finally, a teenage girl stood up and followed her, head bowed, her face hidden under a curtain of honey-blond hair. She seemed reluctant, or maybe just nervous and embarrassed?

She was so beautiful. Kerry struggled to hide her reaction. Her breath caught in her chest and she felt her heart stop, her full and complete attention fixed on the girl—*her daughter*—as the rest of the world melted away.

Kerry watched Dan and Emily take their places near the altar table, where four large blue candles stood in a circle of pine branches and holly.

First Dan spoke, some verses that Kerry had seen printed in her program. She glanced down at the page for an instant but very quickly back up at the altar at Jane, who stood by Emily's side, fidgeting a bit and biting her lower lip. She held a slip of paper in one hand and with the other pushed her hair back.

Kerry finally saw her face clearly. She tried to study and memorize it as fast as she could. Jane had an oval-shaped face, a straight nose, and high cheekbones. A broad, high forehead and deep-set eyes. Kerry thought her eyes were blue, or maybe even hazel, like her own. But it was hard to tell for sure from such a distance.

When it was her turn, Jane read her verses from the slip of paper with a serious expression and lit the candle. While Emily spoke again, Jane looked out at the congregation.

Kerry felt Jane look straight at her. Their eyes connected and held and Kerry felt her breath catch. An instant later, Jane's gaze moved on. She smiled shyly at Sam, the deacon who had seated them and now stood in the side aisle, taking a video on his phone.

The ceremony ended and the family returned to their seats. Kerry could barely see the back of Jane's head. She sighed and sat back against the wooden pew. The rest of the service loomed ahead, and the idea of sitting through it seemed challenging now. She felt so stirred up. She had enough nervous energy to do laps around the churchyard, but forced herself to remain in her place and try to focus on Reverend Ben, who was finishing his announcements.

For the rest of the hour, Kerry felt as if she was playing a secret game, trying to catch glimpses of Jane whenever she turned her head to say a word or two to Emily or to the older woman on her right, whose white hair was neatly pinned in a roll on the back of her head. A French twist, Kerry recalled, was the name of the old-fashioned style. The woman's large pearl earrings and the collar of a fur coat hinted that she was well-off. She held her head high and looked straight ahead, her posture impressive for someone her age.

Kerry wondered if she was Jane's grandmother. She hoped so. It would be some comfort to know that Jane had grandparents, and that they were wealthy. Though it was even more important that they were loving. A grandmother like Claire . . . now, that would be ideal.

She had no way of knowing if the older, well-dressed woman was anything like Claire. The woman did look proud; Kerry just got that impression.

Or maybe that's because her own father had been very well-off and very proud of his money and position. He had provided for all her material needs—clothes, shoes, books, food. Just the minimum, what he thought she needed. No extras or gifts or luxuries. Especially after her mother passed on. Shoes and clothes had to last. If all the girls were wearing a new style, Kerry didn't even bother to ask if she could go to the mall. She knew what her father would say. He didn't allow her to follow the crowd, to make friends with girls he thought might be a bad influence, to take part in activities that might instill the wrong ideas and attitudes and lead her on the wrong path. Which pretty much included all her classmates and anything she wanted to do after school.

He actually used those words, too. "The wrong

path, Kerry. You must be vigilant and resist temptation. It's around every corner, waiting to drag you down. I know it's not easy. But you know right from wrong. Some of these other children never learned that at home. You have no excuse."

He was right, too. When she discovered she was pregnant, she had no excuse. The child's father was a boy in her school whom she had met for secret dates only a handful of times. She hardly knew him. She certainly didn't love him. If loneliness and simple human need for a kind word and a loving touch, or the naivete and the poor judgment of a sheltered seventeen-year-old girl, were not an excuse, she had none.

That was how her father saw it, and he very quickly decided she would be sent away to a home for pregnant teenagers, where she could keep up with her studies. When her baby was born, it would be taken away and given up for adoption. She would never have a chance to hold it or even see it.

And she would not come home, or contact him, ever again.

She'd have a high school diploma and would earn her own way. He was sorry but she had done this to herself. She'd given him no choice. Kerry could hear his words ringing in her ears, even to this day.

The congregation came to their feet. The sudden sound and motion startled Kerry from her memories. Claire leaned closer and showed her open hymnal. "Number two-oh-five, dear. Page three fifty-three."

Kerry quickly picked up her own book and flipped the thin pages to the right spot. She found the verse and tried to sing but mostly just mouthed the words.

It had been hard to come here this morning. Harder than she ever expected. She could never describe the way it felt to finally see Jane, practically in arm's reach.

She had been so anxious this morning, getting ready to come here, that she'd never considered the strange coincidence. She had waited so long and come so far to find Jane, and the first time she would see her daughter again would be in this church, the very same place she had let Jane go.

"God works in mysterious ways," Claire often said. Kerry had always thought that phrase to be just a figure of speech, a convenient cliché. But today, she felt the truth of it deep in her bones. It was more than a coincidence to finally see Jane again in this church. It felt like a message, but one she could not decipher.

It was so hard to remember the past, the forces that had shaped her life. That had conspired to wrench her baby from her arms fifteen years ago, in this very place.

So hard to look back at her younger self, pulled

under by the ink-black despair that had convinced her, for one despicable moment, that giving up her baby was the right thing to do. That giving up on herself as a mother would be best for her child.

Kerry could still remember how, in that crazy, desperate moment, she'd felt her heart torn from her chest, the better part of it left with her little girl. After all these long years, there was still a gaping wound that would never be filled.

She had been through a lot in her life and had taught herself not to look back; that was an indulgence she couldn't afford. She could not dwell on regrets; she had plenty of those. The past could not be changed. But this morning, in this church, she couldn't turn away from the memories and regrets.

The congregation continued to sing along with the choir.

Reverend Ben walked down the center aisle to the rear of the sanctuary, and when the hymn stopped, he raised his hand and conferred a blessing.

"Go in peace. And now, the work begins."

The choir sang a few closing bars without any instruments accompanying them. The pure, bright notes of their voices lifted to the rafters and echoed with harmony. Kerry felt her mood lift, too. She shook off the recollections and secrets of her past and brought herself back to the present. The sanctuary bustled with activity and conversation as everyone made their way out of their seats.

Claire took Max by the hand and Daniel carried Charlotte as Liza followed with the tote bag and coats. It was slow going. The aisle was very crowded, and sitting so far to the front, they had to wait for most of the other pews to empty. Kerry took a moment to search the crowd for another glimpse of Jane. But she couldn't find her.

As she stepped into the aisle to follow Claire, she walked straight into someone. More precisely, straight into a tweed sports coat that covered a pair of broad shoulders.

She jumped back, embarrassed. "I'm so sorry. Excuse me."

The man turned his head and glanced down at her. He was tall, his thick black hair neatly trimmed. Surprise and curiosity flashed in his dark eyes. Then he smiled, a dash of white, even teeth against tanned skin. He had a warm, wide smile with deep dimples on both cheeks. "My fault, I'm sure. I need to have my brake lights checked."

His reply made her smile. She looked away, afraid she was staring at him. But something about him seemed familiar. She just couldn't figure out why.

He turned his attention back to his row and

helped an older woman from the pew. She was about half his height but had the same dark hair, dark eyes, and dimples, Kerry noticed. A relative? The woman walked with a cane but was dressed very stylishly for her age in a blue and red print dress with a dash of red lipstick.

A few steps ahead, Claire glanced over her shoulder. "The line to greet Reverend Ben is so long this morning. Let's go straight to coffee hour. I promised Max a cookie for being a good listener and singing all the songs."

Kerry didn't know Liza very well, but she was almost certainly a mother who didn't reward her children with sugary treats. That was an old-fashioned method, to be sure. But Claire could be excused. Kerry had a feeling Liza would feel the same.

The tweed jacket and the handsome stranger wearing it had disappeared into the crowd. Just as well. She didn't need any distractions right now. If she could catch one more glimpse of Jane, she would live on the precious memory forever.

Kerry followed Claire through the crowd to a community room that adjoined a large kitchen. Long tables with cakes and plates of cookies were flanked by two large percolators. There was an orderly line of adults leading down from the coffee station, but children darted back and forth from the dessert table like flying insects attacking a picnic.

Max tugged Claire's hand and led her to his reward. She laughed at his persistence and surrendered. "I did promise. You're perfectly right. Let's pick out a cookie, any one you like."

Liza and Daniel stood talking to one of Claire's friends, Vera. She was a very nice woman, though very talkative.

Vera was admiring Charlotte, who was suddenly shy and ducked her head into her father's shoulder.

"My goodness, isn't she a living doll. Last time you came, she was a tiny baby, Liza. And is that Max with Claire? He's growing up so fast. How old is he now?"

"Almost five," Liza said.

"Is he really? Time flies. I can't keep track. Speaking of kids growing up too fast . . ." Vera's smile widened as she waved someone over.

Kerry turned to see who was being beckoned. Her breath caught in her throat as Jane smiled shyly and walked toward them.

"Nice job this morning, Janie Forbes," Vera said. "For a moment, I didn't recognize you. I said to Sophie, 'Who's that lovely young lady with Emily and Dan? Do you know her?' "

Jane laughed. "You recognized me. I know you did."

Kerry took a deep breath and forced a smile. Jane stood inches away, and Kerry longed to speak to her but was afraid she might faint on the spot if Jane so much as looked her way. Her head felt light, as if the room were spinning.

Jane was more interested in Liza and Charlotte. "It's so good to see you, Liza. Are you visiting for Thanksgiving? Is this your daughter? She's beautiful."

Liza leaned over and gave Jane a hug. "We finally made it back. It's been too long. This is Charlotte, and that's Max, her older brother." Liza glanced at her son, who was leading Claire with one hand and clutching a cookie with the other.

"They're both adorable," Jane said.

"Completely," another voice agreed. Kerry was so focused on Jane, she didn't notice Emily Warwick walking over to join them. "I remember when you were that age, honey. It doesn't seem that long ago."

Jane rolled her eyes. "Now you'll tell stories about things I did when I was two. Let's not go there, Mom."

Kerry smiled at Jane's teenage exasperation, then felt a pang in her heart. It was so hard to hear her daughter call Emily "Mom." The word struck like a dagger, flung from the blue, finding its mark with cruel precision.

She blinked, hoping her eyes weren't tearing up. Was she going to cry? She couldn't. Not here, in front of everyone.

Claire and Max joined them, and Emily, Jane, and Vera fussed over him, just as they had fussed

84

over Charlotte, giving Kerry a few moments to collect herself.

Suddenly Claire looked up from the children and met Kerry's glance. "For goodness' sake, I've forgotten my manners. Emily, Jane . . . have you met our Kerry? She's been helping me at the inn. I don't know what I'd do without her."

Kerry felt touched at Claire's introduction. No one had ever called her "our Kerry" before. The affectionate term was a balm to her raw emotions.

Emily smiled and extended her hand. "It's nice to meet you, Kerry. How long have you been at the inn?"

"Not that long. A little over a month." Kerry shook Emily's hand, surprised at her friendly, down-to-earth manner. Kerry knew Emily had been mayor of the town for years and had imagined she would be different, more like the executives Kerry had worked for in big offices, always letting the underlings know they were higher up on the food chain. But Emily didn't seem like that at all—just the opposite.

"It feels as if she's been with us forever. She fits right in. Hand in glove," Claire said.

"That part was easy. Claire is wonderful to work for," Kerry said, glancing at the older woman.

"Oh, dear. You make me feel like a boss, and that's certainly not what I am, or ever will be. We're a team, or even a family."

Kerry agreed but didn't reply. Claire and Nolan had been so caring and kind to her, much more so than her real family had ever been.

"It must be fun to live at the inn, Kerry. I love it there," Jane said.

Kerry smiled back but felt tongue-tied. Jane speaking directly to her—and calling her by her name—was an unexpected shock.

There was an awkward pause, then Kerry said, "I watched you light the candle today. It was the nicest part of the service."

Emily looked surprised at the out-of-sync comment, and Kerry cringed. She felt so foolish. What a silly thing to say. She glanced at Jane to gauge her reaction, then looked away, certain that the girl thought she was a total dolt.

But it was true. For her, it had been the best part of the service.

Jane smiled and leaned closer. "Thanks, but don't let Reverend Ben hear you. I'm sure he thinks his sermons are the highlight."

Everyone laughed. Kerry smiled, too, but not only at Jane's quick wit. *I just spoke to my daughter. She's so lovely and smart and clever, I can hardly believe it.*

Vera turned to Emily. "I see that you're the chair of the Christmas Fair again. I guess if you ran the town all those years, organizing our volunteers is not much harder."

Emily laughed. "Between you and me, it's like

herding cats. Luckily, Jessica is going to share the job this year. She's pretty good with cats, as we all know."

Everyone smiled, but Kerry didn't get the joke.

"My aunt Jessica runs an animal shelter," Jane said.

"How interesting." *She's so thoughtful to notice I didn't understand. What a sweet girl.*

"You can count on me for the bake sale, as usual," Claire said.

"Me, too. And I'll take on some handcrafts if that group is slim," Vera offered.

"I was hoping you'd both say that. There's a meeting tomorrow night. I hope you can come."

The women began to talk about the fair, and Kerry acted as if she was listening, but she was actually taking a moment to study Jane, who stood between her and Emily. *So close,* she thought, *like a delicate butterfly poised on a flower petal.* She didn't dare move a muscle and frighten her away.

My daughter is so beautiful. We have the same hair color, except that hers is straight, and mine is wavy. But her eyes are exactly the same hazel color. That's just what I looked like in high school, too, that soft, trusting light in her gaze and expression. It's so strange to see my reflection in her face. I've always wondered what she looked like, but I never expected this.

Kerry glanced at the other women, suddenly

panicked someone would notice the resemblance between her and Jane. It seemed striking to her, uncanny. But no one spared a glance at her or Jane. The women just continued to talk about the fair.

A teenage girl across the room waved at them, and Kerry watched Jane walk over to her friend. Kerry felt her heart deflate. She turned to Claire and touched her arm. "I think I'll step outside for a breath of air."

Claire gazed at her, looking as if she sensed something out of the ordinary was going on. But thankfully, she didn't ask any questions. "It gets a little close in here. We'll be leaving in a few minutes. Let's meet up around the back."

Kerry headed out of the hall and found the first exit. She pushed through the glass doors and stepped outside, then followed a gravel path that led into the village green. It felt good to walk and breathe the fresh, cold air. She needed to clear her head; her thoughts were spinning.

It was a fair, clear day, mild for late November; a real fluke, especially in New England. The forecasters said the temperature would drop tonight and it might even snow tomorrow. She had brought along gloves but stuffed them in a pocket.

She knew New England winters well. She had grown up near Cape Light, at the very end of the peninsula in Rockport. She'd never once returned. *Though I didn't get very far, did I?* Kerry reflected. *Just up to Maine and back.*

Today it felt as if she had come full circle, looping back to Cape Light and this old church, to finally be reunited—in a small way—with her daughter.

She had come back here hoping just to see her, even from a distance. But to actually speak to her, to hear her daughter say her name . . . It was almost too much for her to handle. It would take time to process, to mull it over in her mind, every word, every look. Kerry suddenly wondered what her daughter thought of her. *What sort of impression did I make on her? I'm just the new helper at the inn. She probably won't give me a thought, one way or the other.*

Kerry sat on a bench with the church in view, the dock nearby and the wide blue harbor behind it. The church was decorated for Christmas in a simple but beautiful way. A thick pine wreath hung on the arched wooden doors and a large crèche with almost life-sized figures stood nearby, nestled in a stand of tall trees.

Kerry's heart ached at the sight, a painful reminder of the worst decision of her life. The morning she'd come to Cape Light with her baby, she'd left the church after desperate prayers for help had yielded no answer or sign from above. The crèche scene had come into her sight; Mother

Mary and Joseph standing ready by the empty wooden cradle. In a crazed moment, she gave the baby to their care, tucking her inside the cradle with a note, praying she would be found soon and given a chance for a good life. A better life than Kerry believed she could ever provide.

Today it was clear her prayers had been answered. It also seemed clear that she could never reveal to Jane their true relationship.

Even if I could find the courage, she'll hate me. I don't want to see the hate and anger in her eyes. I'd rather she think of me as a stranger, even a totally forgettable one.

I brought her into this world, but Emily is her mother now. She seems to be a pretty good one, judging from the way Jane has turned out. Jane is smart, mature, and kind. I could never have provided the upbringing she's had. I could have never raised her that well.

I hurt my daughter once, abandoned her. It wouldn't be right to interfere with her life now, to mess up anything. Especially her relationship with her parents. That would be very selfish, certainly not a loving thing to do. And I do love her. She's the only person I've ever really loved in this world, even more than my own life.

Kerry stared out at the harbor, the blue waves ruffled by the breeze. Seabirds swooped and dipped around the dock, looking for a bite to eat.

"Hey . . . is this yours?"

She looked up, startled by the words. The tweed jacket was walking up the path toward her. The handsome man wearing it now had a brown scarf tossed around his neck. He smiled his warm smile and held out a blue and white knit glove.

She stood up and checked her pocket, even though she instantly knew it was hers. "Thanks . . . I must have dropped it."

He reached the bench and handed her the glove. "It's nice enough out now, but you'll need both later. Especially on the island. It can get wicked cold out there."

She stared at him. How did he know where she lived?

As if reading her mind, he said, "I saw you Saturday at the inn. I came to see Nolan. You answered the door."

She stared at him a moment. She did remember now. He had come to see Nolan and Daniel, to look over the porch roof. But he'd been dressed differently, wearing a baseball cap over his thick hair and a ragged field jacket and overalls.

They had barely exchanged a word. She'd merely opened the door and called out for Nolan. She was surprised he remembered her at all.

"I do work at the inn . . . but I'm sorry, I didn't remember you."

His mouth twisted to one side in a funny grin. Insulted or just amused? She couldn't tell.

"Wait . . . now I remember. You're going to

do some repairs? Nolan was talking about you."

"Only good things, I hope?"

"So far. But you haven't done much yet."

He laughed at her tart reply. "True enough. But I might have to move in to take care of all the projects Nolan listed."

He was joking, but it wasn't that far from the truth. She wasn't happy to hear that he was going to be wandering around the inn fixing things indefinitely. She felt a tug of attraction to him, to be honest. But she didn't like the feeling. Romantic relationships never turned out well for her. Not that she'd had many, but enough to know she was jinxed somehow where the opposite sex was concerned.

She was well practiced in giving men the "not interested" message. Some were more persistent than others. Kerry guessed Gabriel O'Hara would fall into that category. But it didn't take long before even men who liked a challenge got the memo and moved on.

"I've never seen you in church before. Was this your first visit?"

Kerry shook her head. "Not really . . ." *My second visit, if you must know. Both have been very memorable.* Of course she couldn't say that to him. "I was only inside once before. This was the first service."

"How did you like it?"

He had so many questions. Too many. "It was

fine. I really don't have time for church right now. Weekends at the inn are busy. Lots of meals to cook and serve."

"So you're a cook there? I thought that was Claire's job."

"It is. I help out in the kitchen and bake a lot. I do housekeeping, too."

"Are you a good cook?" His expression was serious, as if the answer was important to him. Though his dark eyes still held a humorous light.

"Most people think so. I enjoy baking more. I'm a pretty good baker," she said honestly.

"That's good. Dessert is my favorite part of the meal."

Maybe, but you'd never know by looking at him. He was totally fit, from head to toe. She pulled her gaze away, wanting to end the conversation.

Just say it's been nice to meet you and go. She was about to do exactly that, but something in his smile and dark eyes made it hard for her to step away.

"I'm walking into town for a bite of lunch. Would you like to join me? I was thinking of Willoughby's. You might like it . . . as a baker."

He waited for her answer with a hopeful look. Kerry was surprised by the invitation and that it took her so long to answer.

"I'm sure I would . . . but I need to get back

to the inn. I'd better find Claire and the Merritts. They're probably waiting for me."

He just nodded. He didn't seem upset by her refusal.

"So long. It's been nice to meet you." She smiled briefly and headed down the path toward the church.

Why had she said that? The words had just popped out. Maybe she felt guilty for turning down his invitation. It hadn't been exactly "nice" to meet him. More like unnerving. An unexpected encounter in her totally unexpected day.

"It was nice to meet you. I'll see you soon, Kerry," he called.

Even her name sounded different when he said it. And how did he know her name? She didn't remember telling him.

She kept her face forward, resisting the urge to turn around for one last look at him. But she still felt something in her heart tug, like a fish caught on a line.

She ducked her head down and quickened her pace, wondering if he was still watching her walk away. She wanted to be annoyed, to be cynical and curt. To dismiss Gabriel O'Hara as a charming flirt who knew he was attractive and played that card very well.

Somehow, she couldn't write him off that easily. She didn't like facing that fact either.

CHAPTER FOUR

~

When they returned from church, Claire and Kerry went straight to the kitchen to make turkey sandwiches from the Thanksgiving leftovers while Liza took the children upstairs to change their clothes. She had dressed them in their best outfits for church, and the plan was to play on the beach after lunch.

Liza knew it would be a bittersweet beach walk. They were leaving tomorrow. Returning to miles of sunbaked desert, with no crashing blue waves to be found. But she didn't let herself dwell on that thought; she just wanted to enjoy the day.

It was surprisingly mild for November in this part of the country, without a puff of wind. She stuffed a few hats and scarves in a tote bag, just in case.

She called Daniel to take the children down, then changed into a pair of old jeans and a hooded sweatshirt she had found in the closet, along with a pair of worn-out sneakers, perfect for a beach walk.

She yanked up the jeans and sucked in her stomach. Was she crazy to think they would fit after all this time . . . and two pregnancies?

Miraculously, they did. A little snug on the waist, but she left the snap open. No one would see with her sweater and all the other layers pulled down.

She folded the children's clothes and put them in a suitcase. It was almost time to pack up for home. She didn't like that idea either, but forced herself to start. At least she would get a bit done before lunch was ready.

She was glad they had gone to church today with Claire. It had been fun to catch up with old friends and to show off her children. Claire had definitely enjoyed that part of the morning.

Liza hadn't attended church much when she'd lived here. Sunday morning was a very busy time at the inn, especially in the summer. Going to church was important to Claire, so Liza had usually stayed back to take care of the latecomers to breakfast and guests who were checking out or needed help with bike routes or borrowing beach chairs. There was so much to keep a person busy here.

Now that she was older and had a family, she could see joining the church. She already knew practically everyone in the congregation, and it would be good for the children to have a spiritual side to their upbringing . . . something they could rebel against later?

But the musing seemed pointless. They didn't

live here and there was no plan to return. Which reminded her of a difficult task she had to face before they left tomorrow. She still had not spoken to Claire about the inn. She'd promised Daniel she would do it, but simply hadn't found the right moment. Would there ever be one? She didn't think so.

Once or twice, she'd been just about to broach the conversation but lost her nerve. Or she and Claire had been interrupted. And now time was running out. She had to do it today, or tonight at the very latest. She couldn't leave it to the very last minute of their stay and part with Claire on a sour note. That would be the worst thing.

"Liza? Lunch is ready," Claire called from the bottom of the staircase.

"Thanks. I'll be right down." Liza took a deep breath and sat on the edge of the bed, intending to put on the old sneakers. Instead, she clasped her hands together and closed her eyes. "God, you know I don't pray much, but I really need some help today. I need to have this difficult talk with Claire. I can't stand the idea of hurting her feelings, but some things have to be said. Can you help me, please? Can you send me the right moment and the right words to make it go well? As well as possible?" she amended.

She didn't know what else to say. She hardly ever prayed, except when she was worried about the children or Daniel. Then her prayers were

97

more like, *Help, help, help*. But she had once heard Reverend Ben say even that prayer was perfectly fine.

"Can you help me, please?" she added one more time for good measure. Then she opened her eyes, tied her shoes, and headed downstairs.

Later that night, once the children were asleep in their room, Liza began to pack in earnest. She walked back and forth in the bedroom, sorting out everyone's clothing. Daniel packed his own bag, but it was up to her to remember all the odds and ends. With two children under five, there were a lot of those. Something under the bed caught her eye, and she picked up a small pink sock with a bunny face.

"Have you noticed another one like this anywhere?" She held up the sock so Daniel could see it.

"It might be in the bathroom. Wait, I thought it was a hand puppet. I think I stuffed it in the duffel bag with the toys."

Liza yanked the duffel over and checked the contents, a jumble of toys, puzzles, books, and Lego pieces. Somehow, the matching bunny face floated to the surface. "Got it. Thank goodness— it's her favorite pair." She rolled both together in a ball and put them in the other suitcase.

"Do you have a lot more to do? I can help," Daniel offered.

"I'm getting there." Liza took out a few of her own clothes from the standing closet and began to fold them on the bed. "We have a little time tomorrow. The flight doesn't leave Logan until six thirty."

"True. But we still have to get to Boston and return the car . . . all that stuff." He paused. "Did you speak to Claire today?"

Liza felt a fist tighten in her chest. She was afraid to look at him. "No . . . not yet. I'm going to do it tomorrow."

"Liza . . ." She could tell he was trying very hard not to lose his patience. "You promised you'd do it today, on the beach. It was the perfect time to say something."

She sighed and sat on the edge of the bed, her good silk blouse crumpling in her lap. "I know, but we were all having such a nice time. It was such a beautiful afternoon, and Claire and Nolan were enjoying the children so much . . . I just couldn't spoil it."

The beach had been beautiful in the late-afternoon light. The surf swept in so gently, Liza could easily imagine taking a swim, though she knew the water was frigid. It was low tide and the shoreline was long and deep, flat enough to walk on easily, with plenty of tide pools for the children to explore. Nolan found tiny crabs in a large puddle, which fascinated Max and Charlotte. Until Max decided he wanted to catch one of the seabirds, who trotted lightly along the water's edge just beyond his reach. Edison tried his best to help, but he couldn't catch a bird either.

Liza took so many videos, her cell phone battery went down to zero. It was just as well. It was better to enjoy their time at the beach than to try to capture it in a photo or a video. She had all the memories of such a special day safely stored in her heart, where they belonged.

Daniel met her gaze with a resigned expression. "It was a lovely day. A highlight of our visit, for sure. But I thought that after I took the kids and you two were alone, you'd tell Claire what's been on your mind."

"I tried. I really did. We were walking along and I was just about to start. But she suddenly seemed tired, out of breath or something. She said she'd been chasing Max too much. She had to sit down, and I got worried," Liza confessed. "How could I say anything after that?"

Daniel instantly had that doctor look. "Did she have any dizziness or chest pain?"

"I don't think so. Would Claire even tell us if that was the case? She's never once complained about her health. I've never even seen her with a cold."

"Me neither," Daniel admitted. "But she's still human. And getting older. All the more reason to have that talk, honey."

"Yes, I know . . . We sat down a few minutes

and she was fine. She bounded up the steps faster than I can."

"Glad to hear it. But you need to speak to her tomorrow morning, first thing. Just get it over with. You'll feel a lot better."

She knew he was right. "I will. First thing. She gets up very early. Maybe I'll go down and help her get breakfast ready."

"Good idea." Daniel yawned and stretched. "I think we should go to bed now and get a good night's sleep. We have a long day ahead of us tomorrow."

A few minutes later, the lights were off and she heard Daniel breathing deeply on his side of the bed. He had the uncanny ability to fall asleep the moment his head hit the pillow. A talent he'd probably perfected as an intern, when sleeping hours were few and far apart.

It was so annoying. Like right now, Liza thought. She flipped over to her favorite sleeping side, then tried the other, but still couldn't settle down. It seemed hopeless. She didn't even feel drowsy.

Finally, she got out of bed, found her slippers, and pulled Daniel's big flannel shirt over her pajamas for an extra bit of warmth. Then she crept out of the room and down the stairs.

Claire always left a small lamp on in the kitchen, and Liza didn't bother with any other lights. She didn't want to wake anyone.

She filled the teakettle and set it on the stove. Maybe if she had a cup of tea and read a few pages from a book or a magazine, it might make her drowsy?

Or maybe a small snack? Liza knew it wasn't healthy to eat late at night, but she had read somewhere that carbs made you drowsy. She pulled open the fridge and browsed the shelves. She did recall one last slice of pumpkin pie should be in there.

Ahhh . . . there it was. She spotted the dish tucked behind the egg carton and slid it out.

"Liza, is that you? I thought I heard someone."

Liza turned, feeling caught in her midnight refrigerator raid. Claire stood in the doorway, wearing her long blue robe, her white hair uncoiled, hanging down her back in a thick braid. Liza couldn't help but notice her favorite slippers peeking out below the nightwear. A cross between Danish clogs and boiled-wool socks, they could only be purchased from some obscure manufacturer by mail order. The rare but practical footwear was just so . . . Claire.

Liza shut the fridge and strolled over to the table with her prize. "I couldn't sleep. I don't know why. The beach walk was plenty of exercise."

"Maybe you're anxious about the trip back to Arizona. Traveling with small children can be challenging. So many connections to make."

"Maybe." Liza met her gaze and knew it wasn't that. "I'm sorry I woke you up."

"You didn't wake me, dear. I forgot my pill." Claire wandered to the cabinet next to the sink and took out a small bottle.

Pill? Since when was Claire taking medication . . . and for what? Liza tamped down her alarm. "What sort of medication is it? A prescription?"

Claire nodded. She took a small pill from the bottle and tossed it in her mouth, followed by a sip of water. "It's nothing, a little digestive ailment. The doctor says this keeps the stomach acid down. It's my own fault for eating too much."

It was just like Claire to blame herself for the condition. "That happens to a lot of people. No matter how much they eat."

"For my age, I'm blessed with remarkably good health. Some of my friends use little boxes marked with the weekdays to keep track of their medications. But sooner or later something has to give on such old machinery," Claire said with a little laugh.

"Not much, though, and not too quickly, I hope." The condition didn't sound serious, but Liza wondered if Claire was telling her the whole story and not underplaying some problem. "I'd offer to share the pie but that's probably not a good idea if your stomach is upset. I was about to make some ginger tea. That should help you feel better."

"Ginger tea would be perfect," Claire agreed. "Even better than a pill."

The kettle rattled but wasn't quite whistling. Claire stepped toward the stove. "I'll fix the tea," Liza said quickly. "You sit down and rest."

Claire seemed about to argue but finally took a seat at the table and watched as Liza prepared a full pot of tea and set it on the table with two mugs, a jar of honey, and at her own place, the surviving slice of pumpkin pie.

"I wasn't going to indulge," she admitted as she took a small bite, "but I rationalized that it might help me sleep and I won't have pumpkin pie until next Thanksgiving. Unless I make it myself, which might seem odd any other time of year."

"I've always wondered why that is." Claire checked the pot to see if the tea had steeped long enough, then filled Liza's cup and her own. "The Pilgrims only had pumpkins in the fall, but we have the ingredients available anytime. Maybe I'll serve some to the guests in the middle of the summer and see what they think."

Liza caught a twinkle in her eye but still wondered if she was entirely joking. "It would be an interesting experiment."

"I'll let you know if we get any complaints." Claire smiled and sipped her tea.

A bite of pie stuck in Liza's throat, and she washed it down with a sip of tea. Then she took hold of her courage and plunged ahead.

"Have there been any remarks from guests lately . . . about anything?"

The question was vague, but she had to start off slowly and hope Claire would take the hint.

"Remarks? About our pies?" Claire looked confused.

Liza shrugged. "About anything . . . the food, the linens . . . the rooms?"

The light in the kitchen was dim but she did notice Claire's blue-gray gaze drop to her teacup, the soft smile slipping.

Liza waited a painful moment for some reply. It was only a few seconds but felt like hours. She almost started talking again, about to brush her question aside, when Claire suddenly lifted her head.

"I sprinkled chili powder all over a tray of French toast one morning. I had mistaken it for cinnamon. There were a few remarks after that dish was served, I'll tell you that."

Liza was about to laugh at the confession, but Claire looked so serious. As if she were giving testimony at a trial.

"Anyone can make a mistake like that. You were probably in a rush and didn't have your reading glasses handy."

Claire sighed and sat back, squaring her

shoulders, her chin high. "Anyone could use that excuse as well, Liza. But it wasn't the first time, and I have to admit, I've been getting a little forgetful in the kitchen. I need my recipe book front and center when I cook these days. I'm liable to forget about putting clams in the chowder." She shook her head and stared down at her tea. "It's shocking. But I can't deny it."

Liza's heart went out to her dear friend. She could see how hard it was for Claire to make this confession. "Well . . . at least you're aware of it. And you have Kerry now, to help you."

"That was mainly why I decided to look for kitchen help. And I'm not the tornado of energy I used to be," Claire added. "My intentions are good. But these old legs don't like to climb the stairs twenty times a day anymore. They let me know it, too."

"I noticed you were tired on the beach." So it wasn't just a fluke or chasing after Max and Charlotte too much that had tired Claire today. Liza had known that in her heart but had not wanted to face it.

"It comes and goes. I have more gas in my tank some days than others. But generally speaking, I suppose I'm feeling my age, and Nolan is, too. Chores that used to take him a day, like painting a bathroom or patching a leak, stretch into a few. Or even a week's time. He's reluctant to climb up on a ladder these days. I don't want him to either."

Claire's confessions were hard for Liza to listen to. She suddenly felt so guilty, and selfish. For the past few days, she had only been focused on the inn and the neglected repairs. But what about the two people in the world who were as dear to her as her own husband and children?

She reached out and took Claire's hand. "Are you and Nolan all right, Claire? Are there any health issues you aren't telling me about?"

Claire smiled and patted Liza's hand. "Not at all, dear. Dr. Harding says we're both fit as fiddles. We're getting older, that's all." She sighed and met Liza's gaze. "I know the inn isn't quite the way it used to be . . . I know it's not the way you left it. I've been meaning to talk to you about that all weekend, but . . . I just couldn't find a way to work the topic into the conversation."

Liza was surprised and relieved by Claire's words. "I did notice things have . . . slipped a bit, here and there. I wanted to talk to you about it, too. But we've all been having such a wonderful time together and we get to visit so rarely. I guess I didn't want to spoil things."

"I know. I felt the same. But it's best that we get it out in the open before you leave tomorrow . . . Is that why you couldn't sleep? Were you worried about talking to me?"

"I was," Liza admitted. "Mainly because I feel

as if I don't have the right to be critical at all of you and Nolan. I've left you both here, with all this work to do. I've totally taken advantage of you and our friendship. This arrangement was supposed to be temporary, two years at most. Now it's been almost six."

"That doesn't matter a whit to us, dear. We're not watching the clock. Why, if there's anywhere on earth that time stops, it's this island. We love it here. This is our home. You never even asked us to watch the inn for you. We offered, from our hearts, and we're not going back on that promise now. I just hate to feel that Nolan and I have let you down."

"Of course not. I'd never think that, Claire. I just wish you would have let me know it was becoming too much for you. How long have you felt this way?"

Claire looked down and bit her lip. "It's hard to say. These things creep up on a person. It hasn't been long, and we didn't want to worry you, way out in Arizona. We decided to hire Kerry to take over some of my work, and now we found Gabriel O'Hara to help Nolan. We thought with some reinforcements, young and able, we could right the ship before the summer season. I believe we can do it, too."

"Do you think Kerry and Gabriel will be enough? We can hire more staff if you want to."

"It's so quiet right now. There are hardly any

guests, except for the rush around Christmas week. I thought we'd see how these additions work out and take it one step at a time. Besides, it might be too confusing to train and supervise too many new people at once. Don't you think?"

"Good point." It was so like Claire to have a clear, reasonable plan, while Liza felt as if she was flailing. "You've done the right thing, and I think you've found excellent help."

"Thank you, Liza. It means a lot to me to hear you say that."

"What do you always tell me? 'Worry never solved a problem.' Let's not worry about this. Let's just go forward from here. I do think the inn can be back in shape for the season if we focus on what needs to be done and carry through."

Claire looked pleased by Liza's positive attitude. "I do, too. We'll start with a good, solid list. And a schedule. To make sure everything is shipshape in time. I know you don't have much time to work that in tomorrow, before you go, but we'll talk over the phone when you get back to Deep Wells and sort it out."

"We could do that . . . but I've decided I should stay and help you. I don't feel right just dumping this in your lap and running away again." Liza thought Claire would protest. Maybe feel insulted? As if Liza didn't trust her to navigate these choppy waters on her own? She did look surprised.

"I breeze in and out, like royalty on holiday," Liza added, "and take all the glory for owning the place. It's time I put in some sweat equity. It will be fun, getting back into innkeeper mode."

She saw Claire's smile—and maybe even a look of relief in her eyes—and knew she had said the right thing.

"Does Daniel know you want to stay?"

"He'll understand. I'll keep the children with me." Daniel had such long, unpredictable hours, especially lately. He couldn't possibly take care of them, even though he might want to. "Max can miss a week of preschool. Right now, it's all holiday crafts, singing Christmas carols, and parties."

"I'll make decorations with him, and teach him some carols," Claire offered. "We can bake Christmas cookies, too."

"Max and Charlotte will be thrilled to hear they're staying for a longer visit with you and Nolan." It would be good for the children and Claire and Nolan to have more time together, an unexpected perk of extending her stay.

"Uncle No-man will like the idea, too. I have no doubt."

Liza smiled, feeling as if a great weight had been lifted; and with that wave of relief, she felt suddenly sleepy. She couldn't even finish her tea.

She stood up and carried her cup and plate to the sink. "I don't know about you, but I'm ready for bed. I have a feeling I'll sleep like a rock now."

"As you should. You go on, dear. I'll just finish my tea."

"Okay, good night, Claire. Sleep well." Liza lightly touched Claire's shoulder as she left the kitchen.

She climbed the stairs and headed for her bedroom, amazed at how well the dreaded talk had gone. Mainly because Claire was such an extraordinary person. She'd made it easy for Liza to speak her mind and had not bristled with offense, like most people would have, or taken Liza's words about the inn personally.

Claire had been working at the inn for over ten years, maybe even longer. One would assume her pride and identity were wrapped up in the place. But Claire was not like that. She had a solid, separate, immutable sense of self that was not easily shaken or confused. She was so open and honest, focused on solving a problem, not shielding a sensitive ego.

Liza knew that if the shoe had been on the other foot, she wouldn't have handled the situation so objectively. Or productively. It was a valuable lesson.

No matter how old I get, Claire always has something new to teach me. Not just by what she says, but by example, the way she deals with problems, big and small.

Liza crept into the dark bedroom, careful not to wake Daniel, much as she ached to tell him the problem was solved. Not solved, exactly, but at least everything was out in the open, and she and Claire had a plan.

She'd also have to tell him that she and the children were staying for at least another week. An impulsive decision, but she knew he would understand.

Judging from Claire's reaction, Liza knew she was doing the right thing. It was only fair that she stay to help manage this situation. Far better to do it hands-on than from two thousand miles away. She blamed herself for this mess, not Claire and Nolan. It was mostly due to her long absence and benign neglect, and her assumption that the inn was being maintained exactly as she had left it.

She had to stay or risk seeing the inn deteriorate even further. Daniel would certainly understand that.

The next morning, Daniel woke first, before the alarm. He leaned over and whispered, "Wake up, sleepyhead. The little critters will be out of bed soon. Time to leave paradise, I'm afraid."

Liza opened her eyes and rolled over to face him. "I have something to tell you. I couldn't sleep last night, so I went down to make some tea. Claire couldn't sleep either, and we finally had that talk."

Daniel was out of bed, a fresh towel for the shower in hand. He turned to her. "How did it go?"

"Much better than I expected. I nearly chickened out, but Claire knows the inn isn't what it used to be and wanted to talk to me about it, too."

Daniel sat on the edge of the bed. "Well, that must have made things a lot easier."

"Much. But she did admit she and Nolan aren't up to taking care of the place on their own anymore. That's why she hired Kerry and Nolan found a handyman. They were hoping that with more staff, they could get the inn back in shape by the spring. I think it's doable, too. We're going to make a complete list of repairs and a timeline, to stay on schedule."

"That sounds like an excellent plan. You must be relieved."

"I am . . . But I told her I'd stay here to help, for at least a week." She waited and watched his expression. "I didn't think it was right to just dump all this on her and Nolan and run back to Arizona. I can see now that being away so long and trying to oversee the place from a distance probably caused the problem in the first place."

Daniel nodded, his expression serious. "I hadn't thought of it that way, but you might be right. It definitely played a part."

"I'll keep the kids with me. Max can miss

113

preschool. Charlotte will only miss playdates and a Mommy and Me singing class. You're not upset, are you?"

"Of course not. There's a lot at stake here. It's the right thing to do. I'll miss everyone. I wish I could stay to help, too. I'm still handy with a hammer and a paintbrush."

"I'd hire you again in a heartbeat," she said, making him smile.

"Sometimes I wonder why I ever switched from doctoring houses to doctoring people. It was an easier way to make a living, that's for sure."

Liza knew he didn't really mean that, but she heard the note of longing in his tone. Their holiday weekend had been too brief a break for him. His long hours and the growing responsibilities at the clinic were getting to be too much. Liza feared the administrative demands of his job were robbing Daniel of the joy he found in practicing hands-on care with his patients.

"Maybe after everything settles with Dr. Mitchell's retirement and the staff changes, we can find time for a real vacation. I know you could use one."

"First things first. You need to get this place in order. Maybe we'll come back this summer when the Inn at Angel Island will be restored to its former, award-winning glory."

Liza liked that idea. The kids loved the beach, even in this chilly weather. How much more fun it would be to take them there in the summer.

"That gives me even more motivation." She pushed the covers back, got up out of bed, and walked into Daniel's open arms. "Thank you for understanding. I'll miss you, too. But a week isn't so long."

"No, it's not. But will one week be enough?"

Liza pressed her head into his shoulder. She didn't know how to answer. She wondered about that, too.

Chapter Five

Emily had hoped to meet with her sister earlier in the week, but with one thing and another, their schedules didn't mesh until Wednesday. She dashed into the bakery, late, as usual. Jessica was already at a table, looking over a menu.

"Sorry I'm late. Were you waiting long?" Emily sat and shrugged off her jacket.

"Not very. But I don't have much time. I have to pick up three goats in Rowley later."

"You'll have gourmet cheese *and* Zelda's butter."

Jessica grinned. "I wouldn't mind. I love goat cheese. But I'm hoping the Gilroys will take them. I haven't called them yet. I ordered us both the quiche and salad special. Is that all right?"

Emily was such a creature of habit, her sister knew she always ordered the same thing. "It's perfect. I love the quiche here. Maybe we can serve some at Ezra's party. If we have a brunch or something like that?"

"It's a good idea. But what sort of party do you think we should plan for him? A party at night? A brunch? Just cocktails and hors d'oeuvres?

We have to settle that before we figure out a menu . . . And where should it be?"

"Let's decide where first, and then when. And then what to eat. I made a draft guest list." Emily pulled a notebook from her purse and handed it to her sister. "Don't faint, but I'm up to fifty, and there are a lot of people left out."

"Fifty—or more? That *is* a big crowd."

As Jessica scanned the list, Emily chose a small croissant from the basket on the table and took a bite. "These are scrumptious. Pure butter."

"I think Molly tosses in a little flour, but definitely the minimum." Jessica took a bite of the muffin that was already on her bread plate. "Where are we going to put fifty people?"

"How about the Spoon Harbor Inn? They have a big room if we want a lot of guests, and a smaller room if it's just the family. And the food isn't bad," Emily added. "All we'd have to do is decorate a bit with flowers and balloons and show up."

Jessica didn't seem that excited by the suggestion. "I don't know. The place is cozy but a little tired-looking. They haven't changed a thing since Sam and I were married there, almost twenty years ago. It's a little humdrum, don't you think?"

"I wouldn't call the Spoon Harbor Inn boring, exactly. It's . . . reliable."

Before Jessica could reply, the buttery, cheesy

scent of warm quiche lorraine snagged Emily's senses as a dish appeared in front of her, and then beside it, one filled with mixed greens, tossed with a lemon vinaigrette dressing. Emily could smell the fresh herbs.

"Reliably *boring* food, is that what you mean?" asked Molly Willoughby, setting Jessica's quiche and salad on the table.

Emily couldn't help laughing. "This looks delicious, Molly."

"Enjoy." Molly owned Willoughby's, and of course, she had high standards for restaurants. But not every restaurant could serve food as reliably delicious as Willoughby's. "It's a little better than the Spoon Harbor Inn, wouldn't you say?"

"Definitely better. But we're planning a party for Ezra and tossing around ideas. He's going to be ninety-five," Jessica explained to her sister-in-law. "Don't tell anyone—it's a surprise."

Molly's expression softened. "Ezra is going to be ninety-five? That's a biggie. I love that guy. He deserves a nice party. He deserves a medal for putting up with your mother all these years. No offense," she added quickly.

"None taken," Emily assured her. She knew Molly was no fan of Lillian, and the feeling was mutual, to say the least. "Ezra's been the perfect partner for her. He's intelligent, enjoys the same interests, and has a playful side that keeps her on her toes."

"He's the only one who can keep her in line," Molly said as she took the extra seat at the table. "So what are you ladies putting together for dear old Ezra? I think a house party is always the best choice. Not some stuffy inn."

"True, but a house party is so much work," Emily said. "We'd be overwhelmed, on top of Christmas."

"Ezra's birthday is January fifth, and we want to have the party around that time," Jessica explained. "I suppose Mother's house is big enough. But she has a panic attack if one person stops in for tea. I don't think she could handle fifty guests marching through her living room."

"Agreed," Emily said. "We don't want her to know about it anyway. My house isn't big enough, unfortunately."

"Mine is," Molly said. "I'd be happy to host a bash for Ezra. I'll cater everything from here. No one will have to lift a finger."

"Except for you. You're having the family for Christmas Eve, and you have two shops and a catering business to deal with during the holiday rush. We couldn't possibly ask you to do all that," Emily said.

"You didn't ask. I offered," Molly reminded her. "There's nothing like a nice house party. It's so relaxed, and no one is going to kick you out at a certain time. And you know the food is going to be great if I make it for you. That will be my gift—please? Ezra was so good to Matt when he first came to town and so supportive of both of us when we got married. He's such a sweetheart, it's the least I can do for him."

Emily and Jessica exchanged a look. They both got the not-so-subtle hint. Molly wanted to be part of the party planning team. She certainly didn't need the extra work, and they would definitely pay her something toward the food; they couldn't accept it for free. She did love Ezra and was making a persuasive case.

"What if we have it at my house?" Jessica said. "I'll have to run it by Sam, but he won't mind. It will be a little more involved than a restaurant, but if Molly caters it, the extras won't be that hard to pull together. It will be informal and fun, and we can invite as many people as we think Ezra would like to see."

Emily mulled it over for a moment. "I think that will work out great. Dan and Jane will help with the grunt work, moving the furniture and setting up tables and all that. And I'll take care of the flowers and decorations and anything extra."

"You're heading in the right direction now. With my guidance," Molly added with her trade-mark sassy grin. "Aren't you glad I stopped by? It always helps to get some pro tips."

"Very true," Emily agreed. She turned to Jessica. "But when should we have it?"

"How about New Year's Day? It will be easy

for us to trick Ezra into thinking he's going to a family get-together, just to celebrate the New Year. Does that work for you, Molly?"

"Absolutely. I'll still have the extra holiday help on board, and we'll cook for your party with the orders for New Year's Eve and New Year's Day brunches." Molly stood up and smoothed out her apron. "We have time to figure out the food. I'll give you some menus before you go . . . Anyone interested in dessert?"

"Do you have those little cream tarts with the berries on top today?" Jessica asked.

"I love those, too," Emily admitted.

Molly got to her feet. "Two tarts coming right up."

"So it's all settled," Emily said as Molly headed toward a glass case filled with pastries. "And quicker than I thought."

"Yes—once Molly jumped into the conversation. Though I can't say I'm surprised at that," Jessica replied. "All we have to do now is send out the invitations."

"—And keep the plans secret from Mother," Emily added. "She has a way of sniffing out secrets. Like a hound dog tracking prey."

Jessica laughed. "She really does. But the party is less than a month away. We can manage to keep a lid on it for a few weeks, don't you think?"

"I hope so. At least, keep it from her until it's too late to change everything?"

"Fingers crossed!"

The tarts arrived with two forks and a dollop of whipped cream on the side. Emily glanced at Jessica as they both dug in. She was so thankful to have Jessica in her life. They had helped each other through plenty of rough spots. This was a happy time. Surely they could pull together a great celebration for Ezra.

They had been working steadily since Monday morning, but Liza had to admit, it was slow going, a painstaking process to review the inn, top to bottom, in and out, every nook and cranny. To examine with an objective eye and decide where repairs or replacement were needed.

They had started in the guest rooms, inspecting the curtains, the rugs, the paint and furnishings. And the bathrooms, as well. Pitted fixtures, cracked tiles, bathtubs and showers that needed to be resealed. Claire seemed very much in the spirit at first.

On Wednesday afternoon, she and Claire opened the big linen closet on the second floor. A large walk-in closet, it was almost as big as a baby's nursery, with piles of linens stacked neatly on shelves from floor to ceiling.

Liza felt her heart sink, wondering how long it would take to sift through it all. But she took a deep breath and smiled at the scent of crisp, freshly washed sheets mingled with lavender.

Claire grew the herb in her abundant garden and hung it in bunches on the walls.

"It smells wonderful in here. I love the lavender. It clings to the sheets and towels, too."

"Yes, it does. The scent is relaxing. It promotes a good night's sleep. And lavender will chase away moths, too."

The lavender reminded Liza of the many personal touches at the inn that were initiated by Claire, touches that made the place special. She couldn't dwell only on the negatives.

Liza was up on the stepladder now. "Well, it won't chase me away. I can't get enough of it."

A good thing, too, she decided, a few moments later. It was beyond tedious to examine every washcloth, hand towel, bath towel, sheet, and pillowcase. But it had to be done. Liza had realized on Monday that she couldn't take anything for granted. Not any longer.

She checked the towels on the upper shelves while Claire worked on the sheets, stored near the bottom. Liza didn't want to peer over Claire's shoulder, but she couldn't help watching to make sure Claire was a harsh enough judge. She knew how much Claire hated waste of any kind. She had probably let some worn-out linens slip by, feeling too guilty to throw them out if they had some use left.

But that's not how you run a five-star inn. Or even a three-star one. When people stay overnight at a hotel, they want their towels to be thick and fresh, even better than they have at home. It didn't make sense. It was just the way it was.

"What do you think of this one?" Claire showed her a pillowcase. It looked acceptable. Until Liza noticed a faint pink stain on one side. Lipstick, maybe? "I can try some bleach on that mark again. It might be fine."

" 'When in doubt, toss it out.' I'm sure you taught me that."

"So I did. You're right. It's worn thin, even without the mark."

Claire tossed it into the discard pile and checked the next. She was trying to be vigilant, but Liza could see it was hard for her. Each rejected piece was like a silent rebuke, announcing she had been lax on her job.

"Here's one." Liza tossed a bath towel into the growing pile without explanation.

Claire picked it up and looked it over. "Oh my, the hem looks like Edison got at it. I should have noticed that."

"Doesn't matter . . . maybe it got caught in the dryer?"

Liza was sure that was not the case, but it seemed a face-saving excuse.

Claire took off her reading glasses and wiped the lenses on her apron. "It might be time for a visit to the eye doctor. I must need new glasses."

For a moment, Liza wondered if that was the case. There had been a time when most of these worn items would never have escaped the laundry room.

"There's so much laundry to deal with. I'm sure you and Kerry are in a rush to wash it and put it away, to make up the rooms as quickly as you can. I never notice at home when towels and sheets get worn out, until they're almost threadbare." Liza knew she was offering Claire an easy out. She hated to embarrass her. But this was an inn, and the condition of the linen should have been watched more closely. Much more closely, from what she'd seen today.

Claire picked up a few towels and stuffed them in a plastic trash bag. "I'm sure the homeless shelter in Salem can use some of these. The sheets, too. There's still a lot of use in that linen. If you're not fussy, I mean."

Liza cringed. Did Claire think she was just being fussy?

No, she didn't mean that. I'm being overly sensitive because this is hard. Claire is proud and used to being in control here, in her quiet way. Having someone look over her shoulder and inspect everything—even me—must be unnerving.

It seemed cruel to find any fault at all, whether in a leaky faucet or a faded quilt. It seemed like a personal attack on a friend whom she loved and felt indebted to.

But what else could she do? She was here to get the place back on track. The hardest part of that so far was feeling at odds with her dear friend.

And we still have the dishes, glassware, cutlery, tablecloths, and piles of other items to review. This will not be an easy week. Not at all.

Kerry heard a sharp knock on the back door. She set a cover back on a simmering pot and turned from the stove to see Gabriel O'Hara step inside.

"It was open. You look busy. I didn't think you'd mind if I just came in."

She turned to face him and wiped her hands on her apron. He was smiling at her in a way that made her tongue-tied. No tweed jacket and tie today. He was back to painter's overalls and a big blue sweatshirt, though he looked no less handsome, his broad shoulders and bright eyes and sheer energy filling the room along with a blast of cold air.

"Are you looking for Nolan? He just took the children out to the barn."

"Yes, I know. He sent me inside to grab a few tools he keeps in the basement."

Kerry turned and pointed to the basement door. "There's a light on the right. The workbench is at the bottom of the steps. Watch out for his inventions," she added. "They're all over."

He headed for the door but paused at the stove,

126

taking in all the pots on the burners. "Something smells good. What are you cooking?"

"Dinner." She pulled a hot mitt over her hand, hoping to give the hint that she wanted to get back to work.

"Is it stew?" He reached over to lift the lid, but she pressed the lid down with the big mitt. Her hand covered his a moment and she quickly pulled away.

She stared at him, eye to eye. "Don't let the steam out, please. It needs to simmer. My, you're nosy. I bet your mother taught you better manners than that."

Gabriel stepped back, trying to look contrite, but the smile in his eyes gave him away. He was amused at her little outburst.

"Sorry, that was rude. My mother did teach me better manners. Honestly."

She sighed and turned back to the stove, feeling embarrassed.

She was rarely so snappish. So what if he wanted to see what was in the pot? He just got her so rattled. And seemed to enjoy it. "It's paella. For dinner. And the other pot is butternut squash soup, for the guests coming on the weekend. We'll freeze it." She turned and caught his gaze. "Satisfied?"

"I would be . . . if I got invited to dinner. That sounds too good to miss."

She shook her head and had to smile. Was

she blushing now? She hated that. Maybe he'd think her cheeks were flushed from the heat of the stove. "Dinner is a long way off. I wouldn't count on it."

"I'm usually a fast worker, but maybe if I slow my pace, Nolan will invite me."

Kerry turned, shocked again by his boldness. "I wouldn't bet on it."

"Good idea. Let's bet. If Nolan invites me, you'll go out with me this weekend."

What was it with this guy? He didn't give up, did he? "I said 'Don't bet on it.' Not 'Let's bet.' "

He shrugged and smiled. She was sure that he'd heard her; he just liked to tease. And flirt. "Would you like to go out with me? We could have dinner Saturday night. If you're free, I mean." His tone was even more persuasive.

Of course she was free on Saturday. She was free every night of the week. That didn't mean she would agree.

Liza came into the kitchen, saving Kerry from a reply. She carried a trash bag in each hand and dropped them near the back door. "Hello, Gabriel. How's it going? Are you getting anywhere?"

Kerry caught his eye and sent a look that said, *Not with me, you aren't.*

From his sheepish grin, she knew he'd understood. "It's going fine. I'm still pulling out the rotted wood. I just came in for a few tools from the basement."

"Sorry to hold you up. That's the door to the basement." Liza pointed. "Be careful on the stairs."

"Thanks. Kerry just showed me." He headed for the basement, finally, glancing over his shoulder at Kerry one last time.

Kerry ignored him. "Can I help you with those bags, Liza? Is it trash?"

"Not exactly. Old sheets and towels. Claire wants to bring them to a shelter in Salem. Maybe you can put them in her car when you have a chance?"

"I have a chance right now." Kerry pulled off her apron and slipped on her down vest, which hung near the door, then grabbed a bag in each hand and headed out to find Claire's old green Jeep.

The bracing cold felt like a slap on her cheeks, but it was good to get a breath of fresh air. It cleared her head and settled her nerves. With any luck, the small chore would keep her out of Gabriel's path when he came back upstairs.

She headed around the side of the house, looking for Claire's car on the drive. She saw Gabriel's white truck parked near the porch, his ladder and tools on the lawn nearby.

He would be around the inn a lot the next few weeks. She had overheard Nolan and Liza reviewing a long list of repairs they had hired Gabriel to do. She would do her best to avoid him and hope he would get the message she wasn't interested in him. Which had not penetrated so far.

Maybe because you are *interested?* a little voice chided. She couldn't deny it. He was the most attractive man she'd met in a long time. But she had no intention of dating anyone, especially right now. Relationships with men had always turned out badly for her. After her last disaster, she wouldn't risk it anymore. It was safer to spend the rest of her life alone.

The Jeep was unlocked and Kerry fit the bags of donations in the hatch and slammed the gate. She looked up at the clear blue sky and the afternoon sun starting to sink toward the horizon. She could see the ocean across the road. Seabirds circled above the waves, dipping in lazy circles, looking so carefree. Reminding her that she was not free, not really. She had paid her debt but would never be totally free of her past.

Any truly worthwhile man would lose interest in her once he learned how she'd given up Jane and, later, with her life back on track, had ended up in prison. Who would want her after that?

Kerry headed back to the house, ready to tackle more cooking on the list Claire drew up for her every few days.

Would Gabriel really try to wrangle a dinner invitation from Nolan, or had he just said that to see her reaction? Nolan was so sweet and openhearted, it wouldn't take much. He'd be an easy mark for Gabriel's charm. Kerry feared the odds were against her. She would probably lose this bet.

Liza brought the children to the kitchen at six, fresh from their baths and dressed in pajamas. They had played outside with Nolan a good part of the afternoon and looked both hungry and drowsy as Liza helped them into their chairs.

Claire noticed, too, as she took a seat next to Max and offered him a slice of Kerry's warm homemade bread. "Dogs and children both behave far better after lots of fresh air and exercise."

"It was so nice of Nolan to watch them today," Liza said. "I'm sure he has better things to do."

"—Nothing better," Nolan said as he walked in the back door. "Now that Gabriel is climbing on the roof and fiddling with the plumbing, I'm quite at my leisure."

Kerry was at the stove, heating dinner. She didn't even notice Gabriel had followed Nolan inside until she turned from the stove, a large bowl of paella in her hands.

She met his gaze briefly, then stepped over to the table and set the bowl down. He was holding the tools he had borrowed from Nolan's workbench, a long wood saw and a heavy wood planer.

He crossed the kitchen, heading to the basement

door. "Sorry to interrupt your dinner. I'll just put the tools back where I found them and be on my way."

"You're not interrupting. We haven't even started." Claire glanced at Liza and then at Nolan, a question in her eyes. Kerry had a feeling she knew what it was, too . . . and her stomach sank.

"Why don't you have dinner with us, Gabriel?" Nolan asked. "It's getting late; you must be hungry."

Gabriel had already opened the basement door but turned to face Nolan. "Thank you for the invitation. But I don't want to trouble you."

"Nonsense, it's no trouble. All we'll do is set another place for you." Claire rose from her seat and headed to the dish cabinet. "You take care of those tools. Everything is ready."

Gabriel gave Claire a wide smile. "All right, if you insist."

He glanced at Kerry, as if to say, *What else can I do? I don't want to be rude.*

Kerry turned her attention back to the food. Claire and Nolan had made an effort to persuade him, but she was still sure Gabriel had somehow engineered this.

If he expected his presence at the table meant she would go out with him, she'd have to tell him in no uncertain terms that it just wasn't happening. Not on Saturday, not ever.

Gabriel quickly returned from the cellar and washed his hands at the sink. Unfortunately, Claire had set the extra place right next to Kerry, who, last to the table, couldn't avoid sitting next to him—not without taking her dinner to the dining room.

She sat down and spread her napkin on her lap and stared straight ahead, trying to act as if he were invisible. She knew he was glancing sideways at her, wearing that playful, secretly amused smile.

"Let's say grace." Claire bowed her head. She took Nolan's hand with her left and Max's little hand with her right.

Kerry took Charlotte's hand. The little girl thought it was a wonderful game and smiled at her. Kerry smiled back then reluctantly placed her other hand in Gabriel's. He held it lightly, staring straight ahead. His touch was warm, his skin rough with calluses from his work.

Kerry bowed her head and followed Claire's quiet prayer. "Thank you for this day, Lord. For our health and all the blessings we enjoy. Thank you for this wonderful meal that Kerry has prepared. Bless this table and everyone around it. Amen."

Claire lifted her head, then offered Gabriel the platter of paella. "Help yourself, Gabriel, don't be shy." Claire obviously didn't know him well. Shyness was the least of his problems. "We're

133

experimenting with paella. Kerry thought it would be a good dish to serve to the guests."

"I made it with chicken and sausage. But in the summer, we can add shrimp, clams, and mussels. Even lobster," Kerry said.

Nolan served himself. "The streamlined version is fine with me."

"More than fine. It's delicious," Gabriel said after his first bite. "My *abuela* always makes us dishes like this. *Arroz con pollo*, chicken with rice. She sometimes adds chorizo. It's her favorite spicy sausage."

"Your grandmother, you mean?" Liza served her children, dicing the chicken into tiny bits. Charlotte was already eating the rice with her fingers.

"Yes. My mother's family is from Mexico. My grandmother lived with us all the while I was growing up. She helped raise me and my sisters. Now she's got a house of her own in Cape Light."

"How many sisters do you have, Gabriel?" Claire asked.

"Two, Lucinda and Pia. My parents made a deal—my mother got to choose our first names, since we all had my father's last."

"That sounds fair," Nolan said. "It's important to remember our roots and preserve family heritage."

"Gabriel is the name of an archangel who delivered important messages. But I'm sure you know that," Claire said.

"I do. *Abuela* told me that, too," he said with a grin. Kerry recalled seeing him helping an older woman at church last week. That must have been his grandmother. Kerry was not surprised that Gabriel was such a caring, respectful grandson, but she didn't want to dwell on it and give herself a reason to like him even more.

He took a bite of bread and turned to Kerry. "Did you make this, too?"

"Yes, she did," Claire answered quickly. "She started the dough this morning, before break-fast."

"You must have been in the kitchen all day," he said.

"A good part of it . . . but that is my job, you know."

"Where did you learn to cook so well, Kerry?" Liza said. "I don't think I ever asked you."

"Oh . . . here and there." The question took Kerry by surprise. She glanced at Claire, knowing now that Claire had not told Liza all about her background. She had learned to cook while serving a jail sentence. But she could hardly confess that to Liza right here at the table.

"Kerry's a natural talent," Claire said. "She rarely uses a recipe. I still love to cook, but I'm glad we have her here."

Kerry saw Liza's sympathetic look. "We all worked hard today, Claire. You and I battled that linen closet. It wasn't easy."

135

"No, it was not. But it feels so good to check it off our list, doesn't it? Very encouraging. A job begun is a job half done."

Claire was always so optimistic. Kerry had seen Liza, Claire, and Nolan working on their plans to repair the inn this morning, and checking the linens was a drop in the bucket. Kerry wondered how it would all get done in a few months' time.

"And Gabriel has almost completed the porch roof. He'll put the tar and new shingles on tomorrow. Isn't that right, son?" Nolan said.

"If the weather holds," Gabriel said. "The roof was old and needed replacing. Most of the patches on it were about to give way."

"I think Daniel was the last to work on it," Liza said. "That had to be over five years ago."

Nolan helped himself to a dish of salad, then passed the bowl down the table. "So you worked for your father and took over the business. Is that how you leaned your trade?"

"I worked with him when I was in high school but moved away after I graduated college. I had studied business and took a job in an insurance company down in Hartford."

Kerry was surprised to hear he had gone to college. She had planned on college. But after she gave up Jane, she struggled to finish her coursework for the GED and never had the chance to go further.

"Hartford? How did you end up back here?" Nolan asked.

Gabriel had finished his dinner and sat back in his chair. "That's a long story. I'll just say my life hit a rough patch about three years ago and I decided to come home and regroup. I began to work with my father, just to get out of the house, but realized I liked it a lot more than I remembered. And a lot more than working in an insurance office. When my dad retired last year, I took over his business, and here I am."

"Any regrets?" Claire asked.

"Never. I feel so lucky that I'm not stuck in an office crunching numbers in some mind-numbing desk job. I'd much rather dig my truck out of two feet of snow than dig through a pile of forms and memos."

Nolan nodded. "I felt the same way when given the choice between working for a big tech firm or developing inventions on my own."

"Maybe some people love wearing a suit and tie every day and sitting behind a big desk in the corner office. That's fine for them. I like to be my own boss and do things my own way."

Kerry had already guessed that about him, though she wondered what had gone wrong in his city life that had caused him to return here. Some career crisis or failed romance? A divorce, maybe?

"Didn't you work in insurance for a while,

137

Kerry?" Claire was helping Max with a last bite of chicken and rice while he made a little stuffed dog hop across the table.

"I did," Kerry replied. She hadn't bothered to contribute that to the conversation. She much preferred watching Gabriel in the spotlight, being asked questions about his past. "But I don't have any regrets either. I like the work I do now much better . . . Anyone ready for dessert? There's flan."

"Flan?" Gabriel echoed. "My favorite. How did you guess?"

Kerry answered matter-of-factly, "It seemed a good idea, with the paella."

Of course she hadn't made it to please him. She hadn't even known he would be joining them tonight. But his teasing tone made it seem as if she had made it with him in mind. She turned to face the sink, so no one could see her blush.

Gabriel had come to his feet and started clearing the table, though Kerry would have been happier without his help.

"I'll take the flan out of the fridge and get the dessert plates," Nolan offered.

"Save me a slice. These sleepyheads need to get to bed." Liza helped Charlotte out of her booster seat.

Claire took Max's hand. "I'll help you tuck them in. I promised Max we'd continue the storybook we started the other night."

Liza offered Claire a grateful smile as she carried Charlotte in her arms. "I love that story. We'll all listen to a few pages, right, Charlotte?" Charlotte nodded, her eyes already half-closed.

It was awkward to have Gabriel help with the dishes. Kerry kept stepping out of his way as he put plates in the sink or reached around her to load the dishwasher.

She concentrated on wrapping up leftovers and avoiding eye contact. When he started to wash the pots and pans, she had to intervene. "You can just leave those. I'll get them later. Would you like some coffee or tea with the flan?"

He seemed about to argue, but Nolan beckoned him back to the table. "Don't leave me alone with this plate of custard, Gabriel. It's divine. To quote Oscar Wilde, 'The only thing I cannot resist is temptation.' "

Kerry had to laugh at Nolan's worried tone. She was glad to see Gabriel give in and start on his dessert. She kept herself busy cleaning the stove, hoping he would finish his meal and go home.

But Nolan was the first to leave the kitchen, because his cell phone rang. He checked the number and said, "I'd better take this—it's my daughter, Fiona. She so rarely gets a chance to talk."

"Of course," Gabriel said. "I'm leaving soon. I'll see you tomorrow, Nolan. Thanks again for dinner."

"My pleasure, Gabriel. You're welcome any-time." Nolan pressed his phone to his ear and left the kitchen. "Hello, sweetheart . . . Thanks for returning my call . . ."

Kerry knew she was alone with Gabriel, even though she hadn't turned around to face the table in a long time. She just . . . felt it.

She heard his chair scrape the floor and his steps approach her. He grabbed a dish towel off the counter and began to dry a pot. "I thought you said you were leaving these pots until later. I could have done them for you."

"I decided to get them out of the way. I like the kitchen clean in the morning. And it is my job," she added, her tone a little more curt than she intended.

He glanced at her but didn't answer right away. "Dinner was delicious. From start to finish."

She walked over to the table to get some distance from him and started wiping it down with a sponge. "I'm glad it met your standards."

He seemed confused. "I didn't mean it that way . . . Hey, I was only joking this afternoon about the bet. I never expected Claire to invite me. Maybe I shouldn't have accepted, but I didn't want to be rude."

Kerry was at the sink, rinsing the sponge under warm water. "It's all right. I get it."

"Do you really? Why do I feel I've done some-thing to offend you?"

140

He was leaning against the counter, arms crossed over his chest. For the first time not looking nearly so sure of himself. "I sure don't expect you to go out with me if you don't want to. Is that what you're worried about?"

Kerry shrugged. She *did* want to go out with him, that's what bothered her. She could see he was the kind of person who would want to know all about her. Most men she met were mainly interested in talking about themselves, which suited her fine. But Gabriel was different. The type of man who valued family and wanted a serious relationship. The type of person you'd want to confide in. Who, you'd think, might understand. But how could he? How could anyone?

She finally turned to him. "It's nothing. I'm sorry to be curt. I just don't think we should be involved socially since we're working here together."

The excuse had worked for her before, many times. But she could tell Gabriel wasn't buying it.

He cocked his head to one side, his dark eyes sparkling with a playful light. "Do you really think that would be a problem? Has someone said something to you about it?"

Kerry shook her head. Though it would be easy to lie to him, she didn't want to. "I'm sorry. It's just the way I feel. I'm still new here and I need to make a good impression. Especially with Liza taking charge and making changes. And I'm really not interested in dating right now. It's nothing you did or said. It's nothing personal at all."

His almost ever-present smile failed. He nodded, disappointment in his eyes. "Sure . . . I understand."

She felt disappointed, too, almost enough to take back her words. But she fought the urge, hoping he would just go. Enough had been said.

He took his down vest and baseball cap from the coatrack near the back door. "Good night, Kerry. Thanks again for dinner. I'll see you tomorrow."

"I'll be here." No getting away from that, though it could not be the same after this conversation. The flirting and teasing would be over. She hoped so anyway.

He opened the door. "By the way, the flan was just as good as my *abuela*'s . . . but I won't let her know."

The compliment made her smile. She couldn't help it. "That's probably a good idea," she said quietly. He smiled back and disappeared out the door.

Once he was gone, she took a deep breath and finally let her guard down. It had been hard to turn him away, harder than she had expected.

He'd looked genuinely disappointed . . . not just annoyed that he hadn't persuaded her.

Don't worry, she told herself. *Gabriel O'Hara won't be lonely long. Not with those dark eyes and dimples. There are women all over town who would be happy to go out with him.*

She was sure that was true, though it didn't make her feel any better about turning him down.

CHAPTER SIX

$\sim$

I'm sorry. I should have known this would take
longer than a week. Claire and I have been
working very hard and we got a lot done. But
there's so much more we need to do before I can
come home. I can't handle this long-distance,
honey. I hope you understand."

It was very short notice to tell Daniel on Friday
night that she and the children wouldn't be back
on Sunday, as planned. But it had been hard for
Liza to face the fact that it would take another
week, maybe even longer, to get the inn sorted
out.

She heard him sigh but knew him well enough
to feel relieved by the tone of it. It was the sound
he made when he didn't get his way but was
resigned to the change of plans.

"I can't say it's a huge surprise." They had
been in touch every night, though they were both
so tired at the end of the day, the phone calls
were usually brief. "To tell you the truth, Liza, I
don't think you should make any flight reservations until you're certain that you can come
home. This problem might be bigger than you

and Claire think. And more complicated to figure out."

The same thought had crossed her mind more than once that week, though she had not admitted it to Claire. "I know," she said, cutting off further conversation in that dire direction. "We just have to wait and see. What's going on with you? Do you have any time this weekend . . . at all?" She hoped so but doubted it.

"I was going to take off most of Sunday. But since you and the kids aren't coming home, I'll probably work that day. Jim finally announced his retirement. He'll be gone the first week of January. The announcement put everyone in a flurry this week."

Dr. Jim Mitchell had been a professor and mentor of Daniel's in medical school, and he was also the doctor who had persuaded Daniel to join the staff at the clinic years ago. He had established the clinic on his own, with donations and grants, but a short time after Daniel started working there, Jim had given over control to a large nonprofit health organization.

"Jim leaving will be a big loss. But at least you've known this was coming for a while."

"It wasn't a surprise to me, but everyone else is reeling. He's been a big buffer between the staff and the board and always stuck up for us. His replacement might not pick up that banner. That's what we're all worried about."

Liza knew that Daniel dealt with a huge work-load and increasing amounts of administrative red tape. Daniel drew his satisfaction from working one-on-one with his patients, not staring at computer screens and attending meetings. Would practicing that kind of hands-on medicine still be possible once Dr. Mitchell left?

"You certainly don't need your job to be harder," she said.

"No, I don't. I pray it doesn't happen. There's already some buzz that the administration isn't just going to replace Jim. It will be a top-to-bottom reorganization. Maybe even involving some of the other clinics they run."

"What does that mean?"

"I don't know yet. But you're the first one I'll tell when I find out, honey."

"Whatever happens, we'll figure it out."

"Just like we always do." His voice grew soft with affection. They trusted each other and tackled problems together. They had faced challenges before this, but the hard times had drawn them even closer, not torn them apart.

"Love you, honey. We'll be home soon," she promised.

"Love you, too. Kiss the kids for me. I miss those little critters." She heard the smile in his voice. "But you take as long you need. The inn is important to you. To our whole family."

They said good night again and Liza ended the

call, thankful for such an understanding husband. She knew he was just a phone call away but did wish that Daniel were here with her, helping her figure things out. They both seemed to recognize that the easy fix might not do the trick. But what would?

Only one couple was expected for the first weekend in December, checking in on Saturday morning and staying until Monday. Alice Webster had made the reservation during the week, explaining to Liza that she and her husband would be visiting their newborn granddaughter and didn't expect to take any meals at the inn, except for breakfast.

"My daughter's house is very small. We don't want to be underfoot. We just need a comfortable place to sleep. Your inn was recommended very highly by a friend of mine."

At least someone still thought well of the place. Liza took some comfort in that. "That's a very nice compliment, thank you. Check-in time on Saturday is usually eleven o'clock, but your room will be ready whenever you'd like to arrive. We look forward to seeing you."

In light of her extended stay and all the hard work she and Claire had put in that week—not to mention the tense moments they had navigated—Liza decided a day off from their schedule, or even two, might be a good idea.

"I think the work will still be there tomorrow . . . or even Monday," Liza told Claire at breakfast that Saturday. She was feeding Charlotte scrambled eggs and bits of buttered toast, her favorite breakfast. She glanced up a moment and saw Claire smile.

"If you think we can spare the time . . . I told the baking committee I couldn't make the meeting at church today. I think I'll check in with Emily and let her know I'll be there."

She should have known that Claire would quickly find some productive endeavor to fill her day. She rarely sat idle for even five minutes.

"Are you going to start baking for the fair today?" It was only December seventh. The fair was two weeks away. But most baked goods could be frozen and would look and taste perfectly fine at the fair.

Claire had already picked up the phone to call Emily. "First we need to agree on what we want to sell and how much to make of different recipes. We all have our specialties. We might start today at church. Then again, the oven in that old stove is so unreliable. But it is fun to work together. We'll meet again closer to the fair, and bake on our own, of course."

Liza hadn't known how such an abundance of cookies, cakes, gingerbread houses, and every sort of holiday confection ended up at the Christmas Fair. She had thought it all came from

148

random donations. Now she realized it was a well-coordinated effort.

Before she could reply, she heard Claire greet Emily. "Yes, it's me, calling back. I can come to church, after all." She paused and frowned. "Oh . . . I'm glad I called, then. Has someone told Reverend Ben? He needs to get the new sexton to take a look. Carl Tulley was the only one who could talk any sense into that old furnace."

The furnace at the church had broken down. Again. It hadn't been in very good working order when Liza had left town, just over five years ago. It was even more unreliable now. But the church could not yet afford a new one, she gathered.

"How about Sophie's house? Her kitchen is definitely big enough." Claire paused again, listening. "I didn't know that. I'll make her some chicken soup and bring it over tomorrow."

Sophie had a cold; Liza translated that quickly. She didn't mean to eavesdrop, but Charlotte was very slow to finish her breakfast. She had found a crayon and paper on the kitchen table and was happily scribbling zigzags and circles.

Liza looked across the table at Claire. "The bakers can meet here today if you need a big kitchen. And plenty of ovens."

Claire's face lit with gratitude. "Excellent suggestion, Liza. Thank you so much." She quickly returned to the call. "Emily? Liza said we can meet here. We have plenty of cookie sheets and pans. And three big ovens. Everyone can contribute supplies they have on hand, but we have most of the basics in the pantry . . . Twelve noon? That sounds fine. I'll be ready."

Claire hung up the phone. "Problem solved, thank you, Liza. I'm sure there will be some leftovers and factory rejects in it for the inn. We won't lack for misshapen butter cookies or one-armed gingerbread men."

"Max and Charlotte won't even notice."

Claire grinned. "Neither will Nolan."

Liza suddenly remembered the kitchen was more or less Kerry's domain now, and she was very diligent about keeping up with Claire's many lists. "What about Kerry? She may have planned to do some cooking or baking today."

"Oh dear, I didn't even think of that. But the Websters only want breakfast tomorrow and Monday. There isn't any cooking that can't be put off a day or two."

Kerry had been upstairs putting the finishing touches on the room for the incoming guests and walked into the kitchen with a stack of towels in hand. "I think this set can be put in the donation bag. I used the new towels you gave me, Liza. And that lavender soap you brought over from the Gilroys' farm smells like an English garden. Everything is set, but you can check later when you go upstairs."

"I'm sure it's perfect, but I will take a quick peek when I take Charlotte up."

Liza was pleased with the report. She wanted the room to look above reproach, with all the right touches and amenities—the way the inn used to be when she'd been running it. She trusted Kerry to do a good job, but would give it one last check after breakfast.

"Kerry," said Claire, "would you mind if the baking team for the Christmas Fair uses the kitchen this afternoon? I just spoke to Emily Warwick, and the furnace at the church is on the blink again. Liza offered to have everyone come here."

"Of course I don't mind. That sounds like a good solution."

Liza noticed Kerry's surprise at the request. Perhaps she didn't think anyone needed to check with her about such things. Liza always treated her staff with respect, grateful for their time and talents. She was their employer, not the queen of a very small monarchy.

"I'll stay out of your way," Kerry said. "I'm sure Liza has some tasks for me?"

"Liza gave us the day off. Isn't that sweet? I wondered if you could help the group. We old-timers get so stuck in our ways. Same old, same old. I bet you'd have some great ideas for us."

Kerry smiled, looking even more surprised, and a little nervous, too. "I'd love to help you,

151

Claire. If I can. I have some holiday recipes in my baking binder upstairs. There's one for a chocolate Yule log I've made a few times. The French call it *bûche de Noël*."

"I love that cake." Liza sighed, her mouth watering at the thought of the dense chocolate filling and soft sponge cake, rolled together and decorated with shaved chocolate bark. "It's a real showstopper, too. Your group could charge a tidy sum for a cake like that, Claire."

"See, you have a great idea already," Claire said to Kerry. "They'll be here at noon. Plenty of time to get ready." Claire checked her watch and scanned the kitchen like a general surveying a battlefield, about to prepare for the army of bakers that would soon descend. "I hope there's not too much talk. I'm ready for action."

Liza smiled at Claire's excitement. She was a woman of little talk but lots of action, that was for sure.

What would I ever do without her? That was a question she never wanted to answer.

Kerry helped Claire clear the kitchen for the bakers. The invitation to join Claire's friends today had surprised her. She had been touched by Claire's request; it was a real compliment. She'd do anything to help Claire. Kerry had only known the older woman a short time but already felt great affection for her and a great debt for her trust and encouragement. A lot of people would not have given Kerry a chance once they had learned her history. Claire had never hesitated; she'd been encouraging Kerry every day since she started. Kerry's only worry was that Liza didn't know about her past. Kerry wondered if she should speak to Liza herself, but she never found the right time.

There might have been some time to catch her this morning, but now she was busy with Claire, preparing for the bakers, and Liza was getting ready to take the children to a puppet show in town.

"We might not need all the mixing bowls, but you'd better take them all out. Just stack them on the counter," Claire said.

While Kerry handled the bowls, Claire dug in drawers for long-handled mixing spoons, spatulas, rolling pins, measuring spoons, and measuring cups. In the pantry closet, they found stacks of cookie sheets, large and small, along with layer-cake pans of various shapes and dimension, loaf pans, springform, and a big bundt.

"We probably won't use the springform, but Vera will want to borrow it for her cheesecake. She only has one at home. And this is for Sophie's cinnamon spice bundt. I'll drop it at her house this week. She won't be here today—she has a cold."

Kerry nodded into the pile of pans that was

tucked under her chin. She set them on the end of the table, hoping she and Claire had finally set out enough equipment. She wanted a few extra minutes to change her clothes and fix her hair. To look a little more presentable than she looked in her Saturday morning work attire.

You're just nervous because you might see Jane. You don't want Claire to notice that you're acting oddly and start asking questions, do you?

Kerry wasn't even sure Jane would come with Emily. Claire had only mentioned her friend Vera and Emily's sister, Jessica Morgan. Kerry felt too self-conscious to ask specifically about Emily's daughter, fearing that something in her expression or the tone of her voice would give her away.

She would have helped the bakers anyway, of course. But she did hope with all her heart Jane would be among them and she would have the unexpected but precious opportunity to get to know her a little better. A chance to teach her daughter a thing or two about baking? How wonderful would that be?

It's about all I know and all I can do for her. The realization was bittersweet. But it still seemed a wonderful gift from the universe.

Claire finally judged the kitchen ready, and Kerry ran upstairs to change her clothes. She certainly couldn't wear her best dress, but she had to find something nicer than the dowdy sweatshirt and jeans she wore to clean guest rooms. Teenage girls noticed those things.

I just hope Jane will like me. That's what I'm worried about most. Girls that age can be difficult. She might think all adults are stupid and annoying. I have to be prepared for that and try not to take it personally if that's the way it goes.

I'll never get to know her all that well. I'll always be a stranger, an acquaintance. At the very least, I hope she won't think badly of me.

Kerry made tea for the group and served a plate of orange-cranberry scones left over from breakfast. She brought a dish of butter, a bowl of whipped cream, a dish of strawberry preserves Claire had made last summer, and a pot of honey from Potter Orchard. She took a seat at the far end of the table, next to Claire.

The group was very excited, already reviewing last year's bake sale—their triumphs and best sellers, and also some duds.

Emily sat at the opposite end of the table from Claire, large-framed reading glasses sliding down her slim nose as she reviewed the pages of a notebook. *She looks comfortable being in charge,* Kerry thought. *She has such an easy, confident manner.* Kerry admired that. Emily was also pleasant and friendly. Not snobby at all, though some people with her accomplishments and background would be.

Kerry didn't want to find Emily so likable, but she did. Even if it made her heart ache to see Jane's gaze fixed on her adoptive mother with so much respect and pride.

She'll never look at me that way. Never once, in my entire life. That's my own fault, isn't it?

Emily looked up at the group. "What do you think about making the miniature gingerbread houses again? We thought the children would love those but we didn't sell that many last year."

Vera put down her cup, her eyes wide as an owl. "Don't you remember? They all collapsed into a mess of cookies and icing. Did you ever go camping and have the tent fall down? That's what they looked like, covered with gumdrops and peppermint wheels."

Vera looked so serious. Kerry didn't mean to find the baking disaster amusing, but she felt herself struggling not to laugh. At the far end of the table, Jane caught her eye and grinned, silently sharing the joke.

"I think it was a nice idea, but maybe we didn't use the right icing or construction?" Jessica asked the others.

"I don't think it's worth bothering to try again. They took a lot of time to make." Emily made a note in the notebook. "But we do need something for the children, some novelty to catch their eye."

"Pink and green cupcakes? We can top them with peppermints," Vera suggested.

Kerry didn't think that was such a good idea. Most people didn't find green icing appetizing. It just wasn't cute enough for children.

"I have an idea for the kids. I saw this in a magazine." Jane had taken a piece of paper from her knapsack. She unfolded it and showed everyone the picture. "Reindeer cupcakes. Aren't they cute? I'm totally old and I'd love these . . . and the icing is chocolate. Kids always love that."

Emily took the photo, glanced at it, and passed it to her sister and Vera. "These are cute, Janie," Jessica said. "I like the reindeer face."

Vera frowned at the scrap of magazine page. "Yes, it's cute. But it looks hard to make. Even harder than the gingerbread houses. So many pieces for the trimmings. And the icing has to go on just so."

Kerry saw Jane's face fall and felt a tug in her heart. So far she hadn't contributed a word to the discussion. She was not one to speak up in meetings, more apt to keep her opinions to herself.

"I don't think it will be hard," she heard herself blurt. "The antlers are pretzel pieces and the eyes are just candy, like M&M's. It's just three or four pieces. And we can pipe the icing out from sandwich bags. Just clip off a corner and it comes out very smoothly. And who can resist chocolate-iced anything? I bet you'll sell dozens."

Kerry was suddenly self-conscious, feeling all eyes on her. She wanted to shrink down to cupcake size herself and disappear. She hardly knew these women. They had been working together for years. Did everyone think she was the pushy type now—including Jane?

When she dared to glance at her daughter, she saw a small smile and Jane's gaze fill with gratitude. Kerry knew it wasn't the United Nations Security Council discussing a world crisis, but Kerry doubted she could have felt any more gratified to be recognized as Jane's ally.

The cupcake recipe had made its way around the table again to Emily. She looked down at it a moment, then up at the group. "Let's try it. If the reindeer cupcakes seem too hard to put together, we'll only make a dozen or two. We can decorate the others with plain icing. Maybe Jane and Kerry should work on the cupcakes today, and they can trim them right before the fair?"

Had Emily actually paired her with Jane to bake today? Kerry was so surprised and happy, she could barely keep a straight face. "Is that okay with you, Kerry?" Emily's voice broke through her wild, joyous thoughts.

"Yes . . . yes, of course. That'll be great. We'll make a cupcake recipe that will freeze well. Half chocolate, half vanilla?"

Emily nodded and marked her list. "Yes, two dozen of each."

"Now that the children are covered, we need something special for the adults," Claire said. "Some confection we can pack in pretty bags. So you can add it to a gift or use it as a stocking stuffer."

"We do need something in that category," Emily agreed. "Last year's experiment with the truffles didn't turn out well."

Vera spoke up. "Macaroons would be nice. You see them all over in the mall. Very popular and trendy. But I hear they're hard to make. They do look delicate. Maybe you need a special pan or mold?"

"I can't say. I don't think I ever tried to bake them," Claire said in a vague voice.

Kerry waited for someone else to comment. Then took a breath and made a stammering start. "French macarons are complicated, the type with the wafer layers, I mean. But I have an easy recipe for macaroons, which are different. Shredded coconut and condensed milk, with a dash of vanilla or almond extract. They look very nice packed in a gift bag."

Vera frowned. "The recipe sounds simple enough. You can't beat three ingredients. But I tried to make those cookies last Easter, and they stick to the pan something awful."

"Parchment paper," Kerry said. "It makes them slide right off. They freeze well, too, if you want to make them in advance."

"I love that idea," Emily said. "Toasty, tempting macaroons packed in a see-through bag with a bow? We'll sell piles of them."

"We can charge the same as they do at the mall, too. Ka-ching!" Vera said. "More funds for the church's good work, I mean. It's all for a worthy cause."

"Yes, very worthy," Emily agreed. "You'll have to show us how to make the macaroons as well, Kerry."

The group talked for a few more minutes about the confections they sold every year at the booth—star-shaped cookies, gingerbread people, date nut loaves, fruitcakes, and the standard chocolate chip, peanut butter, and oatmeal cookies that everyone loved.

Finally, Claire said, "Well, let's clear off this table. There are plenty of aprons near the sink. And everyone has their assignments. Let the baking begin!"

Kerry had a white cook's apron hooked on the chair and tied the strings around her slim waist.

"Sorry now that you gave up a day off to help us, Kerry?" Claire seemed concerned that Kerry might have been given too much work. Before Kerry could answer, Jane caught her eye and smiled as she sailed across the kitchen to her baking partner.

Kerry's heart beat a little faster as she turned

to answer Claire. "It's the most fun I've had in a very long time," she said honestly.

Claire looked surprised but satisfied. "I still think you're very sweet to help us. And I can't wait to try the macaroons."

"Me neither," Jane said. "They sound easy enough for even my mom to bake," she added quietly.

"Hey, I heard that." Emily came up behind her daughter and handed her an apron.

"Oh, Mom, you're not that bad. Though I heard you might find a new fire extinguisher for the kitchen under the tree this year."

Emily mocked a wounded look for a moment, then laughed. "Funny . . . and true. Don't let me slow you down. I'll just wander around and help where I can."

Kerry pretended to study the recipe while Jane gathered more equipment—a spatula and beaters. It was hard to watch Jane and Emily together. They clearly had a great relationship. Even if she had kept her baby and raised her, would they have developed the same close, loving bond?

How could I ever compete with that? It wouldn't even be right to try. What kind of person would I be to abandon Jane as a baby and then come crashing back into her life and cause a lot of hurt and confusion? That would hardly be a loving, motherly thing to do.

"Look! I snagged an electric beater. I had to

wrestle it away from Vera," Jane whispered, holding up her prize.

Kerry had to laugh. She was glad that Jane had not inherited her shyness. "Good job. Let's be quick with it and pass it along. We have a lot of mixing to do."

"Just aim me in the right direction." Jane brandished the beater and pointed it at the big bowls where Kerry had already added sticks of softened butter and eggs.

"Why don't you cream the eggs and butter together, and then we'll add some vanilla and sugar." Kerry tried not to be overly instructive.

Jane set the mixer in position in the first bowl, then looked up at her. "I just want to say one thing before I turn this on."

Kerry was measuring out sugar and turned quickly.

"Thanks for sticking up for the reindeer. I think the group would have voted them down if you hadn't jumped in."

Kerry felt herself glow. "You're welcome. But I do think they're cute and will definitely sell well."

"I think so, too. But Vera was right. It might be hard to make them look like the picture."

"No worries. They'll look perfect. They'll be the hit of the fair," Kerry promised. She'd make sure of that, if it was the last thing she ever did.

Her time with Jane seemed to fly by. They

were kept busy mixing batter and handling the pans of cupcakes. Kerry tried to find moments here and there to get to know her daughter, to find out her favorite subjects in school—history and political science and English. Her favorite sport—basketball, to play, but she really didn't like to watch any sports on TV. Her favorite foods, books, movies . . .

Kerry knew she was asking a lot of questions, but hoped Jane would think she was only trying to make conversation. Jane asked questions about her, too. Kerry wasn't sure if she was really interested or just being polite. She delivered vague answers with a smile and always found some baking emergency to deflect the conversation.

The kitchen quickly filled with the scent of cakes and cookies being turned out from the three ovens. The bright sun sank in the west, casting the kitchen in a soft light, and soon after that, the sky was dark outside and Claire began turning on all the lights.

"How did it get so late?" she asked the others, as she turned on the lights in the kitchen first and then went out to the foyer and other rooms.

Kerry wasn't sure either. She took a moment to peek into the dining room. The long table was filled with the products of their labor, and even though all the confections weren't decorated yet, Kerry could imagine how wonderful the baked goods would look on display.

Emily had been in charge of counting and wrapping. She had done a good job, but there was still a lot left. "I guess it's time to store the rest until we can meet again and decorate. I'm sure everyone needs to get home."

"It is getting late," Jessica agreed. "But we sure got a lot done."

"And there will be more when we each bake our special assignments," Claire reminded everyone.

Jane left Kerry to help Emily in the dining room. Kerry stayed to clean up the kitchen. Her time with her daughter was coming to an end. She wished with all her heart there was something more she could do or say. Something to let Jane know how precious the hours had been to her.

But she could never do that. *It might even scare Jane, make her wonder if I'm some sort of weirdo,* Kerry reflected. *I have to hold on for just a few more minutes, until they go. I've held this all inside of me for so very long, I can manage a few more minutes . . . can't I?*

Kerry rubbed her forehead. A massive headache had struck from out of the blue. She'd been having such a wonderful day, too. Where had it come from?

Riding a roller coaster of emotions, probably. That will do it, she reminded herself.

"Kerry? Are you all right? You look a little pale," Claire said, taking her aside.

"I'm fine . . . just tired, I guess."

"Of course you are. Why don't you go upstairs and rest? There's plenty of helping hands in here. We're almost done."

Kerry wavered, then decided it would be best to make herself scarce right now. She wanted to say goodbye to Jane but she was afraid her emotions might just bubble to the surface and ruin everything. She couldn't trust herself to keep up the charade one more minute. Hiding out in her room was the best solution.

The women didn't stay much longer. Kerry heard their voices in the foyer as they gathered coats and wished each other good night.

Did Jane ask anyone where I went? Did she miss saying goodbye to me? Kerry knew it wasn't even right of her to wonder.

You forfeited the right to have a relationship with your daughter when you gave her up fifteen years ago. Now you've met her, and you can see that she's fine and has a good life and a loving home. You even had a chance today to spend some time with her. You promised yourself that was the plan, your only reason for finding her. Staying any longer will only lead to trouble.

She shut her door and lay down on the bed. She closed her eyes, but sleep wouldn't come. *I really should go. Before I end up making another terrible decision and living with even more regret.*

CHAPTER SEVEN

꩜

I t was fun to meet at the inn. Much nicer baking there than in the drafty church kitchen," Jessica said. She sat in the passenger seat while Emily drove and Jane sat in the back. "I think our booth is going to be great this year."

Emily nodded, her eyes fixed on her driving. The roads on Angel Island were curvy and narrow at best, and driving over the land bridge always demanded some extra attention. "It's definitely pulling together."

Jane leaned forward in her seat, her head popping up between her mother and aunt. "Kerry had good ideas. She's a really good baker. She taught me some neat things."

"What did she teach you?" Jessica asked. "I could use some baking tips."

"She showed me the difference between folding in ingredients and beating them in. And how to crack an egg with one hand. I can do it, too." Jane sounded very proud of that trick.

"I can't wait to see a demonstration." Emily knew she could never teach her daughter how to crack an egg with one hand.

Jane often came home from school raving about some wonderful new teacher or coach. Emily always thought that was a good thing. There were so many adults who could be a good influence, who could inspire and encourage a child.

So why was Jane's enthusiasm about Kerry so nettling? Emily brushed it off. It was silly to feel that way. *Now my daughter knows how to crack an egg with one hand. It might come in useful someday.*

Jane flopped back in her seat. "She's very nice. I hope she helps us again."

"I do, too," Jessica said. "She promised to lead the charge on macaroons next week. She's just what our baking team needed—a dose of fresh energy."

Emily smiled but didn't reply. Kerry was certainly nice enough, shy but intelligent. She was clearly a professional baker, with advanced cooking skills, but didn't seem the least bit bothered to be matched with a teenager and assigned children's cupcakes. She'd been very kind to Jane.

Still, something about her set off a silent alarm. Emily couldn't put her finger on it, and that was unsettling.

Soon after they crossed the land bridge, Emily dropped Jane off. She was having a sleepover with her best friend, Sara Duncan. Jane tugged her big knapsack from the car and kissed Emily goodbye through the window.

"Have fun. Call me tomorrow morning when you want to be picked up. I can't come before church is over," Emily called after her.

"I doubt we'll be up before then. No worries, Mom," Jane called back.

" 'No worries, Mom,' " Jessica repeated as they drove off. Emily knew she was teasing. "It was fun to have Jane with us today. I'm so glad she decided to be on the fair committee. Did you ask her to help you?"

"No, it was all her idea. I really love having her with us this year. By this time next year, she'll be applying to colleges and she won't have a minute to spare."

"She'll be totally crazed. Even if she does have a spare minute, you won't want to be around her," Jessica warned in a humorous tone.

Emily doubted that. No matter what state Jane was in. She turned onto the Beach Road, where Jessica lived. Even though it wasn't late, it was already dark out. Here and there, she spotted the warm yellow lights of houses through the dense trees that lined the road.

Jessica gazed out the passenger-side window. "I'm glad we gave those reindeer cupcakes a green light. She was starting to look a little crushed at Vera's critique. It's lucky that Kerry jumped in. It's nice that she's helping us so much. She doesn't even belong to the church."

"Yes, it is generous of her. Claire told me she had the day off, too." Emily glanced at her sister. "I like Kerry, I do. But have you noticed anything . . . I don't know . . . odd about her?"

"Odd? How do you mean? She seems shy. I got the feeling it was hard for her to join in the discussion. We've all known each other for years. She must have felt like an outsider."

"Maybe it was uncomfortable for her, at least at first. I don't know . . . she seemed to take an unusual interest in Jane. Even the way she was looking at her. As if . . . well, as if Jane had floated down from a cloud or something. As if she'd never seen a teenage girl before."

Jessica turned in her seat and stared at her. "Now that you mention it, no, I absolutely did not notice that."

"It wasn't just that." Emily was starting to feel foolish, but if she couldn't confide her concerns to her sister, whom could she tell? "Her hair, her eyes, the shape of her nose. Even her gestures, the way she rested her chin in her hand. Jane always does that when she's listening. Didn't you notice a resemblance? It seems very striking to me, now that I think about it. I couldn't put my finger on it before, but that's what is. That's what rattles me about Kerry."

Jessica didn't laugh at her. "Now that you

mention it, I did notice. A little. It must be a coincidence. What else could it be?"

"Maybe they're related. A cousin or something? There's a very good chance that Jane's birth mother lived around here. Jane probably has some relatives in the area. But there was no birth certificate and no way to find them."

Jessica didn't answer for a moment. "I guess that could be. Maybe you could talk to Kerry privately and ask about her family? I mean, you could explain why you were curious. I don't think she would mind."

"I guess I could." Emily felt a chill and knew what her sister was thinking, because she was suddenly thinking it, too. She pulled into the long drive that led to Jessica's house and shut off the engine.

Jessica didn't seem in any rush to leave the car. "After all this time, Jane's mother has never gotten in touch. Do you ever wonder about that?"

"I do. I wonder if she's still alive. Or if she maybe lives far away, even in another country. We did an open adoption, in case Jane ever wanted to meet her. But to tell you the truth, I lie awake some nights in bed, feeling horrified at the thought. And Kerry is just the right age to be Jane's birth mother, if she had Jane when she was a teenager."

Jessica stared at her. "Come on, Em. I think your imagination is running away with you. I sincerely doubt Kerry is Jane's mother or even related to her. Sure, they have similar coloring and maybe hold their forks the same way. But that's just coincidence. I think you have this question on your mind because Jane just had a birthday. She's getting older and she's going to want to find her birth mother. That's what you're worried about."

"Possibly," Emily admitted. "The mind does play tricks."

"I know. Someone says, 'Don't think of reindeer cupcakes,' and that's all you can think about."

Emily offered a small smile, thankful that her sister was trying to lighten the conversation. "I know I should talk to Jane about it, but I keep pushing it off. As if delaying the conversation will keep her from wanting to find her birth mother. Ridiculous, right?"

"It's illogical, but cut yourself some slack. Everyone who adopts a child feels that stress and fear. But you've already gone through this with Sara, in reverse," Jessica reminded her.

"That's what makes it even crazier," Emily admitted.

"I don't think Kerry is Jane's birth mother. But maybe you think she is because you know it's time to talk to Jane and see how she feels about the whole question."

Emily sighed and glanced at her sister. "That's

true. That must be it. Thanks for talking me down from the ledge, Sis."

Jessica leaned over and gave her a hug. "Anytime, pal. You've done the same for me, plenty of times. Well . . . time to get inside and see what new adventures my family has been up to."

"And the animals?" Emily replied.

"That goes without saying." Jessica slipped out of the car, and Emily watched her quick-step up the path to her front door. She waited a moment, almost expecting Zelda the cow to greet her sister, then had to smile at her silliness.

Jessica had given her good advice, as usual, she thought on the drive home. She did have to speak to Jane about looking for her birth mother. *And it shouldn't feel so difficult and frightening, for you of all people,* she scolded herself.

Emily had never been one to dwell on the past. The regrets that, for years, had trailed like frayed threads in her own life had been mostly resolved. Many people were not that fortunate, she knew. When she was only a few years older than Jane, she had eloped with a young man who her parents disapproved of. Tim Sutton was a fisherman, a few years older than her, and she was bound for an Ivy League college, not the life of a fisherman's wife. But a few months before her high school graduation, Tim had won her heart, and her path seemed clear, and much different than the one her parents had set out for her. Her mother objected to Tim most fiercely, her father, less so. Their relationship was carried on in secret. How different might her life have been if her family had accepted him? It had taken Emily a long time to resign herself to the fact that she would never know.

A few days after her high school graduation, she and Tim left Cape Light and were married by a justice of the peace in Maryland. They ended up in Delaware on the Chesapeake Bay, where Tim had a friend who owned fishing boats and had offered him a good-paying job. If she discounted the shock and outrage of her parents—who had communicated by letter that they would have nothing to do with her unless she ended her marriage and came home—her life at the time had been wonderful. While Tim was working on the water, Emily took temporary office jobs and tried to figure out how to start college part-time. But she quickly became pregnant. She and Tim were thrilled. Their love and vision of the future seemed complete. Though sometimes she felt sad and wished that her family could share in the anticipation and joy. But she didn't even write to them, their rejection had seemed so cold and final.

Jessica, nine years younger, was barely ten at the time. Emily longed to be in touch with her younger sister, just to explain that she was happy and hoped they could visit soon. She had no idea what her parents had said. But Jessica seemed too young to be dragged into the conflict, so Emily decided not to reach out to Jessica either.

"When you have the baby, your family will come around. You'll see," Tim would assure her. Emily hoped that was true. But she never got to find out, not the way Tim had imagined it.

A few weeks before the baby was due, a drunk driver ran a red light and slammed into Tim's truck. Her husband was killed instantly and she was critically injured. Their baby was delivered by an emergency C-section and not expected to live. Emily was frail, grief stricken, and dazed when her mother found her in the hospital ICU. Lillian took the situation in hand and convinced—more or less forced—Emily to give up her baby. Lillian's plan was for Emily to return home and pick up her life again, as if the unfortunate episode—her marriage to Tim and giving birth—had never happened.

Emily resisted at first, but the alternative seemed a black abyss she could not navigate. How could she raise the child on her own, without Tim by her side? How could she provide for her baby and herself? She was only nineteen, with just a high school diploma. She could already see that the jobs she was qualified for hardly paid enough to keep a roof over her head. Bringing the baby home to Cape Light and living with her parents was not an option. Her mother made that very clear. Her father was more vague about it, more concerned about her health and recovery. Emily had his sympathy, but after his business had failed and his heart attack, she couldn't look to her father to do battle with her mother on this question.

Finally, Emily gave in and gave up her baby, praying she was doing the right thing and that her little girl would find a happy, loving home. The decision clouded her life ever after. For years after losing Tim, she could never find a good relationship. Sometimes she felt she was purposely depriving herself of a "normal" life, marriage and family. Punishment for giving up her baby. Reverend Ben had offered comfort and counsel, but she could never quite forgive herself.

She tried to find her daughter several times, but the agreement had been a closed adoption and it wasn't easy to alter the terms, even with the help of attorneys and private investigators.

She'd never given up, but hadn't held out much hope either. Twenty-one years later, her daughter found her. It was one of the happiest, most miraculous moments of her life. Emily could still remember how her heart trembled and practically burst. The stunned feeling of disbelief when Sara revealed she was Emily's daughter—Emily had almost been afraid to accept the truth—and the wave of pure, indescribable joy and relief that the long wait was truly over.

How could she deny any mother that gift, that miracle? *But you're not denying Jane's mother the right to meet her.*

She has yet to emerge from the shadows and ask, Emily reminded herself. *You're just worried that someday she will, or Jane will go looking, and you're afraid of what will happen after that.*

You thought you were prepared to be on the other side of this question, that you understood what Sara's adoptive parents felt when she found you. But you didn't have a clue.

Soon after the baking team met at the inn, Kerry convinced herself she had to leave Angel Island. Spending more time with her daughter would only make it harder to go later, and it would be far too tempting to reveal her identity. Every moment with Jane was a bittersweet torture. One she had not anticipated.

But the days passed quickly. On Wednesday morning, she mulled over the problem as she cleaned the big suite for weekend guests. Each time Claire or Nolan asked for a hand here or there, she felt torn. She couldn't quit without some warning and leave them without the help they so obviously needed. They'd come to depend on her and had been so good to her. It wouldn't be right.

But how much notice should she give? Was a week enough? Was two? She didn't have much sense of how busy the inn would be over the holidays. Still, there was plenty of work and few people to do it. It was a terrible time for the inn to lose her help. That fact made her even more confused.

Kerry worked out her frustration on an oak armoire, buffing the finish to a sheen with a soft cloth and lemon oil. She didn't hear Liza enter the room until her employer stood right beside her.

"Fingerprints and dust motes don't have a chance around you, Kerry. I can see that."

Kerry felt embarrassed. She'd been going at the work with zeal. "I was just thinking. I didn't see you standing there, sorry."

"No need to apologize. I'm sorry to interrupt. Do you have a minute? I want to ask you something."

Liza looked serious. Had Claire finally told Liza about the black mark on her past, the time she'd spent in jail?

Kerry took a breath and braced herself. "Absolutely . . . What's up?"

"I was looking over your résumé," Liza said, making Kerry's pulse jump. "I knew you once worked in an insurance agency, but I didn't realize you had bookkeeping skills, and even some management experience?"

Kerry felt her body sag with relief. Liza wasn't going to ask about her past—not the reason she was charged and sent to jail, anyway.

"It was a small office . . . and a very small department. I didn't oversee a lot of people," she said quickly.

"Nonetheless, those skills give you a different perspective on the inn and running it. I know that you haven't been here very long, but you seem to like it. There could be a future for you here, Kerry. A real career path, if you enjoy hospitality work. I can see that you're very responsible. You give every job your all and you really take initiative. That's so important. Claire has nothing but good things to say about you. But I think you know that already."

"Claire's a wonder," Kerry said. "I've learned so much about inn-keeping from her, even in a short time here."

"She is a wonder. She's a national treasure. And has a lot more to share if you're inclined to stay with an eye to advancement?"

Kerry was thrown off balance by Liza's overture. How ironic that she was doing so well here and had just been wondering when to go.

Would Liza be so full of compliments and encouragement if she knew that I have a criminal record? Kerry didn't think so.

Claire obviously hadn't gotten around to telling Liza what she knew. She considered telling her to set the record straight, then thought, *What's the sense of going through that ordeal? It would embarrass us both right now. I really don't plan on staying here. Even if Liza wants to make me Queen of the May Day Parade. I just can't stay. Not for her, or even for Claire.*

"That's a very nice compliment. I'm very grateful to you for thinking of me that way. I love working at the inn and love working for Claire. But I really can't say what my plans are right now."

Liza looked surprised. "That's too bad . . . May I ask why?"

Kerry took a breath, not knowing what to say. She was tired of lying. Even about little things.

Finally she said, "Some family issues have come up that may require me to leave." It was a vague answer, but not a lie. Not really. "I'd like to stay, if I could. I just don't think it's possible."

She watched Liza's expression, waiting for her reaction and hoping she wouldn't ask more questions.

"I'm sorry to hear that. I hope it all works out for your family . . . I didn't mean to put you in an awkward position. I just don't know what to do. You've only arrived recently and you have no way to judge, but the inn is not up to its former standards."

"Yes, I understand. I know you're working on that. We all are right now."

"And making some progress," Liza said. "But the problem is deeper than weeding out worn linen and chipped soup dishes. It's really slipping, and I need to find some way to get things moving in the opposite direction. And fast."

Kerry could see Liza was worried and had lost her optimistic hope that the list of repairs and remedies she and Claire had drawn up, over a week ago now, was going to close the gap.

"I can see this is very hard for you. I don't know what I'd do if I were in your shoes," Kerry said honestly. "But I'd hate to see Claire and Nolan pushed aside or sent out to pasture if they want to stay here. Do you think that might happen?"

Liza looked past her for a moment. Kerry could see it was difficult for her to answer. "I'd hate to see that, too, Kerry. I'd never do anything to hurt them, if I could help it . . . But right now, I just don't know what's going to happen. I'd be lying if I said I did."

"Are you thinking of selling the inn?" Kerry was usually not so bold or straightforward. The question just popped out.

"I really don't want to. But I have to take a hard look at all the possibilities. And that's certainly one of them."

Kerry didn't know what to say. She would find another job somewhere, but it felt awful to think of the inn without Claire and Nolan. And Liza.

They're the heart and soul of this place. The reason it has so much warmth and character. Even if some of the shutters are loose and a few doorknobs stick.

She wanted to tell that to Liza but couldn't summon up the nerve and didn't think it was her place either. Anyone could see Liza loved Claire dearly, like family, and would never intentionally hurt her or Nolan. If anything, Liza's affection and respect for them was making her problem much harder.

"When were you planning to leave?" Liza asked.

"I'm not really sure. I hate to leave you and Claire shorthanded. I'll try to stay until Christmas, or even the New Year, and maybe you'll know what's happening with the inn by then."

"Thank you, Kerry. That would be a great help."

Kerry was glad she had offered. She could see that Liza was relieved by her answer.

Liza smiled. "I'm glad we had this talk. We'll talk more, I'm sure. I'll let you get back to your work. Everything looks perfect."

Kerry thanked her and watched her leave the room. She hadn't intended to box herself in, but now she'd promised to stay for Claire's sake, at least until the foggy fate of the inn was clear. But she didn't regret the promise. She owed Claire as much. Even if her time here was going to be like skipping across a minefield.

"You forgot the oyster crackers." Emily's mother had removed all the groceries from the bags and set them out on the kitchen table for Emily to store.

Emily watched her mother scan the boxes and cans, looking increasingly distressed.

"I did? I don't think it was on the list." Emily placed two cans of chicken noodle soup in the cupboard, one directly behind the other, the way her mother needed the cans to be. Unless the cans were a different flavor. Then they were placed side by side, or one on top of the other, so the labels showed.

"Of course it was on the list. Do you think I'd ask you to buy all that soup and no crackers?" Her mother stared at her. "That wouldn't make any sense at all."

"It wouldn't . . . unless you could eat toast with the soup. That might work. Since you forgot to put crackers on the list?"

Emily could see where this was going. A trip back to the store, she had no doubt. Part of the process. She was used to it. There was always a forgotten tube of toothpaste, a book on hold at the library, a package that had to be mailed.

She and Jessica took turns looking in on their mother and Ezra and doing errands for them. Jessica had covered Monday, so by Wednesday afternoon, Emily was in the hot seat.

"That's just the point, Emily. I didn't forget. You must have overlooked it." Emily's leather tote sat on the counter, and before Emily could stop her, Lillian began sifting through it. "Where's that list . . . I'll show you . . . Here it is." She pulled out a sheet of notebook paper covered with writing and slipped on the reading glasses that hung from a beaded cord around her neck.

Her mother had found a list. But not for the grocery shopping. Emily considered making a lunge to snatch the paper from her mother's hand but thought the move would be far too dramatic. And only underscore her culpability.

"What is this? It's not the shopping list I gave you this morning." Lillian peered at the sheet, then up at Emily. "It looks like a guest list. Are you having a party? With a lot of old people? I notice that Ezra and I are not included," she added, scanning the sheet to the bottom line.

"Of course you are. That goes without saying," Emily replied in a mild tone. She wasn't sure how to play this.

Her mother looked mildly mollified. "What sort of get-together is this? Some senior soiree sponsored by the town? You know I hate those things, all that big band music. I never liked it back then, and even less now."

Even though Emily was no longer mayor, she still volunteered her time and helped plan community activities. She wondered for a moment if she should dissemble and tell her mother she was planning a gathering for the town's seniors.

But her mother had her ways of checking into such stories. The ruse wouldn't last long. *Better to face the music now,* she thought, *swing era or not.*

"It's a surprise party for Ezra. For his ninety-fifth. And that's the guest list. Some of it anyway." The longer she and Jessica talked about the party, the more guests were added. Soon they would reach a number that would be too many for Jessica's large house to hold. They weren't quite there yet. So many people in town truly loved Ezra, it was hard to leave anyone out.

"Your sister is in on this plan, I suppose?"

Emily nodded. She knew it wouldn't take long for her mother's paranoia to kick in.

"Why bother asking? The two of you love to cook up your little schemes. And leave me in the dark."

"Mother, please. We just want to do something nice for Ezra. It's a surprise party, for his birthday. You make it sound like some secret plot against you."

Emily certainly didn't believe in reincarnation, but if there was such a thing, she had no doubt that her mother had been the much-beleaguered but long-running queen of a court rife with treachery. Fending off many a scheme to oust her from her throne.

Which is how she dealt with the everyday world, more or less.

"Why didn't you let me in on the surprise? It's not my birthday." Lillian sounded hurt and offended.

"We didn't tell you for a very simple reason . . ." Emily stopped there, feeling stymied by the question. She couldn't confess that she and Jessica knew their mother would take over the party plans and orchestrate a very grand and very costly celebration.

"We thought it would be so nice to surprise both of you," she said finally.

Lillian stared at Emily in disbelief. "Why in the world would you want to surprise me? I hate surprises. Everyone knows that."

That much was true. Everyone knew of Lillian's aversion to surprises, of any kind.

"It's a lot of work to plan a party. And stressful. We didn't want to trouble you. Won't it be nice to enjoy it as a guest? A guest of honor," she added "Along with Ezra."

"Thank you for your concern. I think. But why should planning a simple party trouble me? Am I a fragile flower, all wishy-washy and over-whelmed by decisions? Like whether the table linens should be cream or blue?"

They weren't planning on table linens. Not so far. Perhaps they'd have to amend that decision.

"So, what are the details, aside from this long, but mostly unimpressive, guest list?"

Emily summarized their plans as briefly as

possible, with as positive a tone as she could muster. She could see that her mother wasn't buying it. Not one bit.

"Jessica's house? That's not very special. And all those people? Complete strangers, most of them. I hate when the meal is served as a buffet. Everyone standing in line, serving themselves. It's like feeding time at the trough. Though the way your sister is running her life lately, I can't say that I'm surprised."

Emily cringed at the last remark. She would delete that from her report to Jessica. For sure. "Molly is sending help to serve the food. The guests won't be serving themselves exactly."

"I don't know why everyone makes such a fuss about Molly Willoughby's cooking. It's a mystery to me, honestly. So many spices and little bits of things floating about. Getting stuck in one's teeth. So bothersome—"

"Those are fresh herbs, Mother. Most people like them."

"I, for one, can forgo the bits. And the exotic flavors. Who knows what she'll cook for this party? You're at her mercy. You can't even get a plain old cup of soup in there . . ."

Or an oyster cracker, Emily nearly reminded her. But why fan the flames? She knew better by now.

"We haven't settled on the menu yet. We'll keep your comments in mind. Those are very good points. We'll find some foods that are classic dishes that everyone likes."

"Good luck with that. Why not just hire someone else? Or find a nicer venue, where you know the food is solid and reliable."

By which her mother meant a dry slice of roast beef or cod, a pile of potatoes, and steamed green beans.

"I'm afraid that's out of the question. We already gave Molly a deposit . . . at least I think Jessica did." Molly had never asked for a cent from either of them, but Emily grasped for some defense. "It's all arranged. We'd hate to cancel on Molly. She's family."

Her mother glanced at her with half-closed eyes. "That woman is no family of mine. Not that I'd publicly acknowledge." She sighed and shook her head. "Let me know how much you put down. Maybe I'll cover it to move the party . . . elsewhere." When Emily didn't answer, she added, "Foolish girls. I wish you'd told me sooner. We could have found a nicer venue and planned a much more sophisticated event. Someplace like the Plymouth Room, in Boston. I hear it's the same as always. Quiet, elegant, the staff waits on you hand and foot. Your father used to know the maître d'. He would welcome us by name."

Her mother's expression softened in reverie. Emily had heard that story hundreds of times and expected she would hear it a hundred more. She didn't dare say what she thought of the Plymouth Room. The few times she'd been there, she felt like she was dining at a wake.

"It's a lovely spot. Maybe next time."

Her mother laughed, a sharp, quick sound. "At my age, Emily, you don't wait for 'next time.' You take your chances when you can. But it sounds as if the die is cast. I suppose there are some details left I can weigh in on? The menu and decorations? The seating arrangements, flowers, and music? Have you decided on all of that already too?"

"Practically none of it." Mainly because they were aiming for a relaxed, low-key get-together without fussy seat assignments and a violin quartet.

Before Mother is done, Molly's waitstaff will be wearing black tie and tails.

Her mother must have noticed her expression. "I'm sure you realize I'll be very disappointed if you exclude me from the rest of the plans. Ezra will surely ask why my chin is dragging on the ground."

Dragging on the Persian rugs, more like, Emily silently amended. But she did get her mother's not-so-subtle point.

"You're in on the rest of it, Mother. No need to worry. Providing we can count on your total discretion?"

Her mother mimicked zipping her lips. "As we said in the day, 'Loose lips sink ships.' I suppose I'll have to settle for these arrangements. No use crying over spilt milk. Or overly spiced soup."

"None at all," Emily agreed.

She heard Ezra's shuffling step approaching and wondered what he had heard of the conversation. Not much, she hoped.

From his cheerful expression as he greeted her, it didn't seem so. "Did someone mention soup? I wouldn't mind a bowl for lunch today, Lily. With a grilled cheese sandwich on the side?"

"Neither would I." She glanced up at Emily.

"I'm sorry, I'd love to make you both lunch, but I have to pick up Jane at school and take her to a music lesson. I'm already late."

"You run along. Where's my apron? I'll be the chef today," Ezra announced in his typically sunny way.

Lillian rolled her eyes. "Why do men make such a fuss when they cook? Women go about the job without a peep, day in and day out."

Ezra laughed. "Some women, you mean. I don't know any women around here who do that. Except for Estrella, and it's her day off."

"Touché, dear," Lillian said. "But I don't think you married me for my cooking. I was completely forthcoming about that."

"So you were, my dear. No question. I can

always call for takeout, but there's no substitute for your sparkling conversation."

Her mother looked satisfied by the compliment. Ezra was a genius at feeding her ego, as well as preparing breakfast and lunch. Emily said good-bye and kissed her stepfather on the cheek.

Lillian followed her to the door and leaned over to whisper, "When are we going to select the menu? I hope Molly Willoughby will let us taste test the items before we decide."

"I'll look into it." Emily could only imagine that scene, her mother and Molly, going head-to-head. The match would be grueling.

"I have a lot of doctor appointments coming up. You need to give me fair warning."

"We will, Mother. Don't worry." Emily said goodbye again and waved from her car as she pulled away. Once she was headed toward the high school, she called Jessica on her cell phone.

Her sister answered quickly. "Emily? What's up?"

"I just left Mother. We're busted. She found the guest list in my purse and I had to tell her the whole thing. Now she wants in on menu plans and decorations. All the 'little touches,' as she'd say. Sorry, but I had no choice. She threatened to spoil the surprise."

"It's not your fault. Mother knows how to get her way. We'll just have to deal with it."

"I guess so. It won't be the first time we've

had to work around her to get something done."

"And not the last," Jessica replied. "If we work together and hang tough, we can hold the line. She won't be able to change our plans too much."

"Agreed, we can handle her. Thanks for the reminder."

"Anytime, Em. But I've got to run. I just picked up some rabbits from a pet shop that was closing, poor dears. Let's talk tonight. I'll call you."

"Good plan. I hope the rabbits settle in nicely. They're lucky you came to their rescue."

"They're very dear. But I'd better find homes quickly, or we'll be inundated with baby rabbits again. You know how that goes."

"No worries, we can give out bunnies as party favors. Ezra would love that idea."

Jessica laughed. "He would . . . But that's one little touch we won't run by Mother."

CHAPTER EIGHT

～

Kerry was the only one who joined Claire for church on Sunday morning. Liza decided to stay behind with the children. Charlotte was being fussy, and Liza also wanted to watch over guests who were not checking out until Monday morning. There was less than a week until the fair and only ten days until Christmas. The volunteers were meeting after church, and Claire didn't want to miss it.

"You two go along," Liza told Claire and Nolan. "I'm expecting Daniel to call. He didn't get to speak to the children last night. They were already asleep."

"In that case, I suppose we will." Claire glanced at Nolan, who looked very dapper in his Sunday outfit, a navy blue jacket, with a dress shirt and club tie peeking out from the V-neck of his sweater vest.

He put down his newspaper and rose slowly, stifling a groan as he gripped his back. He had pulled something out of line playing hide-and-seek with Max last night, but insisted he was fine.

"Just gets knotted up when I sit too long. It's nothing."

Claire watched him slowly straighten to his full height. "You can't go gallivanting around with your back like that. Go upstairs. I'll set you up with the heating pad and the newspapers. Twenty minutes on, twenty minutes off. When I get home, I'll fix you a mineral bath. That should kick it out."

Nolan pressed his hands to his lower back, his elbows jutting out like wings. He squinted with pain. "When you put it that way, I will follow your orders—er, suggestions—dear."

Max tugged on the edge of his jacket. "I'll read you a story, Uncle No-man. That will make you feel better."

Nolan ruffled Max's hair and smiled. "Yes, definitely. Grab some books and meet me upstairs."

Max couldn't really read, but he knew his picture books by heart and could recognize many words on the page. He loved to pretend he was reading to Nolan and Claire and delighted them with his versions of the stories.

Claire herded her husband toward the stairs, the loyal Edison on their heels. She suddenly turned back to Kerry.

"Would you like to come with me to church, Kerry? The service should be very nice. I think the children's choir is going to sing Christmas carols."

Claire always had a reason why the service shouldn't be missed. Kerry wondered if Claire felt a little lonely and wanted some company. She had considered going, mostly because she might see Jane, then decided it was better to avoid another meeting. But now that Claire was encouraging her, the invitation was too tempting.

"Sure. I'll just finish up in here and get changed."

Claire looked pleased. "Very good. We'll leave in a few minutes. I'll get Nolan settled."

A short time later, they were driving toward Cape Light. It was a chilly day, but not so cold for mid-December. The sky was a brilliant blue and remarkably clear.

"I hope Nolan hasn't sprained his back badly. Once it starts up, it's hard for him to shake it off. A warm bath with mineral salts is just the thing if it's a simple sprain."

Kerry didn't know the first thing about mineral salts, but it warmed her heart to see how much Claire cared for Nolan and what a wonderful relationship they had.

She couldn't remember her parents relating in such a close and caring way. Her mother was respectful of her father, but he definitely intimidated and sometimes even frightened her. He scared Kerry, too. She remembered running and hiding in her room whenever he went into one of his angry outbursts.

"I admire your marriage, Claire. It's rare to see two people so happy together, and so compatible. Have you and Nolan been married a long time?"

Claire laughed. "Goodness no, not long at all, compared to some couples. We met six years ago and married soon after. The whole thing took me by surprise. By that point, I was resigned to the idea that I'd never be married, though I came close once or twice when I was young. But it seems Heaven had other plans for me. I never imagined anyone like Nolan. And you know what they say." She looked away from the road to glance at Kerry. " 'Every pot has a lid. Even the bent one.' "

Kerry smiled. "I've never heard that before."

"It's true, my dear, believe me. Nolan was the right person for me, and it all unfolded perfectly. Not my idea of when and how it would be, but in God's time," she added. "You'll find the right person to share your life with someday. I'm sure of it. But don't wait until you're an old lady like me."

Claire made it sound so easy, advising her as if she were any other woman. But she wasn't. They both knew that. There were black marks on her history that Kerry felt would always block the path to finding someone to share her life, raise a family.

"It's nice of you to say that. But I doubt any

worthwhile man will have me. After he learns about my past."

Claire turned quickly and shook her head. "You mustn't think like that, Kerry. You were tricked and taken advantage of, manipulated by someone you trusted."

Kerry would grant that she had been manipulated by Michael Cook, her then-employer and boyfriend. He knew how much she wanted to please him and how she feared the loss of his affection. Even more than the consequences of taking part in his schemes. Michael owed money in all directions and said he'd found a way he could settle his debts so they could have a real future together. He needed her to create false accounting statements and notarize signatures she suspected were forgeries. "Just this once," he'd said. He would never ask again. Without her help, it wouldn't work. They were partners, weren't they? "Now and forever," he'd said. They'd never get caught, he promised, and if they did, he would say it was all his idea. She'd bear no responsibility or blame. He swore that he would protect her, no matter what. "Trust me, Kerry," he'd said. Kerry wasn't even sure now if she had trusted him or believed him. But she had done as he asked.

When they were caught and arrested, Michael didn't protect her one bit. It hurt even more to realize he had never loved her at all.

"I knew right from wrong," Kerry said finally. "I can't blame anyone else for what I did."

"And you've paid your debt," Claire reminded her. "We all make mistakes. We've all done things we're not proud of. We're only human. We stumble, even fall. Perfection is not the point in this life, dear. God knows He didn't make us perfect. I think He only wants us to own up to our mistakes, to ask for forgiveness and try to do better. If someone can't look beyond your past and see all the good in you, they don't deserve you, dear."

Kerry wanted to believe Claire's encouraging words, but in her heart, she really didn't. She thought it best to change the subject.

"I was talking with Liza the other day. She was hoping I could make a commitment to the inn, and eventually take on more responsibility."

Claire looked interested and pleased by the news. "I agree. What did you say?"

It was hard for Kerry to continue. She knew Claire would be disappointed to hear her answer. "I had to say that I didn't think that would be possible. Even though I wish it was. I love working at the inn, Claire, and I love working with you and Nolan. But . . . some family issues have come up. I might need to leave here soon."

Claire's expression fell. "I'm sorry to hear that, Kerry. But I understand. Family comes first.

Perhaps, when the situation is resolved, you could return."

Claire's unsinkable optimism surprised her once again. She always found a chink of light slipping through the darkness, didn't she?

"Maybe," Kerry agreed. Though she couldn't see how. When Jane left for college? But her daughter's shadow would still hover all around this town. Her absence wouldn't solve the problem.

"How did Liza take the news?" Claire asked.

"She seemed disappointed. I was flattered that she thinks so well of my work," Kerry admitted. "But I could tell she doesn't know I've spent time in jail. I wanted to tell her, but it didn't seem like a good moment. But I'm going to. Maybe when we get back from church today."

Kerry had thought the matter over and decided that even if she didn't stay at the inn much longer, Liza certainly had a right to know about her past. She was the inn's owner and it was up to her to decide if she wanted someone with a criminal record working there. She might not. No matter how nice a person Liza was or how well she thought of Kerry.

Kerry knew she might get fired but also knew it was the right thing to do. She was weary of hiding things about herself, lying to the world by omission.

"I'm sorry. That's my fault entirely. I meant

to tell her but it slipped my mind somehow." A flush crept up Claire's fair skin. "I don't think it will make any difference now that she knows you. But I hired you—I should be the one."

"I don't mind telling her. But if you feel it's your place, please tell her soon? She might find out and think I was purposely hiding the information."

Claire nodded. "I'll take care of it right away."

Kerry wondered if she should tell Claire about the rest of her conversation with Liza: Liza's concerns about the inn and its precarious future. Liza hadn't asked her to keep their talk confidential, but Kerry thought privacy was implied. And she didn't want to seem as if she was gossiping.

Besides, wouldn't Claire know even more about these matters than she did? Claire was so much closer to Liza.

The church came in sight and so did a parking space at the top of the village green. Kerry saw the arched wooden doors of the church flung wide open. Reverend Ben stood to one side, his white cassock and blue scapular lifting in the breeze off the harbor as he greeted the congregants.

"A convenient space. We'll be right on time. Thank you." Claire glanced upward a moment as she unclipped her seat belt.

Kerry had never driven with anyone who

thanked the heavens for a parking space, not even her father, who considered himself very religious. But he was devout in a very different way than Claire or Nolan, or anyone she had met at this church so far, including Reverend Ben. Her father's beliefs were rooted in fear, judgment, and censure. Just the opposite of what she had found here.

Reverend Ben greeted them both with a wide smile and a hearty handshake. "Good to see you again. It's Kerry, right?"

"Yes, that's right. Good morning, Reverend." Kerry wasn't sure how he knew her name. They had never been introduced. But she guessed Claire must have told him about her. She knew the reverend well and considered him a good friend.

"Welcome back," he said.

They entered the sanctuary and paused, looking for a place to sit. Vera and Sophie waved to them. "We saved you a place, Claire. Sit with us." Kerry followed Claire to the pew, and the two women greeted her warmly. As did Jessica Morgan, who was walking by with her children. She briefly touched Kerry's arm as she passed. "Hey, Kerry. Good to see you."

Kerry smiled back and took a seat. The deacon named Sam was walking with Jessica, and Kerry realized he was her husband. Jessica's family found seats a few rows away. Kerry soon spotted

Emily, Dan, and Jane sitting nearby, along with Jane's regal-looking grandmother.

All she could see of Jane was the back of her head.

Which is just as well, she decided. *Even if I did come here today, I won't seek Jane out later. It doesn't feel right anymore. Jane is fine, loved and well cared for by one of the most respected families in town. All I need to do now is find a way to leave the inn without causing problems for Claire. It's bad enough that I have to go. I can't leave her with a lot of work she's not able to handle anymore.*

Claire sat reviewing her program. She looked up at Kerry and patted her hand. "I'm glad you came with me. I think we each have some serious concerns weighing on us this morning. What better time or place to offer up prayers for help?"

Kerry couldn't deny that but wondered if Claire could guess the half of her concerns. Claire was so sensitive and observant. So intuitive. Kerry wouldn't doubt that Claire sensed she had come to the village for her own private reasons. But Claire was also too wise to pry.

The service was about to start when Kerry noticed Sam Morgan leading more congregants up the side aisle. It was Gabriel, walking slowly with an older woman who clutched his arm for support. Kerry recognized her coil of silver hair mixed with dark strands and her round, cheerful face. *That must be his grandmother,* she thought. *His abuela.* Gabriel helped her off with her brown coat and a flowery silk scarf. Kerry didn't mean to watch but couldn't help herself. He was so kind and attentive.

A moment before he took his own place, Gabriel looked up and caught her eye. Kerry felt embarrassed to be caught watching him, but he wore a wide smile. Pleased to see her or just to catch her staring at him? A little of both, she decided.

She smiled back and nodded hello. It seemed childish not to. She would avoid him later, she decided. That shouldn't be too hard. He'd be busy taking care of his grandmother.

Ever since Gabriel had stayed for dinner at the inn, almost two weeks ago now, and she'd told him in no uncertain terms she didn't want to date him, he'd kept his distance from her. All the repairs he'd been working on were outside, like the shutters, the drainpipes, and some work on the outbuildings and paths. He was friendly enough if they happened to meet, but no longer took time from his work to talk with her or tease and flirt.

At first, it surprised her that he had given up so easily. *That's what you wanted. What you asked him to do,* she had to remind herself.

It was just as well, she thought now. But it did make her feel sad, as if she had passed up a chance that would not come again for a long time. If ever. Maybe her talk with Claire about marriage had put her in a mood. She would try to concentrate on the service, she decided, and snap out of it.

The organ sounded a sharp, resounding note—the signal that the service was about to begin. Kerry turned to watch the choir's entrance. Instead of the adults in their long robes, a flock of children marched down the center aisle, holding pages of sheet music, many of them staring around, looking timid and confused. Encouraging adults at the head and rear of the parade guided them to the front and center of the sanctuary.

Kerry heard the *oohs* and *awws* of the audience while parents and grandparents raised cameras and phones to capture the performance.

"I wish Max and Charlotte were here," Claire whispered. "They'd like this."

The children sang an Advent hymn to open the service and then a traditional carol, "Away in a Manger." Their voices were sweet, if mostly out of tune. Kerry recalled Claire's words in the car: "Perfection is not the point in this life, dear."

They were doing their best, trying so hard and so sincerely, and their performance was made even more touching by the effort. *Is that the way God sees us?* Kerry wondered.

A young couple came up to light the third

Advent candle. Claire leaned closer and whispered, "That's James Potter, Sophie's grandson. He's a writer but helps the new owners run the orchard. Sophie sold it a few years back," she explained. "That's his fiancée, Zoey Bates. Her folks own the Clam Box Diner. She's studying to be a child psychologist. I think she almost has her degree. They just got engaged at Thanksgiving. Isn't that sweet?"

Reverend Ben greeted the congregation and made a few announcements about events and meetings. ". . . and the Christmas Fair Committee will be meeting after the service today. Anything to add, Emily?"

Emily Warwick stood up. She wore a tailored navy blue dress and a small strand of pearls. The classic style suited her, Kerry thought.

"Just a quick reminder that the fair is next Saturday, December twenty-first. We have a lot of new holiday items for sale, lots of gift ideas and activities for children. Please get the word out and bring your friends. There's a meeting after the service for all volunteers. It's all hands on deck."

"The baking team is set," Claire whispered to Kerry. "No need to come to the meeting if you don't want to."

Kerry nodded. She had hoped to beg off and was relieved that Claire gave her an out.

"—Of course, you'll still lead the charge with

the macaroons this week? Everyone is coming back to bake again on Wednesday."

Kerry had forgotten about that plan. She had been so distracted by Jane that day, she hadn't been paying attention. Had she agreed to "lead the charge"? She must have if Claire said so.

"Yes, of course I will. I promised."

Claire seemed satisfied. "We'll figure out the amounts of ingredients we need and shop this week."

The announcements were over and it was time for a hymn. Kerry opened her book and stood up beside Claire. She focused on the words, but her thoughts wandered.

All these friendly people greeting her this morning, her responsibilities at the inn, and the promises she'd made to Claire's friends . . . They all felt like invisible threads, binding her fast, holding her to this place.

Even if she wanted to make a fast getaway, it didn't seem possible. Not without disappointing a lot of people she'd come to care for.

After the service, Kerry walked with Claire to Fellowship Hall. "Oh, look. Lucy Bates and Zoey brought the food for coffee hour. The food at the Clam Box isn't exceptional, but Lucy's deviled eggs are outstanding."

Kerry had to smile. She had not seen deviled eggs in some time. Perhaps the dish was making a comeback? More likely, it had never been dropped from the menu around here.

"They look good, but I thought I'd take a walk in town. Let me know when you're ready to head back to the inn. I'm not going far."

"Good idea. I'll give you a call. Have fun," Claire added with a smile.

Out on the green, Kerry headed down a path that led toward Main Street. She had often been to the village with Claire or Nolan, to shop or visit the post office and bank. But she had rarely come on her own.

The street was surprisingly busy for a Sunday morning. Many people were out shopping, walking dogs, or just enjoying the day.

The Clam Box Diner looked very busy for a place with "unexceptional" food, she noticed. The line stretched right out the door. She had stopped in there once, when she first came to town in October, to ask if help was needed in their kitchen. The owner, Charlie Bates, was a bit gruff. There were no openings except a waitressing job. She was glad now she had kept looking further.

Still, the appetizing scents of bacon, eggs, and toast wafted her way, beckoning her to cross the street. Kerry had hardly eaten breakfast but decided to walk farther before she stopped.

She did pause to admire the diner's front window, filled with old-fashioned lights and a big plastic Santa Claus, circa the 1960s. The windows of all the shops were decorated with care, she noticed—the flower shop filled with poinsettia and amaryllis, the toy store displaying a giant sled loaded with every toy imaginable. Even the hardware store had an old-fashioned sled parked on drifts of fluffy cotton snow. Shiny power tools, topped by big red bows, filled the rest of the space. The perfect gifts for that handy someone on your list.

Like Gabriel O'Hara, for instance. He was the sort of man you might shop for at the hardware store. Though she never would, she quickly reminded herself.

She gazed up at the trees, where small white lights had been strung on all the branches. All the way down the avenue, each one of the old-fashioned lampposts was decorated with a large pine wreath. If walking through Cape Light didn't get you in the mood for Christmas, nothing could, Kerry decided with a secret smile.

She usually had only a few gifts to buy—for friends or coworkers. But this year, her list was longer. Claire and Nolan, of course. And now Liza, Daniel, and the children. Finding special presents for each of them would be fun, though she didn't have all that much time.

But for some reason, she wasn't in the mood to make those decisions. She didn't want to settle for a pair of gloves or a pretty calendar. She wanted to buy them each a special gift, because they were all special people. Special to her. She might even be gone before Christmas, but that possibility made the idea of giving them each something memorable even more important.

The Christmas season had been a happy time when she was a girl and her mother had been alive. But ever since her mother's death, Kerry had been on her own during the holidays. She knew that her father was still alive and living in Rockport, in the same house where she had grown up. Not so very far from Cape Light in actual distance. But he may as well have been living on the Moon if you were measuring emotion-wise, she reflected.

He had made no attempt to reach out to her since the day he'd stood her up, promising to meet her and her baby in Cape Light, but sending a devastating message instead. After that day, she had never tried to contact him either.

Sometimes friends or neighbors would invite her to their family gatherings. But most years, she preferred to be on her own—to take a long walk by the water or in the woods during the day, if the weather was willing. At night, she would watch favorite movies with a cup of tea or hot cocoa. And enjoy some of the cookies she'd baked and given out as gifts.

Liza and her family would be back in Arizona by Christmas, but Claire and Nolan would probably invite her to spend the day with them.

That's just the way they were. It would be nice to celebrate with the older couple, Kerry thought. But she couldn't even see that far ahead, though it was little more than a week from now.

Kerry had walked up one side of Main Street and come down the other, facing the harbor again. She turned the corner and saw the burgundy and gold trimmed awning of Willoughby's. It was the first place she had stopped when she'd come to Cape Light. Molly Willoughby was straight talking but friendly. Although she'd been very busy, she had taken the time to be kind and helpful when Kerry had asked about a job in her kitchen. Molly didn't need help at the time but suggested posting a notice on the bulletin board in the café. That turned out to be a great idea, since that's how Claire had found her.

Kerry had been so focused on finding a job that day, she hadn't tried any of the bakery's delicious-looking food. She was hungry enough now for a bite and was also very curious, after all she'd heard about Molly's culinary talent.

Though Willoughby's was another popular spot, Kerry was willing to brave the line she found inside. There was a line for the bakery and another for ordering a meal from the menu. She found the very end and browsed the choices on a paper menu.

"Is this secret research for the inn, or are you actually hungry?"

Gabriel. She would know that husky, teasing voice anywhere. "Claire doesn't send me on spy missions. Though I may report back to her," she said, turning to face him. He stood close behind her. Too close. She couldn't tell if that was on purpose or because the space was crowded. Probably a little of both.

"Either way, seems you're here for lunch. Why don't we have some together?"

His tone was so hopeful, his dark eyes so persuasive. She knew that she shouldn't encourage him, but was there really any harm in eating with him? He knew where they stood by now. She couldn't deny that she enjoyed his company. There was something so upbeat about him. She was already smiling and he'd barely said hello.

"All right. Let's sit together. But I'll take care of my own check."

Her ground rules seemed to amuse him, as she might have predicted. "I accept your terms . . . but only if I can carry the tray," he replied in a formal tone.

Kerry had to laugh at the counteroffer. "If it means that much to you."

Pleased by her answer, he picked up another menu as the line inched forward. He looked very handsome today, wearing a brown leather jacket with an Aran-knit sweater underneath and a pair of new-looking jeans.

Why is a guy like Gabriel so interested in me? She couldn't figure it out. She knew she was attractive enough, but she hardly played the game, like most single women her age. She had made it very clear she wasn't looking for a relationship, and he seemed the type who wanted the real deal, a commitment and a future with a woman he would love and admire.

Most men were drawn by a challenge, she had learned. They liked to pursue a woman who seemed out of reach. But she wasn't just playing hard to get—she *was* unavailable. Totally. She had tried to tell him that. She liked him, more than she wanted to, and she didn't want to lead him on or hurt his feelings.

Hey, slow down. It's only a chicken salad sandwich on a brioche roll. You're not going to break his heart by sitting with him for a few minutes. Sorry, but you're not that much of a heartbreaker, she chided herself.

"So, what are you having, Kerry? I'm thinking of a cappuccino and pastry. But I don't even know the names of half the things in that case." He pointed to the top row of delectable-looking confections. "I think I like those. I don't remember the name, though."

"Napoleons," she said.

"Can you make them?"

"The pastry has to be properly chilled and rolled out several times, but yes, I can."

211

"How about one of those?" he asked, pointing to the next treat.

"Cream puff. Not so hard. The dough gets very stiff. Lots of egg yolks. The pastry cream inside is sort of tricky."

He pointed to others, moving from row to row—an éclair, a petit four, a miniature fruit tart, a cannoli.

"Yes . . . yes . . . and yes." She was starting to laugh, despite herself. "The cannoli shell isn't baked. It's like a crepe, wrapped around a metal tube and deep-fried," Kerry explained about the last pastry in the row.

Gabriel looked impressed. "Why don't you open a bakery? I bet you'd do very well."

She shrugged. There were a million reasons why that couldn't happen, but his suggestion was a nice compliment. "For one thing, there's already a very good one in this town."

"That's true, but look how crowded it is. If you had a bakery in town, too, we would have been served our food by now."

He looked very sure of this conclusion, and his convoluted logic made her laugh. "I can't even reply to that," she admitted.

He smiled down at her, catching her gaze. "Got you there, right? By the way, you should definitely laugh more. You have the prettiest smile I've seen in a long time."

Kerry stared at him a moment, then looked

away. She felt her cheeks redden and couldn't answer that comment either. *Do you see now why you shouldn't have agreed to this?* a little voice reminded her.

"Hey, Kerry!" Kerry turned toward the entrance and saw Jane walking in with her father, Dan Forbes. Kerry had purposely avoided her at church this morning, but couldn't help feeling pleased at Jane's warm greeting.

Jane quickly walked over to meet her. "I saw you in church with Claire. My mom's still at the meeting. My dad and I got bored so we came here for a snack."

"I just stopped in for lunch," Kerry said. "And this is my . . . my friend, Gabriel," she added, thinking it was rude not to introduce him.

"Nice to meet you, Jane." Gabriel smiled at the teenager.

"Hey, Gabriel." Kerry could tell Jane was wondering if she'd interrupted a date.

"The line is so slow here," Kerry said, hoping to distract her. "Can we order for you and your dad?"

"It's okay. We're on the faster line. I just want to try the macaroons."

Kerry had already checked out Willoughby's version. It wasn't a French macaron, made with wafers, but she'd wager there was whipped egg white in the mixture. "Their recipe is probably more complicated than mine. But maybe you'll want to make some like that on your own some-time."

"That's what I was thinking. I've started a food diary, with notes and photographs." Jane pulled a little black book from her sack-shaped purse. "I read somewhere that all serious cooks keep one. Do you?"

Kerry smiled at the question. "No, I don't. But that's a great idea. Maybe I should start one, too."

"You should. Then we could compare our notes." The woman behind the counter handed Dan a bag, presumably filled with macaroons, and Dan gave Jane a look, silently asking if she was ready to leave.

"We're going to head back," Jane said. "See you . . . Have a nice lunch." She glanced at Gabriel again, and Kerry cringed a bit. Jane did think it was a date, a predictable teenage interpretation. But it still made Kerry feel self-conscious.

"Thanks, Jane. See you soon."

As Jane followed Dan out of the shop, Gabriel said, "She's very sweet. Do you know her folks, Dan and Emily?"

"Um . . . not really. Claire asked me to help with the bake sale for the church fair, so I've met Emily a few times. Jane is part of the group, too. She's very interested in cooking."

"She seems very interested in you, too."

Kerry wasn't sure how to reply.

"Can I help the next person on line, please?"

Their turn to order, finally. Kerry felt relieved that the conversation was interrupted.

They found a table at the front of the café with a view of the park and harbor. They were just settling in when their food orders arrived. Kerry was impressed. "That was fast. It's so busy in here, I thought it would take longer. That's a very efficient kitchen."

"Have you worked in many restaurants?" he asked.

"Not really. Just a large inn up in Maine, and now Angel Island."

And the food service at the low-security prison where she'd served out a sentence of almost two years. But she didn't include that.

"The type of cooking I do is much easier," she explained. "It's almost like cooking in someone's home."

"Not quite, from what I can see. I think you work very hard. But that's a positive way to look at it."

If he knew what she had been through, he would understand why she felt her life was so easy now. Most of her life, anyway. "I was very lucky to find a job at the inn. I'd been asking all over town, and Molly Willoughby suggested I put up a flyer on the bulletin board in here. Claire saw it and things just worked out."

Because she's such a special person and was

215

willing to give me a chance, she wanted to add.

"I think it's more than luck. I think some things are just meant to be," Gabriel said. "A friend of mine was supposed to fix the porch roof, but he was all booked up, so he passed the job to me. Now my schedule is filled with projects at the inn. Funny how things work out, right?"

Kerry took a bite of her sandwich and nodded.

She had thought about checking on Jane for years until some invisible hand had pushed her in this direction. Once she arrived in Cape Light, things started to fall in place, almost too quickly. She had not only met her daughter, but was getting to know her more each day. Building a strange but precious friendship, she reflected.

"And I got to meet you," he added.

His words pulled her from her wandering thoughts. She didn't know how to reply. Was he saying that their meeting was "meant to be"?

"Um . . . yes, you did." She shook her head. "Sorry. My mind was just wandering a bit."

"What made you move down here from Maine? I don't think you ever said."

"I grew up around here, out in Rockport," she began, wondering how to frame a plausible and mostly true answer. "But I moved up to Maine when I was about nineteen. I always planned to come back," she added, "and it just seemed a good time."

"Rockport is very pretty. Do you go back there much?"

She concentrated on her sandwich, wondering how she could avoid all these personal questions. "No, not at all. I don't really miss it," she added.

It was a charming town. The gracious old homes and long pier filled with shops and art galleries drew visitors year-round. But the winding streets and seaside village were shadowed by too many memories for her. She could never see the place the way a tourist would.

She could see he was curious about her reply and wanted to ask more. "I mean, it's hard to miss Rockport, living here. Cape Light and Angel Island are just as nice as Rockport, maybe more so."

"They are. I missed this place, even though I loved living in Boston while I was there. Most of the time, anyway. I came back a lot, especially in the summer."

"Were you unhappy in the city? Is that why you came back here?"

She recalled he had said something like that the night he'd had dinner at the inn with everyone. Had he given a specific reason? She couldn't remember.

"I'd hit a low point in life, I guess you'd have to say. My father needed some help with his business, so I came back to give him a hand, and it all worked out."

She could see that this was a hard subject for him to talk about. She would be the last person to press with more questions.

She glanced down at her sandwich, as if it had just landed on her plate. "This chicken salad has some very unusual seasoning. I think I'll make some notes. How's the Napoleon? It looks good."

"I'm not having any trouble with it." He smiled at her, and she felt relieved. He hadn't taken offense at the way she had diverted the conversation. "Would you like a taste?" Kerry was curious to taste the pastry. If only for her new food diary, she thought with a small smile.

"Sure, but just a small bite. Thanks."

Gabriel passed her the plate, then watched her sample the pastry.

Kerry held the morsel in her mouth a moment, savoring the flaky crust and cream filling.

"On a scale of one to ten?"

"The crust is flaky and crisp and the filling is light and delicious." She paused to formulate her rating, half teasing with the drama. "I'm giving it a nine, only because I prefer plain powdered sugar on top, but most people love the icing."

Gabriel laughed. "I'm in the icing group myself, but I might have guessed you're a purist. Did they teach you food tasting at cooking school, too?"

"Not a great deal. That skill is for more advanced study than I had." She hoped he wouldn't ask now where she had studied cooking. She didn't want to lie but she wasn't ready to share her entire life story.

They were seated near parents with two small children about Max and Charlotte's ages. The kids had finished their treats and were starting to fuss. But the mom and dad took turns entertaining them long enough to finish their own treats and cappuccinos.

"It's hard to bring kids that age to a restaurant. You have to give the parents credit for keeping them busy," Kerry said, noticing that Gabriel was also looking at the children.

"They're doing a great job," he agreed. "You're very good with Max and Charlotte, I've noticed."

"Thanks. They're not hard to take care of. They're really sweet kids." Kerry took a sip of her coffee. The light mood suddenly dispersed. She had a feeling about where the conversation was going—not a place she was comfortable.

"I'd like children someday," Gabriel said. "I was married in my twenties, but we didn't get a chance to start a family. I'm thirty-seven now. I don't think it's too late, do you?"

Was he wondering if she was interested in having children, too? The question seemed implied, but she wasn't going to answer it.

"Not at all. People have children at all ages now."

She wanted to know more about his marriage,

but didn't want to encourage more personal talk. "Gee, it's getting late. I'd better call Claire. She must be wondering what happened to me."

Kerry took out her phone and dialed Claire's number. Claire picked up quickly and explained she was in another meeting and had totally lost track of time. "I'm so sorry, dear. I'll call Nolan and ask him to pick you up."

"That's all right. I'll call a cab or something," Kerry replied.

Gabriel, who'd been listening, asked, "Do you need a ride? I'll drive you back."

Kerry didn't really want to accept his offer, but it seemed the easiest solution. "I'm at the bakery with Gabriel. He'll give me a ride to the inn. Problem solved," she told Claire.

"Very good. See you later." Claire sounded pleased and they ended the call. Gabriel looked pleased by the solution as well, Kerry noticed as they left the café.

What's the difference if you spend another twenty minutes with him? It won't change anything, she told herself as they walked to his truck. But deep inside she knew that every minute she spent alone with Gabriel did change things between them, and did draw them closer, whether she was willing to admit it or not.

They drove through the village in silence—a comfortable silence, Kerry thought. He seemed content not to talk, and so was she. They arrived at the land bridge, and he turned to her. "I always love this last stretch of driving back to the island. You almost feel as if you're driving right over the water."

"I know what you mean. I love the view from the middle, when the water is all around. And the cliffs are pretty, too."

At this point of the ride, the famous cliffs on one side of the island were clearly visible.

"Oh, the cliffs, right. They're shaped like angel wings. Some people say that's how the island got its name. But it's really because of the legend."

Kerry turned from the window to face him. "I didn't know there was a legend."

He smiled, his gaze fixed on the road. "Really? I'm surprised Claire didn't tell you. It's an interesting story. Back when this area was just settled, in the mid–sixteen hundreds, a deadly pox spread through the village on the mainland. It was highly contagious, and the town elders decided to move all the infected villagers to the island. To quarantine them there. The sick folks had weekly visits for a while, until winter set in. It was particularly harsh, and traveling to the island by the land bridge or boat became impossible. It took until spring before the villagers were finally able to reach the island. They didn't expect to find any survivors." Kerry waited, bracing herself for an unhappy ending. "They could hardly believe it when they found everyone on the island was not

221

only alive, but completely cured, and in excellent health. All through the winter they'd had good shelter and clothing. And plenty to eat and clean water to drink. They were better off than most of the villagers on the mainland."

"And how had that happened?" She smiled at him, waiting for the answer. He'd said this was a legend, not a factual story.

"The quarantined islanders claimed that a group of wise and compassionate people had visited them many times during the winter and had taken care of them. They thought this group had come from the village, but the villagers didn't know anything about such visits. Once the quarantined group got home, they set out to look for these helpers. They traveled to all the settlements in the area, but never found the people who had saved them. They decided they must have been visited by angels, and that's how the island got the name it has to this day. Ever since those sick villagers were saved, the island has been thought of as a place of healing, even in the most hopeless and impossible situations."

His final words struck a chord, reminding Kerry of her own reason for coming here. "It is an interesting story. Quite a tall tale."

"A historian from a university came here years ago and did a lot of research. He wanted to disprove the legend. But all the basic facts panned out. There were even written accounts from the quarantined group about the visitors who had nursed them back to health. Of course, he could never verify if they were angelic beings or not." Gabriel glanced at her. She couldn't tell if he believed the legend or not. Was he just teasing her by looking so serious, trying to see if she would fall for it?

"You can read his research paper in the library. I'm sure they have it."

"Maybe I will," Kerry said, though she doubted she would be in town long enough for that. "Do you believe it?"

He smiled and nodded, his dimples deepening. "I do. But more based on personal experience."

"Really? Have you been visited by an angel, too?" She was teasing him now, but she could see that, even though he was smiling, he was still serious.

"I can't say for sure. I do know the last part of the legend is true." He was quiet a moment, then said, "Looking back, I'd have to say that returning here saved my life. I was in a very dark place a few years ago. My wife died in a strange accident. She was kayaking with a friend and their boat tipped over. Her friend swam out, but Jenn was trapped underneath and drowned."

"I'm so sorry. That's heartbreaking." Kerry felt awful for him. Kerry had assumed his marriage had ended in divorce. She didn't realize he'd gone through such a tragedy.

"It was heartbreaking. I always thought of myself as such a grounded person, but I didn't deal with it well. Everything just unraveled. I drank a lot and lost my job. I didn't see any reason to get up in the morning. I was sinking pretty fast. Luckily, I came back here. Helping my father gave me some purpose, and being in this place helped me pull my life together again. I realized a lot of the goals and values I'd had back in the city didn't work for me anymore. I wanted something different from life. Something simpler. Did I ever see an angel?" He smiled. "Maybe not, but I've heard that they're mostly invisible. I have felt them hanging out around here. I'm almost positive about that."

She wondered if he was joking with her now, ending the sad story on a light note. He had to be, right?

"I don't know the first thing about angels," she admitted. "I certainly won't argue with you."

Kerry was still stunned by his admission. He always seemed so stable, cheerful even. She found it hard to picture Gabriel lost and confused, in the desperate state he'd described.

But even Gabriel O'Hara was not perfect. *Would his own missteps help him understand the mistakes I've made?* She was tempted to think so. But losing someone you love is very different from breaking the law, she decided. It wasn't the same thing at all.

Kerry had been so interested in their conversation she hadn't even noticed that the inn was coming into view. Gabriel pulled up the driveway and stopped in front of the porch.

"Thanks for the lift. I hope it wasn't too far out of your way."

"Not at all. I enjoyed the company."

Kerry had enjoyed his company, too. He was not only handsome and charming. He was also a caring, thoughtful person who had been through tough times, just as she had. She felt wistful that their tentative friendship could never amount to anything.

"I enjoyed the story. Thanks for enlightening me." She stood next to the truck but hesitated to slam the door.

"I have a lot more stories, no worries. See you tomorrow, Kerry."

"See you." She slammed the door and waved goodbye through the window. Then watched him drive away.

As she climbed the steps and entered the inn, Kerry did look forward to seeing him and was glad that she only had to wait until tomorrow morning. She really didn't want to feel that way, but she did.

CHAPTER NINE

～✑～

L illian thought if she visited the bakery at ten, it would be fairly quiet and empty. She was surprised to see she was mistaken. There wasn't an empty seat to be found at the many tables, and a long line of customers waited in front of the counter.

"You'd think more people would be at work on a Monday morning," she murmured to her helper, Estrella. "Is there some holiday I'm unaware of? They're always making up new ones."

"No, Mrs. Warwick. I don't think so." Estrella gently held her arm as they made their way toward the counter.

"Maybe they're giving something away," Lillian replied.

"There's an empty seat for you. That couple just got up. Why don't you sit and tell me what you'd like?"

A seat had opened up a few steps away, right next to the window. A fortunate location. There were so many mothers killing time with peevish toddlers, and old people like herself, planted for the duration with their sudoku and crossword puzzles, her claustrophobia was kicking in. "Phobia of rubbing shoulders with the riffraff," Ezra had diagnosed it.

"A seat by the window *is* preferable. Good thing you spotted it." Gripping Estrella's arm, she set off at a quick pace—quick for her, anyway.

A few other customers had followed them inside and were also searching for empty seats. Lillian glared at them as she shuffled by, displaying her cane and uneven gait to full advantage, lest they dare to consider beating a poor, defenseless old lady to her prize.

Estella held the chair steady as Lillian sat, then waited patiently as she loosened her silk scarf and caught her breath.

"What would you like, Mrs. Warwick? The croissants are very good," she suggested. "Light and crisp, the way you like them."

She did make the favorite pastry sound tempting. But Lillian did not want Molly Willoughby to see her enjoying anything cooked here.

Lillian glanced at the huge display of bakery items. Breads of every shape and type, baskets of rolls and scones, brioches and croissants as well. The glass case was filled with cakes on one side; Danish pastry, cupcakes, brownies, and cookies on the other.

The woman could bake, that was not the question. But a birthday cannot be celebrated by bread alone . . . or even cake, for that matter. It was the soups and entrees and such that concerned her, the dishes that would be served at Ezra's party.

She tugged off her leather gloves and set them down neatly, one on top of the other, then glanced at Estrella. "Coffee, black would be fine. I've changed my mind. I don't feel very hungry, after all. But I would like to speak to the owner, Molly Willoughby. Perhaps you can send word through someone at the counter?"

She had not been forthcoming with Estrella about adding this stop on their morning errands. In all the times her helper had taken her to town, Lillian had never once requested a visit to the bakery. But today, after her weekly appointment at the hairdresser, she had directed Estrella to drive here.

As she waited for her coffee and an audience with Molly, Lillian peered at the diners nearby. A young man dug into a pile of mashed avocado on toast with gusto. A revolting mess, in her opinion, though she knew the dish was all the rage these days. His companion appeared to be eating some interpretation of eggs with Hollandaise sauce, but, butchered with the usual Willoughby flair, it was practically unrecognizable. Was there not a simple plate of pancakes or plain old scrambled eggs? Lillian looked about but didn't see any such. No sense mincing words with Molly Willoughby when she showed herself. She would tell her straight out. That was the best way to deal with the woman; she already knew that much.

They'd had run-ins many times before, when Molly was merely a housekeeper mopping Lillian's kitchen floor. Emily had even hired Molly to prepare meals at Lillian's house. Always a disaster, no matter how clear the instructions. Perhaps she could produce a perfect brioche, but she could not manage to produce a simple roast chicken, boiled potatoes, and edible green beans. And she did not do well with criticism, that was for sure.

Lillian had always found her to be a stubborn woman, very opinionated and proud. How she had managed to build a successful business was a mystery. Who could get along with such a person? Her overbearing personality had to be a liability. Lillian felt sure of that.

Emily and Jessica are no match for Molly. But I certainly am.

Estrella returned with a paper cup of coffee and carefully set it before Lillian. "Mrs. Willoughby will be right out to see you."

"Thank you. You can bring the packages to the post office and pick me up when you're done."

Estrella agreed and left Lillian with her coffee. She took a testing sip—far too strong, and burnt tasting. She might have known. She put it aside and gazed out the window.

Molly had found a good location for this store,

hadn't she? Right across from the rolling green park, playground, and harbor. A short distance away, Lillian could even see the church roof and steeple and a fragment of the village green.

"Enjoying the view, Lillian?"

Lillian recognized the voice instantly but took her time giving Molly her attention. "I was just noticing that your bakery is in a busy spot. Probably a big reason for its popularity."

Molly smiled. "I'm not sure if people stop in because they've been at the park, or if it's the other way around now."

Touché, Lillian thought. But she was not distracted from her mission.

"To what do I owe the honor? Did you come to talk about Ezra's party?"

"That's it exactly. I asked Emily if she could set up a tasting session so we could choose a menu, but I don't think she's been in touch with you about that?"

Molly shook her head. "Haven't heard from her lately. But I have a catering menu handy. We can go over it together."

"How efficient. Let's do that." Lillian watched Molly bring over a large printed menu, leather bound, and a notepad. The notepad would not be needed, Lillian wanted to tell her, but decided not to bother.

Molly opened the menu and handed it to her, then sat down at the table. "Jessica said it will be an afternoon party. I think a mix of hot and cold, brunch and lunch dishes would work well."

"Perhaps," Lillian murmured. She glanced down the selections, unable to even imagine some of the combinations and preparations described. What was sriracha sauce? Some unspeakably spicy potion, she'd wager.

"I can probably bring out samples of most of the dishes listed. We're serving both breakfast and lunch right now."

Lillian snapped the menu closed and set it aside on the table.

"To be perfectly frank, nothing here whets my appetite. If I wouldn't eat it, how can I, in good conscience, offer it to our guests?"

Molly squinted at her as if she wasn't sure she'd heard correctly. Then she looked as though she might laugh but was doing her best to hold it back.

"Perhaps you don't believe that," Lillian pressed on.

"Honestly? I'm not surprised. I know you've always turned your nose up at my cooking, Lillian. I can see the way you wander around the buffet table every Christmas Eve with an empty dish, as if I'm only serving . . . stale bread and water."

Molly usually hosted the family Christmas Eve party. Molly was one of Sam Morgan's sisters, and Sam had married Jessica, so Lillian was obliged to attend Molly's party or forgo spending the holiday with her children and grandchildren. Molly and her husband, Matt, had a large, luxurious house, well-suited for entertaining. Oddly, all the guests—with the exception of Lillian—believed she served the best food, too.

"There's nothing wrong with bread with water. I wouldn't object to that choice at all. But you'd probably put some exotic spices in the water and smear the bread with a condiment that was unrecognizable . . . and too spicy for most palates."

Molly let out a slow breath, like a little steam engine, Lillian thought. "Point taken. If there are dishes you'd like us to cook that are not on the menu, we can certainly handle that. Does Ezra have a favorite? Let's start with that."

It was actually a good suggestion . . . if Lillian had been in the mood to negotiate. But she was taking no prisoners today. She was determined to shake loose of Willoughby's Fine Foods and Catering.

The truth was that Ezra was still an adventurous eater, far more than his aging digestive system would tolerate at times. He would enjoy most, if not all, of the exotic plates on Molly's menu. But Lillian certainly was not going to admit it.

"Ezra likes what I tell him to like. We are of one mind in the dining department. And while I appreciate your accommodating attitude, what guarantee do I have that even if you try to prepare some dish I suggest, it will taste good? I recall the few times my daughters hired you to cook for me. A simple roast chicken and boiled potatoes seemed beyond your much-touted skills."

"Below. Not beyond. There's a big difference. It sounds to me like you should have this party catered by a hospital kitchen—or a school cafeteria—if that's the sort of the cuisine you're looking for."

Lillian smiled and nearly sighed aloud with relief. Finally, she'd gotten to her. Molly had developed somewhat thicker skin since her younger days. She'd had a shorter fuse when she was younger. Though not by much. Lillian knew she was cracking.

"Your reply only tells me you have no understanding of my concerns, and even less interest in providing the sort of food I'd prefer for my husband's celebration. I don't think that's a very good basis for this collaboration, do you?"

Molly's face was beet red, her large hazel eyes bugged out, and her mouth a tight line. Lillian braced herself for an explosion.

"I should have known the minute I saw you here. Fine, if you don't want me to cater Ezra's party, suit yourself. I certainly don't need the business. Especially during the holidays. I was doing it as a favor for Emily and Jessica. Go find someone who will serve poached cod and mashed potatoes if that's what you like . . . and canned peas on the side."

Molly had raised her voice, and customers were watching. Lillian felt totally calm, even relieved. She had won the battle, and faster than she expected.

"Good. We understand each other. Finally." Lillian lifted her chin. "I hear a deposit has changed hands. Will there be some refund? We're certainly canceling your services with fair warning."

"Deposit? I was doing this as *a gift* to Ezra."

No one had told her that. Lillian paused, wondering if she had gone too far. But a person like Molly needed a full frontal attack. Nothing less would have saved the day.

No wonder her daughters were so keen on this choice. They were pinching pennies, it seemed. Not that anyone would ever call her a spendthrift, but she knew when it was necessary to pay for the best, and it certainly wasn't to be found at Willoughby's.

"A well-intended gesture. But our family hardly needs charity. You get what you pay for, I suppose." Lillian shrugged. "I hope you'll be able to attend, though we understand if you're busy with your work."

"Oh, I'll be there, Lillian. Don't worry. For Ezra," she added. *And now, to spite me,* Lillian thought. "I really don't know what you ever did to deserve a man like him."

"God works in strange ways, doesn't he?" Lillian spotted Estrella through the window, returning to pick up her up. "Here's my ride. I'll let you go back to work. I've taken up far too much of your time already, I'm sure."

"Yes, you have. I can't say it's been a pleasure, Lillian. But I can say it's been real. As usual."

Lillian felt the same about her. It was refreshing, actually, to deal with a person so forthrightly. Most people couldn't take the heat. She had to grant Molly Willoughby that.

Liza was stealing a few moments Monday morning to go over the accounts and the reservations that had been booked so far for December. Audrey had just picked up Max and Charlotte to take them, along with her own little ones, to the youth center in town for an hour of tumbling. Though Liza had wanted to join the fun, she decided to stay at the inn and make the most of the quiet.

It was already the sixteenth, less than ten days until Christmas. She could hardly believe that her extra week's stay had stretched so far. Yesterday, while on the phone with Daniel, they faced the fact that she would not be bringing the children home for the holiday and decided he would come back to the island.

It seemed the logical thing to do, and he hadn't objected. She wanted to vent about the inn, how sprucing up the place and running a tighter ship hadn't made a difference so far. Registration was flat and outgoing guests were leaving subtle but snide comments in the registration book. The latest had been a doozy. She would have to speak to Claire about it.

Daniel had pressures and concerns of his own. The closer the date for Dr. Mitchell's retirement came, the more muddled Daniel's position at the clinic had become. The board had offered him a promotion, a job as the supervisor, but he didn't want it.

"It will mean less time with patients? Is that it?" Liza had asked.

"Not just less. I doubt there will be any. A higher salary and a fancy title, but that's not why I came out here. You know that."

Liza certainly did. "What are you going say?"

"I'm not sure. I have to hear them out. Maybe I can negotiate something in between? We'll talk when I come back. I don't have to answer until the New Year."

Liza was relieved to hear that. Either their lives were completely dull and routine or there was too much going on. She hoped to have the situation at the inn settled before she and Daniel had to sort out his job prospects. But it might not fall into place so easily.

Claire peeked into the cozy space below the staircase that Liza used as office. "Do you still want to check the glassware today? I can start on my own in the dining room if you're not ready."

Liza cleared her throat. She had something to say to Claire; it was best that it didn't wait. "I do, but I think we should talk first. Come on in, take a seat." She shifted aside so that Claire could sit in the extra chair.

Claire sat down squarely facing her. She looked curious but not alarmed. "What is it, Liza? Is something wrong?"

"I'm sorry to seem petty. I know that we've all been working very hard to bring up the standards here. But a few hours after the MacGregors checked out, I found a nasty comment about the inn online. It had to be her. She describes their room perfectly . . . and the lunch I served them yesterday."

Claire looked alarmed. "What did she say?"

Liza had printed out the comment, posted on a popular travel site. She hesitated to read the whole diatribe aloud. Even an edited version was cutting.

" 'We've stayed at this inn often when visiting this part of New England. The island is unchanged, but this inn is not what it used to be. Two of three drawers in the dresser stuck, and the closet smelled musty. The toilet ran all night, and my husband had to get up and shut off the water valve so we could sleep . . .' " Liza deleted a jab about Claire's banana bread tasting too salty. " '. . . I had specifically asked for gluten-free foods, and was promised it was no problem. The squash soup and an omelet I was served must have had gluten. I am still in distress from the reaction.' "

"Oh dear . . . that's awful." Claire's complexion had lost its usual color. She pressed a hand to her cheek.

Liza leaned closer, feeling guilty now for sharing the harsh comments. "Claire . . . I'm confused. You told me the blue bedroom with the water view was ready and all the issues on the list had been addressed."

"I did say that. I know I did. I suppose, I got confused. I was thinking of the smaller blue room, on the garden side, the one with twin beds. Nolan intended to repair the plumbing in the larger room," she continued. "It's just that little plastic arm in the tank that needs replacing. I could do it myself if I had a minute . . . or if I had remembered."

Liza didn't know what to say. "Maybe I should have checked the room myself. But I didn't want you to feel that I didn't trust you and had to look over your shoulder."

"Yes, I know. You trusted me and I let you down. I can't understand what happened with that woman's soup. I do have portions of gluten-

238

free soup in the freezer. I must have marked one wrong. I used to be so good with the tiniest details. I need to make myself more notes and pin them everywhere."

"That might help," Liza agreed, though she wondered if it really would.

"I can see this is very troubling for you, Liza. And discouraging. After all our hard work the last two weeks or so."

It was discouraging, but Liza thought Claire felt bad enough about the mix-ups. "I don't mean to blow this out of proportion. It's just one visitor. And I will reply to it online and maybe even offer her some discount on another stay. But I'm not sure we're making much progress, Claire, and I don't know what else to do."

"I understand," Claire replied in her calm, straightforward way. "And I think I know why."

"You do?"

"It's Nolan and me. Maybe managing the inn is too much for us. If I can't even keep the blue room on the seaside and the one on the garden side from getting mixed up, I'd say that's a bad sign."

"It was a little senior moment. I should have double-checked before they came," Liza said, giving her a quick out.

Claire shook her head. Liza felt a knot of dread tighten in her stomach. Claire was really serious. *She's trying to tell me something important, and*

239

I need to listen. Even if it's not what I want to hear.

"It's not just the senior moments and forgetting a guest's particular requests. I'm afraid that the inn is too much for us to manage physically, Liza. These old legs can't climb the stairs ten times a day anymore. Nolan thinks he's still twenty-five, able to climb ladders and chase the children around. But reality catches up. We had a serious talk last night about all this. While I rubbed ointment on his back," she added with grin. "We still have our health, thank heaven. Plenty of our friends are in far worse shape. But how many more years will we be this able-bodied? Not only to do most of the work around here, but to travel and see some sights on our bucket list. You know how much Nolan loved to roam when we met," Claire reminded her.

Liza didn't even know Claire and Nolan had such a list, but she did remember Nolan's rambling spirit. He had been living on his sailboat when he'd arrived at Angel Island, attempting to cruise down the Eastern seaboard when a storm broke the mast and the boat capsized just offshore from the inn. They had all run out to the beach, and Daniel had rescued both Nolan and Edison from the sinking wreckage.

"I do remember," Liza said.

"Then you know that this is about as long as he's ever settled in one place. He has a pile of travel magazines and brochures on his desk, and he studies them every night. We think it's high time we choose one from the stack and buy some tickets. There are no promises in this life, dear, and at our age, every day's a gift."

Liza was stunned. This was not the way she had expected the conversation to go. "I understand," she said finally. "Why didn't you tell me this sooner? I hate to think managing the inn has been a burden for you and Nolan."

Claire sighed and looked away. "I didn't want to let you down. We promised to stay on as long as you needed. I didn't want to go back on my word and make problems for you. Especially since you live so far away and your life is so busy with the children right now."

Liza reached out and touched her hand. "That's just like you, Claire, always putting other people first. I just wish you'd said something."

"Nolan has been quietly nudging me to talk to you, at least about having some time off to travel. His feet are getting itchy again. I'd like to travel, too. I've rarely been off this island, as you know. There are so many corners of the world I'd like to see. We thought that by bringing in more help, we could take a few weeks abroad in the fall, when the busy season is over. But maybe it's not that simple," Claire added. "Kerry told me that you spoke to her last week about staying on and taking more responsibility. But it seems she can't make any commitment right now and might even be leaving us soon."

"She told me there's a family situation that may need her attention. It's really too bad. She's an excellent employee, a real find. But when you think about it, we only hired her for house-keeping and cooking. Even if she could stay, it would probably be too soon to load her up with a lot of responsibilities."

"Perhaps. But please don't underestimate her just because she was reluctant to be promoted. She's a wonderful young woman. She just doesn't realize her own worth. Nolan and I have tried to build her confidence. Which is another reason I would be sorry to see her go . . . There's something I haven't told you." Claire took a breath and squared her shoulders, and Liza braced herself for another revelation. "Kerry has been through some hard times in her young life, before she learned to cook and bake and started hotel work."

"Hard times? What do you mean by that?"

"You know that she worked in an insurance office, as a bookkeeper? She was tricked by her employer there and ended up in serious trouble. An odious man, if you ask me, who was also her boyfriend at the time. He exploited her feelings for him, her vulnerability, and persuaded her to break the law. Some sort of insurance fraud situation. I don't understand it entirely. But the bottom line is that Kerry notarized a forged signature on some documents, at this man's direction. When the authorities caught up with him, she was in trouble, too. She was sent to jail for almost two years. She made good use of the time, learning how to cook, and took more advanced courses when she was released, then found a job at a hotel in Maine before she came here."

Liza was distressed to hear about this dark chapter of Kerry's past. Kerry hardly seemed like a person who had spent time in prison. Well, whatever she imagined that sort of person to be.

"Are you sure about all this?"

Claire nodded. "I meant to tell you sooner, but I thought it was best if you got to know her a bit. If you saw how hard she works, and how talented and good-hearted she is. She's had such a rough road. I suspect there's more, in her childhood maybe, that she hasn't even told me. This job means a lot to her. *We* mean a lot to her."

It seemed from Claire's appeal she was afraid that once Liza knew about Kerry's past, she would ask her to go. But Liza could see that Kerry's light shone brighter than her history. On the other hand, when Liza thought about it in a cooler, more logical way, was it smart to trust someone who had such a blot on their record? To trust them around valuables and even her children?

"I suppose I feel bad for her, too. If she really

was used and tricked, as you say. But do you really think we can trust her now? I mean, how would we know?"

"Do you think I shouldn't have hired her? Do you want to let her go?" Claire asked.

"I'm not sure," Liza said honestly. "I do know it was naive of me to assume she was someone you could train to take on more authority. Perhaps it's best that didn't work out, after all. She thinks she might leave soon. I suppose the problem may take care of itself."

Claire didn't answer. Liza knew that look. She was hoping Kerry wouldn't leave but didn't want to say it aloud.

Liza sighed. "The point is, with you and Nolan stepping aside, I'm not sure what to do. Maybe I should hire a manager? I can call an employment agency that specializes in the hotel business and start interviewing people. You and Nolan would still live here, of course, and help out as much or as little as you choose. None at all, if you like. But maybe you could assist and train someone new first, to get things rolling?"

"Of course we would. We're not heading off for foreign lands quite so quickly. I think that's an excellent solution."

Claire seemed pleased but Liza didn't feel nearly half as satisfied with her own suggestion. "It will never be the same as you running the inn, Claire. I wonder if it would even solve the

244

problem of jumping back to the top of the list of the best inns in New England. I can't see how anyone new could maintain the character and charm Aunt Elizabeth established when she ran it with you."

"I suppose that's a risk," Claire replied. "But all change involves risk, one way or the other."

Liza's worries weren't settled by that observation either, though it certainly rang true. "What other choice do I have? I can't just sell it . . . can I?"

She thought Claire would instantly object to the idea. But her expression remained thoughtful and detached. "I think you can do anything you want, Liza. Make any choice you think is best. What do you really want? What's best for your family? Those are the questions you need to answer now, dear."

"Oh, Claire . . . what I really want is for things to never change. And I also know that's impossible."

For you and Nolan to be content running the inn while I live in Arizona, she could have said. *For this place, which is so much a part of my past and identity, to be watched over and cared for by people I love and trust.*

But Liza knew now that well had run dry and she had to come up with an entirely new plan.

Claire seemed to sense her thoughts without Liza saying another word. She leaned over and patted her hand. "It's funny how life changes. We don't even notice what seems, in hindsight, inevitable. Like a faucet dripping into a pot until suddenly it's filled to the brim and spills over. But change is the only thing we can really count on. 'To every thing there is a season,'" she added. "You'll figure this out, dear. I know you will. Nolan and I will help you in any way that we can and support any decision you come to."

Liza had to smile. "I do know one thing. I'm so fortunate to be figuring this out with you, Claire."

Anyone else would have reacted to this conversation in a million other ways—by being angry or upset, opposing her or making her feel guilty. As usual, Claire smoothed the rough edges with her insight and understanding, offering Liza her wisdom and support.

"Of course I'll help you sort this out, Liza. The inn has been my life for decades. I love it, and Nolan does, too. But your welfare and happiness certainly mean more to me than four walls and a roof. A leaky one at that," she added with a cheeky grin. "No matter how lovely this place is, you and your family come first in my heart. And always will."

Liza blinked back tears. She didn't know what to say. She put her arms around Claire and hugged her close. Claire was so much more than a friend.

It was frightening to think of all the changes

that might come if she really sold the inn. It might be just four walls and a leaky roof, but this place was the glue that held them all together. If she did really sell it, would she lose Claire and Nolan, too?

Claire seemed able to read her mind again, or at least to sense her fears. "Don't worry, Liza. We'll help you figure this out. Now ask God to help you, too. Pray for the best possible outcome for everyone. Even if you can't imagine now what that might look like. He makes a way where there is no way. I know you've heard me say that before, but it's true."

Liza nodded and wiped away a few tears that had slipped down her cheek. She wasn't nearly as spiritual and trusting a person as Claire, but she certainly hoped that was true.

CHAPTER TEN

⌒

"W e're lucky Molly is even speaking to us."
Emily had just arrived at Jessica's house.
They were going to drive back to the village to
pick up their mother next, then up to Newburyport, to the Bradford Arms Hotel.

Lillian had decided that a private room should
be booked there for Ezra's party, one large
enough just for the immediate family to enjoy
a formal sit-down dinner. Dignified waiters in
dark suits would serve them, barely uttering a
word. Emily could easily imagine the scene, even
though she didn't want to.

"Molly has a good sense of humor. She's taking
this on the chin. Though I'm waiting a few more
days to visit the bakery," Jessica confessed.
"Mother was fast on her feet, setting up this
appointment at the Bradford Arms."

Jessica wasn't quite ready to leave, and Emily
sat at the kitchen table while her sister placed
some breakfast dishes in the sink and wiped off
the counter.

"Fast turnaround, even for Mother," Emily
agreed. The confrontation with Molly had been

on Monday, and it was only Wednesday now. "She must have had this idea in her back pocket."

Jessica grinned. "Very likely. She probably even made the appointment before she visited Molly. You know how this will go, don't you?" She turned to Emily, not waiting for a reply. "It's going to be a tenth of the guests and ten times more expensive than we wanted it to be."

"And no fun at all—except for Mother," Emily added. "I hope it's a bit more cheerful there than the Plymouth Room. But I doubt it."

Jessica moved about the kitchen, putting away cereal boxes. "I think we're stuck with her choice. There isn't much time left. Every decent place will be booked by now. It's the holidays."

"I'm sure she knows that, too. She knows she's got the upper hand now. I can't even imagine the demands she's liable to make."

"I can imagine, but I'd rather not," Jessica admitted.

"Mother is like an imperious diplomat, negotiating for her little monarchy. She doesn't expect to have all her demands met," Emily reminded her sister. "She can't possibly. She just wants to raise the bar, to make sure we hustle and at least try to do her bidding."

"Well put. That is the way she operates."

"To put it another way, we'll do our best and ignore the rest. As long as Ezra is happy. That's what matters."

Jessica had taken her coat from a row of hooks near the back door and slipped her purse strap over her shoulder. "Yes, this is all for Ezra. Not for Mother. We need to remind her of that."

"How easily she forgets," Emily replied, rolling her eyes.

"Oh, for goodness' sake. You just reminded me of something."

Emily assumed it was some animal emergency. "Do you need to run out to the barn for a minute? That's okay, we have time."

Jessica shook her head and walked back to the table. "Remember how we talked about finding pictures of Ezra and making a slideshow? Darrell took a box of photographs down from Mother's attic the other day and I started looking through them this morning."

An old shoebox sat at the end of the table. Jessica slid it toward Emily and flipped open the lid. "There were several boxes like this one in the carton. It will take a while to look at them all. But right on top, I found this little book." She lifted a small book, bound in black leather, from the pile of photos in the shoebox. Emily noticed the binding looked cracked and the pages were yellowed. "It's Ezra's handwriting, unmistakably." Jessica handed the book to Emily and waited for her to open it.

Emily saw a row of names written in neat,

square printing on the left side of the page, a column down the middle with some abbreviated comments, and a column on the end with a check mark and date, and sometimes a word or two.

"What is it? A record about his patients?"

"I thought so, too. At first. Then I looked more closely at the comments." Jessica waited a moment and smiled. "It's a prayer ledger. Ezra wrote about people he knew in need of prayer, and in the last column, he recorded prayers answered and how." Jessica's smile widened, her blue eyes sparkling. "Isn't that sweet?"

Emily had to smile, too, at the idea of it. "It's more than sweet, it's very special and amazing. He's truly devoted his life to healing the world, in more ways than one." She looked back at the book, better able to decipher the notations now. "It's also scientific in a way. As if he'd been recording the results of an experiment."

"Good point. I hadn't thought of that. I did notice how many people he's prayed for. I recognized so many names. Every page is filled. I bet that's not the only one like that in the carton. I bet he filled up a pile of them."

"I bet you're right." Emily closed the book carefully and set it back in the box. She came to her feet and slipped on her coat. "That makes me feel even sadder about not holding a big party for Ezra. He took care of this town for decades as the only doctor for miles around, and when he wasn't ministering to their physical ills, he was tending to his patients' souls.'"

Jessica sighed. "I feel the same, and the same about the party now, too. But it seems there's nothing we can do."

A few moments later, they set off for the village to pick up their mother. The conversation turned to other matters on the drive over, and Emily was glad for a break from party planning.

They soon reached their mother's grand house on Providence Street, a large, rambling Victorian that stood three stories high, distinguished by its Mansard roof. The same steely gray color with black shutters and white trim for as long as Emily could remember. Her mother could never entertain the idea of any other combination.

Emily pulled up the long driveway. "Here we are. Right on time. Though I'm sure Mother will make some remark about us running late."

"She purposely sets her clocks a few minutes fast so that *everyone* is late," Jessica said with a grin. She turned to Emily with a more serious expression. "Do you really think Ezra will enjoy the stuffy, formal party she's planning?"

Emily sighed. "I don't think it would be his first choice. But you know Ezra—he's pleased with any gift at all. And any gesture of affection or appreciation. I think, deep down, he'll know it's Mother's idea of a wonderful tribute. Even if it isn't exactly our idea of one."

Jessica considered her words as they got out of the car. "I guess you're right. Ezra is easy to please, and he does understand Mother. It will make him happy just to see her proud and pleased to give him a party that meets her lofty standards."

"Which is another example of how much he loves her. Though I've never been able to understand why." Emily's confounded expression made Jessica laugh.

"Me neither," her sister whispered back.

There was no way to avoid Gabriel. He was working inside the house now, painting the bedrooms and bathrooms upstairs. Ever since she had spent the afternoon with him on Sunday, Kerry couldn't even pretend that she wanted to avoid him.

She enjoyed his surprise visits to the kitchen during the day, seeking an extra cup of coffee or in search of some supplies in the basement. She knew he was actually seeking her company, and while the commonsense voice in her head insisted nothing could come of it, another, uncommon-sense side was drawn to him, like a moth to a flame. His charm and warmth had worn down her willpower. She could no longer keep him at a distance, even if she wanted to.

On Wednesday morning, Kerry had just put up a pot of potato-leek soup when Claire came into the kitchen, dressed for the cold in her puffy down coat, thick gloves, and short leather boots with laces. "Nolan is back with the pine roping and wreaths. Can you come outside and help us decorate the porch, Kerry?"

Kerry wiped her hands on a kitchen towel. "Sure. I'd love to."

The inn was being dressed for the holidays, like an elegant, aristocratic woman attended by her maids in a former day, Kerry thought. Gabriel had been assigned to bring down boxes and containers from the attic, each labeled with the contents within—special ornaments and decorations not only for the tree but for each room, every fireplace mantel, mirror, and possible area of the inn that could be decorated. Kerry wasn't sure how Liza and Claire kept track of it all, even with the labels.

She already knew they were starting outside today. It was all hands on deck, and she was glad to get out of the kitchen for a while. And, if she had to admit it only to herself, for the chance to spend more time with Gabriel.

Out on the porch, she found a pile of Christmas wreaths on a table. Although they weren't big, there were a lot of them, and two large ones were set to one side. The wreaths were bare, but she guessed Claire would stick bows on them or do something to dress them up.

Gabriel was on the far end of the porch, already

up on a ladder. With a hammer in hand, he tapped at small nails as he secured swoops of pine along the edge of the porch roof.

Nolan stood by as his assistant. "Here's another nail for you. Hold on. This stuff has gotten all tangled."

Gabriel turned on his perch and caught sight of her. "Another elf has arrived to help. A cute one, too. But she looks like the mischievous kind."

Kerry felt herself blush. She hoped Nolan hadn't heard Gabriel's greeting. Claire was coming up the steps with a basket of greenery hooked over one arm. Kerry thought she had heard, judging from the smile in her eyes.

"Let's decorate these wreaths. I have sprigs of holly and pine cones. Some bits of white branches might look nice, mixed in. And I found a spool of red ribbon for bows."

Kerry set to work, fitting the holly twigs into one of the pine circles. The red bows would complement the bright berries. "There are so many wreaths. Where will they all go?"

"We hang them in the windows, with wire. It's a little tricky to get them straight, but it looks lovely when it's done. The large ones will go on the front door and the barn."

Kerry sifted through the basket as she finished the first wreath. Claire's selections looked very natural, not like the gaudy trim on most wreaths for sale this time of year.

It didn't take very long to decorate the wreaths, but hanging one in each window took more time. She and Claire managed the first two. Then Gabriel came over to help them.

Without asking her to stand aside, he came up behind Kerry and reached around her as she struggled to hammer a small nail above the window frame.

"Here, let me," he said, his mouth so close to her face she could feel his warm breath. When she turned toward him, their faces were barely an inch apart.

She stepped aside, feeling breathless. Luckily, Nolan and Claire had gone inside to find more wire. She walked to the railing, a safe distance away, and watched him work.

"It's not even with the others. I think it needs to hang more to the right."

He peered at her over his shoulder. "Are you sure? It's a pain to hammer in these little nails. I've smashed my fingers to bits this morning."

Had he really? Or was he just vying for sympathy? "I thought you were better at your job than that. Aren't smashed fingers very amateur?"

"Very funny. I think you need to be sure before you make me hang this one again. You're standing much too close. Go stand in front of the door, then see what you think."

Kerry wondered why that spot on the porch was his idea of a good vantage point. It didn't make sense, but she did as he asked. Then studied the window again. "Sorry, it's still in the wrong spot."

He winced, seeming annoyed at her insistence. "Let me see for myself."

He put the hammer down and strode toward her. Then he put his hands on her shoulders and moved her a few steps back.

"Stand right here and tell me, is it still hanging funny?"

She nodded and he sighed. "You might be right . . . but I just noticed something else."

Before she could object, he took hold of her shoulders, dipped his head, and kissed her, a soft searching kiss on her mouth that warmed her down to her toes.

She felt herself melt toward him for a moment, then pulled back and started to object. "Gabriel—"

He shrugged. And pointed above. "Mistletoe. That's allowed. I've heard it's bad luck if you don't kiss someone."

"I've never heard that." She glanced at the offending greenery, then back at his handsome, teasing expression. "And that's not even mistletoe. It's a sprig of holly." She stood back, her arms crossed over her chest. "Very funny."

He shrugged. "I guess I need a lesson in holiday greenery. You could help me brush up."

Claire came outside through the front door. "We found more wire and some twine. This should be enough for the rest."

"Great. Let's get back to work. Kerry?" Gabriel said, as if it had been her idea to goof off.

"Yes, let's hop to it now," Claire said. "We have a lot to do out here before the bakers arrive. I hope we have time to set up, so everyone can go right to work."

On Sunday afternoon when Claire had returned from church, she had told Kerry that the baking team would meet today at the inn to make macaroons and asked Kerry if she would be available to direct them. *As if there is anything more important on my calendar,* Kerry had thought at the time.

She had worked out the amounts of ingredients needed to make all the cookies the group had planned, and Claire bought the supplies on Tuesday.

"Everything's ready," Kerry told her. "All the mixing bowls and spoons are out, and I lined all the baking sheets with parchment paper. I even made some extra copies of the recipe, so the bakers can work in teams again."

She hoped Jane would be her partner again. If it didn't work out that way, she'd be disappointed, so much so it might be hard to hide it. But it would be a gift just to be with her again, she reminded herself, even in a large group of busy, chatty women. If that was all she was given today, she'd take it.

Claire seemed pleased. "Splendid. We'll get

right to work when they come. The fair is on Saturday. We're cutting it close this year, but many hands make light work, and quick work, too."

Kerry smiled but didn't reply. Not too quick, she hoped. The minutes moved so slowly while she waited for Jane to come today, but she hoped time would slow down this afternoon. Precious minutes instead of years, that's all she would have with her daughter. But she counted herself lucky to steal even that much.

"Here's another wreath to hang, Gabriel," Claire called out to their helper, who was moving the ladder. "By the way, that one on the left is off center. Could you fix it first, please?"

"I thought so, too, Claire. But Kerry said it looked fine."

Kerry was speechless. That was the wreath she'd told him to move! She felt like whacking him with a pine branch but restrained herself. She also felt laughter bubbling up, and even more, recalling how he'd tricked her into giving him a kiss.

Talk about mischievous elves.

It was finally time for the Christmas Fair volunteers to arrive. Kerry changed from the sweater and jeans she'd worn that morning. She wanted to wear something nicer than work clothes to see Jane, but nothing so dressy it would look silly for baking.

She finally chose a long denim skirt with a dark blue tailored blouse on top and short boots. The skirt was so long that she didn't need tights, and she was glad of that. She couldn't find a pair anywhere and felt so jumpy, it was like getting ready for a first date.

It was a bit like a date, she thought, but not the first. *Possibly the last,* she realized, a bittersweet feeling sweeping over her. She just wanted to leave Jane with a good impression, some idea of who she was. *So if she ever thinks of the woman who taught her how to break an egg with one hand, or bake macaroons, she'll have a fond feeling. Is that too much to ask?*

Kerry wasn't sure who she was asking. God, maybe? Was she finally able to pray again, after all the years when she'd pushed back any stirring of faith? Just to spite her father. She had realized that long ago, but still could not summon up whatever it took to talk to God again.

I guess we're back on speaking terms, she thought, feeling surprised. *Claire would probably say it's never too late, and You've been waiting for me to check in. I don't know if it will help,* she admitted honestly. *I don't know that I have any right to ask You favors. I'm just thankful to have a little more time with my daughter today. Even if she'll never know how much I love her.*

Down in the kitchen, she tied on an apron and turned on the ovens, so they would be heated to the proper temperatures for the recipes. She fussed over the ingredients, rearranging spices, measuring cups, and mixing bowls.

Claire walked in and smiled. "Don't you look nice. Almost too pretty for kitchen work."

"I had some pine tar on my jeans, so I thought I'd change."

"Are you nervous?" Claire asked. "Anybody would be."

Kerry didn't know what to say. Had Claire guessed? Did she suspect something? "Nervous? How do you mean?"

"To be teaching the group the recipe. I'm afraid I volunteered you without asking first. I know you're a private person, Kerry. I didn't mean to put you on the spot."

Kerry knew she really meant "shy." She sighed with relief. "I don't mind giving a few baking instructions. It's different than having to make conversation. Do you know what I mean?"

"I do." Claire smiled. "It's something you know so well, it's your domain, so self-consciousness drops away. The kitchen is all yours today. I know you'll do a great job."

Kerry had been so focused on Jane, she hadn't worried about instructing the other women. But it was just as well that Claire thought that was the reason she seemed nervous.

A few minutes later the women arrived and were bustling around the kitchen, finding partners and space at the table to work. Kerry moved about the kitchen, greeting everyone and making sure they had a bowl, a spatula, and cookie sheets.

As much as she wanted to partner with Jane, she waited to see if her daughter would prefer to work with someone else today—Emily, perhaps? Or her Aunt Jessica? But Jane quickly came to the head of the table, where Kerry had set up her own place. "Reporting for duty," she said, brightly. "I've been practicing my egg cracking, too. Want to watch me?"

Kerry couldn't help smiling. "I'd love to. Maybe later—there aren't any eggs in this recipe."

Even Jane's disappointment at the news was charming. "Rats. I was psyched."

"You can mix the ingredients while I help the others." Kerry stepped aside so Jane could be the main cook on their team.

Jane looked pleased by the promotion. "Great. But if I'm messing anything up, just let me know."

Kerry touched her arm. "You'll be fine. If Max can do it, you can."

Her encouraging comment made Jane laugh. But at the far end of the table, Claire's partner today was Max. He wore a small apron that Claire had found in the linen closet, and knelt on a chair in order to reach the bowl and spoon. He looked very serious as he glanced at Kerry then up at his Aunty Claire.

"Thank you for leading us in the final project for the bake sale, Kerry," Emily said. "I guess we can get started if everyone's ready? Isn't Liza going to join us?"

"Something's come up," Claire said. "She needs to be in her office. She said to start without her."

Kerry wondered about that. This morning at breakfast Liza seemed sure she would be baking. Kerry suspected the emergency had to do with the future of the inn. But she couldn't think about all that now.

"If everyone's ready, I'll get started," Kerry began. "I left a few index cards out on the table with the recipe, if you want to see it written out. It's really so simple, even Max will have no trouble.

"The bowls are large enough to hold a double recipe, which should make about sixty to seventy small macaroons of the size you'd want for gift bags," Kerry went on.

As Kerry explained, Jane demonstrated how to mix the three ingredients and drop the batter on the lined pans.

"—This part is tricky. Usually, I'd just use a teaspoon measure for each and dip the spoon in warm water to keep the batter from sticking. But we want these to look professional, so I'm going

263

to ask you to try piping them from those small plastic bags I've prepared."

Kerry held up one of the sandwich bags she'd left at each spot. One corner had been snipped off for an opening. Next, she showed the women how much to fill the bag and how to squeeze out the batter so it made a spiral pattern.

Jane seemed uncertain, doing it on her own. She filled the bag but made a face. "It's sticking all over the plastic. I've messed up all this batter, Kerry."

Kerry calmly shook her head. "No, you haven't. Just push it down, like toothpaste. But don't let it come out of the opening yet."

She showed her how for a minute and let her do the rest. Jane's expression quickly brightened. Vera had the same problem, but Sophie Potter showed her how to fix it.

"This is the way to pipe it out. Point it down, squeeze, and give a quick twist of the wrist." Kerry executed a perfect spiral macaroon, then felt surprised when the women let out a unified sigh of admiration.

"Nicely done. You make it look easy, Kerry," Vera said. "I think it might take time to get the hang of that technique."

"This is a very forgiving batter," she assured them. "The cookies will still taste great, even if every one isn't perfectly shaped."

The women set about their work in earnest,

taking turns squeezing out the batter, which was certainly the hardest part. There were soon several sheets of macaroons in the oven, baking with a sweet, tantalizing scent. And even more were lining up, waiting their turn.

Emily had been helping Jessica, mostly looking on, Kerry noticed. She claimed she didn't want to jinx Jessica's bowl by even touching it. As the macaroons came out of the oven and cooled, Emily took the trays into the dining room, where she had set up an assembly line for packing bags and decorating them.

Jane removed the pans of cookies she and Kerry had made. She carefully set them on the cooling racks and turned to Kerry, looking proud. "They look so good. I wish I could eat one right now."

"They're much too hot. But we'll definitely find a few crumbly ones to taste test." She winked at Jane, and her daughter laughed.

Jane put three more pans in the oven and set the timer again. "I think these will cook a little faster," Kerry warned her. "The oven is even hotter now."

"Right." Jane nodded and reset the timer, cutting off a few minutes from the alarm. "Would it be hard to dip them in some melted chocolate? I saw that in a magazine. It looked yummy."

"Good idea. It's not hard at all. I have some bittersweet chocolate in the pantry that we can use. Why don't you ask your mom what she thinks?" Kerry added, remembering that Emily was in charge.

"Thinks about what?" Emily had just come back into the kitchen for more macaroons and stood right behind them. Kerry wasn't sure how long Emily had been standing there. Kerry had been feeling so cheerful and relaxed in Jane's company. Now she suddenly felt stiff and self-conscious.

She glanced at Emily, then pretended to check the oven. *I just feel guilty about "stealing" her daughter. My daughter, really, and not even stealing her.*

Just a little more time, please? she wanted to say. *You'll have her forever.*

The buzzer went off. Jane jumped with surprise. "I'll check. I smell something bad. I hope I didn't burn that batch."

Kerry saw her grab a dish towel and peer into the hot oven. A puff of smoke drifted out, stinging Kerry's eyes. Jane looked distressed. "Oh, no . . . did I burn them?"

Kerry didn't think so. Some crumbs had fallen to the bottom of the oven, that was all. But before she could reassure Jane, she saw her grab for the hot cookie sheet with just the thin towel covering her hands.

"Jane, wait. Let me get it with the hot mitts—"

It was too late. Jane tugged at the edge of the cookie sheet and a split second later pulled

266

back in pain. But by then, the cookie sheet was off balance and suddenly flying through the air, aimed right for Jane's leg. Kerry pushed her aside and tried to catch it before it hit the oven door. The mitts protected her hands, but the hot pan landed right on her leg and for a moment stuck to her denim skirt.

She muffled a groan as she pushed it off. It clattered to the floor, along with a few dozen cookies. She slammed the oven shut and gripped the top of her leg. It hurt so much.

All around her, chaos erupted in the kitchen. Everyone ran to her aid. Quick-thinking Claire was already at the sink, wetting down a clean cloth with cold water.

Emily, who was standing closest, was the first to grab her arm and help her to a chair. "Kerry, you poor thing. You must be in agony."

Kerry couldn't answer. She felt tears well up in her eyes but didn't want to cry. Jane stared at Kerry over Emily's shoulder. She was crying, and it hurt Kerry's heart to see her tears fall.

"I'm so sorry, Kerry. It's my fault. I was such a stupid idiot—"

"No, don't say that." Kerry took a deep breath. "It wasn't your fault at all, Jane."

Emily's gaze was troubled. Kerry knew she'd noticed how Kerry had pushed Jane aside and taken the hot pan on her own leg, rather than let Jane be injured.

Before Emily could speak, Claire stepped forward with an icy compress. "This should help for starters. I'll just lift your skirt a bit so I can get at the spot."

Claire carefully folded the denim over Kerry's knee, exposing the burn on her thigh. Kerry winced and closed her eyes. The fabric had almost stuck to her skin. The burn was a triangle shape, not very large but bright red, as if she had been branded by the hot metal. It had struck just above the birthmark, purplish in color and almost heart-shaped, at the top of her knee. Kerry had been embarrassed by the mark when she was younger but hardly noticed it now.

Claire covered the burn with the cold, wet towel. "Hold that on the spot. I'll get some aloe."

"Aloe would be good," Emily agreed quietly. She stared at Kerry's leg, then back up at her face. Her skin had gone ash white. Kerry wondered if she was the type who got light-headed at the sight of blood or injuries, though Kerry would have guessed she was just the opposite.

Then she realized. Emily had seen the birthmark. She knew. Kerry's mother had been born with the same mark, in the exact same spot. Jane had it, too, Kerry remembered.

Emily stood up and took a deep breath. "Do you need anything? Maybe some ibuprofen?"

Kerry couldn't even look at her. What was she thinking? Was she going to tell Jane? Tell everyone? Kerry wanted to run from the kitchen and hide in her room, but a quick escape was impossible.

"Claire keeps some in the cupboard next to the sink," Vera said.

Vera, Sophie, and Jessica hovered around her, concerned and sympathetic. Jessica brought a fresh ice pack and a footstool, then helped Kerry put her leg up.

Sophie rubbed her shoulder. "Poor thing. Maybe we should take you to Dr. Harding."

Their kindness and care were almost overwhelming and made her feel even more guilty about the way she was deceiving them. All of them, including Jane. She heard the kitchen buzzer sound again. "Don't worry about me. The macaroons need you right now."

Vera and Sophie grabbed hot mitts and headed back to the oven. Only Jane remained. She sat next to Kerry and took her hand. "I know you don't think it was my fault, but I was such a clumsy idiot. I'm so sorry you got hurt because of me, Kerry."

Kerry felt her heart break. She squeezed Jane's hand. "Don't say that, Jane. It wasn't your fault . . . and I think you're absolutely perfect."

Emily returned with the pain pills and a glass of water, and Kerry quickly let go of Jane's hand. She didn't dare meet Emily's gaze. She took the water, swallowed back the tablets, and swung her leg down from the stool. Maybe she should speak to Emily privately, right here and now, and let her know she posed no threat. But Emily had drifted into the dining room with Jane, where the group was packing cookies.

Claire appeared with a bottle of aloe. "This does wonders for burns. Let me help you get upstairs and we'll patch you up. I think you should lie down awhile and let the ice and aloe go to work."

Kerry nodded, not wanting to cause any more bother. She came to her feet and held her skirt away from the wound. The ice had numbed the pain and she felt a lot better.

"I'll be fine. I think you're needed down here. The show must go on." She tried to hit a light note and almost managed.

Claire looked reluctant to let her leave alone. "All right. Take your time on the stairs. I'll check on you in a little while."

Kerry headed to the foyer at a slow, hobbling pace, relieved to be out of the spotlight. She climbed the steps slowly, as Claire had advised, and recalled how her daughter had taken hold of her hand. She didn't feel the stinging burn at all.

CHAPTER ELEVEN

When Liza emerged from her office at five, the bakers were gone. The only evidence of their visit was the sweet scent of toasted macaroons that perfumed the air and the piles of cookies on trays in the dining room, waiting to be packed.

Before she could comment on the sight, Claire said, "I still have some baking to do, and we didn't get to pack all the cookies. I hope you don't mind. Kerry had an accident and we lost some time. Everyone had to leave by five."

"An accident? Is she all right?"

Claire quickly told her how Kerry had been burned when Jane Forbes had dropped a hot cookie sheet. "Kerry jumped in the way, so Jane wouldn't be burned. I didn't want Jane to feel any worse than she did already, so I didn't say anything at the time. But it was a very brave thing to do, so selfless to protect the girl like that."

"Yes, it was," Liza agreed. "How is Kerry doing? Does she need to see a doctor?"

"She's resting now. I checked on her a little

while ago, and she was sleeping. Maybe she'll come down for dinner."

"I hope so," Liza said. "If she's not up to it, I'll stop by her room. I'm sorry I wasn't able to help."

Liza could tell Claire wondered what had possibly kept her from at least peeking out the door during the commotion. "I did hear some-thing going on out here. But I was in the middle of a meeting on my laptop. I couldn't step away. An important meeting," she added.

"About the inn, I assume," Claire said evenly.

"Yes, it was about the inn." Liza knew she had to tell Claire and Nolan very soon about the meeting. There would be no better time to deliver this news, because it wasn't good news at all.

"I was meeting with executives of the Colonial Inns of New England. They own and manage a group of top inns and small hotels in New England. They've contacted me many times over the years to see if I'd ever sell this place."

Claire's expression was thoughtful. Liza was surprised to see she was not upset. "Are they interested?"

"Yes," she replied. "Very. They wanted to visit tomorrow, but I put them off until Friday."

Claire looked surprised now. "That's only two days from now. It doesn't give us much time."

"None at all. But we have been cleaning and making repairs. I'm sure they don't expect the place to look perfect, especially since I'm willing to let it go." It was hard to say the last phrase aloud. Claire's gaze searched her own and Liza knew what she was thinking. "I'm not sure if I really am, yet," she said honestly. "This could be a very long process. They may visit dozens of times, and there will be meetings and negotiations. I might not sell it to them at all. But they asked to visit, so I said it was all right."

"I think it's a good first step. No reason to delay. We'll work all day tomorrow to brighten things up. I wish we had longer but we'll all do our best."

Liza felt relieved. She had dreaded telling Claire about the solution she was considering. But Claire's reaction gave her courage. Selling the inn seemed unthinkable. How could she ever let go of this place? But the more Liza considered the idea, the more it made sense and seemed the best decision for everyone.

Kerry was lying on her bed with an ice pack on her leg, exhausted but not asleep. She had heard the voices of the baking committee in the front hall and the sounds of their cars pulling away from the inn. Soon after, Gabriel knocked on her door. He quietly called her name and waited for her to answer. She wanted to but was afraid he'd see she was upset about something more than a small kitchen burn and she would be tempted to

273

tell him the whole story. She knew she couldn't do that. She held her breath and stayed very still. A few moments later, she heard him walking away.

She must have dozed off after that, because Claire's soft voice at her door woke her. Kerry knew Claire would worry if she didn't answer and quickly rose and let her in.

"I brought you a fresh ice pack. Is it helping any?"

"It's helped a lot. The aloe helped, too."

Claire didn't look convinced. "Are you sure? Maybe Dr. Harding should take a look tomorrow. You don't quite seem yourself, dear."

Claire's clear blue eyes and kind expression seemed to draw Kerry's confidence up from the depths of her soul. Like bubbles rising in a pot of boiling water. If there was one person in the world who might understand and not judge, it had to be Claire.

But could Claire understand when she'd been tricked, too? Kerry had lied to Claire about the reason she had come to Cape Light and the reason she wanted a job here at the inn. She had paid back everyone who had been kind to her with lies. That was another reason she had to go.

"Maybe I just need a good night's sleep. It's been a busy day," Kerry said, hoping the generic reason would satisfy Claire's concern.

"Perhaps." Claire didn't seem entirely convinced. "Dinner will be on the table in half an hour. Would you like to eat up here? I can make a tray."

The idea of continued solitude was tempting, but Kerry thought it best to join the family. "Oh, no need for that. I'll be down in a few minutes."

Claire looked pleased to hear that. When she left, Kerry sat on the window seat and stared out at the dark sky and the ribbon of blue water at the horizon. The sun had just set and fading light tinged the clouds purple and lavender. Such beautiful sunsets here. Kerry knew she would miss that, too.

She didn't know what to do. She had never wanted her true identity known, and certainly not revealed this way. But God moves in mysterious ways. She'd often heard that said.

This is His way of telling me I've gone too far and I must go before anything worse happens. Will Emily tell Jane who I am? Some instinct told her, *No.*

But I must talk to Emily. It's only right. I have to let her know I mean no harm to anyone, and Jane never needs to know who I really am.

Kerry was shocked to hear that the inn might be sold and that potential buyers would be visiting on Friday. She never thought Liza would consider such a thing.

But when Liza told her at the dinner table,

she did her best to hide her surprise. She could see that Claire and Nolan had already heard and seemed to accept the news calmly, and even with a positive attitude. She tried to do the same.

"The Colonial Inn Group is a very reputable organization. I checked them out on the Internet, right after Claire told me," Nolan said. "Family run. They'll make some updates, but they'll leave the character of the place intact. Not like some big hotel chain that's liable to wipe away all the personality and years of history."

Kerry knew Nolan was trying to be supportive, but she noticed Liza wince, then, finally, force a smile. "I did some digging on the Internet today, too. I think they will preserve the inn's character. That's one of the reasons I considered talking to them. And it's just talk right now," she reassured everyone. "Far from settled."

"These things take time. Like we say in baseball, 'It ain't over till it's over,' " Nolan replied.

"Absolutely," Liza agreed. "We have a lot to do tomorrow. The executive committee will be here at ten on Friday. That doesn't leave much time."

Liza seemed nervous, and with good reason, Kerry thought.

"Don't worry. We'll be ready," Claire promised.

"Absolutely," Kerry added. "We have a solid team."

"Thanks. I know we do." Liza cast a grateful look her way. Kerry did feel a binding spirit with everyone at the table, more than any place she had ever worked before. But the inn was very different from any place she'd ever worked or lived. It was too bad that she had to leave soon.

True to their promises, Liza's team had the inn ready for a full inspection on Friday morning. Every shiny surface was polished, every fingerprint wiped clean. The guest rooms each looked ready for a travel magazine exploring the finest inns of New England.

When Kerry came down to the kitchen at half past seven, it seemed as if no one had dared to eat breakfast, lest a toast crumb drop onto the floor or an empty coffee mug appear in the sink.

Except for the children, who were just finishing bowls of cereal. Liza spooned a final bite into Charlotte's mouth, and Claire whisked away the bowl. Max had already finished his. Nolan cleared his place and wiped off the table and Max's chair.

"Edison, you missed a piece. Right there." Nolan directed the dog to a stray Cheerio that quickly disappeared. "Any on Charlotte's side? I'll send him over."

"I'm not sure. Let him check," Liza replied. "Do you think the prospective buyers need to know we use a fur-covered vacuum in here?"

"He's not included in the deal. No matter how much they offer." Nolan sounded so serious,

Kerry had to smile. She stepped over to the sink and got to work, drying a pot that sat on the drainboard.

"Thank you, dear. But have some coffee and a bit of something for breakfast. They won't be here for at least two hours. Liza wanted the children dressed and fed early. Audrey is going to watch them today. Liza needs to give her full attention to the guests."

The inspection committee, Claire really meant. With all Liza had found in disrepair over the last few weeks, today's visit had to be unnerving for her. Kerry hoped there wouldn't be any surprises.

"She will need to focus. I was going to offer to babysit, but it's probably best if the children are out. I can take care of the guests when they check in," she offered.

In addition to the executive group, at least six guests would arrive in the late afternoon. Not a full house, Claire had noted last night, but enough to make the place look busy.

"That would be a help. Liza wants me to stay with her, most of the time, to answer questions."

Liza had already told the people at Colonial Inns that Claire and Nolan were part of the deal if they wanted to stay on. There would be no sale otherwise. It was important that the visitors had time with the older couple, too.

But Kerry knew that she was not important. Her job could be filled easily, and she had already told Liza it was unlikely she would stay long.

"How else can I help? Is there something more I can do before they come? Would you like me to take care of my usual jobs today or leave the inn for a while, too?"

Claire's eyes suddenly widened with alarm, and she pressed a hand to her cheek. "Thank goodness you asked. I almost forgot . . . When we were cleaning up yesterday, I put the boxes of cookies in my car, but I never brought them over to the church."

"I can do it. I'll take them over right away."

"Would you, dear? That would be a big help. The church will be swarming with volunteers, and you know how chatty my friends are. Once I go in, I'll never come out."

Kerry had to agree. Claire would get stuck there, socializing. And talking about the latest development at the inn. Kerry wondered how many people had heard by now that the inn might be sold. Liza had asked them to keep it confidential, but news had a way of traveling in a small town like Cape Light. Especially news like this.

She wasn't sure what Gabriel thought of the situation. He had stopped by yesterday, to help with the last-minute cleanup. But they hadn't had any time to talk privately. Which was just as well, she thought now. For a moment or two, she had allowed herself the pleasant fantasy of

279

a real relationship with him, but these sudden changes outlined the truth very clearly. Her days here were running out. She could almost hear a ticking sound, like a wind-up kitchen timer. Very soon, the buzzer would sound.

As Kerry pulled away from the inn, she noticed a caravan of three large SUVs arrive. The inspection committee, she had no doubt. She was glad that she wasn't there to welcome them, though her heart went out to Liza, who had put on such a brave face. Kerry knew that deep inside, she had to be torn in two.

The church parking lot was busy, with cars pulling in and out and people carrying cartons and decorations into the church. Kerry double-parked near the back door. She didn't plan on staying long. She searched the parking lot for Emily Warwick's car. Relief swept through her when she didn't see it. She had expected that Emily would be here, watching over the preparations. But maybe she was coming later, or had left for some reason?

Don't wonder why, just take your chance while the coast is clear. Kerry jumped out of the car and grabbed the boxes of bagged cookies.

I do want to speak to her about Jane, Kerry thought as she walked toward the church. *But I'm not ready yet. It might even be better to write her a letter. I can say what I really want to say.*

280

No more, no less. There's no chance of losing my nerve or of the words getting all jumbled up. That's what I'll do. I'll send her a letter. I'm sure she'll understand.

The church was filled with congregation members, upstairs and downstairs, each intent on a different job. They were setting up tables in the Fellowship Hall and all down the corridors, into the area in front of the sanctuary.

She recognized Vera coming toward her, her face just visible behind a pile of boxes. "I have the rest of the macaroons and some gingerbread people Claire made," Kerry told her.

"That's swell, dear. Just follow me. Jessica and Sophie are decorating our table."

"I will, thanks." Kerry headed out to Fellowship Hall. At least Vera hadn't asked her about the inn. It would have taken a long time to extricate herself from that conversation.

Jessica, Sophie, and Jessica's husband, Sam, were decorating the bake sale area to look like a gingerbread cottage. There was a stage-set type of frame, made of plywood, propped up against the table and painted to look like the front of a cottage, trimmed with white icing, gumdrops, and candy canes.

Kerry stared at it in wonder. "Wow. That's amazing."

Sam bowed his head and smiled. "It's not great art, but it does send the right message . . ."

" 'Got milk?' We've got cookies to go with it." Sophie smiled at her joke. "And reindeer cupcakes, come to think of it."

"And a ton of macaroons. Here are the rest of the bags and Claire's gingerbread."

Jessica took the box and set it on the floor by a side table. "Thank you, Kerry. How's your leg?"

So much had happened in the past few days, Kerry had forgotten about the burn. "Much better. It looked a lot worse than it was."

"That's good to hear." Kerry turned to face Emily, who was standing behind them. She must have walked over from the opposite side of the hall. It looked as if she had just arrived; she was still wearing a long down coat, a plaid scarf slung around her neck.

Kerry felt her heartbeat quicken. She wasn't sure what to do or say. "I have a few more boxes in the car. I'd better get them—I'm double-parked."

She knew her exit was abrupt. She hadn't even paused to greet Emily. But all she could think of was putting distance between herself and Jane's adoptive mother.

She was already heading for the hall's exit when she heard Emily say, "I'll help you, Kerry."

Kerry glanced at Emily over her shoulder. How could she refuse?

In a few quick strides Emily caught up to her,

and they walked side by side to the glass doors that led to the parking lot.

Kerry stared straight ahead. *I won't say anything. Maybe she'll lose her nerve and won't ask me any questions.*

Claire's Jeep was parked near the door. Kerry walked over and lifted the hatch. She could feel Emily watching her, standing very close now.

"There are just a few boxes left. I could have handled it. But thanks."

Emily didn't reply. Kerry glanced at her, and Emily said, "You're Jane's mother, aren't you? I saw the birthmark on your leg, when you were burned. Jane has the same one, in the same place, too." Her voice was low and even. As if they were having a normal conversation about the weather or some other mundane subject. Though there was nothing mundane about it, Kerry thought. It was one of the most important conversations of her life.

Kerry couldn't meet her gaze. She could barely answer. "I know . . . my mother had one, too."

"That's why you came to Cape Light, to find Jane. Am I right?"

"Yes, that's true." Kerry felt relieved to admit it. "I knew that you and your husband had adopted her. I read it in the newspaper. I knew that you were the mayor here back then and probably a good person. But I wanted to see for myself, to make sure Jane was happy and well taken care of. That she had a home in a loving family," she quickly added.

"Dan and I would do anything for Jane. We couldn't love her more," Emily said.

"I can see that. You're a wonderful mother. Jane thinks the world of you." It pained her to admit it, but she knew that was true. "You have a wonderful bond with her, and I'd never want to take that away. I've hurt her enough. I did the unthinkable, abandoning her at this church. I loved my baby very much. I didn't really want to give her up. And I've lived to regret it every day. After what I did, I have no right to ask her to accept me. I didn't come here for that. I hope you believe me."

Emily met her gaze and held it. Kerry wished she would say something. She had no idea what Emily was thinking. She expected her to be defensive. To doubt her claims of not wanting to hurt Jane.

But her expression softened, and Kerry saw only sympathy in her eyes. "I believe that you didn't want to give her up and that you do regret that decision. And even that you came here with good intentions, as you say. But I've watched you and Jane together. You must feel differently now that you've gotten to know her, even for such a short time. You must have some urge to tell her who you really are."

Kerry couldn't deny it. "Sometimes I do. It's

284

very tempting. She's so sweet and kind," she said, remembering how Jane had taken her hand to comfort her. Kerry took a steadying breath. "But I won't tell her. I promise you . . . Has she ever asked about me?"

Perhaps it wasn't even right to ask that question, but she couldn't help it. Would Emily even admit it if Jane had asked?

It took Emily a moment to answer. Kerry could see the question was hard for her. "Only once, a few years ago. She doesn't seem ready to talk about the issue yet." She watched Kerry's reaction. "I know that must make you feel bad. I'm sorry, but it's true. She doesn't seem ready to talk about her birth mother. I'm sure someday she will be. But now doesn't seem to be the right time, Kerry. I don't think so anyway."

Kerry felt her eyes fill with tears, but she didn't want Emily to see her cry. Despite all her claims of not wanting to crash into Jane's life, some small part of her had still hoped Jane had been curious about her and wanted to find her, too. Learning that she wasn't hit her harder than Kerry had expected.

"What will you do now? Will you stay here?" Emily asked the question in a casual tone, though Kerry knew she had to be worried about her answer.

"That was never my plan. I can see that it's better if I go. I'll stay until Christmas. Liza and

Claire need my help until then. I'll probably go back to Maine. I have a few friends there and can find a job easily. Can I keep in touch with you, in case Jane ever wants to find me?"

Emily reached out and touched her hand. "I want you to. I'll let you know what's going on with Jane from time to time. And of course I'll let you know if she ever decides to look for you. We won't have to look far."

Kerry was touched by her promise. Some people would have never been able to talk all this out so calmly, without recrimination and threats. It made her see once again that her daughter was fortunate to have been delivered into Emily's care.

"Thank you. That means a lot to me."

Emily shook her head. "No need to thank me, Kerry. I understand what you're going through . . . more than you think. I know that we both love Jane and only want what's best for her."

It was hard to speak. Kerry could only nod her agreement. Emily was not her adversary, she realized. Their connection was the opposite, a silken thread, invisible and gossamer thin, binding them together for the rest of their days in their mutual love for Jane.

When Kerry returned to the inn, she found plenty to keep her occupied while Claire and Liza guided the group of executives from the attic to the cellar and beyond—all the outbuildings, the gardens, and the beach. Kerry spotted the group from various windows as she worked. With Liza and Claire in the lead, they moved from one place to the next, like a herd of sheep in down jackets and mufflers.

She prepared for the incoming guests, setting out coffee, tea, and homemade cookies as an afternoon offering. She checked them in, took care of special requests, and answered all their questions. Only one couple asked for dinner, and they wanted to eat on the early side.

Kerry spent the rest of the afternoon preparing their meal and also a meal for the family. Liza and Claire had taken the caravan of executives on a tour of the island. There wasn't much to see besides a small village center with a general store that was also a post office, a tea shop, and an emergency medical clinic that was manned by volunteers. There was a quaint cobblestone square with a fountain that had a lovely view, she recalled. Visitors loved to pose for photos there.

The rest of the island was fairly empty, except for old houses like the inn that dotted the land-scape and clusters of fishing shacks clinging to the cliffs here and there. Claire had told her there were many laws that preserved open spaces and kept eyesores of mini-mansions and condo developments from popping up everywhere.

287

The only substantial change on the island had been to the waterfront on the northern shore. About seven years ago a high-speed ferry began to run between Newburyport and a dock on the shore that was largely deserted. The waterfront around the ferry landing had been renovated, with a boardwalk full of shops and cafés and other conveniences for beachgoers.

"Your prospective buyers will want to see that," Claire had reminded Liza the night before.

Liza had agreed. "It's not much, but at least they'll see that Angel Island is trying to enter the twentieth century."

"Twentieth? Did you forget that we're in the twenty-first, my dear?" Nolan asked with a laugh.

"I didn't forget. We're not moving along that fast."

Everyone laughed, agreeing. But Kerry thought that made the inn even more valuable. Something about the inn and even the island remained untouched by time. How rare was that?

Though Kerry was curious to hear about what the visitors had thought of the inn, Claire and Liza were both quiet during dinner. She knew the day must have been hard for them, making so much conversation and answering so many questions. Aside from that, the emotional toll of acting upbeat and positive about the situation must have been exhausting. Kerry felt sure that Liza did not feel at all upbeat about the idea of letting the inn go.

She didn't feel it was her place to press them, but Nolan had no such scruples. "So . . . what did the inspection committee think? You've hardly told me a thing."

Liza glanced at Claire as she cut the breaded chicken Kerry had made for the children into small bites. "It's hard to say. George and Nina Foster—they own the company," she explained to Kerry. "They were playing their cards close to their vests. But I'd say their reaction was mainly positive. Wouldn't you, Claire?"

"Yes, very positive. Of course, one or two of the others pointed out problems and drawbacks here and there. But there's bound to be at least one naysayer in any group."

"Bound to be," Nolan agreed. "You probably won't hear anything more until after the New Year. None of these big companies are doing any work now."

Liza had taken a bite of her own dinner—chicken with artichokes and mushrooms in a white wine and butter sauce. "They didn't admit that, Nolan. But I think you're right. Like I said last night, this is a long process. It might take months before they make a decision. I'm surprised they didn't put off this visit until January. I'm glad for that. I would have dreaded having that appointment hanging over our heads. Now we can relax and focus on the holidays."

"I was thinking the same thing," Claire said.

"By the way, Kerry, this chicken is delicious, and I want to thank you for holding down the fort today," Liza said. "You did a great job."

"It was nothing." Kerry had been glad to be busy at the inn after her visit to church. Her conversation with Emily had shaken her to the core. As many times as she had imagined how it would be to talk so openly with Jane's adoptive mother, the reality had been very different. And very . . . *final,* Kerry realized. She still hadn't processed it all.

"Will Daniel be here tomorrow or Sunday?" Claire asked Liza.

"There was some last-minute glitch at the clinic, of course. But he promised he'll catch a midnight flight tomorrow and be here Sunday morning. The kids want to wait for him to decorate the tree."

"Of course they do. We're all looking forward to decorating the tree," Claire said "After the guests are taken care of in the morning, I'm going to the fair. I don't need to help at the booth this year, but I want to see how it all turned out. Would you like to come, Kerry?"

She was curious to see the fair, after hearing about it all these weeks. But she hesitated to agree. Jane would be there. And Kerry had practically promised Emily that she would leave Jane alone from now on, until she left town.

"Don't you need me here, Liza? There are a lot of guests this weekend. I bet you want them pampered and happy and no one posts a grumpy review online right now."

Liza was wiping Charlotte's mouth and hands. The little girl had feasted on the broccoli crowns and melted cheese Kerry had made for the children as a side dish.

"A grumpy review would be more than annoying," she agreed. "But I think I can handle the guests. You go with Claire. She needs a chaperone to make sure she doesn't stay there all day."

"And buy out the place," Nolan added.

Claire's cheeks flushed. "I'm a very careful shopper. I mainly buy handmade items, things you can't find in stores anymore. It's all for a good cause."

"A very good cause, dear," Nolan replied in a sweeter tone. "And who couldn't use one of those ski hats Sophie knits? Or a birdhouse or letter opener whittled by Digger Hegman?"

Claire's expression brightened. "Exactly." She glanced at Kerry. "We'll leave at noon. It will be in full swing by then."

Kerry could see she had no choice. All she could do was reply, "I'll be ready."

CHAPTER TWELVE

~~~

The parking lot at the church was ten times busier on Saturday than it had been the day before. Kerry gazed around at the cars and the people walking in and out of the church. "It looks like the whole town is here, not just church members."

"The whole town and then some. It's a very popular holiday fair." A note of pride rang in Claire's voice, and Kerry understood. Here, nearly all of Claire's friends seemed to be part of this warm, vibrant community that was so much a part of Cape Light.

The hallway that led to Fellowship Hall was very crowded. Kerry and Claire walked with the throng of people heading toward the fair. Children wearing pageant costumes—shepherds, wise men, even sheep—streamed out of a classroom and wove in and out of the adults, eager to reach the fun. Kerry saw Reverend Ben following the group, greeting church members on his way.

"They must have been having a last rehearsal for the pageant," Claire said. "All the children are so excited for Christmas by now."

They had reached the hall, a large space that had been miraculously transformed with decorations and booths all around the perimeter, and in the middle, a tall Christmas tree.

The bake sale booth was ringed by a line of people eager to purchase the baked treats. Kerry saw Vera and Jane there, taking care of customers, and hoped Claire didn't want to visit the booth first. Kerry turned away. She wasn't ready to face her daughter yet. "Why don't we start at this end and work our way around to the bake sale?" she suggested.

"Good idea. Let's save the best for last," Claire said. "If we get separated, I'll meet you there."

Gilroy Goat Farm's booth was the first one they came to. Audrey and her husband had created a beautiful display of their cheeses, soaps, skin creams, dried lavender bouquets, and wreaths. "It's a wonderful booth, Audrey," Kerry said. "I want to buy everything."

"Let me know what you like. Friends and neighbors discount," Audrey whispered with a wink.

Lavender and soap from the Gilroy Farm were in almost every room of the inn. But Kerry bought some for herself, knowing she would be gone soon and would miss the lovely fragrance. Claire had already wandered off to Sophie's booth, where Sophie sat at a table displaying jars of apple butter, fruit preserves, and honey.

Kerry was about to join Claire when a display of children's books caught her eye. She picked one up, attracted by the illustration on the cover, a delicate watercolor of whimsical animals—chipmunks, otters, and a jaunty little fox.

She began to page through the book, skimming the story. "What lovely illustrations," she said to the woman sitting behind the table. "Is this a book by a local author?"

"Very local," the woman replied. "In fact, you're looking at her." She smiled, and Kerry checked the cover. *Written and illustrated by Jean Whitman.*

"You're Jean Whitman?"

"That's me. And that's my first book. The first in a series."

Kerry had noticed other picture books on the table. She glanced at the back cover of the one she was holding, *Oscar Goes to Town*. It was filled with enthusiastic quotes from reviewers. "I know someone who will love this." Kerry took out her wallet and paid for it. "Could you sign it for me, please?"

"I'd be happy to. Who shall I sign it for?" Jean asked, pen in hand.

"A little boy named Max. He loves all kinds of animals. His father is a doctor, but I think Max will grow up to be a veterinarian."

Jean smiled as she wrote an inscription on the title page. She closed the book and handed it back to Kerry. "My email address is on the back. Please let me know what Max thinks of the story."

Kerry nodded then remembered she might not be around to read Max the story. The thought gave her a sad feeling.

"Have a Merry Christmas," Jean said.

"Same to you."

Another customer approached Jean, and Kerry scanned the hall to see where she should shop next. Sawyer's Tree Farm had a large booth with Christmas trees, ornaments, and all kinds of wreaths and greens. A handmade ornament might make a nice gift for someone on her list. She noticed bunches of mistletoe tied with red ribbon and arranged in a basket. *Maybe I should get some of that for Gabriel, so he finally knows what the real stuff looks like.*

Then she decided it was best not to encourage him in that direction. He would certainly take her little joke the wrong way.

She was about to leave Jean's booth when a rack of photographs caught her eye. She recognized scenic spots around Cape Light and Angel Island—Main Street at night, the famous lighthouse, the woods and the marshes.

Kerry walked closer and picked up a photo of the Angel Island cliffs, taken at sunset. Behind the island's ragged edges, radiant beams of light broke through the clouds, reaching toward infinity. The rocky ledges could have been carved by the wind and sea, but Kerry could not help but think of the story Gabriel had told her. The view the photographer had captured really did look like wings. She glanced at the signature in the corner of the frame—Grant Keating. The name was familiar to her. Probably a member of the church, she realized. She walked back to Jean Whitman and waited a moment until she was free.

"I'd like this photograph, too."

"Nice choice. One of my favorites," Jean replied as she wrapped the frame in paper. "The photographer is my husband, so I'm not the most impartial judge."

"I think it's beautiful. You must be very proud. And he must be proud of your books, too."

"That's kind of you to say. We have a little shop at the end of Main Street. Come and visit sometime."

Kerry liked her very much and appreciated the invitation. "I'll try," she promised, not knowing what the future would bring.

She strolled over to a booth run by Grace Hegman and her elderly father, Digger. Grace was another of Claire's friends. She had come to the inn once or twice since Kerry had been working there, but Kerry had never actually met Grace's father; she'd only seen them in church together.

Delicate in build, almost birdlike, Grace was a quiet woman, devoted to her father's care. Digger had been a clammer and lobsterman in his younger days and still dressed as if he might be headed out to sea at any minute, his dark blue knit cap pulled down over wiry white hair, the edge of the hat meeting bushy eyebrows. He wore a thick sweater and overalls and whittled a bit of wood.

Kerry saw the toy cars, boats, and houses he'd made on their table, though she knew Grace mainly sold antiques at her store, The Bramble. From the look of the wares on display, it was an intriguing place. There were delicate china cups with flowery patterns, ceramic figurines, crystal perfume bottles, and antique lamps.

A pair of opera glasses. Interesting, though she didn't know if anyone on her list liked the opera. Right next to that, a compact pair of binoculars and a small round leather case with a loop and snap, for a belt maybe? She thought it might be a stopwatch, but she found a compass inside instead.

The face was faded yellow with pale red and green markings. A delicate arrow with a scroll-shaped tail hovered above the circle of degrees.

"That's a fine old piece," Digger told her. "A real collector's item. You could never lose your way with a real compass in your hand. Not like that GPS gadget people use these days. A compass will never fail you like a silly old cell phone."

The old man had a point. How many times had the GPS been guiding her somewhere when her phone's power ran out?

"Does it still work?" Kerry asked, balancing the compass in the palm of her hand.

Digger squinted at her; his small, dark eyes were amazingly bright. "Of course it works. Unless they moved the North Pole when I wasn't looking. I think I'd hear about that."

"I think you would, too," Kerry agreed with a laugh.

The compass seemed the perfect gift for Nolan. He would appreciate the craftsmanship and maybe even use it on his sailboat. Now that Claire and her husband planned to travel, the gift was symbolic, too, she realized.

"I'll take it," she said, handing it over to Digger.

"Smart lady. I was going to keep that for myself, but Grace wouldn't let me." For an old man, his fingers were very nimble. He quickly made change and slipped the box into a paper bag. "I hope this helps you find your way, young lady."

"Oh, it's not for me. It's a gift for someone on my list."

"I still hope you find your way. I think you will." He gazed at her and nodded; his knowing look gave her a chill. How had he sensed her troubled heart? She didn't believe anything she had done or said could have given her away. Was he senile and just said random things to strangers? It was uncanny. Then again, maybe it was a coincidence.

Before she could answer, Grace walked over. "How are you, Kerry? Catching up on your Christmas shopping?"

"I am. I just found a nice gift for Nolan, but I still have a few more to find."

"That table in the corner is all markdowns, but I put some nice pieces there. You ought to take a quick look," Grace advised.

Kerry hadn't noticed the table. Nothing to lose by browsing another minute, she decided. Grace's markdowns included several silver sugar spoons, some with bent handles, and a pretty but dented set of candlesticks. Kerry picked up a letter opener with a monogrammed handle. It looked very grand and didn't cost much. But she didn't know anyone who would use such a thing.

Right next to that, she saw a lovely triptych frame made of sterling silver. The carved design was very delicate. It was polished and hardly scratched with a mellow patina that made Kerry imagine how many photos it had proudly displayed. Three spaces, she noticed. This would be perfect for Liza to hold pictures of her family.

She checked the price—not quite in her budget, but Liza had been so nice to her, and it was the perfect gift. She couldn't pass it up.

She brought the frame to Grace, who smiled as she set out some tissue paper to wrap Kerry's prize. "You have a good eye. I forgot that I put this back there."

"I'm going to give it to Liza, for pictures of her children and Daniel."

"Very thoughtful." Grace checked for the price sticker and pulled it off, then peered at it through her reading glasses. "I forgot to mark this one down. Everything back there is twenty percent off. I need to give you the discount."

Kerry shrugged. "That's all right."

Grace shook her head. "Says so right on the sign."

Kerry had seen a sign on the table but hadn't worried about it. "That's very nice of you, Grace. I appreciate it."

"That's all right. It wouldn't be fair if I didn't. I think Liza will like this. It's just her style."

"I think so, too." Kerry took the package, feeling satisfied with her finds. And all within her budget.

She found a funny, cuddly cat puppet for Charlotte at the toy shop table and a box of moose tracks chocolate nut brittle for Daniel at a booth run by a Boy Scout troop. She had heard it was his favorite treat, which he only allowed himself on Christmas, since he was mindful of eating only healthy foods.

She still hadn't found the right gift for Claire

and was about to give up when she came to a table with a sign that said *Winkler Tearoom*. Where had she seen that sign before? In the island's village center. That was it. Across from the General Store.

Daisy Winkler was an eccentric old woman, wearing a long green velvet dress topped by a colorful beaded shawl. Wild red-gray hair framed a friendly face. "Have a look," she said to Kerry. "You might just find a treasure."

Among the teapots and bags of loose, fragrant tea, Kerry spotted a china heart, cream-colored with pale blue flowers. Forget-me-nots? She thought they might be. It was Limoges china, she was almost positive. Her mother'd had a few small pieces and prized them. Kerry lifted the lid, which was attached to the bottom with a small gold hinge. Inside the heart, she found a small scrap of paper folded in half, only slightly larger than the slip inside a fortune cookie. Was it the price?

Kerry unfolded it and found a quote from Eleanor Roosevelt:

Many people will walk in and out of your life, but only true friends will leave footprints in your heart.

The words seemed to perfectly describe her feelings for Claire.

Claire had helped her so much in such a short time. She'd taught her about inn-keeping, and cooking, too. But more than that, Claire had believed in her, valued her skills and talents. She had always treated her with respect, and never looked down on her because of her past. To the contrary, she thought better of Kerry than Kerry often thought of herself. At least, when she'd first arrived here.

But Kerry could see how, little by little, Claire's encouragement and high expectations had worn on her, like water on a stone, and forever changed her. Once she left here, she might never see Claire and Nolan again, however good their intentions to stay in touch. But Kerry knew she would always hold Claire in her heart, and would always draw strength from her wisdom, encouragement, and gentle affection.

She folded the paper again and carefully put it back inside, then snapped the lid closed. "I'd like to buy this," she told Daisy.

"For yourself?"

"For a friend," Kerry corrected her. "For Christmas."

"You must have a very special friend to have chosen this one."

"She is," Kerry said. "I didn't see anything else that seemed right for her. This is perfect."

"Someone nearly bought it this morning, but they put it down at the last minute. It must have been waiting for you," Daisy replied.

"Maybe," Kerry agreed, though she could

hardly see how the heart could decide who it would go home with.

Kerry was so happy with her purchases, she had almost forgotten her reservations about coming to the fair. But there was no avoiding the bake sale booth forever.

Claire had just emerged from Sophie Potter's booth and waved to Kerry as she walked over to meet her. "Looks like you found a few things that you liked."

"More than a few. I finished my list."

"I did, too. Let's visit the bake sale booth," Claire said. "I want to see how our macaroons are selling. Like hotcakes, I bet."

Kerry nodded and followed Claire, feeling a little nervous. She had noticed Jane at the booth earlier. She was sure Jane had been trying to catch her eye and wanted to say hello, but Kerry had ignored her glance.

They came closer to the booth, and she no longer saw Jane among the volunteers. She felt a strange mixture of relief and disappointment. She would stop for a quick visit and persuade Claire to head back to the inn. That would be the best thing to do.

"It looks wonderful. What a great display this year. So professional." Claire lavishly praised her friends. The display of confections really was very eye-catching and professional, Kerry thought.

"We had it set up the usual way this morning," Vera explained. "Then Molly Willoughby came by and changed it all around. She brought all the cake stands, from her shop, I suppose. They do highlight those reindeer cupcakes nicely."

Jane's reindeer cupcakes, Kerry nearly corrected her aloud.

Jane had ended up with the assignment of decorating them at home on her own. No small task. Kerry thought the novelty cakes had come out perfectly. She imagined Jane spending hours placing the pretzel antlers and M&M eyes and noses. She couldn't help feeling a rush of pride in her daughter. Unfortunately, or perhaps for the best, Jane was not here to receive her compliments.

The booth was so busy, there was little chance for Claire to chat with her friends. Kerry bought cupcakes for Max and Charlotte, even though the inn was stocked with cakes and cookies. These were a special treat, Kerry thought, and would delight them. Finally, it was time to head to the car. As she and Claire made their way through the crowd at the fair and came out to the corridor, Kerry again felt half-relieved and half-deflated that she had missed a chance to speak to Jane. *At least I saw her at a distance. That's probably the best I can hope for now.*

They had just reached the exit when Claire abruptly stopped and pressed her hand to her cheek. "Oh dear, I forgot my blue tote. I must have left it in the bake sale booth."

"I'll run back and get it. I'll meet you at the car," Kerry said. Claire was very able for her age, but Kerry knew she could maneuver through the crowd much faster.

Claire agreed, and Kerry headed back to the fair. The bag was spotted easily, on a chair next to Vera where Claire had been sitting. The volunteers hardly noticed when she returned to fetch it. She had just stepped into the long hallway that led back to the exit when she heard someone call her.

"Kerry? Wait up . . ." She knew it was Jane and turned slowly, careful to control her expression while inside she churned with a mixture of joy and pain.

Jane ran toward her, carrying several rolls of paper towels. Someone at the booth must have sent her on an errand, Kerry realized.

"I saw you walking around the fair, but you were too far away to say hello. How's your leg?"

Kerry had all but forgotten about the kitchen accident. It seemed so long ago. So much had happened since Wednesday.

"It's all right. I don't even notice it. Your cupcakes are a big hit. I bought some for Max and Charlotte. The booth is selling out."

"Are they really?" Jane knew Kerry was exaggerating but seemed pleased to hear it.

"You did an awesome job on the decorating. It must have been hard to do that many."

"My mom helped me. She has a knack for breaking the pretzels just right."

Kerry forced a smile but felt her heart fall like a stone when Jane mentioned Emily. Of course Emily had helped. She imagined the two of them working together in the kitchen, and it seemed so unfair. Why should Emily have her forever? *I'm her mother . . . and I'm nothing to her. Not even a friend, really.*

A wave of envy and even anger washed over her. The words "But I'm your mother, Jane. Your real mother" crowded the tip of her tongue, about to tumble out.

But somehow, she caught herself. "Well, she did a great job. You both did. The fair is terrific. You should be very proud."

Jane smiled shyly at the compliment. "Thanks. I didn't do that much. My mom should get all credit. And Aunt Jess," she added. "I'd better get back with these towels. Before Vera calls nine-one-one." Kerry laughed. She could easily imagine it.

"Will you be in church tomorrow?" Jane asked.

"Gee, I don't think so. There are a lot of guests at the inn this weekend. I'll probably need to stay and take care of them."

"If I don't see you, have a great Christmas," Jane said as she headed back to the fair.

"You, too. Have a wonderful Christmas, Jane."

She watched her daughter disappear into the crowd and felt a piece of her heart go with her.

She couldn't stay here. Not even until Christmas. She'd never be able to keep her promise to Emily.

Emily was not the last to leave church, but almost. A crew of cleanup volunteers had arrived at five, making the last job of the annual fair a bit easier. But she wanted to be sure every trace of the fair was cleaned up in time for tomorrow's Sunday morning service.

"Go home, Emily. I'll stay until they're done," Reverend Ben had told her. "This year's fair was a great success. If you don't believe me, even Sophie said so."

Emily had taken over the committee a few years ago from Sophie Potter, who had come up with the idea decades ago.

"It's not that I don't believe you, Reverend. But that's high praise from Sophie. I think I will go home now and rest on my laurels."

She pulled up to her house feeling exhausted, but the sight of her older daughter and son-in-law's car in the driveway was like a shot of adrenaline. Boston wasn't so far away, but she didn't see Sara nearly as much as she would like. Sara's hours as a reporter for the *Boston Globe* were long and unpredictable. She was often on tight deadlines or working on the road, covering important news stories.

Luke worked for an organization that helped at-risk children. Kids who were always getting into trouble at school or with the law. About fifteen years ago, he had opened up a center to help children like that in Cape Light, and now he did the same in cities and small towns around the country.

Emily was proud of both of them, though she did wish they lived closer and she saw them more often. *But that's what holidays are for,* she reminded herself as she hurried to the front door.

Inside, the house was surprisingly quiet, though the suitcases and coats in the living room were proof of Sara's arrival.

"I'm home. Where is everyone?" Emily called out as she shrugged out of her coat.

Sara stepped out of the kitchen and smiled. "Dan and Jane left to get the tree, and Luke went to buy groceries. He wants to make everyone dinner instead of going out."

Emily and Dan had planned to take Sara and Luke out for dinner tonight, someplace special to celebrate their homecoming.

"A relaxing dinner at home would be nice," Emily admitted. "But I don't want him to go to so much trouble. We can order takeout. You're here to relax."

"It's no trouble. And we will relax, don't

308

worry." Sara stepped over and gave Emily a hug. "I'm sorry I couldn't make it in time for the fair. Jane said it was the best ever."

Emily smiled. "She would say that . . . but even Sophie Potter gave me a compliment. And she invented it."

"I hope it was good. You look exhausted, Mom. If you don't mind me saying."

"I will sleep well," Emily admitted. Though now she wondered if she would, even feeling as tired as she did. The conversation she'd had with Kerry Redmond had kept her up last night. It was no wonder she had bags under her eyes today. She would have rather run three church fairs than have had that talk with Kerry.

Sara was at the counter, fixing a tray of appetizers—cheese, crackers, and olives. She opened a bottle of wine and poured two glasses. "Let's go inside and toast to the chair of the Christmas Fair," she suggested.

"I'm only the cochair. Your aunt Jessica is my partner. But I'll have a sip in her honor as well."

Relaxing by the fire with Sara was just what Emily needed to unwind. She flipped off her shoes and stretched her legs. "I'm finally starting to feel like the holidays are here. How long can you and Luke stay?"

"Until New Year's Day. We both have loads of vacation time. If my office needs me, I can always work from here."

Emily was glad to hear that Sara had managed a long visit.

"You'll be here for Ezra's party. That's good."

"I can hardly wait. Do you think he'll be surprised?"

"As far as we can see, he has no idea. But it's not going to be at Aunt Jessica's house. Your grandmother pulled the plug on that plan. She wanted a much smaller party with a fancier atmosphere, so we booked a private room at the Bradford Arms in Newburyport."

"That Bradford Arms?" Emily wasn't sure if Sara was impressed or about to laugh. "Should I wear opera-length gloves and a fox fur?"

Emily shrugged. "I'm going with a basic black dress, but you'd blend right in with that outfit. We hope Ezra likes the party. But we really have no say. She's simply taken over."

Sara grinned. "I understand. I'm sure you and Aunt Jess fought the good fight."

"We did," Emily insisted. She sipped her wine, her thoughts wandering. She was so lucky to have both of her daughters with her tonight. Her talk with Kerry Redmond had made that point abundantly clear. It was a blessing she'd never take for granted again.

"Mom . . . is something bothering you? I mean aside from Grandma hijacking Ezra's party. And feeling tired from the fair?"

Emily forced a smile. "I'm fine, honey. Just

tired. I'd say I'm getting too old to run that event, but Sophie did it until she was . . . eighty-five? I've still got over twenty years to go."

Sara wasn't letting her off the hook so easily. Emily could tell by the way she looked at her. Her daughter was a reporter, and her skills at reading people were well honed. She smelled a story and she wasn't giving up.

Emily sighed. "The strangest thing happened this week. Not that strange, really. I should have expected it. I didn't want it to happen. That's why I kept telling myself I had to be imagining things . . ."

Sara took another sip of wine, but Emily knew she was listening intently.

"Jane's birth mother is in town. On Angel Island, actually. She came to find Jane. We had a talk and she promised that she wouldn't tell Jane who she really is. She claims that she just wanted to make sure Jane was all right, that she's being raised in a good home and is well taken care of. I didn't believe her at first, but I think now I do."

"Wow . . . that is big." Sara hesitated a moment. "What's her name?"

"Kerry Redmond. She works at the inn, helping with the housekeeping and cooking. She's an excellent baker. She helped with the bake sale at the fair. I don't know if that was intentional, or if Claire North persuaded her to get involved. It turned out to be a way to meet Jane. They even baked together. I had no idea who she was, of course. But something about her set off my radar. Intuition, maybe? I mentioned it to your aunt and she thought I was crazy." Emily laughed, looking back. "Jane does bear a striking resemblance to her birth mother. But it seems I'm the only one who noticed."

"So you got to know her a bit, too? What do you think of her?"

Emily thought over the question for a moment. "I think she's a good person, deep down. Despite tricking us to get closer to Jane. She's a little reserved, but very kind, and she does love Jane. She even stepped in the way of a hot pan so Jane wouldn't get hurt."

"That's brave," Sara said.

"It was," Emily agreed. "Kerry seems resourceful and intelligent. I'm surprised she's a domestic helper—she seems capable of much more. I get the feeling she's been through some difficult times. She told me that she never wanted to give Jane up, but she knew she couldn't raise her on her own. She was just a teenager and had no one to help her."

Sara sat back and gazed at Emily, her head tilted to one side. "That's a familiar story," she said quietly. "I doubt many mothers want to give up their children. But they do it out of a greater love. You'd know something about that, Mom."

Emily glanced at her daughter. She felt a wave

of guilt—but for giving up Sara as a baby? She believed she had resolved that by now. Maybe for the way she'd treated Kerry? She could have made things easier for her. Is that what her daughter was hinting at?

"Of course I do. I never judged her. I understood what she'd been through. Even though I was a widow when you were born, the circumstances were probably similar."

"I know you understood, and even sympathized . . . What are you going to do about it?"

Emily had asked herself the same question. While a voice inside said, *Let it be. You dodged a bullet there. Kerry Redmond isn't making any demands. Why should you speed up the process?*

"I'm not sure what to do," Emily confessed. "Jane hasn't asked about this whole question in a long time. I don't think she's ready to meet her birth mother."

"Just because she isn't talking to you about it doesn't mean she isn't thinking about it. For all you know, she could be talking to her friends, or even looking for Kerry online." Sara paused and caught Emily's gaze. "I can see it's hard for you to be on the other side of this table, Mom. I understand. But I don't think you've been fair to Jane's birth mother by keeping them apart, no matter what the woman said to you. I don't think you're being fair to Jane either. And I'm surprised," she added, before Emily could reply, "because you're always such a fair-minded person."

Sara's quiet words fell like a blow. Emily respected her daughter's opinion and hated to look anything less than perfect in her eyes. "I'm not being fair, is that what you're saying? Even though Kerry told me, more than once, she didn't want to upset Jane? Maybe she's not ready to meet Jane either. Bringing them together right now might not be the best thing."

Sara didn't answer for a long moment. "Do you really believe that? . . . Never mind, you don't have to answer," she added quickly. "I really think you need to ask Jane how she feels about meeting her birth mother before you dismiss the possibility completely. You said Kerry is leaving town soon so she won't be a bother. Something could happen to her while you're waiting for Jane to be ready. How would you feel, knowing Jane had a chance to meet her and you prevented it?"

Emily had not thought of that. She wanted to argue that Kerry was a young woman in excellent health. The chances of anything happening to her were slim to null. But she also knew tomorrow was not guaranteed to anyone—young, old, or in between. She had learned that harsh lesson when she lost Sara's father in the blink of an eye.

They heard the back door open and grocery bags rattling. "Sara, I'm back. Can you help me with the groceries?" Luke called.

"Coming," Sara called, getting up from the couch.

"I'll help, too." Emily slipped her shoes on and followed Sara to the kitchen. She prepared herself to greet her son-in-law, to put herself in a more holiday, family reunion state of mind. They were going to have fun tonight, enjoy a good dinner and decorate the tree.

She pushed aside thoughts of Kerry Redmond, and her sad, appealing expression. Still, the last thing Kerry had asked echoed in Emily's mind. "Has she ever asked about me?"

I didn't treat Kerry as I should have. I know how much she wants to tell Jane who she is, and how much she fears that moment, too. Did I take advantage of her? Her guilt and self-doubt. She brought Jane into the world. Surely she has rights I can never lay claim to?

Claire filled Nolan's mug with more coffee, and then her own. They'd just finished their Sunday breakfast. "At the risk of sounding overly concerned with worldly matters, I'm eager to hear how much money the fair raised for the church this year," Claire admitted.

"You could never sound too concerned with worldly matters, dear," her husband assured her. "Everyone wants to know that. You all worked so hard, I hope it was worth the effort."

"It always is, no matter how much is collected.

The fair is about fellowship and service to the community. I think people in town would feel a loss if the church ever stopped holding it. Don't you think so, Kerry?"

"Can't say that I'm an expert after only one visit, but it seemed like a popular spot." Kerry had served an early bird breakfast to the guests, a frittata with roasted vegetables and cheese that she had prepared the night before.

They had all checked out early, too, in order to attend a wedding in Essex, and would not return tonight. Kerry stood at the sink rinsing breakfast dishes and was about to attack a pile of pots.

"Will you come to church this morning? It should be a very nice service—The Twelve Gifts of Christmas. Lots of special music, stories, and poems, just for the children. It's very unique. Liza is going to take Max and Charlotte."

"And we're going to look for a Christmas tree after that," Nolan said. "Liza wants it up and all but decorated by the time Daniel gets here."

The service did sound unique, and the afternoon plan sounded like fun, too. But Kerry had made a plan of her own last night and was going to follow through on it. She was only waiting for everyone to leave.

"It sounds lovely, but I'd better stay here and finish the breakfast dishes. I'll clean up the empty rooms and get the laundry going. Once Daniel gets here, no one will want to hear the vacuum running."

Claire rose and carried her breakfast plates to the sink. "I suppose that's true. You're so conscientious. But I hope you'll come with us Tuesday night, for the Christmas Eve service? I'd hate to think of you all alone here then."

Kerry didn't know what to say. She didn't want to lie. "I won't be, don't worry."

Claire seemed satisfied with the answer. She hurried off to get ready for church. Nolan was still at the table, working on a crossword puzzle, smartly dressed and ready for his day, as usual. He peered at her over his reading glasses. "Can I help you, Kerry? Wash those pots or something?"

"I'm fine, Nolan. Maybe you should do the puzzle in the sitting room. I'm going to run the electric broom in here and then mop the floors."

"I'll be out of your way, then. No problem."

Kerry quickly cleaned the kitchen and set the dining room back in order. She did want to carry through on all her duties, everything she had told Claire she would do here while they were at the service.

A short time later, Liza and her children, along with Claire and Nolan, left for the village. Kerry calculated she had at least two hours, maybe more. Claire would surely want to stay for the coffee hour this morning.

Kerry ran up to the second floor and quickly

cleaned the guest rooms, changed the linens, dusted, and cleaned the bathrooms, then loaded the washer. She made one last check in the rooms before heading to her own room. Her closet and the drawers in her dresser were empty, and the bed linens removed. Her belongings were packed in one small suitcase and knapsack. The convenience of a modest lifestyle, she thought with a wry smile. She had wrapped her Christmas gifts for the family last night, and now she carried them downstairs, along with her suitcase. She carefully set the gifts near the fireplace and left two envelopes on the mantel, one addressed to Liza and one to Claire and Nolan. It was too hard to say goodbye to any of them. Especially to Claire.

Kerry had never been very good at goodbyes anyway. She hadn't written a note to Gabriel, but had left his gift with the others. She hoped he would understand. Maybe someday, when she summoned up enough nerve, she would get in touch with him and explain. It felt much too hard now.

Yesterday, she had almost revealed her identity to Jane. But that shouldn't happen. She couldn't risk hurting Jane again, in any way. Her daughter's life was happy and secure. *What more could I ask for her? What more could I ever give her?*

Kerry found her jacket and waited by the front door. Her ride was due any minute. There was plenty of time to reach the train station in Cape Light and catch the northbound train. Once she was settled in Maine again, she would let Emily Warwick know where to find her. She was doing the right thing, the best thing for Jane. That's what counted most.

Ten minutes later, as the taxi headed toward the village, Kerry watched the scenery roll by, the views of the seashore and island landscape she had come to know and had taken for granted. She would miss this place, that was for sure. There were many coastal towns in New England, and many islands, too. But this place was special, maybe even magical, as Gabriel had told her. It was hard to leave Angel Island behind.

The taxi suddenly swerved to the shoulder, and the driver hit the brakes. The vehicle bumped along for a moment or two and came to a lurching stop. Kerry felt her seat belt press her back against the seat, the fabric taut. "What was that? What happened?"

The driver turned to face her, looking pale. "Are you all right, miss?"

"I think so. But what happened? Do you have a flat tire or something?"

"A rabbit. It jumped out into the road. I didn't want to hit it, so I pulled to the side, and the car skidded on the shoulder." He took a steadying breath. "Don't worry, I'll have us back on the road in no time."

The motor was still running, and he shifted into drive. Kerry heard the wheels spin, but the car moved barely an inch. Sand flew up against the windows. She felt as though she were caught in a desert dust storm.

"Oh, boy . . . maybe I can back out. That might work." He shifted again and turned to face the back of the car, maneuvering the wheel with one hand.

Kerry heard him hit the gas and felt relieved as the taxi slowly moved backward. The driver started to smile. But the car stopped, stuck again, the spinning wheels sounding even more frustrated and futile now.

"Oh, brother. I'm sorry, miss. Let's get out. I'd better call the dispatcher for another car."

"I guess so." Kerry unhooked her belt and carefully stepped out of the taxi. She was wearing boots and didn't mind stepping in the mixture of sand and soft mud.

She did mind missing her train and her connection to the main line and a train that would get her up to Bar Harbor that night. She wasn't sure when the next connecting train would pass through.

She pulled out her phone to find out, but the Wi-Fi signal on the island was spotty and she couldn't connect to the Internet.

Luckily, the taxi driver's phone worked. "Another cab is coming out to pick you up.

They're a little short on staff today. It will take about half an hour."

"Thirty minutes? That long? Maybe I should call another cab service."

"Be my guest. But it takes at least twenty minutes from the village to the island. I doubt anyone can get you faster."

Kerry thought that was true. She was just feeling so frustrated. The driver walked around the other side of the car with his phone as he explained the situation to his boss. She leaned against the back of the taxi, phone in hand, her suitcase at her feet. She heard the light tap of a car horn and looked up. A truck pulled up across the road. Gabriel O'Hara's truck. He opened the door and jumped out.

"Having some car trouble?" he asked.

"The taxi is stuck in the sand." Kerry felt her cheeks get red. Of all the people to catch her running away today, why did it have to be him?

"I see . . . Are you going someplace?"

"Just up to Maine for a few days. To see friends." She knew he was suspicious and hoped he wouldn't ask more questions.

Gabriel surveyed the stuck taxi. When the driver came back, he said, "I don't have any chains in the truck, but I can go get a set and try to pull you out."

The driver waved his hand. "That's all right. A tow truck is on the way. If anything happens to the taxi, I'm toast. I'm toast already for the screwup."

Kerry felt sorry for him. He was a very good person to go to so much trouble to avoid hurting a rabbit. "Can I call your boss and put in a good word for you? It certainly wasn't your fault."

The driver smiled. "Thanks. I'll be fine. He'll get over it. He's my brother-in-law."

The explanation almost made her laugh out loud. She should have known it was something like that in this town.

"I can give you a ride," Gabriel said. "Where are you going?"

"To the train station. I missed the train I was planning to catch, but there must be another one coming soon."

He grabbed her bag but glanced up at her with his trademark mocking grin. "I wouldn't count on it, but I'll take you there anyway."

With a sigh, Kerry let him take her bag. Then she climbed into the truck. They drove in silence for a few minutes.

"It's a funny time to leave the inn," he said finally. "I thought you were all so busy."

"We were . . . but all the guests left this morning." Kerry didn't say more. That was true. She wasn't lying to him.

"Your suitcase is sure heavy for a quick visit."

"I'm a bad packer. I can never decide what

to bring on a trip." That wasn't a lie either, not really.

"So you just pack everything." It wasn't a question. When she glanced at him, she could tell from his expression he knew she was leaving town for good.

"I'm leaving. I have to. I can't explain why, but trust me, it's for a good reason."

"All right. I trust you. But why don't you grant me the same honor, and try to explain what's going on?"

Kerry considered his words for a moment, then shook her head. "No, I'm sorry . . . I just can't."

"Can't, or won't?"

She sighed. "What's the difference? It amounts to the same thing."

"I think you can, if you tried. Look, if you're in trouble, I just want to help. Someone's hurt you somewhere along the way. I can see it's hard for you to let down your guard. But I just want to help. You don't have to do everything yourself."

She was about to argue with him, to deny everything he'd said about her. But he'd read her like a book, hadn't he? She was exactly like that.

"It's good of you to say that, Gabriel . . . and I believe you. But no one can help with this situation. I brought it on myself, and I'm the only one who can work it out."

She heard him take a deep breath. His only answer was the set of his jaw. He looked totally frustrated with her. She didn't blame him. She knew he must see her as a woman drowning in rough water who refused to take hold of the rope he offered.

Suddenly the truck swerved and bumped along the shoulder of the road. It was a much heavier vehicle than the taxi, and she felt herself bounce in her seat, her head touching the upholstery above a few times.

Finally, the truck came to a stop. She turned to face him. "Were you avoiding a rabbit, too?"

"No . . . I'm avoiding letting you make a big mistake by running away from here. Maybe I don't have a right to know what's really going on, but I think you should tell me."

She felt a sudden rush of anger at him. "You were correct the first time. It's my private business. I'll handle it. Why should I tell you?"

"Because . . . I care about you. And in my book, that counts for something."

His straightforward reply surprised her. She felt the rug pulled out from under her. Just when she was getting up a good head of steam to keep him at a safe distance, he had to say something like that. "That wasn't fair," she mumbled.

He almost laughed. "Maybe not. But it's true . . . even if you don't feel the same. Doesn't matter."

She did feel the same about him—that was just the problem. "You think you want to know all about me, but if you did, you'd be surprised."

He sat up, looking encouraged. "Try me. I'll let you know."

"I mean, really surprised. I'm not who you think I am. I've done a lot of things I'm not proud of."

"Haven't we all."

"Not like me . . . I've spent time in jail." She looked at him, waiting for his reaction.

He did seem startled a moment. Then he forced a calm expression again. "For what sort of crime?"

"Fraud. I notarized documents that I knew were fraudulent."

"I don't believe you'd do something like that, Kerry. Someone must have tricked you into doing it. Or threatened you?"

She swallowed hard. "I did it to please someone, a man I was involved with. I did it because he wanted me to. Even though I knew it was wrong. He was not a good person. But I thought I loved him. I would never say he tricked, or even threatened, me. I take full responsibility for what I did, and I went to jail for it."

She had known that if she hadn't followed his wishes, he would have pushed her aside and found someone new. That was the unspoken threat, and the idea had terrified her at the time.

Gabriel's expression was uncharacteristically serious. She knew some of the wind had been knocked from his sails. "Is that why you're leaving? You're afraid someone at the inn might find out about that?"

She shook her head. "Not at all. Everyone there knows. Claire knew when she hired me. I couldn't hide it. I didn't want to. She didn't judge. She was kind to give me a chance, and I've tried to do my best for her."

"Anyone can see that . . . Now that I've heard that, things make more sense. Why do you act as if you don't like me?"

She had to laugh. "Is it so inconceivable a woman might be able to resist your charm?"

"A few. But not too many." She knew he was teasing now, but not entirely. "I thought maybe it was my background. You didn't want to date someone with my heritage."

His words surprised her. "No . . . not at all. I never thought about it." She imagined his family just like Gabriel—warm, relaxed, caring. She would have liked meeting them, if things had been different. Much different.

"So, you still didn't tell me. If it's not because of your past, why are you leaving this way? I bet they don't even know at the inn, do they?"

"No, they don't. I left some notes for Liza and Claire. I hope they understand."

"I hope so, too, if you told them as little as you're telling me."

Gabriel waited. The silence was drawing her

326

out, like the dull ticking of a clock. "What you just told me doesn't change my mind about you, Kerry. That's all in your past. The person who did those things doesn't even exist anymore. I see the person you are now. You have to do better if you want to shock me."

Get rid of me, he really meant. She sat back and squared her shoulders. Well, he wanted to know all about her. She would tell him everything. *Let's see if he's still so keen on me.*

"All right, I'll tell you. But after this, you have to take me to the train station or I'll get out and call a taxi. I'm leaving. Nothing is going to change that."

He answered with a nod of his head, his dark eyes making her forget for a moment what she wanted to say.

She took a deep breath and began to tell him, as simply as she could, how her mother died when she was thirteen and how hard it was to live alone with her strict and distant father, who was so judgmental and rigid in his beliefs. She told him how she began seeing a boy in secret and became pregnant, and how her father demanded that she give the child up. But one week before the baby was born, Kerry turned eighteen. She realized that she no longer had to obey her father. She refused to give up Jane and tried her best to take care of her baby on her own, but it became impossible. She couldn't stand to see her baby suffering, moving from shelter to shelter with her. That was not the life she wanted for her daughter.

She told him how her father had agreed to meet her, to help her, then sent a curt message saying that he couldn't compromise his beliefs and values. She had taken this path, despite his guidance and advice, and now she had to deal with consequences on her own. "I was supposed to meet my father on the village green, in Cape Light. When I knew he wasn't coming, I went into the church. I prayed, but I didn't hear any answers or any visions. No angels jumped down from the stained-glass windows to help me," she added, remembering his story about the island. "I was desperate and out of my head a bit, I guess. The only idea I had was to pin a note on Jane and leave her to be found. I already heard people stirring around in the church. So I left her in the crèche, out in front. I started walking, I didn't even know where I was going. By the time my head cleared, maybe a half an hour later or even less, Emily Warwick had found her."

"Emily Warwick? Your daughter is Jane Forbes?"

"She is now." Kerry turned away and brushed a tear from the corner of her eye. "I saw police searching the church. I was afraid to come forward. I knew no one would give her back to me. I was an unfit mother. I'd proven that beyond a doubt. I didn't deserve to have her. That's what people would say, and that's what I thought, too. That was the answer to my prayers, losing my baby. Giving her a chance to have a better life than I could ever provide. And she has that, and her parents are devoted to her. I'm leaving because I don't want to ruin that for her."

Gabriel looked confused. "Ruin that for her? She has a right to know who you are."

"When she's ready, she'll look for me. I won't be hard to find. I'm going to stay in touch with Emily."

"Did you tell Emily you wouldn't let Jane know you were in town, is that it?"

"I did, but that's not really the point. She never asked me not to tell Jane. It was my decision. Completely. I've hurt her enough. I don't want to mess up her whole life."

"Maybe you think that's the reason. But I think you're leaving because you're afraid of your daughter's reaction. Afraid she'll be angry with you, and afraid you can't handle that. But what if you can get her to understand and forgive you? Eventually? Over time? What if you show her that you love her so much, it doesn't matter if she's angry? You still love her and you're not going to give up. You say she's a great kid. That her parents did a good job with her. Well, that's what a good person does, eventually. They forgive the ones who hurt them."

She sighed and stared at him. "It's easy for you to say. What if she never talks to me for the rest of my life? What then?"

He shook his head and tossed his hands up. "You're right. It's easy to give advice. All I know for sure is that running away doesn't solve anything. You carried this problem here, and you'll carry it away with you. You need to stay and at least try to fix it. The real problem is, you don't think you're able to. I think you are. I think you can figure out a better solution than hiding out in Maine and waiting for a phone call that may never come. Maybe all you need is to believe in yourself a little more, Kerry. I believe in you. You made a few mistakes, just like the rest of us. But you're a good person. Despite anything you've done, you're worthy of your daughter's forgiveness, and her love, too. That's her choice to make, Kerry. Not Emily Warwick's . . . or even your own."

His words hit a few nerves, she'd grant Gabriel that. Still, she wasn't convinced revealing herself to Jane was the right path. But maybe it was rash to run off, like someone was chasing her. She had promised Claire and Liza she would stay through Christmas, and they did need her help. When she thought about it, she knew she was going to miss spending Christmas at the inn with the circle of people who had shown her such warmth and respect, as if they were family.

"All right. I'll go back." She checked the time. "Oh, no. We'd better hurry. They might be home by now."

Kerry hoped that lunch after the service and the tree shopping had taken longer than expected. She hoped that her notes hadn't been found and read. She'd really have some explaining to do then.

"Buckle up. We'll be there before you can say 'Claire North's award-winning chowder.' " Kerry would have laughed at that quip but she barely had time to snap her seat belt before the truck spun in a hairpin U-turn and gunned down the two-lane road, back toward the inn.

She felt her head pressed back against the headrest as the scenery whizzed past. "I'd like to get there quickly. But in one piece. Aren't there police out here, giving out speeding tickets?"

"They don't like to waste their time. They never catch anyone." Gabriel cast her a mischievous smile. "And I know all their hiding spots."

She didn't doubt it. Gabriel O'Hara knew a lot of things and had given her something to think about today, too. Focused on the road, he didn't speak, and neither did Kerry. He reached over and covered her hand with his, and she felt his support and understanding, and his affection for her, too. It made her feel stronger, as if she could figure this out if she tried a little harder.

CHAPTER THIRTEEN

~

I s that Daddy's car? Is he here?" Max had been watching out the window for at least an hour with ferocious intensity, his small face pressed to the window in the front parlor, causing a cloud of mist on the glass. A miniature watchman, dedicated to Daniel's arrival.

Nolan trotted over to the window and peered out, too. "Not yet, Max. Just another car passing. He'll be here soon. Don't worry."

He ruffled Max's hair and returned to Kerry. They had been working together to set the tree in its stand and string the lights on the branches so that it would be ready for the ornaments by the time Daniel arrived.

Claire kept Charlotte occupied, looking through the ornaments and letting her play with the empty Christmas stockings. "We're going to hang these on the fireplace, and Santa will put toys and treats in them for you." Charlotte peered into a stocking to check if anything was inside yet, then looked back at Claire, frowning with disappointment. "Not yet, darling. It won't be full until Christmas morning."

It would be chock-full, too, Kerry knew, judging from Claire's shopping spree at the fair. With Charlotte's help, Claire hooked each stocking onto the edge of the fireplace mantel, and Kerry thought of the envelopes she had left that morning. She had scooped them up right after she'd walked through the front door. She had beaten the family back by minutes, just enough time to put her suitcase upstairs and hide all evidence of her misadventure.

When Claire asked what she had been up to all morning, besides the housekeeping tasks, Kerry said, "I ran into Gabriel. We just talked for a while."

It was a misleading version of the facts but not that far from the real story, and Claire seemed pleased by her answer. "No-man! I see car lights!" their lookout called.

Nolan pulled back the curtain. "Yup, that's your daddy. Let's get the door."

Max had already jumped off the couch and was hurling his little body across the foyer. Excited by the sudden activity, Edison jumped up and chased him, barking with every step.

Liza must have been watching from her room. She ran down the stairs and straight to the front door as well. It was already open, and Kerry heard Daniel's low voice talking to the cabdriver.

Kerry stood back with Claire and Nolan as Daniel filled the doorway, his wife and children covering him in hugs. He embraced them, his arms stretched wide open, filled with love. Kerry saw his eyes squeezed shut. "I missed you guys so much. Did you miss me? A little?"

"We missed you, Dad. We really missed you," Max said, hugging Daniel's leg.

Liza lifted her head from Daniel's shoulder and whisked away a few tears. She was laughing, too, Kerry noticed, the combination like a sun-shower on her beautiful face.

"I'll get your bag, Daniel. Good to have you back." Nolan stepped forward and grabbed the suitcase.

"It didn't feel like Christmas without you, but now it does." Claire gave Daniel a quick hug and headed toward the kitchen. "Are you hungry? I saved you plenty of dinner, and there's some soup and fresh bread Kerry baked this afternoon if you just want something light to eat."

"I'll start with the soup and bread while the rest of the food is warming up. I starved myself in the airports, knowing what was waiting for me at the end of the rainbow."

"If you've reached the end of a rainbow here, my friend, it's not a pot of gold, but a pot of Claire's chowder waiting for you," Nolan told him.

"That's even better, in my opinion," Daniel said.

Kerry hadn't found a chance to greet Daniel

yet. She wasn't sure he'd even noticed her. But as he took his usual seat at the table, he smiled at her. "Good to see you, Kerry. Liza told me you've been a great help to her around the inn the last few weeks, and with the children. I appreciate that."

"No need to thank me. It's good to see you back."

Max climbed his father's knee and patted Daniel's cheeks with both his hands, as if to make sure his father was really there.

"Do I look chubbier, Max? I've been eating too much fast food with no one home to cook for me."

Everyone laughed, though Kerry was still thinking about Daniel's compliment. Had Liza really said that? His words made her feel recognized and appreciated. She often felt invisible in a group. But not at the inn. Although she had only known these people for a short time, she would never forget them or the way they made her feel.

It was fun to trim the tree. Max hung most of the ornaments, with the help of the adults. Charlotte was lifted and guided to hang many of them, too.

Kerry could recall the last time her own family had put up a Christmas tree, the year before her mother had died. She was about twelve and still enjoyed the tradition at an age when most adolescents were afraid to look childish. Chances for merriment and frivolous activity were too rare in their household to pass up.

She remembered her mother, already sick by then, but her face calm and beautiful, happy as a child's, lit with a glow from within as she watched Kerry place the ornaments. At the time, Kerry had thought her mother was just enjoying the usual Christmas tradition. Later, she realized her mother knew what was happening, and what was to come. But she wasn't just savoring her last Christmas tree; she was watching Kerry. That was the real source of her joy.

Kerry brushed aside the bittersweet memory as Liza drew her attention. "Here are some for you to hang, Kerry." Liza pulled two more ornaments from their wrapping. "They're perfect. You must do the honors for us."

Liza handed her a tiny rolling pin attached to a tiny wooden spoon, and a second ornament in the shape of a tiny chef's hat.

Kerry met Liza's gaze and laughed. "Let's see . . . here's a good spot. Right next to the gingerbread man."

"Excellent," Claire said. She was in charge of the angels, Kerry noticed, and there were many, all different styles and materials. She hung them from the highest branches, standing on tiptoe.

Max tugged on her sweater. "Can you help me, Kerry?" His hands were full and she couldn't see what he was holding.

"All of those, Max, at once?"

He nodded, showing her a handful of bears. "It's a family. Like the story. They want to be on the tree together, or they'll get lonely."

She lifted him up and they chose a branch long enough to hold the furry trio. When she set him down, he looked happy and relieved by the job he'd done.

He was barely five and already understood. He knew he belonged to a family, too.

Tonight, it felt as if she really did belong here, with the lovely people in this room, who all cared for her in their own way. She was glad now that she hadn't left today. After a little persuading from Gabriel. She had to give him some credit. She would have missed out on all of this. For tonight, and all through Christmas, she would cling to this feeling. The sweet memories would sustain her when she finally did go away.

The children were so excited, it was hard to get them into bed and settled down for the night. Charlotte was the first to fall asleep in her crib, curled on her side with her floppy-eared bunny. Liza stood in the dim light and sang a soft lullaby.

In the next room, she heard Max persuading Daniel to read him one more story. Liza stood in the doorway, expecting Daniel to fall asleep first, but moments after a few pages were read in a low, soothing tone, it seemed as if some invisible hand had pulled the plug on their lively little boy. His dark eyes closed, he fell into a deep sleep, his head tilted to one side, resting on Daniel's shoulder.

Daniel and Liza exchanged an amused look but dared not make a sound. Daniel closed the book and slipped off the bed. He kissed Max's cheek softly and smoothed the blanket.

They tiptoed to their room and softly closed the door. Liza adjusted the child monitor on her night table.

"That was quite a homecoming," Daniel said. "A parade down Main Street tomorrow, right? What should I wear?"

"Oh, any old thing . . . and your crown, of course. Your subjects will expect that."

Daniel hugged her tight and kissed her. "If I'm a king, you're a queen."

She grinned. "To paraphrase Bette Davis, 'I'm queen of this dump,' that's for sure."

Daniel frowned. "It's not a dump. It's just not up to your royal standards—but getting there, I hope. After all the improvements. You never told me what the group from Colonial Inns said. Did they contact you yet?"

"Just to ask for more paperwork. I sent them a bunch right before the visit. I doubt we'll hear anything until after the holidays."

"It's not likely," Daniel agreed. "How do you feel about it now? Did meeting them help you make up your mind if they do make an offer?"

"I'm not sure. I've talked to a few other inn-keepers. The Fosters have a good reputation. I think they will take good care of the inn, and at least retain most of its character. Of course, there will be changes. I can't control that. I can either hand it over to someone else or run it myself. I can't have it both ways, Daniel. Even though I wish I could."

Daniel's expression was thoughtful and sympa-thetic. He touched her shoulder. "You don't have to sell it if you don't want to, Liza. It's still just a possibility. We can figure out something else to do. I'm here now; we can talk this through."

She looked at him and smiled. "I know. Seems almost too good to be true. I keep thinking I'm imagining you and talking to myself."

Daniel laughed. "That concerns me. You should see a doctor."

The line made her laugh. But she soon felt sad again, thinking about the inn and all she faced sorting this problem out.

"If I sell it—and it's still a big if—I have to admit, I'd feel as if I'm betraying Aunt Elizabeth. She put so much of herself into the inn. It was her life's work, even more than her painting. She trusted me with it, Daniel. How can I just sell it?"

"I understand. But I knew Elizabeth long before I ever met you. I know she never would have wanted it to be a burden for anyone. Elizabeth was a free spirit. She would never judge you for doing what you think is right, Liza. Even Claire and Nolan want to come out from under the burden of running it. Would Elizabeth have wanted that for her dear friend Claire? Think of the change as doing the right thing for them, too."

Liza nodded. It was good to have her husband here to talk things through. It just wasn't the same on the phone, or even over the computer.

"Enough about the inn. What's going on at the clinic? Have they told you anything more yet?"

"I got an answer yesterday right before I left. I wish I could say it's all settled, but it's still up in the air. The administrators say it's fine if I don't want the promotion. But if I want to keep working with patients, I'll be transferred to some other clinic."

From his expression, Liza could tell he wasn't happy with the choice. "But you've been there so long now, Daniel. Almost six years. You have seniority. That must count for something."

"I thought so, too. Apparently not. They said it's nothing personal, just a budget and staffing issue."

Liza dampened down her anxiety. It never helped to worry about something that hadn't happened yet; she'd learned that lesson well by now. "Where would they send you? Did they say?"

Daniel shook his head. "I don't know yet. That seems to be unclear as well. The organization runs clinics on one other reservation in Arizona, as well as reservations in New Mexico and Montana. I don't have to accept either choice. I can look for another job. It shouldn't be too hard to find one right where we are now."

"That's true," Liza said. "But it's not like we planned to stay in Deep Wells forever. It was only supposed to be a temporary situation. I think this question is bigger than just your work situation, Daniel. Much bigger."

If Daniel left the clinic and found another position, in a practice or at a hospital, Liza feared that would be it. They would be settled in the Southwest. They had made a few friends where they were living, but the children still weren't in grade school. They hadn't bought a house, or joined a church, or made many of the connections Liza expected to make in a real home. They hadn't put down roots there. Did they want to?

Daniel stroked her cheek, his touch soft and loving. "We're both tired. It's been a long day. Let's put this pot on a back burner, alongside the simmering situation with the inn."

She had to laugh at his metaphor. "Good idea. Good thing we have an eight-burner stove."

"We can't figure any of this out yet. It's foolish to keep worrying. When the time comes, we'll make the right choices. I'm sure of that. Right now, I just want to relax and have fun with the kids."

He was right. As Claire had told her, the only thing you can depend on in life is change. It's best to focus on the essential and unchanging bedrock: raising the children, and the bonds of family and friendship. To take life moment by moment and give thanks for what is right in front of you. Like time alone with your husband whom you have missed for weeks and finally being together for the holidays. Liza promised herself she would do just that.

"The children are so excited. I hope they don't burst like balloons before Christmas morning."

"A lot of parents feel like that right now. I've never seen it actually documented," Daniel added, in what Liza called his "doctor" voice. "I mean, in a medical journal."

"Thank you, dear. That's reassuring." She kissed him lightly, then got up to change into her nightgown. "You're right. Let's focus on the kids and make this a great Christmas. Not just for them, but for everyone."

It would be their very last holiday under this roof with Claire and Nolan, she almost added. But Daniel already knew that. There seemed no point in reminding him.

The Monday morning plan was another trip to Sawyer's Tree Farm, and then the Clam Box for lunch. Even though they had their tree, Liza and Daniel wanted to take the children on the pony cart ride. The line had been very long on Sunday, and Liza had promised Max they would come back when Daniel was with them.

There wasn't enough snow yet for Jack Sawyer to hook up a sleigh, but the beautiful white ponies pulled an open cart, a picture from a fairy tale with their long, braided manes and holiday garlands and sleigh bells around their necks. The side boards of the cart had been painted a bright, shiny red with white and green trim; the flat bed was filled with benches and cushions where parents and children sat back and enjoyed a leisurely ride through the winter woods.

Liza ducked into her office for a minute to check email and send a few answers to guest inquiries while Daniel took on the long process of dressing the children for cold weather. When Liza emerged a few minutes later, Charlotte was in her snowsuit, her arms sticking out straight. She rocked from side to side as she walked. Max only had his hat on. Daniel was holding his coat and trying to figure out the mitten situation, how the string connecting both mittens ran through the coat sleeves to keep the pair from being lost.

Liza walked over, fixed the mittens quickly, then slipped the coat up her son's arms. He was able to zip it up himself now and did the job proudly.

Daniel smiled with relief. "They're ready. Finally. I'm ready for a nap."

"Really? Here's some news that might wake you up." Liza opened her phone and showed him an email from George Foster at Colonial Inns.

Daniel read it quickly and stared back at her, his mouth gaping open in shock. "He wants to make an offer? So quickly? They only came here three days ago."

"I know." She let out a long breath and read the note over. "I can hardly believe it myself. I didn't even send them that much paperwork—records of occupancy going back a few years, profit and loss statements, that sort of thing."

"I guess it was enough. They must have liked the place more than they let on. Do you have any idea of how much the inn is worth?"

"I spoke to Betty Bowman. She did some research and compiled a record of recent sales for small hotels and B and Bs in the area. She gave me a ballpark figure for the value of the business and the property. She's heard of the Fosters. She's sure they'll make a fair offer, and she'll negotiate for me. It would be a good sum of money, Daniel. We wouldn't have to worry about our finances— or your job situation."

"I'd welcome Betty in our corner any day. She's very sharp and knows her business. When will they let you know? Did he say?"

"Right after the holidays. He also said they would allow Claire and Nolan to continue living here as long as they want. When it's all said and done—*if* it's all said and done," she clarified, "I think we should give Claire and Nolan some share of the proceeds. They've put their heart and soul into this place."

"I agree. Totally. There will be a lot more fine print to work out. But it seems we really don't need to worry about this anymore, Liza. It's practically settled."

"Almost." Liza nodded and pulled a hat from her jacket pocket. "It's just happening so quickly. It will take me a while to catch up . . . and to decide for sure."

"I understand. Maybe a pony ride through the woods will clear your mind."

"Sounds like a good remedy, Dr. Merritt." Liza grabbed a knapsack with things she needed for a day out with the children, then followed Daniel, Max, and Charlotte to the car.

It was a brilliantly sunny day with clear blue skies, the weather crisp but not so cold they'd worry about the children getting chilled. Liza tried to focus on the family fun and look on the bright side of this unexpected news. Daniel seemed happy and relieved. He assumed the question was settled. Maybe it should be, she reflected. But it didn't feel that way to her, deep in her heart.

There were still a few odds and ends to collect at church—baskets, trays, and cake stands—that had been used at the bake sale. Emily stopped in on Monday morning and sifted through a stack of platters and trays in the church kitchen, looking for the masking tape on each item that was marked with either her or Jessica's initials.

Reverend Ben wandered in, holding a coffee mug that said *Got Faith?* in bold white letters on a blue background.

"Good morning, Emily. Did you find what you're looking for? A few pieces may have been stored in the cupboards by mistake."

"I think I've got everything, Reverend. I just want to make sure these things belong to me or Jessica. I went home once with Sophie's favorite cake pans. You'd think I'd stolen a Rembrandt."

He laughed and filled his mug. "Would you like some coffee? I just made it. I shouldn't drink the whole pot by myself. Carolyn says it's bad for my blood pressure."

Reverend Ben had such a calm, low-key personality, Emily doubted even a major dose of caffeine could raise that vital sign much. "I will have some, thanks. Jane had to get to school extra early—a special review for a chemistry test this afternoon—and I missed my second cup."

The minister smiled, probably recalling his own days of child rearing. He and his wife, Carolyn, had two children, a son and daughter, adults now who had given them several grandchildren.

"I remember that bleary-eyed drive to the high

school well. How is Jane? She just had a birthday, didn't she?"

"Yes, she just turned fifteen." Emily sipped her coffee. "It's impossible to talk about her birthday without thinking of the morning I found her."

"I feel the same," Reverend Ben said quietly. He had been the first person on the scene, after Emily.

"And remember how you encouraged us to adopt her. Even though Dan thought we were too old to start a family." Emily had understood Dan's reluctance. He'd just given over the newspaper to his daughter, Lindsay, and also had a grown son from his first marriage.

"I remember that, too. Though once Jane was in your care, Dan turned into Mr. Mom."

Emily laughed. "He really did. He says now that taking care of Jane as a baby was one of the best times of his life. He'd been working so hard to build the newspaper when he was young, he'd missed out on so much with Lindsay and Wyatt."

"How is Jane doing? She'll be off to college soon."

Emily fought the urge to roll her eyes. Everyone had been telling her that lately. "Not so soon. But she's already talking about applications and entrance exams. Her career plans change by the hour, so please don't ask what she's interested in studying. The answer right now is 'everything.' "

"As it should be." Reverend Ben smiled. "She's

in a time of enormous transformation. Trying on new identities, trying to figure out where she fits in the world. That's a long process. But when you're that age, it's both exciting and painful at times. She's lucky to start out on such solid ground, blessed with parents like you and Dan."

"Thank you, Reverend." Emily was touched by the compliment, but felt she didn't entirely deserve it. "There are . . . special issues because she's adopted. I'm not sure I've been dealing with them that well lately."

Reverend Ben didn't reply, but his calm blue eyes encouraged her to say more.

"Jane's mother has come to Cape Light, to look for Jane. She kept their connection secret, but I figured it out. I won't explain how. That's not important."

When Emily thought back to the series of events that had led to the startling revelation, she felt it was not a random, one-in-a-million chance. She was meant to see the birthmark on Kerry's leg. She was meant to know Kerry's true identity.

"—What's important now is how I've acted on the information. Or maybe failed to," she admitted.

"What do you mean? You didn't tell Jane, is that it?" He wasn't judging her, Emily knew that. He just wanted clarity.

"No, I did not. Jane's birth mother told me, more than once, that she had never come with the intention of revealing herself to Jane." Emily caught herself from admitting she was talking about Kerry Redmond. She could at least respect Kerry's obvious need for privacy. "She told me that she doesn't want to upset Jane's life. Especially if Jane hasn't tried to find her yet."

"So, you're not sure whether or not to go against the birth mother's wishes? Is that it?"

Emily sighed. "I'd like to say that it is, but that's not it at all. I think she's afraid to meet Jane. I know I was afraid to meet Sara, as much as I tried so hard to find her. You know what I went through, the guilt about giving her up that paralyzed me sometimes."

"You walked the same road as this woman," Ben said. "You know her deepest longing and her fears."

"And I still wasn't fair to her. I know it's irrational, and even unethical. But my primitive, lower brain is telling me I can't risk sharing Jane, not even with her real mother. I'm afraid I'll be eclipsed and pushed aside. I'll lose Jane's love. I know it's crazy, but I can't seem to help how I feel." Emily felt some relief speaking so honestly. "I've spoken to Sara about it. And to Dan, of course. They both understand. Dan isn't sure what to do about it either. He tends to think it's the birth mother's choice. Which suits me fine. Too fine, I think."

"I understand that as well. It's only normal,

Emily. You're on the other side of the same coin you shared with Sara's birth mother, years ago. Surely you see that?"

"I see now that I never realized how hard it must have been for Sara's adoptive mother to share Sara with me. She's always been supportive. And now, Jane's birth mother has been so agreeable, not making any demands. I've allowed her to let me off the hook. I can tell that she hasn't forgiven herself for giving up Jane. And I've taken advantage of that."

Emily had sought Reverend Ben's counsel so many times during her own struggle. He'd advised her, encouraged her, lifted her from her doubt and harsh self-judgment. One day in particular, his wise words had broken through her clouds of guilt and doubt like radiant sunshine.

"If God forgives you, Emily, you must forgive yourself. Do you think you're wiser or have some higher authority? God expects us to make mistakes. He knows you're not perfect. He loves and forgives you anyway. It's up to you to do the same."

Now he met her gaze and set his empty mug in the sink. "If you can see that you've taken advantage of this woman, then you know what you should do. You don't need me, or anyone else, to tell you."

"I do know. I wish I could make myself do it, but I don't seem able to. But ever since I spoke with Jane's birth mother on Friday, I can't stop thinking about it either."

The question was a dark shadow hanging over Emily's Christmas. She really wished that Kerry would just leave town, as she had said she planned to do. That would solve the problem, wouldn't it?

"God will help you figure this out. He will find the best possible solution for everyone if you place it in His hands."

Emily wanted to believe that. Reverend Ben had such strong faith; she tried to draw on it, like a bee hovering over a sweet flower. "I'll try, Reverend. I really will."

He smiled and clasped her hands. "I know you. I know you'll do your best. That's a lot. Believe me."

Emily met his gaze and sighed. *If I can live up to even half of Reverend Ben's faith in me, maybe I can do the right thing.*

CHAPTER FOURTEEN

～❦～

There were no guests staying at the inn over Christmas. Kerry wasn't sure if Liza had told everyone that the inn was closed for a few days, or if no one had called to book a room. Either way, it made the holiday and family time much more relaxed for everyone, including her, she realized on Tuesday morning, the day before Christmas.

The family planned to attend the Christmas Eve church service at five and come home for a special dinner. She and Claire had been working on the menu for a few days—wild mushroom soup, roast duck with plums, and an array of vegetables and side dishes. Kerry woke up early to start the bread dough, which needed hours to rise. She was also going to bake a chocolate hazelnut torte and make a trifle for dessert. The elaborate, layered masterpiece made her think of her lunch in the bakery with Gabriel. She could take a photo of the large crystal bowl with many layers of pastry cream and lady fingers within and send it to him, she thought. With a note that said, *I can make this, too.* The message would make him laugh, but of course she would never do that. These last few days she'd been thinking more about a good time to leave the inn than her future here. Even a future with him.

The children were excited at the breakfast table. Daniel and Liza could hardly keep them settled long enough for cereal. "I'll take them outside to play," Daniel said, scooping the kids out of their chairs. "That will tire them out a bit. Christmas can't come soon enough."

"Thanks, honey. It can hold off a little for me. I still have some presents left to wrap," Liza said. "But not much else to do, except to get them ready for church later."

"The service starts at five," Claire reminded her. "We ought to get there on the early side if we want to sit together. The whole congregation will be there."

"What time is it over? I'll have dinner ready," Kerry said.

Claire looked shocked by her reply. "Aren't you coming with us?" Kerry remembered then that she had promised Claire she would join everyone at the Christmas Eve service. It would be one more chance to see Jane—and Gabriel—she thought. And she didn't want to seem churlish by hanging back. She really did feel part of the family and knew she would enjoy attending church with them, even if only to please Claire. It seemed so important to her.

"Sure, of course I'll come. I'll make sure everything is ready for dinner before we go."

Claire looked relieved at her answer. "We'll do that together. There's plenty of time."

There was plenty of time, but the day still passed quickly. After lunch, Kerry wrapped a few last-minute gifts in her room and then dressed for the service. She chose her best outfit: a burgundy-colored dress of soft knit fabric, with a round neck and long sleeves.

Through all her hard times, she had somehow managed to hold fast to a set of gold earrings and a long gold necklace that had belonged to her mother. It was the only good jewelry Kerry had ever owned, and many times, when she'd needed money, she had been tempted to sell it. But she was always glad later that she never did.

When she put it on she felt her mother's spirit near, like a gentle hand on her shoulder, settling her nerves and giving her the strength to do what she knew she must. To leave this place and all these wonderful people very soon—without ever telling Jane her true identity.

But first, you can enjoy Christmas Eve and Christmas Day, she reminded herself as she dabbed on a bit of lipstick. And *that's saying a lot.*

Church was just as crowded as Claire had predicted. *Maybe more so,* Kerry thought as

354

Nolan drove into the parking lot. But they were still early enough to find a space. Daniel's car pulled up right beside them and they entered the sanctuary all together. *Like all the other families here tonight,* Kerry thought. *Families that are happy together and love each other.* Could she really leave all this behind?

But the truth of the matter was that very soon Daniel and Liza would return to Arizona. The inn would be sold, and Claire and Nolan would depart for distant lands. *We seem like a loving family tonight, but we'll soon be dispersed in all directions. Like a pile of Max's building blocks tumbling down on the kitchen floor. They'll all go their own ways. And I will, too.*

The organ sounded the sharp, bright notes of the opening hymn, and the congregation came to their feet as the choir marched into the sanctuary, singing "Joy to the World." The carol was one of Kerry's favorites and never failed to lift her spirits. Instead of feeling blue about the days to come, she felt her heart fill with gratitude for the blessing of simply being here. She wouldn't let herself miss it by looking too far ahead.

The hymn concluded and Claire squeezed Kerry's hand as they sat down. "I'm glad you came tonight," she whispered.

"I'm glad I came, too."

Reverend Ben thanked the choir for the lovely hymn and made a few announcements. Kerry's gaze wandered around the sanctuary. She already knew where the Warwicks liked to sit and spotted them easily. Jane sat between her grandmother and a young woman with long, dark hair whom Kerry had never seen before. Should she try to speak to Jane tonight, just to wish her a Merry Christmas? The fair was over and it was impossible to know if she would see Jane again before she left.

If it happened by chance, that would be all right. But it was best not to seek her out. She'd had some time with her daughter, more than she had ever expected. She had to be satisfied with that.

She didn't see Gabriel. Had he missed the service? She doubted that, though anything was possible.

When it was time for the Scripture readings, she realized that Gabriel must have been sitting behind her and out of sight. He walked up the center aisle in a dark blue suit, with a stark white dress shirt and a red tie. He looked so handsome standing at the pulpit, she felt her breath catch.

"The first reading is from the book of Titus, chapter three. Verses four through seven."

Looking as solemn as Kerry had ever seen, Gabriel began to read the Scripture, his voice deep and clear. " 'Not by works of righteousness which we have done, but according to his mercy he saved us . . .' "

Tonight, the familiar passage yielded deeper meaning. God didn't expect perfection. Even a person who'd made mistakes, as she had, could be touched by His mercy and kindness. The sudden insight gave her hope.

Right before Gabriel closed the Bible and stepped down from the pulpit, he looked out at the pews. Kerry thought he'd found her in the crowd, and offered a small smile, but she couldn't be sure. She might wish him a Merry Christmas tonight. There would be no harm in that. Would they spend any time together before she left? She wanted to give him the photograph, but the package could be passed along by Claire or Liza. That might be best. Saying goodbye would be so hard. It seemed better not to try.

Reverend Ben had returned to the pulpit. "Our second reading is from the Gospel of Luke. Chapter two, verses eight through twenty." He paused and adjusted his glasses. " 'And there were in the same country shepherds abiding in the field, keeping watch over their flock by night,' " he began.

As he continued, Kerry noticed that he barely glanced at the Bible that stood open before him on the lectern. She wondered if he knew the long Scripture passage by heart. His tone was serious but also brightened by the excitement and joy of the story that described the amazing appearance of angels announcing the birth of Jesus to the shepherds. And how the shepherds set off that very night to find the newborn baby.

When he was done, Reverend Ben closed the Bible and gazed out at the congregation, blue eyes twinkling behind his glasses. The sanctuary was silent, his audience waiting to hear what he'd say next.

"Once again, just like the shepherds who have heard the spectacular news of our Savior's birth, we return to the manger in Bethlehem. When I read this passage, I usually find myself in the role of a shepherd, imagining how it felt to see angels flying about in the night sky. And imagining how it felt to hear their astounding message that would forever change history.

"Just toward the end of the story we are told, 'But Mary heard these things and held them in her heart.' And this year, I began to think about Mary. A teenage girl, far from home, without the help of her mother or anyone familiar to her when her time came. Except for her husband, Joseph, of course . . . and we all know how useful men are in such situations." His slight eye roll made everyone laugh.

"How did she manage? Forced to give birth to her first child in a stable, with so little to aid or comfort her? Or to comfort and protect her newborn child? Our manger scenes invariably include a rough, wooden crèche for the infant, but I doubt she had even that modest luxury. No, Mary had little more than her motherly instincts and her bountiful love. As I thought more about her, I began to see how this naive and untested young woman, who had probably never been beyond her small village before, might be seen as the hero of this story. Showing such remarkable courage and strength, conquering her fears with faith, hope, and most of all, love. Love for the child about to be born in such difficult circumstances.

"Mary is always shown as so calm and compliant. But I imagine she must have been afraid. She must have harbored some doubts during that long, dark night. At the very least, she must have been surprised by the way things were turning out. She couldn't have expected to give birth in a stable of all places, even in that day and age. And yet, Mary holds steady, the calm at the eye of the storm. Because?

"Because, above all, she is a mother and her deep, unflinching love for her child is her guiding star, her motivation and inspiration. The wellspring of all the strength, courage, and hope she needed that night, and in all the years that followed."

He paused, his expression thoughtful. "How often we speak of God as our Heavenly Father. But tonight, when I think about Mary, I realize that we might also say—and maybe, more accurately, too—that God loves us as a mother loves. As Mary loved her newborn infant, her

359

only child. With her whole self, her whole heart. A love that is not earned but freely given, no matter our flaws and missteps. A love that goes the limit, makes any sacrifice, forgives any slight. Surely, Mary's role in this story is at the heart of the message of Christmas. A message that we are all so deeply loved. More than loved—cherished, prized. And from this day forward, we are asked to be messengers of that bountiful, unconditional love. To share it with one another, and with the entire world. Tomorrow, on Christmas Day and every day. To follow the bold, brave example of Mary and her son."

He took a deep breath. Kerry did, too, feeling deeply touched by his words, which seemed to hold special meaning for her. She knew that later, when she had a moment or two alone, she would think about all he'd said.

Reverend Ben smiled. His warm gaze swept over the congregation. "I wish you all a beautiful, blessed Christmas."

As the minister returned to his seat, the choir began, "Hark! The Herald Angels Sing." It was another of Kerry's favorite carols, and she sat back, enjoying the blending voices and harmonies.

"Now it is time for us to share our joys and concerns." Reverend Ben stood before the altar and gazed out at the congregation. "Who would like to start?"

Many people raised their hands. Most spoke about feeling grateful to be united with their loved ones, young and old, for the holiday. Or about special Christmas gifts and blessings that had already arrived. Others asked for prayers for relatives and friends who were sick or facing challenges.

Kerry was too shy to stand and speak her heart so publicly. But she silently offered up thanks for all the blessings in her life—for the people who not only had offered her friend-ship, kindness, and affection, but had made her feel more hopeful about the way her future could be.

For meeting her daughter and spending time with her these last few weeks, of course. And for finding out that, without a doubt, Jane had been raised by parents who could not love her more or have given her better care. *Of course I wish that I could have raised Jane on my own, but I have to be grateful for the way Jane's life has turned out. I couldn't have asked for more for her.*

Claire raised her hand and Reverend Ben called on her. "Yes, Claire? Do you have a joy or concern to share?"

Claire stood up, squared her shoulders, and looked around the sanctuary. "I think by now most of you have heard that the inn will soon be sold. I know that many friends are concerned for Nolan and me, but frankly, we're very pleased about this big sea change in our lives. It seems sudden in a way, and yet, we've been moving in that direction for a while now. So it's not so surprising, after all."

Nolan smiled up at her and she rested her hand on his shoulder. "Nolan and I will still live at the inn and continue to attend this church. You're not getting rid of us that quickly," she added, making everyone laugh. "But we are looking forward to seeing the world and have already made plans for our first adventure, a trip through the Mediterranean, including stops in Egypt, Greece, Turkey, and Israel. Not to mention the long cruises Nolan has planned for us on his sailboat, down to Montauk Point and up to Bar Harbor. We're very thankful for the way everything has worked out and are truly looking forward to the New Year."

As Claire took her seat, Kerry noticed many people in the congregation whispering to each other. Either they had not heard about the inn being sold, or they were surprised by Claire's positive view of the situation.

She also noticed Liza and Daniel share a quiet word. Liza looked happy but wistful. Kerry imagined that it would have been hard for her to stand up here and announce the inn was being sold. She must be relieved that Claire took that task on herself. And relieved that Claire sounded sincerely happy to be starting a new stage in her life.

Claire always finds the good in any situation and any person she meets. I need to remember that lesson, because there is good to be found. Though it isn't always easy to see.

The service ended with the last notes of Handel's "Hallelujah Chorus." The voices in the chorus were remarkably strong. Kerry felt the final notes vibrate right through her, her heart lifting as the melody climbed higher and higher.

She had never thought much about the music at church. It was just there, in the background, the same as when she was riding in an elevator or shopping in a store. But she suddenly understood how music could be much more in church, a way of expressing feelings that were impossible to put into words.

After Reverend Ben gave his final blessing, the aisles filled with the congregation, most of them trying to get on line to wish Reverend Ben a Merry Christmas.

Kerry wove a path in a different direction, to an exit at the side of the church that was far less popular tonight. She would catch up with the others later, maybe wait for them out at the car, she decided. She dodged a cluster of children scampering by in their holiday outfits, velvet dresses for the girls and clip-on ties for the boys.

She had hoped to say a few words to Gabriel, at least to wish him a Merry Christmas. But she saw him guiding the same older woman he'd escorted to church before to the minister's receiving line. The woman Kerry assumed must be his grandmother. She once again felt a wistful sadness that she would never get to know his family now. Or spend more time with him. He had helped her so much this last week, stubbornly drawing out her secrets and accepting her anyway. She still wanted to thank him for that.

Kerry slipped out the exit and found herself on a path to the village green. Before she could figure out the direction of the parking lot, she felt someone tap her shoulder.

"Kerry? I've been trying to catch up with you. The church is so crowded tonight."

She turned to find Emily Warwick, the last person she would have expected to seek her out.

"It is . . . Merry Christmas," she added.

"Merry Christmas, Kerry. Are you having a good holiday?" Kerry could see she wanted to say something more but was having trouble finding the right words.

She wants to make sure I'm going to leave soon, as I promised, Kerry decided. "I am. I might stay until New Year's Day, but no longer. I'm not sure yet," she said, preempting Emily's question.

"Thanks for letting me know, but that's not why I was looking for you." Emily glanced over her shoulder. She seemed nervous, which wasn't at all like her.

Standing behind the glass doors of the church,

Kerry saw Jane and a young woman behind her, who touched Jane's shoulder in a reassuring way. The two had been watching the conversation.

"I know what you said. But I've been doing some thinking and I want you to know . . . I think you should tell Jane."

Kerry was stunned. Where had this come from? She thought that was the last thing Emily wanted. She didn't know what to say.

Before she could reply, Emily said, "I know how hard it is. I'm not just saying that, believe me. But I don't think there will ever be an easy time, and you'll regret it when you go . . . And none of us can tell what the future holds. You may never have another chance."

"Yes, I know," Kerry admitted. "I've tried not to dwell on that possibility . . . Did you tell her already?"

Emily shook her head. "I wouldn't do that. I told her that you might be leaving here soon and I wanted to say goodbye to you, privately. She wants to say goodbye to you, too. You don't have to tell her the truth if you don't want to . . . but I think you should. I *know* you should."

Kerry had not been prepared for this. Her head spun along with the pinpoints of starlight in the dark night sky. She stared at Emily and back at Jane in the doorway.

She remembered what Gabriel had told her—that she'd come here with this burden, and she would take it with her if she didn't step up and tell Jane who she really was. And she remembered how he had said that he believed in her. It helped her grab on to her courage.

No excuses now. You've waited so long. This is it.

"All right. I will tell her. You're right. There's never going to be a better time."

Emily turned toward the church and waved. The young woman with Jane encouraged her to go outside while she stayed behind. Kerry watched Jane walk toward her. She knew Emily was standing there, inches away, but it suddenly seemed that she and Jane were the only ones who existed. The village green, the church, the entire world melted away as her daughter came to join her.

"Hey, Kerry. Merry Christmas."

"Merry Christmas, Jane." Kerry felt nerves jump in her stomach. She tried but couldn't return Jane's warm smile.

"I'm feeling a little chilly out here. I'll meet you back inside, Janie." Emily touched her daughter's arm as she left them, but not before exchanging a glance with Kerry.

Jane didn't pay much mind to Emily. Her attention was fixed on Kerry. "Mom said you're leaving. Because the inn is being sold, is that it?"

"Not really. I never planned to live here that

long." Kerry felt her mouth go dry but pushed on. "I came for a certain reason. I was looking for someone. Someone I love very much and think about . . . well, almost every waking minute. I was worried about them and wanted to make sure that they were all right."

Jane looked confused and even concerned. "Did you find them?"

"I did, Jane . . . It was you. I was looking for you. I'm your mother," she said finally. "Your birth mother."

"*You?* You are?" Jane was stunned and took a step back. "All this time . . . why didn't you tell me?"

"I'm not sure. I thought I was doing the right thing by not telling you. I wanted to make sure that you were happy and loved and had a good family. That's the only reason I came here. I didn't think I deserved to tell you. I'm still not sure now that I do."

"You tricked me. You tricked everybody." Jane's voice rose. She looked angry and confused. "I've imagined what my birth mother would be like. I never thought it would be you."

Kerry wasn't sure what to make of that. Was it a compliment or an insult?

"I imagined what you'd be like, too. But anything I imagined never came close to how wonderful you really are. I am just . . . amazed by you. I know you're angry with me. Maybe

367

this is all too much, and too quickly. All I want you to know is how much I loved you and how hard it was for me to give you up. I was so afraid and alone. I was barely three years older than you are now. I didn't think I could provide for you. It broke my heart. I thought it was the only solution, the best thing for you. I did it because I loved you so much. Not because I didn't want you. That's what I really need you to know."

Jane shook her head. "Well . . . okay. What am I supposed to say to that?" Jane was about to cry. Kerry wanted to reach out and hug her close but didn't dare.

"Jane . . . I'm sorry. Please try to believe me . . ." Kerry took a step toward her but Jane stepped away.

"I can't talk about this anymore . . . I have to go." She turned and ran back to the church. Emily was waiting by the door for her. Kerry watched Jane run inside and fall into Emily's waiting arms, crying on her shoulder.

Kerry turned away. She didn't want Emily or Jane to see her.

She was crying, too. It had turned out just as she had feared. Maybe even worse. Jane would never forgive her.

Kerry was shaken to the core by her encounter with Jane, but there was so much excitement when everyone got back to the inn, it was easy to hide her feelings. She focused on working in the kitchen with Claire to get their holiday meal on the table.

Once everyone was seated, they joined hands, and Claire led the family in a blessing over the meal. "Thank You, dear Father, for the bounty of blessings we are about to enjoy on this beautiful holiday. Not just the wonderful food on our table, or the gifts under the tree, but those gifts from You that are far harder to see and much more precious. Our health, happiness, and all the love we share. Amen."

"That was beautiful, Claire. Thank you." Daniel's voice was thick with emotion.

"Well said, my dear," Nolan agreed, patting his wife's hand.

"Can we open presents now?" Max looked around at the adults, his expression so hopeful, Kerry had to smile.

"Not yet, Max. First, we're going to have this delicious dinner that Kerry and Claire made," Liza said.

"Then we'll have dessert," his father added, "and sing some carols by the Christmas tree. And after that, we'll open just a few presents. Because Santa is coming soon, and you have to be asleep so he can leave the toys he's bringing under the tree."

Max didn't look very happy about the plan. He sighed and took a bite of bread. "I guess I can wait," he said finally. "But I wish time would hurry up."

Nolan laughed. "Funny you should say that, Max. I wish time would slow down. Maybe we can work on a machine that could speed it up for you or slow it down for old folks like me."

"That would be a good machine to make, Nolan. I can help you."

"I'm sure you can. Someday," Nolan said, smiling warmly at the little boy.

Kerry and Claire brought dessert and coffee into the parlor, where they continued their feast and sang favorite Christmas songs, a livelier medley than those they'd sung in church. Finally, Max and Charlotte were allowed to choose one gift each to open in advance of Christmas morning. They were both thrilled with their choices—a new, advanced Lego set for Max and a playhouse with a family of little furry critters dressed in tiny clothes for Charlotte.

Charlotte quickly brought one of the critters to Kerry, the little girl doll. "Look! Look!" she said, handing it over.

"Oh my, she's adorable, Charlotte. She looks just like you."

Kerry wasn't sure if Charlotte had understood everything she'd said, but the girl lit up with a smile.

It was easier than Kerry had expected to focus on the happy moments and put aside thoughts of

Jane. One thing did seem clear. Her hours at the inn were numbered. There seemed no reason at all to remain here.

Christmas morning was an explosion of activity, squeals of delight, and a storm of wrapping paper. Kerry remembered jumping out of bed early at that age and being so excited to see her presents, but she had been an only child in a quiet household, while Max and Charlotte had a circle of adults looking on and cheerfully adding to the mayhem.

Once the children were done unwrapping their gifts, the adults had their turn. Everyone seemed thrilled with their gifts from Kerry and touched by her thoughtful choices.

Kerry received gifts, too—from Liza, a classic cookbook that Kerry had wanted for ages, and a bottle of expensive perfume. Liza always wore the scent and Kerry had admired it. Claire gave her a hand-knit sweater that Kerry had been eyeing at the fair. "Blue, to bring out your eyes, dear," she said. And a beautiful silver bracelet. Kerry knew she would always treasure it.

After the morning's hectic burst of energy, the day passed at a leisurely pace. The children played with their new toys, and the adults read new books or dozed by the fireside. They all enjoyed an early dinner, a rib roast and Yorkshire pudding that Kerry had made.

371

She had just finished cleaning up the kitchen when she heard a light tap on the back door. She expected to see the Gilroys, who had been invited for dessert. But instead, she saw Gabriel, leaning over to peer through the small windows at the top of the door.

She quickly pulled off her apron and walked over to let him in. If only he'd given her some warning. She knew she looked a mess, her hair going in all directions after standing at the hot stove all afternoon.

But when he smiled at her as he walked in, she forgot to feel self-conscious. The way he looked at her, she might have been a celebrity in an evening gown and jewels, walking down the red carpet.

"I just stopped by to say Merry Christmas. I tried to catch up with you in church last night, but I lost you in the crowd."

"Merry Christmas," she replied, happy he had surprised her. "I thought you must be having dinner with your family today."

"In a little while. The inn is on my way. I have a gift for you." He held a small package, neatly wrapped with red and white striped paper and a green bow. He offered it to her, looking suddenly shy.

"Thanks. That's very sweet of you. You didn't have to do that."

"I know I didn't have to do it. I wanted to."

Curious, she tore off the wrapping paper. It looked like a book, bound in red leather. There was a gold stamp on top of a knife and spoon crisscrossed, but she didn't see a title.

She glanced at him, feeling puzzled.

"It's a food diary. You said you wanted to start one, remember? I guess you could write stuff down in any sort of book, but I found this in a gourmet store in Newburyport." He took the book from her and opened the cover. "It has a place for the date and location of the food you want to write about and a space for possible ingredients or a recipe. And here's a spot to stick a photo."

Kerry took back the book and flipped through the pages. "Wow, this is great. I have all these little scraps of paper stuck into cookbooks. Now I can keep everything in one place and find it when I need it."

He looked pleased at her reaction but not totally convinced. "Do you really like it?"

"I love it," she insisted. She did, too. "That was very, very thoughtful of you. This is going to help me take my cooking game to a new level."

"Your cooking game seems fine to me. But I'll be happy to sample any new recipes you master."

If only, she thought with a wistful smile. She wouldn't mind cooking for Gabriel every night. But she quickly swept that thought from her head.

"I have something for you, too. Wait here, I'll

get it." Kerry ran upstairs to her room, taking a very quick stop at the mirror to comb her hair and add a dash of lip gloss. She grabbed Gabriel's gift and brought it back down to the kitchen.

"Here you go. It isn't much, but I hope you like it."

"I'm sure I'll love it." He looked as excited as Max had a few hours ago and quickly tore away the paper. She could tell by his slow smile that he did love the photograph and was surprised by her choice.

"This is beautiful. I'll hang it over my desk so I can always be reminded of the legend." He looked over at her and met her gaze. "And you," he added.

Kerry felt the color rise in her cheeks. "I'm glad you like it . . . When do you need to leave for dinner? I hope you're not late."

"I have plenty of time. It's not very cold out. Would you like to take a walk on the beach?"

Kerry thought that was a good idea. Maybe she would try to say goodbye to him. At least warn him that she was leaving soon. It seemed only fair. *We can't really talk privately here. I'm surprised we weren't interrupted already.*

A few moments later, they were headed down the gravel drive to the road. A long wooden staircase across the road led down to the beach. Kerry went down first, with Gabriel following close behind.

"I'm glad I brought my gloves and scarf, but it's not really that cold out. Not for late December around here," Kerry said.

"I hear there's a big storm on the way," Gabriel replied. "It happens like that sometimes. A deceptive spell of mild weather, then *whamo*."

Kerry laughed at his weather forecast. "Is that an official term meteorologists use?"

"Only the really smart ones." Kerry had already reached the sand, and Gabriel hopped down the last step. He smiled at her and took her hand. Kerry felt her heart jump. It didn't seem right or fair to him, but somehow, she couldn't let go.

They soon reached a strip of smooth, packed sand that made it easy to walk along the shoreline. The sky was clear with a few low white clouds. A flock of hardy gulls trotted over the sand and dashed in and out of the waves, looking for food.

"I wonder if seagulls celebrate Christmas," Gabriel said.

"I doubt it. Though they'd probably be happy finding just a few bags of potato chips under their tree and a bushel of clams."

"I think that would do it for them." Gabriel glanced at her and squeezed her hand.

They walked along in silence for a few moments, then Kerry said, "I'm glad you persuaded me to stay longer that day my taxi got stuck in the sand. I'm glad I stayed for Christmas."

Gabriel smiled. "I am, too. I hope you stay

even longer. I think you know that by now."

Kerry felt her breath catch. She wished he hadn't said that, but now she couldn't avoid telling him her plans.

"I do . . . and I wish I could stay. But I wanted to tell you that I've decided to go. I spoke to Jane. She knows who I am. So there's no reason for me to stay here any longer."

Gabriel suddenly stopped walking. He turned to her. "You told Jane that you're her mother? What did she say? How did it go?"

Kerry shook her head. "Not well. Not well at all. She was very angry and upset. I think she hates me. I doubt she'll ever want to speak to me again."

Gabriel put his hands on her shoulders, steadying her. "Kerry, don't say that. She was shocked by the news, I bet. I'm sure she'll go through a lot of emotions, processing this news. But I don't think she'll be angry forever."

"She's upset that I abandoned her when she was a baby. I tried to explain that I did it because I loved her so much but, of course, she doesn't understand that. How could she?" Kerry sighed and stared out at the rolling blue waves. "And she's angry because I tricked her. She thought of me as a friend and feels like I deceived her, hiding my true identity. I guess I did," Kerry added. "But I never planned for that to happen. It seemed the right thing to do at the time."

Gabriel gazed down at her. She could see that he didn't know what to say. He pulled her into his arms and she couldn't stop herself from falling into his warm, comforting embrace.

"This is all very hard to navigate, Kerry. I don't think anyone gets through this situation perfectly. You did your best. Jane will see that, in time. And she'll forgive you. I know she will."

A few tears slipped from Kerry's eyes, and she brushed them away with her hand. "I hope so. Maybe someday we can be in touch and have some sort of relationship. Years from now, probably."

"Sooner than that, I bet. Jane's been raised by good parents. I think they've taught her to be a kind and generous person. And she's been attending Reverend Ben's church her whole life, so I know she's been taught about forgiveness, too. Because that's what good people do. They forgive each other. And someday, she'll forgive you."

Kerry couldn't answer. She wasn't sure she agreed, but it was good to hear him say the words she longed to hear. She trusted him and took heart in his advice and insight. It would be so wonderful to have a person like that by her side, to help her through her life.

But that could never be now. She had just told him that, more or less.

They walked a bit farther, then turned and

headed back to the steps. The sun was sinking toward the horizon, and the breeze off the waves was colder.

"When will you leave? Do you know yet?" he asked.

"I'm not sure. But before the New Year."

"Taking the train again? I could drive you up to Maine. That wouldn't be any problem."

His offer touched her heart. But if she dared accept it, she wondered if they would ever leave town. He'd surely talk her into staying again.

"I'm booking a bus ticket this time. Thanks for the offer, but . . . I don't want to put you out of your way."

He looked like he might argue with her, then stopped himself. "All right. Once you're settled, will you get in touch with me?"

"I will," she promised. She didn't want to cry. Not in front of him. Maybe they would stay in touch, she thought. Though it would be difficult and not quite the same.

At the bottom of the stairs, he turned to her. "I wish we could have spent more time together, Kerry. I hate to see you go. But I know there's nothing I can say to stop you, right?"

Kerry couldn't answer. He was tempting her now almost beyond her limits. She suddenly did want to stay, if only to see where this tentative relationship might lead. But the reasons pressing her forward—the promise she had made to

Emily, Jane's anger and rejection—were too strong.

"I wish I could stay, too. But I think you understand why I'm leaving. I hate to say goodbye. Let's just not, okay?"

"Okay." He looked like he might say more, then dipped his head and kissed her, a soft, searching kiss that made her head spin.

She held him close a moment, and finally, they slowly parted.

They began to climb the steps as the sun sank below the dark blue sea.

Christmas Day is over, Kerry realized. *So is my time on the island.*

CHAPTER FIFTEEN

ᕙ

Jane seemed her usual self during Christmas, but Sara could see that underneath the smiles and teenage squeals of excitement, her little sister was brooding, even hurting. Sara knew why, too.

Jane was torn between holding on to her anger and an urge to run to Kerry, to claim the mother she had always wondered about. Sara could recall the battle inside her own heart and mind almost too well. She also knew that even though a solution seemed impossible, there could be a resolution, one that was happier and filled with more love than Jane had ever imagined.

The day after Christmas passed quietly at the Forbes house. There was cleaning up from the holiday to take care of and sorting out of the piles of gifts under the tree. Dan and Luke played chess in the afternoon while Sara and Emily took a long walk through the village. Jane mostly stayed in her room, which made Emily worry. Sara promised she would speak to her.

That night, while heading to the guest room, Sara found Jane lounging on her bed, her earbuds in place. She was reading a cookbook Sara had given her for Christmas, *The Complete Encyclopedia of Baking*. Jane was very focused on a page that featured a photo of a huge pie with a crisscross crust. Sara had to knock on the doorjamb to get her attention. "Earth to Janie Forbes? Can you read me?"

Jane finally yanked out an earbud. "Oh . . . hey. I didn't see you there."

"Obviously. Can I come in?"

"Of course, silly." Pulling out the other earbud, Jane sat up and made room on the bed. Sara walked in and sat down next to her.

"Heading to bed early?" Jane asked.

Sara nodded. "I've hit cookie overload, how about you?"

"Definitely." Jane grinned. "I went over the top this morning with gingerbread for breakfast."

"Yeah, I saw you. That was bad. But it is Christmas." They shared a complicit grin. "I was thinking, let's do something fun together while I'm here. Just me and you."

Jane sat up straighter, looking interested. "Sure. Like what?"

"I don't know. Some activity that burns off a few cookies? We'd have to drive north awhile to go cross-country skiing. Or . . . is the pond behind the Morgans' house frozen yet? We could skate there."

"Jessica always has their big skating party this

week, remember? I'm not sure what day it is."

Sara did remember, now that Jane mentioned it. In the week between Christmas and New Year's, the Morgans opened their pond to all the skaters in town and served hot cocoa and popcorn all day.

Sara hadn't gone for years but always remembered the event to be lots of fun.

"That would be great. Is that what you want to do?"

Jane quickly nodded. "But some of my friends will be there. It might not be that much fun for you."

"I don't mind sharing you with your friends for a little while. I'd like to meet them. We can do something on our own after that. Go into Newburyport and shop or have dinner? I bet we'd find some good sales up there now."

"I do want to exchange that dorky sweater Dad got me." Jane rolled her eyes. "I didn't want to hurt his feelings. Luckily, it doesn't fit."

"That was a lucky break." Sara met Jane's gaze. "So, how are you doing otherwise, aside from a dorky sweater and too much gingerbread?"

Jane pushed her hair back and looked away. "Okay. I guess. It's great to have a break from school. And fun to have you and Luke here."

Sara could tell her little sister knew what she was asking but was avoiding the subject.

"We love hanging out with you, too. I think

you're old enough to come to Boston and visit us on your own now."

"Tell Mom and Dad that."

"I will," Sara promised. "What I really meant was, what do you think now about your talk with Kerry? It's a big deal to meet your birth mother for the first time. Believe me, I know."

"I know you do. But that's just the thing. It wasn't the first time. Not even the second, or the third—or the fifth. Kerry tricked me. She made me be her friend and taught me all that baking stuff. And I never knew who she really was. That wasn't right. She should have told me." Jane's voice rose on a note of ire and indignation. Feelings she had a perfect right to, Sara knew.

Sara hadn't meant to upset her sister, but she knew that the feelings had to come out if Jane was going to move on to a better place in this situation. She rested her hand on Jane's shoulder.

"I understand. You have a perfect right to feel angry. But I also know that when I came to town and found Mom, I did the same thing. For some reason, I just couldn't work up the courage to tell her who I really was. And she was always so nice to me . . . It got very complicated when it really should have been very simple."

"I know what happened with you and Mom. You've both told me the story. This isn't the same. I don't need Kerry. No matter how nice she acts. She lied to everyone. Not just me."

Sara paused, wondering if anything she said to Jane would make a difference. Maybe it was too soon to talk about this. Had Jane walled off her heart to Kerry so completely?

"No, it isn't the same. No one's experience could be. That's the first thing I learned as a reporter. This is just one side of the story. My side. When I did tell Mom who I was, I was very angry at her, too. I felt the way you do. Why did she give me away? How could anyone do that and still claim that she loved me? But finally, I came to believe what she said, that she did it because she loved me and wanted me to have a good upbringing. At the time, she didn't think she could give me that. When I believed all that was true, I was able to let her into my life and forgive her. At least, to start to do that."

Jane stared straight ahead, hugging the thick cookbook. "I understand what you're saying. But I can't forgive Kerry. I don't really want to."

"I think that's true. You can't forgive her if you don't want to. Forgiveness is a choice. And a process. Sometimes a long one. It doesn't happen automatically. And it doesn't have to mean that you're excusing Kerry's actions. I think she's already told you she's very sorry for the way things worked out."

Jane stared straight ahead, trying hard to hold on to her anger. "What about Mom and Dad? They'd feel pretty bad if all of a sudden, I had another mother. I don't want to hurt their feelings that way. They're my *real* parents."

Sara remembered very well the confusion about which parents were *real*. That would take a long time to sort out, if ever. Jane felt confused and disloyal about sharing herself. Sara had been through that, too.

"I think Mom and Dan can handle it. I think they always wanted you to find your birth mother and have a relationship with her, if that's what you want. I know they would try very hard to make it work if it made you happy."

She waited for her little sister to answer, but Jane stared at the carpet, looking lost in thought. "I didn't lose anything or need to choose sides when Mom came into my life," Sara added. "It gave me *two* wonderful families. You won't lose anything either if you get to know Kerry better. She's part of you, Jane. She's in your DNA, whether you ever say another word to her or not."

"I've thought of that, too." Jane put the book on her night table and sighed. "Mom came with an entire herd of Warwicks. Kerry seems alone. I don't think she has any family."

"I know. Mom said that about her, too. Maybe she'd like to be part of our family," Sara said quietly.

"Maybe. If the crazy tribe doesn't scare her off." Jane glanced at Sara with a small smile. "We'll have to save Grandma for last."

Sara grinned. "Good point. You think about it. If you want me to call Kerry at the inn, or you want to call her yourself, we can make a plan to see her again. Maybe go out to lunch or have tea at the bakery?"

Jane's smile vanished. "I guess I do need to think about it."

"I understand." Sara leaned over and hugged her. "You're pretty cool for a fifteen-year-old."

Jane rolled her eyes. "You're my sister. You're supposed to think that."

"Not necessarily. You could have been a real nerd. The way I was at your age." Sara smiled down at her. "So, I know we've pigged out this week. But I expect you to bake at least one decadent recipe from that book before I go. Just sayin.' "

She left Jane's bedroom, peeking over her shoulder as she turned down the hallway. Jane was already sticking in her earbuds and reaching for the cookbook.

But working out her feelings about her birth mother, too, Sara hoped. She prayed that Jane let Kerry into her life, if not right now, then someday. It would be such a great loss for Jane if she decided not to.

On Saturday morning, Liza cleared up the breakfast dishes with Kerry's help, while Daniel lifted the children from their booster seats, about to lead them upstairs to get washed and dressed for the day.

"How many layers should they wear?" Daniel asked. "Where are we headed?"

Liza turned from the sink. "The Children's Museum in Boston would be great, but it's a long ride. I think there's a museum in Newbury-port that would be fun for them. I can check online."

"Max and Charlotte might be too young, but the Morgans are having their skating party today. They'll just squeeze it in before the snow comes," Claire said.

The weather forecast was calling for snow, coming in on Sunday, Liza had heard. They weren't sure yet how much would fall. They were flying back to Arizona that Friday, on the third, and she couldn't imagine it would delay their flight, no matter how much snow fell. But some part of her hoped it would.

Liza glanced at Daniel. She loved the skating party. It would be crowded, but they didn't have to stay long. "What do you think? Max has already tried skates once. He loved it."

"Future Bruins star," Daniel said proudly.

"I'd like to get on skates again. Even though I might regret it," Liza said with a laugh. "We could take turns watching Charlotte? We don't have to stay very long."

"I'm up for it if you are. Let's see if Audrey is

bringing her boys. Jessica always sets off a space for the little kids."

Liza felt cheered by the idea. As much as she loved Christmas, sometimes the days after were a letdown. She wanted to enjoy every moment they had left at the inn.

Daniel took each of the children by the hand. "We have our marching orders. Thermal underwear below, snow-proof on top."

"I can finish here," Kerry said to Liza. "You need to get dressed, too."

"Thanks. It always takes longer to leave the house than we think."

Liza was following her family into the hallway when her cell phone rang. She pulled it from her back pocket and checked the screen.

George Foster, the CEO of Colonial Inns.

Her hand fumbled as she answered the call. "This is Liza," she said in as steady a voice as she could manage.

"Good morning, Liza. I hope I'm not calling too early?"

"Not at all, George. We're just about to take the children out for the day. How can I help you?"

More records were needed for their research, she suspected. Did she really want to dive into her files today? No. Maybe he was calling to let her know they had decided not to make an offer on the inn after all. That could be it, too.

"You can help me by accepting our offer, I

388

guess," he said with a laugh. "But I need to put it forward first."

Shocked, Liza abruptly sat down on the stairs. She pressed the phone to her ear, willing herself to focus on his words.

"—The property needs some work, but we did love the place. The location is unsurpassed. We think it would fit very well with our brand. For the inn and property, we'd like to offer . . ."

He named a figure that took Liza's breath away. She felt a little light-headed and took a deep breath. "I have to be honest, George. I didn't expect to hear back from you so quickly. And on a Saturday."

"Well, we met yesterday and talked it through fairly quickly. We were all impressed. A property like this doesn't come on the market every day. We know we're the first to see it and we'd rather not get into a bidding situation. So this offer stands for . . . oh, let's say, end of next week, until January third?"

"That seems fair."

"I hope that's enough time for you to decide. I certainly don't expect an answer right now. I'll email the contract we've drawn up, and you can contact me anytime with questions."

"Thank you, George. I'll print it out right away. We're working with a real estate agent, Betty Bowman of Bowman Realty in Cape Light. She might be in touch with you as well."

"That would be fine. I look forward to hearing from her."

Liza said goodbye and put her phone aside. She felt stunned.

She had never imagined selling the inn would be so easy, or happen so quickly. She wasn't ready to hear that someone wanted to buy it, though the offer was far more than even Betty had predicted. She had to tell Betty right away. She could already hear her squeal of delight.

But she had to tell Daniel first. Of course he would say they should accept. It was enough for them to put both children through college and buy a house somewhere, and have a comfortable nest egg for their retirement—or whatever they wanted to do.

Could they dare refuse this opportunity? It might never come again. She had listed the reasons why selling was the best choice a thousand times. Logically, she knew she should feel happy. Elated, even. But a heavy weight, like an anchor, dragged on her heart, keeping her moored in one spot.

Could she really sell this place? It was suddenly all very real, and she wasn't sure that by January third—or anytime soon—she would feel absolutely sure it was the right thing to do.

A short time later, Liza came back downstairs and asked Kerry, Claire, and Nolan to meet her in the kitchen. "This won't take long," she told them. "George Foster called this morning. He's made an offer to buy the inn. Daniel and I have talked it over, and I'm ninety-nine percent sure I'm going to take it."

She waited, watching their expressions change from curiosity to surprise. Daniel was in the parlor, watching the children, so she could answer questions without distraction. But she suddenly wished he were at her side, she felt so weak in the knees.

Claire's face flashed with sadness for a moment, but she faced Liza with a resigned smile. "That was fast work. They must love the inn and see how special it is. That makes me think they'll take very good care of it. I'm so happy for you, Liza. This has all been settled so swiftly."

"I am, too," Nolan chimed in. "What good news. What a great relief for you . . . and for all of us. Now we can move forward with our plans and know that this place will be in very good hands."

There was a lump in Liza's throat. She ignored it and tried to act as happy and relieved as they seemed to think she should be.

"Daniel and I are very pleased. I haven't gone over all the details in the contract yet. Betty is going to help me. But they seem a reputable and fair organization. I doubt there will be any surprises."

Kerry had been quietly listening. It was hard

for Liza to read her reaction. "Congratulations," she said finally. "I'm very happy for you and Daniel."

"Thank you, Kerry. If the deal goes through, Claire and Nolan can still live here if they like and help out part-time, or not. If you want to stay on, too, I'll give you a very good recommendation."

Kerry looked surprised by her offer. "Thank you. That's very thoughtful of you. But since everything is settled here, I think it's a good time for me to head back to Maine."

Liza took in Claire's reaction. She could tell Claire wasn't surprised at the news, but wasn't pleased about it either. "That's your decision, of course, but I want you to know, you don't have to go. I'm practically certain you can stay. The Fosters couldn't stop talking about those cranberry scones you baked."

Kerry sighed; she looked torn. Liza could see she really did want to go—for whatever reason— and now they were making it hard for her.

"It's all right. Please let me know if there's any way I can help you, Kerry. With a reference or anything at all."

"Thanks, Liza. I will. And good luck again. I'm sure this is a huge step for you. But sometimes, the choice that's best for everyone is the hardest one."

Somehow Liza knew she was talking about her own choices, too.

"You'll stay through the New Year, I hope?" Claire said. "Until Liza and Daniel leave?"

"I'm not really sure yet." Kerry replied. "I'll let you know."

"Of course. No pressure." Liza had a feeling Kerry would leave sooner, rather than later. Seeing her go would be hard, the beginning of the end in a way.

Daniel appeared in the kitchen doorway. "How's it going? Audrey's here. The kids are getting a little antsy."

"You go on, Liza. Enjoy the day," Claire encouraged her. "You have nothing to worry about now. None of us do."

Liza smiled, but didn't reply. Trust Claire to put the best and brightest spin on the news. She would need to remind herself of Claire's words all day.

Ever since their talk, Kerry had secretly hoped that she would hear from Jane, or even Emily. A slim, wishful hope that her daughter regretted her harsh words, even a little. She knew such a change of heart was less than unlikely, but she couldn't help hoping. When no word came by Saturday and Liza announced the inn was all but sold, there was no reason to stay on the island any longer.

She quietly packed her belongings that night. Everything still fit in her one small suitcase and knapsack. She hardly slept a wink, and in the morning, woke up with the first light and wrote out three short letters. One for Claire, one for Liza, and this time, one for Gabriel. She would leave the first two in the kitchen and would mail Gabriel's from the bus station.

She had moved around a lot after leaving Rockport, where she was raised. She was well-practiced in putting people and places behind her. But this place and this group of people were different. She had let down her guard and let them into her heart. Especially Claire. And Jane, of course. The very thought of her daughter all but drained her resolve to go. She wouldn't let herself think about Jane at all, until she was far, far away.

Kerry knew she would miss everyone at the inn for a long time. Which made her remember why she had always kept her distance before—and would do so again from here on out.

On Sunday morning, she ate breakfast with the family and carried out her morning tasks. Everyone was in a hurry to get to church. Liza and Daniel were due to leave for Arizona on Friday and wanted to attend one last service at the church.

Talk about the weather was also a big distraction. Nolan turned up the kitchen radio and everyone grew quiet so they could listen. "A massive front of frigid air, sweeping across the

Great Lakes and upper Midwest states, is due to hit New England sometime late this afternoon. It will bring low temperatures, high winds, and snow. How much of the white stuff remains the question, folks," the forecaster added. "Could be anywhere from six to twelve inches. If it slows down and hangs around awhile before moving out to sea, we could be looking at even greater accumulation . . ."

"Six to twelve? That's enough for me." Nolan turned the volume low again. "We'd better take out the shovels and check the snowblower when we get back from church, Daniel."

"Good idea. Let's pick up some bags of ice melt in town."

"At least you don't have to worry about flights being canceled," Claire said to Liza.

"Probably not," Liza said. "Since we don't leave until Friday, I doubt our plans will be affected."

Kerry had to agree, but wondered if her own plans would be. If she got an early start today, she might make it to Bar Harbor by tonight. She would at least reach Portland.

A short time later, she heard everyone bustle out of the inn, and then watched from her bedroom window as both Claire's Jeep and the Merritts' rented SUV drove away. She had already called a taxi and was waiting on the porch with her bags when it arrived.

It was the same taxi company as the last time. There was only one in town. But a different driver was behind the wheel this morning, she noticed. She was almost sorry to see that.

"Where to, miss?"

"The bus station, please. My bus leaves in half an hour. Do you think we'll get there in time?"

"I don't see why not," he said as they turned onto the road that led to the land bridge.

She watched out her window as the inn grew smaller, then disappeared from view. She turned and stared straight ahead, trembling with emotion. She wasn't going to let herself cry, because she knew it wouldn't change anything. She'd learned that long ago.

Claire unlocked the inn's back door, and Liza followed with Max and Charlotte. The little ones mimicked Claire as she stopped on the door mat and stomped off the snow that clung to her shoes.

Nolan and Daniel had headed straight to the barn to check the snowblower, pile more wood for the fireplace on the porch, and put the shovels in a handy place for digging out.

"It's a good thing we didn't stay in town for lunch," Claire said. "It's starting to accumulate."

Liza had noticed that as well. Daniel had turned on the wipers full force by the time they'd reached the land bridge. "It's reached here a lot earlier than they said. Maybe it's a fast-moving storm and will pass by quicker than they predicted."

"We can hope. In the meantime, I'll start on some grilled cheese sandwiches and heat up the potato-leek soup Kerry made last week. I think that combination won the popular vote."

"I'll set the table. The kids can play in the parlor awhile. Let me get some toys out for them."

The kitchen was spotlessly clean, as Kerry always left it. But the house had an empty feeling. Liza couldn't put her finger on it.

She walked to the staircase and listened, then called up the stairs, "Kerry? We're home. Claire's making lunch. Do you want some?"

She didn't hear a sound. Maybe Kerry was in the shower? It seemed late for that. She always left a note in the kitchen if she went out.

Liza settled Max and Charlotte in the parlor with their Legos, then returned to the kitchen. The soup was warming on the stove and Claire was cutting thick slices of the delicious honey-oat bread Kerry had baked yesterday.

"I think Kerry's gone out. Did she leave a note in here?"

Claire glanced at the table. "I don't see one."

The oak server near the basement door caught Liza's eye. She didn't see the usual scrap of paper, but something far more serious-looking. Two envelopes, the one on top marked with her name in Kerry's neat, square printing. She picked them up. The one on the bottom was addressed to Claire. She had already guessed that. Claire was busy grating a hunk of cheddar and hadn't noticed.

Liza opened her envelope and quickly read Kerry's message.

A thank-you note, mainly. But one that made her eyes well with tears. She knew there was no way to delay telling Claire, though she wished she could. Kerry was gone. Liza felt a sad hollowness deep inside.

She stepped over to the stove and touched Claire's shoulder. Then held out the note to her. "It's from Kerry. She left this morning while we were at church. She said she's sorry, but it was too difficult for her to say goodbye."

"Oh . . . oh my." Claire took the envelope and stared down at her name. "I thought she might leave this way . . . She's a dear person. I wish we could have helped her more." Claire looked up at Liza. "I always had the feeling that she came here for an important reason. Maybe she'll come back and visit someday, when she's ready."

"Maybe," Liza replied. Though she doubted Kerry would be in touch again. Maybe for a job reference, but not in the way Claire meant.

Claire sighed as she assembled the sandwiches on the cutting board. "I'm going to miss her help and her wonderful cooking and baking. I'll miss her quiet company and friendship, too. Very much."

Liza felt the same. She noticed that Claire had not opened her envelope. "I can work on the sandwiches if you want to read your note?"

"That's all right. I'll read it later." Claire tucked the letter into her pocket and turned her attention back to the stove. "I can easily cook and say a prayer for her at the same time. That she'll be safe in her travels and has made the right decision by leaving here. And that she'll find peace in her heart."

Liza wished the same for Kerry. No matter the mistakes of her past, Kerry had such a good heart. She deserved to find some happiness if anyone did.

CHAPTER SIXTEEN

E mily and Dan were alone in the kitchen Monday morning, though it was almost nine. Emily turned away from the window and poured herself a mug of coffee. "There's at least twelve inches out there, and the drifts are even higher. Did they say when it will stop?"

"Sometime this afternoon. Where is everybody? How can they sleep through the noise from those snowplows?"

"They stayed up to watch an old movie. Let them sleep in as late as they want. No one's going anywhere right now."

Dan filled a bowl with cereal. "It's not a bad week for a heavy snow. All the schools are closed anyway, and a lot of businesses, too."

"That's true." The snowfall had been fun yesterday. It made the house feel cozy. Sunday afternoon had passed at a leisurely pace, reading books and playing Scrabble while Sara and Luke put together a wonderful stew for dinner. This morning, Emily felt claustrophobic, staring at the blurry whiteness.

"It's so cold. I think we should raise the heat.

We don't want a pipe to freeze, honey." She could have said, "Freeze again. Like last year." They'd already gone through that annoying situation.

"I kept the faucet in the basement trickling last night, just in case. You better call your mother. She's probably in a state and will expect you or Jessica to visit via dogsled."

"Jess probably has enough dogs for that, but I'm not sure about the rest of the equipment." Emily had to laugh at his prediction.

No sooner had she said the words than her cell phone rang.

Dan raised an eyebrow. "Should I check the garage for a sled?"

Emily made a face. She picked up the phone, expecting to see her mother calling, but found the number of the Bradford Arms Hotel in Newburyport on the screen instead.

It was the catering manager, Jeffrey Shelton. Calling to iron out some details of the party, she expected.

"Good morning, Ms. Warwick. Sorry to call so early, but I thought you should know right away. We have some bad news, I'm afraid. There's a plumbing situation at the hotel. A pipe broke last night, and the Emerson Room is flooded. The room won't be available for your stepfather's party. I'm so very sorry."

Emily felt a wariness building but didn't panic. "These things happen. I'm sure you can

401

find another room we can use somewhere in the hotel?"

"I've checked all availability, but it just isn't possible. All the private dining rooms are booked for New Year's Day. I'd hoped to fit your group at a long table in the regular dining room, but there's simply no space to accommodate the reservation. We can offer a private room at our sister hotel, the Battle Green Inn in Concord? We'll certainly reduce the charge considering your inconvenience."

"Concord? That's a lot farther than we wanted to travel," Emily said honestly.

She also knew for certain that her mother didn't think much of the Battle Green Inn. A rustic place, with low, beamed ceilings and faux Colonial decor. Her mother hated places like that. Emily could almost hear Lillian's response: *Where the waitresses swish around in puffy white hats and long dresses that look like nightgowns and hand out doughy popovers all day? I'll pass, thank you very much.*

"Can I talk it over with my sister and get back to you? I'll let you know for sure sometime today."

The catering manager thought that was a good plan and apologized again before hanging up. Leaving her with the problem.

"Now what?" Emily said aloud.

"What's going on? Some problem with the party?" Dan asked.

"Yes, a huge one. A pipe broke and they just canceled our reservation."

Emily quickly dialed Jessica. Her sister picked up on the first ring. "Emily? Is everything okay? Any problems with the storm?"

"Not at our house, but the Bradford Arms just called. A pipe broke in the room we booked and we can't have the party there."

Emily quickly explained the situation—and the offer of a backup room at the Battle Green Inn in Concord.

"Mother hates that place. I took her there for lunch once. She sneered through the entire meal."

"I know. I don't think we should even mention it to her. But what can we do? The party is two days from now. We can postpone it, I suppose. Until they can find a room for us."

"That's one possibility. But it seems a shame to miss out on surprising Ezra for his birthday. I'd offer our house, the original plan, but I have a problem with the heating system in the barn and we had to bring a lot of the animals inside last night. I've no place to put them until the heat back there is working again. That will definitely take two or three days, with New Year's Eve tomorrow."

Emily could picture her sister's house—crates of rabbits and chickens tucked into the family room and kitchen. Maybe a goat or two in the laundry area? Cats and dogs always roaming free. And she couldn't forget the baby piglets. Once she'd even been greeted by a huge macaw, who had swooped down and picked off her hat. "How do you do?" it had squawked at her. Emily wondered if Jessica's talking birds knew how to sing "Happy Birthday."

"Can you imagine Mother dealing with the four-footed party crashers?" Jessica added.

"Let's not even go there. The Spoon Harbor Inn doesn't meet her standards either. And I doubt they would have room for us anymore. It was almost booked solid when I called weeks ago."

"Mother's house is large enough for the family," Jessica said. "But I don't think she can deal with the stress of having so much company. We'd have to clear out all the breakables. That would take at least a week, and we only have two days. And who would cook?"

"Molly is the only one I can think of." They both knew that battlefield was not worth visiting again.

"What about the Inn at Angel Island? Maybe they would take us," Jessica said. "As a favor to Ezra?"

Emily hadn't thought of the inn. *Maybe I blocked it from my mind, because of Kerry.* But she couldn't rule it out just because it would bring Jane and Kerry back together.

"It's worth asking Liza," Emily said. "But with the inn being sold, and Liza and Daniel going back to Arizona this week, I doubt they'll agree. Even for Ezra. Do you think Claire could do the cooking on such short notice?"

"It's just the family. And she has Kerry to help her."

"Yes, she has Kerry," Emily echoed. Would a forced reunion with Kerry and Jane be a good thing—or a bad thing? She had no idea. She did know that she and Jessica were desperate.

"The inn is so lovely. Mother can't object. Can she?"

"I don't think we can worry about Mother's objections. The goal is to have a nice party for Ezra on New Year's Day. If the inn is available, it could be the relaxed celebration we originally planned. With lots of his friends and former patients included. Before Mother demanded the white-glove treatment."

"Good point, Em. We need to return to Plan A and keep Mother in the dark about this switch as long as possible."

"I had the same thought. I'll call Liza right now and let you know what she says. Can you deal with Mother and Ezra today?"

"I just spoke to them. Everything is fine on the Providence Street front. Later, when the snow stops, Sam and I will go over with some groceries and dig them out."

"In Sam's truck, I presume. Not via dogsled?"

Jessica laughed. "I did consider it. None of my dogs are that well-trained."

Next, Emily dialed Liza and explained their predicament.

"Ezra is going to be ninety-five? That's amazing. He really does deserve a party," Liza agreed. "It's very short notice, but there aren't any guests here now. How many do you expect?"

"The party started off big. We wanted to include Ezra's friends and a lot of his former patients, who would love to be part of the celebration. But my mother cut it down to just the immediate family. That's only twelve."

"Everyone loves Ezra. I like the first idea much better."

"You do?" Emily was surprised that Liza would consider the idea at all, much less encourage a longer guest list.

"The more I think about it, the more I like this party idea, Emily. It seems fitting that we should hold one last, big bash before the inn changes hands. I bet you'd include the same people in town we'd invite for a grand finale."

"Does that mean you'll do it?"

"Absolutely. I know Claire will be happy to work on it, too."

"It isn't much time. Can we really pull it together in two days?"

"We'll have to hustle. Maybe Molly can help

with the cooking. She must have parties to cater for on New Year's Day anyway."

Emily already knew that was so. "Bring in Molly if you need to. That would be fine with me and Jess. Just don't mention it to our mother, if for some odd reason she happens to call. Which she probably won't," Emily added. "We're keeping the final arrangements a surprise for her as well."

"How sweet. That makes it even more fun," Liza said.

"We hope so," Emily replied, crossing her fingers. "And of course you have Kerry. She'll be a huge help in the kitchen."

"Kerry left yesterday. While we were all at church. I knew that she planned on going back to Maine soon, but not quite when. She explained in a note that it was hard for her to say good-bye. I was fairly certain she could have stayed on and worked here after the sale, but she seemed determined to be on her way."

Emily was shocked by the news. Even though Kerry had promised that she would leave town by the New Year and not interfere with Jane's life. To hear that she was actually gone somehow didn't seem right. Not for Kerry, or for Jane.

Emily agreed to come up with a final number of guests and figure out a menu with Liza by the end of the day.

Sara and Jane strolled into the kitchen, both

wearing big plaid bathrobes and fuzzy slippers. "Who have you been talking to all morning?" Sara asked. "You can't be managing the snow-plows in the village anymore."

When a big storm like this one struck while Emily was mayor, she had often slept in her office in order to manage the cleanup.

"No, but I have been managing a party crisis," she replied. "We were booted from the Bradford Arms. A pipe broke in the room we had booked. Your Aunt Jessica and I have been trying to figure out where to move Ezra's soiree. By some stroke of dumb luck, Liza just agreed to have it at the inn."

Emily noticed Jane's sleepy expression suddenly grow alert. "I thought Liza sold the inn."

"Almost. It hasn't changed ownership yet. She was very encouraging about holding a big party for Ezra. Not just the family. She wants to close the inn with one last bang."

"Wow, that is a lucky break." Sara sat at the table warming her hands on a mug of coffee. "We can all help set up and decorate. Can Claire and Kerry cover the cooking in such a short time?"

Emily knew this part of the story would be harder to relate. "Liza is going to ask Molly to cater some of the food." She paused and took a breath. "Kerry isn't there. She's gone back to Maine."

Jane turned and stared at her mother. "What

do you mean? She's not at the inn anymore?"

Emily shook her head. "She left on Sunday. Liza knew she was planning to go soon, but Kerry didn't actually say goodbye to anyone. She just left them notes."

"Did she leave me a note?"

"I don't think so, honey. Liza didn't mention it." Emily walked over to Jane and rested a hand on her shoulder. "Kerry promised me that she would get in touch once she was settled. I'm sure we'll hear from her soon."

Jane looked up at her. "You knew she was leaving, too?"

Emily couldn't lie. "Yes, I did. I didn't know when, but she said that was her plan."

Jane turned away. She looked like she might cry. "I should have been nicer to her. I wish I could have talked to her before she left. Can you find out where she went, Mom? Maybe Liza knows."

Emily stroked her hair. "I'll ask her, honey. I promise. We'll figure it out. Kerry loves you. Once she hears that you want to speak to her again, she'll be in touch. I can promise you that."

Emily met Sara's gaze over Jane's bowed head. Her older daughter's expression echoed Emily's concern. They had to find Kerry and let her know Jane's feelings had changed. Jane's rejection on Christmas Eve had been so harsh. That was probably the real reason Kerry had left town so abruptly. Maybe she wouldn't get in touch. Maybe she'd given up all hope of ever having a relationship with Jane.

Emily hoped that wasn't so. How and when had her own feelings about Kerry shifted so radically? She really didn't know. She did pray that heaven would help send Kerry back to Cape Light, so that things could be set right between Jane and her birth mother.

The snow tapered off around noon, and by two o'clock the sun was out. And so was everyone in the neighborhood, shoveling out their driveways, Dan and Luke included.

Jessica swung by in Sam's truck to pick up Emily, Sara, and Jane and take them to the inn. Molly was on the way in her own truck. Considering the tight timeframe, Liza thought it would be best to meet face-to-face and nail down all the plans in one bold stroke. Emily had to agree.

Only half the long driveway at the inn was cleared, but enough space to park the truck and walk the rest of the way to the porch steps. Emily spotted Daniel Merritt working with another man to clear the snow.

Liza welcomed them, and Claire was waiting in the kitchen with a pot of tea and a plate of home-made cookies. "Thanks so much for coming. I hope the ride wasn't bad?"

"Not at all. The roads in town are almost clear," Jessica said. "A little less so out here."

"I think we got more snow than town," Nolan said. "We're working with two blowers and have barely made it halfway to the barn."

Daniel and his helper came in the back door. They brushed snow off their jackets, leaving a small drift on the doormat.

"How's it going, guys? I can come out and help you again," Nolan offered.

"We're doing fine, Nolan. Just stopped for a warm-up break." Daniel poured himself a mug of tea and one for his companion. He was a dark-haired young man Emily had seen at church, though she didn't know his name.

Liza had left to answer the doorbell and returned with Molly.

"Neither snow, nor sleet, nor rain can keep me from party planning. I knew I was destined to cook for my darling Ezra. It was just a matter of time before the wheel of fate turned around." Molly's take on the strange course of events made Emily smile.

"I can't argue with that. You were our first choice."

"Don't I remember. But I can be a team player, too. Where's Kerry Redmond? I hear she's some quality competition in the kitchen."

"She definitely is, Molly. But we won't be running a bakeoff tomorrow. Kerry left on Sunday," Liza explained.

"Really? Well, no worries, my friends. I'm sure

we can manage. I can ask a few of my crew to work overtime if necessary."

Jane, who had been quiet so far, stepped closer to Liza. "Mom said she left you a note. Did she leave me one, too? Maybe you didn't find it yet."

Liza looked surprised by the question. "No, honey. We didn't find one for you. If she gets in touch, would you like me to tell her something?"

Jane's boldness suddenly drained away. "Just that I . . . I wanted to thank her for teaching me so much about baking. And that I wish we could have talked some more."

Emily's heart ached to hear her daughter's request. The room was suddenly quiet. Everyone had heard it, she realized, though she doubted that anyone but Jessica and Sara understood the real meaning of Jane's words.

"I'll absolutely tell her that," Liza promised. "I wish she was here to help us."

"I do, too," Jane said.

A few moments later, the three men left to tackle more snow, and the conversation turned to the guest list, the menu, and all the necessary trimmings that would make the gathering special.

Emily felt overcome by a sudden wave of doubt. "Do you really think we can pull this off in time?"

Claire touched her hand. "If a candle will doubt, it will go out. Do your best, and let God do the rest."

"It's going to be a squeaker, but you all know how I love a challenge. And aren't there gangs of helpful angels out here?" Molly gazed around the kitchen, as if she expected to see a few washing the dishes.

"I've heard those stories, too," Emily replied. "While you're lining up prep cooks and servers, don't forget to call in a few."

Gabriel was already in his truck, on his way to look for Kerry, when Nolan had called and asked to borrow a snowblower. He'd been annoyed to have to waste time with a stop but couldn't refuse his friend the small favor. Once he was there and started up the machine for the other men, he felt obliged to help Daniel while Nolan went inside to warm up again.

Somehow, his reluctant generosity had put him exactly at the right place at the right time, and he had overheard the one message that would make Kerry willing to return.

He had expected to argue with her about coming back but now doubted that any persuasion would be necessary. *In fact, she might even thank me,* he thought, as another bus station came into view.

He'd already stopped at three, following the route from Cape Light to Maine. The roads were almost clear. Buses and trains were running again. His only hope was that the buses on the road were still few and far between, and that she would have to wait along the way.

Anyone who knew what he had set off to do would have told him he was crazy. Looking for her tonight was like searching for a needle in a haystack. That was why he hadn't told anyone where he was going or why. He would follow her all the way to Bar Harbor if necessary. She wasn't going to get away from him that easily.

The bus station looked like all the others. Fluorescent lights and rows of plastic chairs filled with weary travelers. A few posters that advertised scenic spots did little to cheer up the dreary atmosphere. Students, parents with small children, old people, all of them wearing tired and dazed expressions. He searched the faces carefully but didn't see her.

A row of ticket agents worked behind a glass window. He checked the lines. Maybe she was booking a seat on a different route?

He saw a woman who looked like her and nearly called her name. But when the woman turned, his heart fell. It wasn't Kerry. Only wishful thinking.

He walked out of the station and dug his hands into his jacket pockets. It was already dark and cold again. She wouldn't wait outside. That wouldn't make sense.

He climbed into his truck and stared out the windshield. There was a diner across the road. He hadn't noticed it before. He had been driving for three hours and felt hungry, but he didn't want to stop to eat. He might miss her somewhere up the road.

While he debated sparing a few minutes to grab a sandwich, the diner's door opened and Kerry walked out.

She fumbled with her suitcase, knapsack, and a bag of take-out food. He jumped down from the truck and walked over to her. Finally, she looked up and recognized him, and her mouth dropped open. "Need some help with your bags, ma'am?"

She straightened to her full height and hugged the knapsack closer. "No thanks. I can manage."

"Surprised to see me?"

"Yes. And no." She met his eyes for only a second then looked away. "I wrote you a letter. You'll get it later this week."

"What does it say?"

"Oh, a lot of things. It doesn't matter now. I did say I wasn't coming back to the island. I think you know why, too. If you've come to persuade me to go back with you, please—there's no reason to put yourself through that. To put both of us through it."

He stood back and sighed. "Stubborn as a mule. I knew you would be. I'm not going to argue with you about coming back. Honest."

"Really? Then why did you drive all this way?"

"I have a message for you. From your daughter.

She was upset when she found out that you were gone, Kerry. She heard that you left notes for Liza and Claire, and asked Liza if there was one for her, too."

"She did? Really?" Kerry's voice was hoarse with disbelief. "You're not just saying that, are you?"

"I'd never lie about something like that. I know what it means to you. I was standing right there. I heard every word. She gave Liza a message in case you got in touch. Jane said she wants to speak to you. I think she's really sorry for the things she said. I think she's ready to have a real relationship with her birth mother."

Kerry stared at him a moment and then took a deep breath. The message had shaken her. He could see it was taking a minute or two to sink in. "How do you know all this, Gabriel?"

He explained how Ezra's party was being moved to the inn and how the Warwick women and Molly Willoughby came to figure out the plans.

"Claire and Liza miss you, too. They keep wishing you were there to help with this huge event that was just dumped in their laps at the last minute. Everyone wants you to come back, Kerry. Including me. I think you already know that."

Kerry didn't say anything, but he could tell her resolve was softening. "I'll need to make apologies for running out the way I did."

"Everyone will be so happy to see you, it won't matter at all. They don't want apologies, Kerry. They just want you back."

She sighed and finally showed him a small smile. "All right. I'll go with you. Sure beats waiting for a bus that never comes."

She hoisted her knapsack to her shoulder and rolled her suitcase with the other hand. Gabriel stopped her and easily took both pieces of her luggage, leaving her with just the brown paper bag.

He was so elated that she was coming back, he felt as if he were walking on air. But he didn't want to gloat too much.

"So," he said as she climbed into the truck, "anything good to eat in that bag?"

"Just a burger and fries. If you're hungry we can share it."

"Thanks. I guess it will have to do. Until you can cook something for me."

"Is that why you tracked me down? Because of my cooking?" Her tone was a mixture of insult and amusement.

"You are an amazing cook, Kerry. No question. But that's the least of it."

He turned to her and did what he'd promised himself he wouldn't do, in case it scared her away again. He pulled her close and kissed her, feeling a bone-deep happiness when she melted into his embrace.

It was hard to let her go and start the truck. But somehow, he managed. They drove off, heading back to the highway. He glanced at her, watching through her window as the road flew by, taking them closer and closer to Angel Island. He knew he had been meant to find her and bring her back there.

Sometimes, you *can* find a needle in a haystack. If Heaven is on your side.

Chapter Seventeen

When Emily returned home Monday evening after her visit to the inn, she felt somewhat optimistic that the hasty plans for Ezra's party there would actually work out. Molly, Liza, and Claire were all professionals and seemed to thrive on the challenge.

"The only thing left is persuading Ezra and my mother to show up," she told Dan.

"No small matter," he said.

"I know, but Jessica and I have a plan. I'm going to visit them after dinner and see if I can trick them into going there tomorrow."

"Want any backup? I can come if you want me to."

"That's sweet of you to offer, honey. But I think I'd better go alone. I don't want my mother's radar going up."

"I hear you. We all know how sensitive that warning system is."

Emily took his words to heart. She was a woman on a mission, entering a landmine zone.

When she arrived at the house, her mother

answered the door, immediately suspicious to see her there. "Emily? I didn't expect you here tonight."

"I was just driving by and thought I'd look in on you. How did you do with the storm?"

"You know very well. We spoke on the phone three times today, and your sister came by around noon. Didn't she tell you?"

Of course, her mother neglected to give Sam any credit for the visit, though Emily was sure he was the one who had shoveled the driveway and all the paths.

Emily followed her mother into the living room. "Yes, she did tell me." Emily paused. "Where's Ezra? I have some news about his party," she whispered.

Her mother looked interested, as if the reason for this mysterious visit had been solved. "He's in the kitchen," she whispered back. "Snacking on something bad for his health, I'm sure. What is it? Tell me quickly."

Emily quickly related the bad news about the Bradford Arms Hotel. "They offered us a room at the Battle Green Inn, for a reduced rate."

"I wouldn't hold the party there if they offered it for free." Lillian seemed more annoyed than disappointed. "With all this snow, perhaps it's better if the party is postponed a week or so. Ezra's real birthday is Saturday, the fifth. You or your sister can have the family over for a birthday cake. We'll find out when the hotel can reschedule and surprise him then."

He would be surprised a lot sooner than that, Emily hoped. Her mother would be, too. "Good plan," she said.

Her mother sat down on the couch and picked up a book from the end table, a thick novel that took place in England during the Great War. Emily had been meaning to read it but had heard it was heavy going.

"By the way, I had a call from Liza Merritt. She's invited us to the inn on New Year's Day," Emily said. "She's having a big New Year's Day party. It's all very last minute, but she wanted to have a big, grand finale celebration before she gives up ownership. We don't have any plans now. I think it would be fun to go."

Ezra walked in. He carried the newspaper folded to the crossword puzzle tucked under his arm, with a slim yellow pencil stuck behind his ear. His hands were occupied by a bowl of popcorn, as her mother had predicted. Though it wasn't a very large bowl, and Emily thought it was a fairly healthy snack.

"Who do you mean by 'us'? We aren't included in that roundup, are we?" Her mother sounded wary, but not because she suspected anything, Emily decided. She was just wondering why she was on Liza's guest list.

"Of course I mean you and Ezra. Liza asked

for you specifically. She's inviting everyone they know—from the village and church and island. It will be a wonderful way to bring in the New Year."

"A party at the inn? I'm all for it," Ezra announced as he got comfortable in his favorite wing chair. "We don't kick up our heels on New Year's Eve anymore, Lily. I'd like to do something festive to ring in the new. Emily says the whole town is going."

"That's exactly why I won't attend. That's not a social event, it's a cattle call."

Emily sighed. Had she slipped up here? She should have remembered how her mother despised any gathering where she'd be obliged to rub shoulders with what she called the "riffraff."

"If it is a cattle call, then I'm a stubborn old bull. You can stay home if you like, dear. But I will attend." Ezra looked up at Emily. "There's a lot of college football on that day. She probably doesn't want to miss the games."

Emily stifled a laugh as her mother scowled. Her mother detested football, college or professional. Ezra was just pushing her buttons. And he knew how to do it, too.

Finally, her mother shrugged and opened her book. "Go if you like. Enjoy yourself. It will be a perfect time to catch up on my reading and write up my resolutions for the New Year."

Her mother made resolutions? That was news to

Emily. She couldn't imagine what they might be.

Her mother started reading, and Emily could see the discussion of this question was solidly closed. She had no idea how to persuade her mother to change her mind. At least they still had tomorrow. Maybe they would think of something.

"I'd better go. It's getting late. I just wanted to make sure you were both fine."

"Snug as two bugs in a rug," Ezra replied with his usual, sunny smile. He glanced at Emily's mother. "One's a humbug," he added quietly.

Lillian sniffed but otherwise acted as if she didn't hear him.

"Good night, Mother." Emily leaned over and kissed her cheek. "I'll bring you groceries tomorrow if you need anything."

Her mother looked up briefly. "I'll let you know. Thank you."

Ezra rose and put his newspaper aside. "I'll show you to the door, dear."

Once they were out in the hallway, Ezra leaned closer and said, "What time will you pick us up on New Year's Day?"

"Do you think you can actually persuade her to go?"

"Don't worry. She thinks she's calling my bluff and I won't leave her here alone. But she'll be the first one to blink, mark my words. What time should we expect you?"

"Around a quarter to three. It doesn't take long

to get there." The guests had been told to arrive by two thirty, so everyone would be in place for the surprise.

Emily hoped he could persuade her mother in time. She could hardly take him alone to his own party. And if she told her mother why her presence was imperative, her mother would put up an unholy fuss when she learned she had been tricked. She might refuse to come on those grounds alone.

Emily leaned over and kissed Ezra's dry cheek. "I'm counting on you, pal. Don't let me down."

He smiled and winked behind his wire-rimmed glasses. "Never fear, my dear. I know how to navigate these tricky currents by now."

His words were some comfort. If anyone knew how to handle her mother, it was Ezra. The ball was in his hands now, which seemed awfully ironic to Emily.

New Year's Eve day was bright and sunny, boding well for the party, Emily thought. Everyone in her household loaded cars with party supplies and headed to the inn. There were tables and chairs to set up, furniture to move, and decorations and balloons to hang.

Not to mention all the food preparation, which was definitely not Emily's turf. But Jane planned to help in the kitchen all day and had even brought her own apron.

Liza had asked them to come in through the back door today and into the kitchen, so there wouldn't be a lot of mud tracked into the front of the inn. Emily knocked, but the door was unlocked. She stepped in, tote bags hanging from each arm and a pile of boxes in her hands. Sara and Jane followed. Dan and Luke were still emptying their cars.

"Reporting for duty. Where should I put all this stuff?" Emily called out.

Liza rushed toward them. "The kitchen table is fine for now. We'll sort it out in a minute . . . Kerry, could you help with the coats?"

Had Liza really called for Kerry? Emily thought she must have imagined it. She turned quickly and could hardly believe her eyes.

It was Kerry, standing at the stove with her back toward them. She slowly turned and smiled, then walked toward them.

"Hello, Emily," she said. "Let me take your jacket."

She turned to face Jane. "Hello, Jane. Liza said you might come today. Would you like to help in the kitchen?"

Emily's heart beat wildly, imagining that Jane must feel the same. Jane stood wide-eyed, staring at her birth mother. "I thought you left. Liza said you went back to Maine."

"I did leave. But I decided to come back. Now I'm glad I came in time to help with your

425

grandfather's party. Claire and I could really use another cook in here. What do you say?"

"I'm not a real 'cook' yet. Not like you guys," Jane said. "But I can help if you tell me what to do. I've been reading new cookbooks all week," she added, suddenly seeming shyer than Emily had seen her in a long time.

"Really? Maybe you'll teach me a few things." Kerry smiled and lightly touched Jane's shoulder. "And maybe we can talk a little before you go. Just you and me?"

Jane nodded. "I'd like that."

Emily felt a sudden lightness deep inside, as if a heavy burden had lifted off her heart. She gave a silent prayer of thanks. Things between Jane and Kerry were going to be all right, she realized.

When Emily and Dan arrived at her mother's house on New Year's Day, Emily had her fingers crossed in her pocket as Dan knocked on the front door.

Ezra answered, looking very dapper in a gray plaid sports coat, a pale yellow shirt, and a red bow tie. He wore black trousers and black wing-tipped shoes, buffed to a high gloss. Emily never saw those in the stores anymore. She was pretty sure he sent to England for them.

"Happy New Year!" he greeted them cheerfully. "Is everything all right? I expected you a while ago."

Emily had purposely come late, to be sure that all the guests would be in place for the surprise. "Just some last-minute tasks around the house. It's so hard for me to get out the door sometimes."

"All the time," Dan chimed in. "You know Emily. Punctuality is not her strong point."

"A trait she did not inherit from me." Emily's mother appeared. She was nicely dressed in a lavender twinset that complemented her white hair and blue eyes. Emily was not surprised to see her ever-present string of pearls and matching earrings. But the lovely outfit was still no guarantee that she was coming.

"Shall I help you with your coat, Lily?" Ezra already had on a navy blue topcoat and a silk muffler. He turned to his wife, holding out her long mink.

Her mother scowled. "You'd really go to this hoedown without me, wouldn't you?"

Emily held her breath. Did she have to spill the beans and pay the price? They'd never get to the party at all if that happened.

Ezra thrust out his chin. "I've known Liza Merritt since she was a little girl and visited her aunt in the summertime. I've known Claire North even longer. And I helped Daniel study for his exams when he decided to return to medicine. I hate to see all of them go. It's a big loss for this community. Attending their party is the respectful thing to do. So I'm going."

"So I concluded from that lovely speech." Her mother rolled her eyes, though she did look a bit mollified.

"I won't enjoy myself very much without you at my side," Ezra added.

"Really." Her mother brushed off the comment, and Ezra answered with a mild smile. "All right. If you're going to make such a fuss. But I'm not staying long. I'll call a taxi for myself if I need to."

"I'll remember, dear. Don't worry." Ezra turned to Emily and winked. She wanted to hug him but restrained herself.

They arrived at the inn to find cars parked all along the circular drive and up to the barn in back. "When you said the whole town, I thought that was an exaggeration," her mother said. "I believe they invited everyone in Essex County."

"The more the merrier, Lily," Ezra said.

"People will say that. But I don't agree."

Molly had hired help to park the cars, which made maneuvering the seniors into the house much easier. Emily had texted her sister from the land bridge with a heads-up on their arrival. There was nothing more to do now except to stand back as Ezra headed for the front door.

Ever the gentleman, Ezra held his wife by the arm and ushered Lillian in just steps ahead of him. Emily watched her make her halting way into the foyer, using her cane.

Had it been a bad idea to plan a surprise party for a ninety-five-year-old man? Would the shock of it be too much for him? Or her mother? Emily had a sudden panicky thought, then realized it was far too late to worry about it.

A shout of, "Surprise! Happy Birthday, Ezra!" from a throng of voices seemed to shake the very foundation. Molly had given out New Year's Eve noisemakers, and the cheer was punctuated by toots from plastic horns.

Ezra stood back and touched his heart with his hand. Then he let out a huge laugh of delight. "What in heaven's name is this?"

"What indeed," Emily's mother echoed, though not nearly as cheerfully.

Jessica stepped forward. "Happy Birthday, Ezra. We wanted to do something special for you, and all these lovely people want to help you celebrate."

Ezra gazed around at the crowd—his family, friends, neighbors, church members, and so many former patients, all gathered to celebrate and honor him. His eyes filled with tears.

"My word, I can hardly believe it." He turned to Lillian. "Did you know about this?"

Emily's mother's eyes were wide as saucers. "I certainly did not," she replied in an indignant tone.

But her ire was quickly drowned out when Digger Hegman stepped forward and started to sing, *"For he's a jolly good fellow, for he's a jolly good fellow . . ."*

Carolyn Lewis, the reverend's wife, was at the piano in the front parlor and played a robust rendition of the song.

Molly stepped forward, wearing her kitchen apron, and gave Ezra a big kiss on his forehead that left a red lipstick mark. "I love this guy. He's the greatest."

Ezra was delighted and beamed with happiness as everyone sang along. If Emily had ever thought for one moment the party was too much bother, she knew now she would put up with ten times as much work and hassle to see that look on his face.

Sophie Potter took Ezra's arm. "Come along, Ezra. Everyone's been waiting for you."

Emily's mother turned to her. "Did a pipe really break at the Bradford Arms?"

"Yes, it did. I didn't lie—about that part."

"Just all the rest, I see. You and your sister got your way, after all. I bet you're both very pleased."

"We are, Mother. And you should be happy, too. Look at Ezra. He couldn't be happier, surrounded by so many people who love him and are delighted to be here, celebrating his birthday. And a life well lived."

Lillian's cold stare turned from Emily back to her husband. Emily watched her expression soften. "We'll still have the dinner at the Bradford Arms. I'm not giving up on that. But he does look happy. Maybe this stadium of fans was needed. He loves the attention. I hear it's beneficial for one's health at our age. Encourages the good brain chemicals."

"I've heard that, too. Good brain chemistry for the both of you, I hope."

Emily knew that she and Jessica were not forgiven. Far from it. But at least their mother would not walk around all night in a snit because she'd been outmaneuvered.

That would make Ezra happy, too.

After all the guests were gone and Molly's crew had left, Liza hung back in the kitchen with Claire and Kerry, finishing the last tasks of the cleanup. What could be done that night, anyway.

Considering the mob of people who had celebrated in every room, the mess was ninety-nine percent cleaned up and the inn was just about set to rights before they finally shut the lights and locked the doors. There wouldn't be much to deal with tomorrow.

A good thing, too, since she had to concentrate on packing up for Arizona. Upstairs, in the bedroom, Daniel was still dressed, stretched out on the bed, reading a medical journal. He sat up and patted the space next to him. "If I was a doctor,

431

I'd prescribe a hot shower and ten hours of sleep."

"Where is a doctor when you need one?" She sighed. Had she sat down once since noon? She didn't think so. "At least I'm exhausted for a good cause. Ezra couldn't have been happier. He must have thanked me ten times. I barely had anything to do with it."

"More than barely, I'd say."

"Emily and her family did most of the heavy lifting. And Molly's food certainly helped lighten the work in our kitchen. I'm so glad that they asked me to hold it here. I wouldn't have thought of having a big bash like that to close down the inn. Well, maybe I would have thought of it," she amended, "but I might not have gone through with the idea. It worked out perfectly this way."

"So you're feeling better about the sale now? Is that what you mean?"

Liza wasn't sure how to answer. She wanted to be honest but didn't want Daniel to worry about her.

"I won't say I'm happy about it. That wouldn't be true. Part of me is still hanging back, just not able to accept it's really happening. But we've discussed the question thoroughly and we both agree it's the best solution. Not ideal. But we don't live in an ideal world. You've said that yourself," she reminded him.

"So I did." He took her hand in his. "I have

something to tell you, now that the party is over. I didn't want to distract you yesterday, or today, for that matter."

"What is it? Is something wrong?" His tone made Liza nervous.

"Nothing's wrong, honey. In fact, you might like this news. I had a call from the clinic's head administrator. Remember I appealed to him about the transfer?"

Liza nodded. "I do. What did he say?"

"He says he can't—or simply won't—let me stay at the clinic. Not unless I take the promotion. And we know I don't want that. So it's either accept the transfer or resign."

Liza held her breath. "What did you say?"

"Door number two. I'm officially unemployed. I guess I should have told you sooner."

Liza smiled at his penitent expression. "Is that the part I'm supposed to like?"

"The thing is, we always planned to come back East. Maybe this is the time to do it. Before the kids are older and we really put down roots. I don't want to drag my family around to someplace new and start all over again. I don't think that's fair. I've put in my time on the reservation, and I can always go back as a volunteer for a few weeks at a time. I'll make sure that any new job will allow that."

"That's true," she agreed. She was starting to like this news.

"What do you say? Did I pull the plug prematurely?"

"I'm surprised. But I'm happy we can move back. I didn't want to say anything, Daniel, but the last few weeks, I really saw how much I've missed New England. The ocean and the snow . . . and just, everything."

He leaned over and hugged her. "I guess that's a yes?"

She nodded, her head pressed against his shoulder. "A *big* yes. Thank you. This feels like a gift to me. One I was afraid to even ask for at Christmastime."

"You're very welcome. You need to thank the clinic administrator a little, too. He more or less gave me the idea."

"But you took a lemon and made lemonade. That counts a lot in my book." She leaned back to look at him. "Now I need to ask you something. Would you mind very much if I call off the sale and we live here?"

Daniel laughed. "I was thinking the same thing. But I didn't want to push you." He paused, his expression suddenly serious. "I know you love the inn. But do you really want to take all this on again? I'll still have long hours, practicing somewhere. I won't be around much to help you. Claire and Nolan will be thrilled to hear our news. But they don't want to work here twenty-four-seven anymore either. In a few weeks, they'll be traveling through the Middle East and who knows where else."

"I know what you're saying is true. But I do have an idea of how to solve all that." She sat up and took a breath. She felt so happy and excited, bubbling over with energy, when a few minutes ago, she was a sleepy heap. "I have a feeling Kerry will stay, once she knows the sale is off. With a little training from me and Claire, she can be my second-in-command. We can hire Gabriel to be the official property manager. He's basically doing the job already. I'll have a whole new team to help me. With Claire and Nolan to offer their experience and wisdom, as needed, it will work out fine."

Daniel squinted at her. "Have you been thinking about all this secretly?"

"Not really. Though I did daydream a bit, wishing things were different and imagining how it *could* work."

He leaned over and kissed her forehead. "If this is what you really want, I'm all for it. You know I love this place, and I'll help you as much as I'm able."

"At least we know now we can sell it off pretty quickly if we ever want to," she joked.

"In theory. Not that I believe it will ever happen."

"Not if I can help it," Liza whispered.

She hugged him close and closed her eyes,

feeling relieved and at peace. She was finally home, in the place where she and Daniel had fallen in love and gotten married, and would raise their children and grow old together. She would never have to leave here again. Liza's heart overflowed with gratitude for the way everything had turned out. Just as Claire always said, Angel Island was a magical place. Liza knew she would never doubt it now.

Their invitation had said, *No gifts, please. Your presence is our present.* But of course, Ezra had received piles of gifts from his many guests. Emily brought a load over in her car on Thursday morning and carried them inside.

Her mother and Ezra had just finished break-fast. Emily noticed that instead of reading the newspaper, as Ezra always did, he was studying the stack of greeting cards he had received the night before, quite engrossed in deciphering the handwritten notes in each one.

"Good morning, Emily!" He glanced up a moment to greet her. "Wonderful party. I can't thank you enough."

"No need to thank me, Ezra. It was a pleasure for Jessica and me, and everyone who helped, to put it together for you."

"A dubious one, I must say," her mother replied. "You must be exhausted from managing that mob scene last night . . . Are those more gifts? We hardly know what to do with all the trinkets he's unwrapped already."

Leave it to her mother to find a way to complain about too many birthday presents. "I'll come by one day this week and help you sort them out."

"I'm delighted with the gifts, Emily. All very thoughtful," Ezra said. "People didn't have to give me anything. I just loved seeing everyone. And talking about old times. That was a marvelous slideshow you made. It was very touching to see those old photos."

"Sara and Luke worked on that project. Jessica and I just chose the pictures."

It had been fun to see Ezra in his younger days, as a skinny boy with oversized ears. A gangly young man in a military uniform. And later, looking very serious in his white lab coat with a stethoscope slung around his neck.

There were even a few photos of Ezra with Emily's father, Oliver, and her mother, in their younger days. They'd all been friends back then. Ezra and Emily's father had been rivals for Lillian's hand. Ezra had lost the contest and never married, perhaps just waiting for the day he could claim Lillian as his own.

Her mother sighed. "Walking down Memory Lane is highly overrated, in my opinion. Please don't invade my privacy that way when I'm ninety. I don't want any slideshows either." She turned to her husband. "I'm glad to see you're

437

still tickled pink by the affair. But it was not the one I'd planned for you. Not by a long shot."

"I know, dear. I bet you ordered champagne and caviar for me. But sometimes hot dogs and beer are all right, too. In fact, just the ticket."

Ezra's party had been far more elaborate than that humble fare. But Emily knew what he was trying to say.

"The ticket for you. But not for me," her mother insisted.

"Don't worry, Mother, when you're ninety, no hot dogs. We'll make a note of it." Emily shared a grin with Ezra. How would they surprise her mother when her turn came around? Emily decided to save that riddle for another day.

Right now, no one—not even her mother—could deny that Ezra's party had been a great success. The perfect tribute to a wonderful man, who was showered with the well-earned love and respect of so many people. Emily was glad she'd helped give him that. He certainly deserved it. And so much more.

It was barely ten o'clock, not very late, but the inn was already quiet. Claire and Nolan, along with the Merritts, had gone up to their rooms early. Kerry was about to follow but stood waiting for water to boil so she could make a cup of tea.

Everyone was tired from the party yesterday,

438

and from the rest of the cleanup. Not to mention the excitement of hearing that the inn was not going to be sold, after all, and the Merritts were going to stay.

Kerry felt as if her life had changed overnight, from darkness to light. Liza had asked her to stay and train to be her assistant manager. And even better, Kerry had talked with Jane, and her daughter was starting to forgive her. Jane wanted them to spend time together and get to know each other. Kerry's heart was so full, she couldn't ask for more.

She wasn't sure how it had happened, but the New Year that had seemed so dim, and even hopeless, as she'd sat waiting in the bus station now looked bright and full of promise.

The kettle whistled, and she poured the hot water in a cup, then realized that someone had been tapping on the back door. Who could be visiting now? *One of the Gilroys from next door, probably,* she thought.

She peered out as she pulled open the door. She was surprised to see Gabriel, standing in the dim light. He had been at the inn all day and had left after dinner. Why was he back now?

She stood aside as he walked in, along with a gust of cold air. "Did you forget something here?"

His keys or phone, she suspected. What else would be too urgent to wait until tomorrow?

He reached in his pocket and took out a letter then held it out to her. "I found this in the mail when I got home."

Kerry took a step back, as if the slim white envelope were about to explode. "Oh. Right . . . What about it?"

"I read it, of course. A few times. Did you really mean what you wrote in there?"

The letter had not been long, but Kerry had been honest about her feelings for him. Maybe too honest, she realized now. She had thanked him for his friendship, even though she knew she'd made it hard for him most of the time. And she'd thanked him for talking so much sense into her when he had found her stranded on the road. Both times. But mostly for encouraging her and believing in her, even when she had not believed in herself.

She'd admitted she would miss him and was sorry they'd never had a chance to know each other better. Maybe that was the worst thing she'd said. Or the best, depending on how you looked at it?

She stole a glance at him. He was waiting for her answer.

"Well, did you?"

She nodded quickly. "Why would I lie? I thought I'd never see you again."

He laughed quietly and shook his head. "A letter like this isn't a very good way to get rid of a guy, Kerry. I can promise you that."

She shrugged, not knowing what to say. She felt embarrassed now. "You came to look for me anyway. You hadn't even read the letter."

"I did. And I don't think you ever thanked me."

"You're right. Thank you. I was just remembering how sad I felt, sitting in that bus station. How bleak my life looked. But look at me now. Everything's worked out. Even Jane," she added. "We had a good talk. I think we have a chance at a real relationship. One I never thought would be possible. I guess I need to thank you for that, too."

He smiled, his eyes shining with a warm light that touched her heart. "I can't take credit for that. You and Jane would have gotten together sooner or later. I am glad it's all working out with her. I had a much more selfish reason for bringing you back." He held out the letter. "You told me how you feel about me, so now I want to tell you how I feel."

Kerry felt her mouth go dry. Was this really happening? Her heart was beating so loudly, she was afraid he could hear it, too.

"I've never met anyone like you, Kerry Redmond. The minute you looked into my eyes, I was hooked. You infuriate me, fascinate me, and know how to put me in my place. You amaze me and touch my heart. I think about you all the time and just want to be around you. Now we'll

441

be working here together again, and I guess my wish is coming true, too." He waited for her to say something but she couldn't speak.

"Does it bother you to hear me say these things?"

Kerry shook her head. "I'm glad you came to find me. You amaze me, too," she admitted quietly.

Did she dare admit more? She didn't have a chance. Gabriel closed the space between them in two swift steps and took her into his strong arms. He kissed her gently at first. Then their embrace deepened. Kerry felt lost, but this time, in the arms of a man whom she would trust with her life. Gabriel was nothing like other men she'd known. He was kind and honest and would never hurt her.

When they finally eased apart, she rested her head on his chest. She could hear his heart beat in time with her own.

"Do you still think we shouldn't date because we're working together?" he asked.

Kerry laughed softly. "I think it will work out."

"Yeah. I do, too," he replied. She knew he was talking about something more. A future together.

Not too long ago, she would have run from a good man like Gabriel, for a hundred reasons. Most of her own making. She was different now. The shadows that had chased her for years had melted into the light. She had put the past behind her and opened her heart—to Jane, to Gabriel, and to a whole new world that she'd found on this island.

Maybe the world wasn't new, Kerry thought. Maybe it was just the way she was looking at it? *That's something Claire might say,* she realized. *I'll have to ask her about that tomorrow.*

After his initial surprise, George Foster was much more gracious about Liza's change of heart than she had expected. Liza called him early on Friday morning. She was due to give her final answer and didn't want to put it off.

"It's a fine old inn, and if I were in your shoes, I'd have a lot of trouble letting it go myself," he confided. "Good luck to you, Liza. I think you know what to do. I feel certain the Inn on Angel Island will be strong competition for us again this summer," he joked. "If we can be of any help down the road, just let me know."

Liza thanked him again. She appreciated his good wishes, and his vote of confidence.

Daniel had also made important calls that morning, getting the ball rolling in his job search. Matthew Harding, Molly's husband, was eager to meet with Daniel once he heard that Daniel was moving back to the area. Matt was a family doctor who had taken over Ezra's practice in town over fifteen years ago. A position in his office might not work out for Daniel, Liza reminded herself, but Matt knew all the doctors in the area and would certainly help get the word out.

The sun was strong and the temperature mild for early January. The children had been so housebound by the snow, Liza decided to take them for a walk on the beach after lunch. There were a few drifts piled near the cliffs, but the shoreline was clear, the waves rushing in and out along the flat sand as they always did.

At the bottom of the steps, the children rushed ahead of her. She felt her heart expand with happiness. This was the place she was meant to be. She felt so lucky to be able to stay here.

As they walked toward the jetty, Liza noticed a fisherman on the beach, wearing high waders, a heavy jacket, and a hat. He'd been surf casting but now held his rod and reel in one hand and a plastic bucket in the other as he made his way along the shoreline toward them.

The gap closed a bit more and she recognized him, then lifted her hand and waved. It was Reverend Ben—she should have known. He came to this beach year-round to surf cast.

"Hello, Liza. It's a good day for a beach walk. I'm surprised we're the only ones around."

"I am, too. Catch anything today?"

"Oh, you know me," he replied with a shrug and a small smile.

Everyone knew he rarely caught any fish, for all his efforts. And when he did, he usually threw them back. The minister had often told Liza he never fretted about his fishing luck. He really came for the quiet and time close to the sea. It was more of a meditative practice, he said, than a sport.

The children were chasing seagulls a safe distance from the water. They knew not to venture too far from her, and Liza felt free to chat for a few minutes.

"That was a wonderful party New Year's Day. It was good of you to hold it at the inn last-minute. Emily told me the whole story."

"We were happy to help. I thought it would be a fitting way to close our doors, but I have some big news. I changed my mind about the sale. We're moving back East and I'm going to run the inn again."

Reverend Ben's head tilted back in surprise. "Are you really? That is big news. How did this all come about?"

She quickly explained why Daniel had resigned his job and how they'd always planned to return, so this seemed the perfect time.

"It's amazing the way things have worked out. Claire told me to pray for the best possible outcome for everyone. I thought that meant selling the inn, but this answer is better than anything I ever expected or imagined."

"Claire is a very wise woman. I couldn't have given you better guidance." He stabbed his rod in the sand and pulled off his waterproof gloves. "I'm sure she was happy to hear about your change in plans."

"She was," Liza replied, though the two small words hardly described Claire and Nolan's joyous reaction. "I've missed Claire very much. She and Nolan aren't getting any younger. That's another good reason to return."

"An excellent one," Reverend Ben answered with a warm smile. "I look forward to seeing you around town now."

"And at church," she added, knowing he was far too polite to put pressure on anyone about Sundays. But she would see him at church soon, to offer thanks for the way all her problems had sorted out.

Their future seemed bright as the sun above and filled with blessings. Liza knew she could never ask for more than that.

Books are produced in the United States using U.S.-based materials	Books are printed using a revolutionary new process called THINKtech™ that lowers energy usage by 70% and increases overall quality	Books are durable and flexible because of Smyth-sewing	Paper is sourced using environmentally responsible foresting methods and the paper is acid-free

Center Point Large Print
600 Brooks Road / PO Box 1
Thorndike, ME 04986-0001 USA

(207) 568-3717

US & Canada:
1 800 929-9108
www.centerpointlargeprint.com